Praise for Legac[y]

"An amazing adventure ... Fans of ricl[...] will anyone interested in the complexities of humanity." —*Fresh Fiction*

"Skillfully interweaves Cherokee lore and human nature at its best and worst." —*Booklist*

"[Mary Crow is] a kickass Atlanta prosecutor." —*Kirkus Reviews*

"Mary proves a captivating protagonist. The mystery and suspense are eerily entrancing." —*Romantic Times*

"Readers will take a few deep breaths ... A fascinating mix of Cherokee customs and folklore plays an important role ... Sallie Bissell has created a set of characters that are realistic and full-bodied." —*Mystery Scene*

Praise for Call the Devil by his Oldest Name

"A deftly written thriller that grips you from beginning to end. Sallie Bissell's protagonist, Mary Crow, is one of the toughest and sharpest investigators in the genre and totally captivating. A riveting read with a conclusion that shocks even the most intuitive reader." —Nelson DeMille, *New York Times* best-selling author of *Word of Honor*

"*Call the Devil by his Oldest Name* has it all—nail-biting suspense, poignant human drama, non-stop action, an intriguing locale, and no small doses of humor. Heroine Mary Crow's spirit and guts make her impossible not to love. Once again, Sallie Bissell delivers herself a magnificent novel." —Nancy Geary, author of *Regrets Only*

"Ties with *The Narrows* by Michael Connelly as the best mystery of the year so far." —*Nashville City Paper*

"Tightly wound ... offers a disturbing look into contemporary Appalachia; very well done." —P.T. Deutermann, author of *The Last Man*

"Bissell's strong writing and clever, didn't-see-that-coming denouement will keep readers enthralled... She may soon be keeping company with the likes of Tami Hoag and Sandra Brown." —*Publishers Weekly*

"An extremely exciting crime thriller about an obsession taken to extremes... a pulse-pounding, adrenaline-pumping novel that the audience will remember long after finishing the last page." —*Midwest Book Review*

Praise for A Darker Justice

"[A] fast-moving story, elegantly told, in which Bissell... weaves a palpitating web of sinuously deadly suspense." —*Los Angeles Times Book Review*

"For thriller fans who value action." —*Booklist*

"Bissell's Mary Crow is one of the most intriguing characters in today's mystery genre." —*Tulsa World*

"At the end of this book, I felt I had read a masterpiece."—*Deadly Pleasures*

Praise for In the Forest of Harm

"A top-notch thriller... the pressure builds steadily... [in] this taut debut... [a] solid page-turner." —*People*

"Hair-raising... harrowing." —*Publishers Weekly*

"Bissell tightens the screws slowly and expertly... A shrewdly imagined female actioner, tailor-made for audiences who would've loved *Deliverance* if it hadn't been for all that guy stuff." —*Kirkus Reviews*

"In the mode of Patricia Cornwell... Bissell masterfully drives the plot with... gut-wrenching suspense." —*The Ashenville Citizen-Times*

Music of Ghosts

The Mary Crow Series
In the Forest of Harm
A Darker Justice
Call the Devil By His Oldest Name
Legacy of Masks

SALLIE BISSELL

A Novel of Suspense

....

Music of Ghosts

MIDNIGHT INK
WOODBURY, MINNESOTA

MIDNIGHT INK

FIRST EDITION
First Printing, 2013

Book format by Bob Gaul
Cover design by Lisa Novak
Cover photo © Alex Stoddard
Editing by Nicole Nugent

Midnight Ink, an imprint of Llewellyn Worldwide Ltd.

Library of Congress Cataloging-in-Publication Data
Bissell, Sallie.
  Music of Ghosts: a novel of suspense/Sallie Bissell.—First Edition.
      pages cm.—(Mary Crow; #5)
    ISBN 978-0-7387-3584-9   5162 6777 05/13
1. Crow, Mary (Fictitious character)—Fiction. 2. Women lawyers—Fiction.
3. Mystery fiction. I. Title.
  PS3552.I772916M87 2013
  813'.54—dc23
                              2012043010

Midnight Ink
Llewellyn Worldwide Ltd.
2143 Wooddale Drive
Woodbury, MN 55125-2989
www.midnightinkbooks.com

Printed in the United States of America

For Carter Bissell, my fair-haired boy.

ONE

Never had Lisa wanted to go to the haunted house. Saturdays they usually went clubbing in Asheville or hiked up to some hidden away waterfall. But Chris Givens had talked up the infamous Fiddlesticks cabin all week, ultimately persuading them that an overnight in a haunted house would be a nice break from cleaning up bird shit. "I'll take my camcorder," he told her, as they banded a fierce little sparrow hawk. "If we get any cool video, we can sell it to one of those ghost buster shows on TV."

"But Nick wants us at the sports park ceremony," Lisa replied. "He's going to fly Sequoia."

"Not til noon the next day," said Chris. "You'll be back in plenty of time to help Nick with that eagle."

So now she stood, along with the other five interns of Pisgah Raptor Rescue Center, breathless and sweaty in front of a small, dilapidated cabin that huddled at the end of a twisting, pine-shrouded path. With broken windows and mildewed chink, the structure looked more sad than haunted; a beaten place where light and energy had packed up one day and never returned. Though Lisa did not believe in ghosts, something about the place made her shudder.

"So what's the story up here?" asked Ryan Quarles, a blonde, broad-shouldered sophomore from Duke.

"This is where the Fiddlesticks murders happened." Chris pulled a video camera from his backpack. "Let's go check it out before it gets dark."

Givens climbed up on the rotting porch and beckoned them forward. As he pointed his camera at them, they made their way up the disintegrating steps. Though Lisa longed to stay outside in the last slivers of daylight, she took a deep breath and climbed up to the rickety porch. She was the daughter of a governor, a prideful man. She dare not let anyone think she was scared.

With Chris filming away, she lifted her chin and stepped over the threshold. Immediately a chilly dankness raised goose flesh on her arms, reminding her of mold and mildew and the pale, disgusting little toadstools that grew beneath fallen logs. As her eyes adjusted to the near darkness, she fully expected to see pentagrams carved on the walls, the bones of small animals offered up in sacrifice. Instead, she saw the detritus of expeditions much like their own. Beer cans and cigarette butts littered the floor while the walls bore the names and initials of the countless couples who'd come before them. In the dimness she saw that someone had spray painted "Class of '77" on the ceiling; someone else had written "I love KISS" over the small fireplace. As stupid and lame as the ancient graffiti was, she found it comforting. The six of them were just part of a stream of people who'd spent the night here and then gone on with the rest of their lives.

"What a place," said Ryan. He surveyed the living room, stopping in one corner to lift a dust-covered beer bottle. "When did you last see a Schlitz beer?"

"Never heard of it." Rachel Sykes gaped at the graffiti on the ceiling. "But I think my mother graduated from high school in '77."

They were staring at all the old tags when suddenly, Chris lowered his camera and cocked his head toward a dark room to the right. "Did you guys hear that?"

"Hear what?" Rachel frowned.

"That noise," he whispered. "It sounded like someone groaned."

They turned and listened. All they heard was silence.

"I think you're imagining things." A rising senior at Carolina, Abby Turner was their self-appointed skeptic.

"No, I'm not," said Chris. "I heard something. Come on!"

Lisa followed as he led them into what turned out to be an old kitchen. Small and dirty, it had a rusty old-fashioned pump that once spewed water into a chipped iron sink. More beer cans littered the room, and their feet crunched desiccated animal turds and moth cocoons as they walked across a cracked linoleum floor. Though they heard no more groans, Lisa wondered if anybody else felt the oppressive coldness, or smelled that sick toadstool stink.

"So tell us." Tony Blackman ducked under a scrim of dusty cobwebs that drooped from the ceiling. "What were the Fiddlesticks murders?"

"Fiddlesticks was the best fiddler in North Carolina," said Chris, doing a slow pan of the room. "Years ago, he had a steady gig down in Jackson County, every Saturday night."

"How many years ago?" asked Abby.

"Back in the 1950s," Chris replied. "One Saturday in March they had a big wind storm, and the dance ended early. Fiddlesticks

3

got in his truck to come home, but a tree had blown across the road, so he had to park and walk. Usually, his wife left a candle on in the window for him, but that night, everything was dark. Scared that something had happened to her, he hurried to the cabin and opened the front door."

"Let me guess," said Abby. "He found the devil inside, waiting to have a fiddle contest with him."

"He found his wife inside," Chris said somberly. "Naked in front of the fireplace, screwing another man."

"Whoa, dude!" said Tony.

Chris continued. "Anyway, Fiddlesticks went crazy—pulled out the straight razor he kept in his boot. Cut off the man's balls, slit his wife's throat. Then he sat down and played his fiddle while they bled to death."

Chris returned to the living room and pointed at some dark splotches on the floor. "Those are bloodstains. They say Fiddlesticks haunts the place—that some nights you can still hear the fiddle music. And the screaming."

For a moment they all stood staring at the floor. Lisa wished more than ever she'd stayed home. Though her father had always admonished her to be brave, a dark thing she could not name lurked here. It held its breath and listened while they talked, watched them through the cracks in the wall.

"I'm going back outside," she told Chris. "I'm really cold."

Chris turned his camera on her. "Awwww, is the governor's daughter scared?" he asked, clucking like a chicken.

"No," she said. "Just cold."

"I'll come with you," said Rachel. "This house is gross."

The two girls walked back outside, shrugging out of their backpacks and huddling together on a fallen log beside an old fire pit.

"Maybe we should build a fire," suggested Rachel. "Gather sticks and kindling."

Lisa cupped her hands and held them to her mouth, trying to generate some heat. "Let me get my hands warm first."

"Good idea," said Rachel. "It's about fifty degrees colder on top of this mountain." Blowing on her own hands, she noticed Lisa's fingers. "Hey, you didn't lose your mom's ring, did you?"

"No, I left it in my room. I was afraid something might happen to it up here."

Rachel looked at her, her pretty brown eyes concerned. "You seriously are not enjoying this, are you?"

Shaking her head, Lisa turned the collar of her jacket close around her neck. "I hate the forest at night. I hate camping. I hate Chris running around claiming to hear noises nobody else hears. But most of all, I hate that house."

Rachel frowned. "You think it's haunted?"

"I don't know what it is," said Lisa, watching as the setting sun made the jagged windows glow bright orange. "I'll just be glad when this night is over."

———

An hour later they sat around a sputtering pine-knot fire, built by Ryan and Tony. They'd eaten the sandwiches they'd packed back at the dorm, now Chris was filming them as they passed around a saltshaker and a bottle of Cuervo Gold. Though Lisa usually didn't drink, she swallowed the fiery liquid eagerly, hoping it would turn the night benign. Ever since the sun went down, Chris had kept them on edge, hearing noises, seeing shadows, claiming to feel spots of cold clammy air. At first the tequila made it all seem absurd and funny, but then the talk returned to what had gone on at the cabin.

"Hey, Chris," said Ryan. "What finally happened to this Fiddlesticks character?"

"Nobody knows," Chris replied, his face reflecting the glow of the fire. "He just walked into the woods and disappeared."

"Oh, please." Abby rolled her eyes. "Don't you think it's odd that nobody ever knows what happened to the person who did the killing?"

"That's not the point, Abby," said Rachel. "My anthropology professor said that ghost stories sprout up when someone breeches accepted behavior. They function like warnings about what not to do."

"But why does the maniacal killer always vanish?" Ryan took a swig of tequila and passed the bottle to Lisa. "I mean, didn't the cops investigate? Did they ever catch this guy?"

Chris shrugged. "Artie claims he's still hanging around. Says he's sees him sometimes at the bird barn, staring out from the woods."

"Just like that guy over there?" asked Tony softly, pointing to the dark pines that clustered on the other side of the clearing.

They all turned, looked. A shadowy figure seemed to be standing there, staring at them.

"Holy shit!" cried Chris. He pointed his camera toward the trees while everyone leapt to their feet. The girls huddled together, frightened. Tony and Ryan grabbed two thick limbs, previously destined for the fire. Everyone held their breath, waiting to see what the figure would do when, suddenly, it turned and dissolved into the woods.

"Come on," said Tony, holding his limb like a club. "Let's go get him."

The two boys took off, heading for the trees, Chris following with his camera. "I knew something was wrong with this place," Lisa whispered.

"It's okay." Rachel put her arm around her. "It's probably just Tony's idea of a joke. He's been drinking since way before supper."

"What if it isn't a joke?" asked Abby.

"Then we'll deal with it," Rachel said firmly. "There are six of us and only one of him."

———

Ultimately, they chalked their ghost up to shadows. The three boys scoured the woods for the better part of an hour but came up with nothing. Then they watched Chris's video of the event. From a distance, the shape did look human. But as Chris had run to get closer, he'd lost his focus on it, and the picture became a jerky montage of boys waving branches, running through shadowy trees.

They returned to sit around the fire, but a light rain started, turning the glowing embers into a smoking, sizzling heap.

"Come on," said Chris, grabbing his gear. "Let's get set up inside the house."

They followed him, scooping up their backpacks as they hurried inside the house. While he set up his camera on the mantel, everyone unrolled their sleeping bags in the living room—Rachel and Tony together, Abby opting to spread out near the kitchen. Her heart still thumping from seeing the shadow man, Lisa unfolded her bag beneath the front windows, as far away from those bloodstains as she could manage. *Just get through the night,* she told herself. *Get through the night. At first light tomorrow morning, you can head back to the center.*

"Want some company?" asked a voice behind her. "If we spread our bags out double, we can sleep together. We'll stay warmer that way."

She turned. Ryan Quarles stood there, sleeping bag in hand. Lisa hadn't planned on a bed companion, but after the dark woods and the bloodstained floor and the shadow man outside, she wasn't going to turn one down. Though Ryan was no Nick, together they could stay warm, and maybe safe from whatever haunted this house.

"Sure." Gratefully, she unzipped her bag and spread it double, lying down on the side nearest the wall. He unzipped his bag, and laid it on top of her, like a blanket. He pulled off his boots and was lying down beside her when Chris Givens made an announcement.

"Okay, we're rolling," he said. "This camera's got a wide angle lens, so nobody do anything that you wouldn't want seen on TV."

"Hi, Mom," Tony sat up and waved at the camera.

"Also no flashlights, or e-readers, or iPads," said Chris. "We don't want any electronic interference. And don't say anything that you don't want my EVP recorder to pick up."

Tony did a fair rendition of the Crypt Keeper laugh. "Good-night everybody!" he said. "Pleasant dreams!"

"You okay?" Ryan asked her as Chris turned off the last flash-light.

"Yeah," she said, her throat growing thick as she tried to gulp down her fear.

"See you in the morning, then," said Ryan, rolling over to turn his back to her.

———

For a long time she lay awake listening, waiting for something to happen. Chris sneezed a couple of times; the rustling from Rachel and Tony's corner indicated if not quiet sex, then at least some vigorous feeling-up. Finally, all the turning and bumping noises faded into sleepy moans and soft snoring. *How good it will be to get home*, she thought. Back to her own bed, back to her little sparrow hawk, back to Nick, the man she loved. As she thought of him, her eyes grew heavy. Soon she began to dream. She was back in their dorm. Nick was knocking on the door, full of sweetness, playing a tune for her on his fiddle. How sweet the music sounded! How lush his notes!

Abruptly, she woke up. For an instant she didn't know where she was, then everything grew clear. Nick wasn't playing any fiddle for her—she was in this cold stink of a cabin, sleeping next to Ryan. Trying to re-enter her dream, she closed her eyes. Suddenly, she heard an odd noise. A high, lilting sound, almost like a birdcall. She cocked her head toward the window. For awhile she heard only silence, then the sound came again. This time it was closer—a high, cascade of notes.

Someone was playing a fiddle, outside, in the trees beyond the house!

It's Chris, she told herself. *Or Tony. Playing some stupid trick.* But when she sat up to peer around the fireplace, she saw them both in the dim light, Chris beneath the other window, Tony with an arm wrapped across Rachel's shoulder.

Suddenly, the music came again—this time so strange and beautiful that the hair lifted on the nape of her neck. Parts of it sounded like a tune Nick sometimes played. But every time she thought she recognized it, the notes would change, making the tune discordant, yet somehow seductive.

Beside her Ryan gave a soft moan. She turned to look at him. He made a funny, chewing motion with his lips, but did not awaken. Trembling, Lisa looked at the other sleepers. Everyone lay still, undisturbed by the music.

———

She sat there, wondering if she was dreaming when suddenly, it all made sense. *Nick* had been the man Tony saw. Nick was sorry for the way he'd treated her and had come up here to make amends. What better way for a fiddle player to apologize than to serenade her out of her cabin?

Trying not to wake Ryan, she eased out of the sleeping bag, picked up her hiking boots, and tiptoed toward the front door. She managed to open the thing with only one soft squeak, and she closed it behind her without making a sound. Padding down the rotting stairs, she stopped and put on her boots. The notes seemed to be coming from the woods, directly in front of the cabin. "Nick?" she whispered as loudly as she dared. "Is that you?"

She heard no reply, just more notes. This time they teased and beckoned, pulling her forward.

Her heart leapt. She squinted through the trees as thick clouds raced across the moon, turning the landscape first dark then amazingly bright. She took several steps forward in the light, thinking she saw him, but the clouds obscured the moon again, turning everything dark.

"Where are you?" she called. "I can't see."

She thought she heard a muffled laugh coming through the night, soft as an owl's wing. Then the notes began curling around her legs like the tendrils of some hungry, night-blooming vine, pulling her step by step away from the cabin, deeper into the woods. She did her best to follow the music, but every time she thought she'd found it, it seemed to turn and come from a different direction.

Nick's teasing me, she decided as the night sky darkened again and she felt her way into a thick stand of pines. *He wants me, but he doesn't want the others to know. Still*, she thought, *this is awfully far away*. She couldn't even see the cabin anymore.

"Nick?" she called, growing nervous.

Again he answered musically, with notes that were sometimes lush as velvet; sometimes sharp with little teeth. She peered into the darkness, but the trees grew too thick, too close together. Then, suddenly, the music stopped.

"Nick?" She looked around. "I can't see you. Please come out!"

For a moment, everything grew silent. Somewhere behind her, she heard a twig snap. She caught a flicker of motion in the corner of her eye as she felt something go around her throat. She tried to pull it off, tried to scream, but it was too tight. All she could do was suck air into her lungs, flail against rough hands that seemed to be everywhere—pulling her hair, tearing her clothes. As brilliant fireworks exploded behind her eyes, she realized that this was the *thing* inside that cabin. Now it was here. She was the one it wanted.

She was the one Fiddlesticks was playing for tonight.

TWO

"Jerrrryyy!"

His mother's voice came so suddenly up the stairs that he jumped, nicking himself as he shaved. He winced when his razor sliced into his upper lip; in the bathroom mirror he watched as his white shaving cream turned pink with blood.

"Damn!" he cursed, eyes watering from the sting of the cut. He rinsed his face and looked at the damage. A deep nick, just below his left nostril. When it scabbed over, he would look like he had snot on his upper lip. *Terrific*, he thought. *The most important day of my life, and I'll look like I've been picking my nose.* As he pressed a small bit of toilet paper against the cut, his mother bellowed again.

"Jerryyyyy!"

He jerked open the bathroom door irritated, thinking he was probably the only sheriff in North Carolina who shared a roof with his mother. "What, Ma?"

"Get the phone! Boots Gahagan's on the line."

"Aw, shit!" he whispered. Boots Gahagan worked the day shift in dispatch and called him at home only in an emergency. Already he had the governor coming at noon to open the new sports park—now Boots was going to pile something else on his plate. He hurried down the hall, picked up the phone beside his bed.

"Hey, Boots." He answered matter-of-factly, as if it was no big deal that his mother had called him to the phone. Though Eleanor Cochran was a widowed economics professor currently recovering from breast cancer, he knew a few of his staff members secretly snickered about their boss's living arrangements. "What's up?"

"Just got a 911 about a possible homicide."

"A homicide?" He sat down on the bed. He didn't need any dead bodies today—he had every available officer in dress blues, providing snappy, spit-and-polish security for the honorable Ann Chandler. "Where?"

"East side of Burr Mountain," Boots reported. "A camper. Friends found her, in the woods."

"You're sure it's not an accident? Somebody didn't take a header off a waterfall?"

"Didn't sound like it. A college boy called, crying like a baby. Said some *thing* tore up a girl at the old Fiddlesticks cabin."

He felt a little catch in his gut. People had gone ghost hunting at Fiddlesticks for as long as he could remember. He had gone there himself, back in junior high.

"Who's on the scene?" he asked.

"Saunooke. He just called for a detective. Whaley's still on vacation and Tuffy Clark's on crutches, so I called you."

Cochran rose from the bed and re-hung his elegant black dress uniform back in his closet. "Okay. Tell Saunooke I'm on my way.

13

And call Tuffy Clark. See if he can hobble down to the station in case this turns out to be something."

"Ten-four."

Sighing, he hung up the phone and walked over to open the little blue velvet box on his dresser. Inside, a diamond ring glittered with icy fire. Not huge, but of excellent quality, according to the jeweler. He'd bought it last week, the first truly romantic act of his life. He thought his second romantic act would take place later today, when he planned to kneel in front of Ginger Malloy and ask her to marry him. Now, he had a bad feeling that Boots Gahagan's phone call had just put his romance on hold.

He hid the ring in the top drawer of his dresser and hurried back to finish shaving. As he re-entered the bathroom, he saw that his mother had remained at the bottom of the stairs, unabashedly eavesdropping on his conversation. She'd taken up mystery writing since he'd been elected sheriff, and she spent most of her mornings scribbling about a mother-and-son detective team. Much to his chagrin, a small press in Charleston had published her first novel, touting her as "the author who lives with crime every day."

"What's going on?" she called up the stairs, full of curiosity.

"Some kid found a body up at the Fiddlesticks cabin," he replied. He never told his mother anything that she wouldn't read in the paper—he just told her a day before it came out in print.

"Oh my God," cried Eleanor. "A homicide?"

He hated it when she used police lingo. "Don't know yet."

Re-lathering his face, he started to scrape the whiskers from the other half of his upper lip and thought of his own trip to the Fiddlesticks cabin. Butch Messer had heard that some high school boys kept a stash of condoms up there, and he wanted a share of them. "Pearl Ann Reynolds let me feel her tits after the last football game,"

Messer had confided, his tone both proud and nervous. "I'm gonna need some rubbers pretty soon!" They'd doubled up there on Messer's Honda, their hearts brimming with the prospect of actually needing a condom. They'd approached the cabin cautiously, the tall dark pines around the place seeming to whisper all the old legends they'd heard growing up. They'd just inched their way inside the front door when a face popped up in one of the broken windows. It stared at them with hideously wide eyes, growling like a bear as it grinned a death's head kind of rictus. Instantly, they forgot all about condoms and raced back to the Honda, terrified. When they finally got home, Messer got off his motor bike shamefaced, urine staining the crotch of his jeans.

Cochran shook the memory away and called down the stairs. "Hey, Ma—what exactly went on up there?"

"At the Fiddlesticks cabin?" Eleanor climbed the stairs to stand in the hall.

"Yeah."

"Fiddlesticks was a man named Robert Smith, who came home one night and found his wife with another man. He cut them up with a knife and sat there fiddling while they bled out." Pausing for a moment, she started clapping her hands in a kind of old jump-rope rhyme. "*Fiddlesticks killed her with his razor. Slit her throat and then forgave her.*"

"What does that mean?"

"The police caught him while he was putting flowers on her grave. He may have killed her, but he still loved her."

"When did all this happen?"

"Well." She frowned. "I was in the fourth grade, so it must have been about 1958. All the boys in my class were terrified—they said if you walked through the woods alone, Fiddlesticks would come and cut off your tallywhacker."

Cochran frowned. "Your what?"

"Tallywhacker. Fourth-grade slang for *penis*."

Cochran leaned against the doorjamb, grateful that his tallywhacker was safe beneath his bathrobe. "So they didn't catch him right away?"

"He hid out in the hills a good while. We weren't allowed to leave our yards for weeks." She ran a hand through the white, down-like hair she usually concealed with a blue Duke cap. "That was the first time everybody started locking their doors at night. Aunt Frankie slept with a shotgun under her bed for the rest of her life."

"What finally happened?" asked Cochran, trying to keep his mother on task. Gossip and memory could sidetrack her pretty easily.

"They found him guilty of murder. Sent him to the gas chamber, as I recall."

————

Ninety minutes later, Cochran pulled in behind Saunooke's squad car, parking on what was locally known as Fiddler Road. It was no more than two ruts that snaked through the trees, overgrown on both sides with wild grapevine and thick tangles of rhododendrons. He got out of his cruiser and gazed at the path. Narrow, it twisted so that you could never see more than ten yards ahead of you. But even beyond that, an odd stillness hung here, as if everything from the birds in the sky to the lascivious red blossoms of the trumpet vines stood silent, watching to see what he would do. *Just like that afternoon with Messer,* whispered a voice inside his head.

He smiled at his edginess but still reached for the twelve-gauge pump Winchester that rode in the front of his car. "Up here, I guess I'm still thirteen," he said quietly. "At least I've gotten past stealing condoms."

He kept the shotgun pointed at the ground as he hiked the last half mile to the cabin, watching for snakes and clambering over several trees that had fallen across the path. As the battered old place finally came into view, he made careful note of his first impressions. It was 11:41 a.m. and the sun had just begun to peek over the east side of the ridge, warming the cool, uncomfortably humid air. A family of crows perched high in a pine tree about fifty yards east of the structure, keeping a beady-eyed watch on Rob Saunooke, who stood talking to five young people clustered around the steps of the front porch. One girl wept into a boy's arms, while another girl stood stony-faced between two other, taller boys. The college students all wore pricey outdoor clothing and kept their backs toward the crow-filled pine tree. Cochran observed them discreetly for a few moments, without announcing himself. Saunooke seemed to have everything under control, though he kept looking nervously toward the path. Deciding it was time to help the young officer out, Cochran made his presence known.

"Saunooke," he called.

His most recent hire turned, looking relieved to see someone with a badge and a gun. "Yes, sir?"

"A word."

Saunooke left the five standing in front of the cabin and hurried over to Cochran. "Hey, boss," he said, wiping sweat from his forehead.

"What have we got?"

"Big trouble, I think." Saunooke solemnly handed him a driver's license.

Cochran studied the laminated card. It belonged to one Lisa Carlisle Wilson, a twenty-one-year-old white female, from 2339 Cleveland Mews, Raleigh, North Carolina. Though Lisa was a pretty, curly-haired girl with a pert little kiss of a mouth, it was her name that caught his attention. It sounded alarmingly similar to Jackson Carlisle Wilson, the former governor who'd long ago dragged Pisgah and the other western counties of the state into a reasonable semblance of the twentieth century.

Cochran frowned at Saunooke. "This girl isn't kin to old Governor Carlisle Wilson, is she?"

Saunooke nodded. "His daughter, according to her friends. Usually just goes with Wilson as her last name though."

Cochran frowned at the five standing in front of the cabin. "Which one is she?"

"She's the victim," Saunooke replied.

"Are you kidding?"

Saunooke shook his head.

"Dear God." Cochran looked at the girl's driver's license again, but this time saw her father—an old style, ball-busting politician who had, on more than one occasion, convinced the entire state that shit was Shinola. Carlisle Wilson would eat Pisgah County for breakfast once he found out about this. *This must be my lucky day,* Cochran thought. *Not one but two governors to contend with.*

He took a deep breath. "Okay," he said to Saunooke. "Tell me what you know."

"She was one of six summer interns at that raptor center on the other side of the mountain," he replied. "They heard about the Fiddlesticks cabin and hiked over here yesterday afternoon. They were making some kind of movie about spending the night at a haunted house."

Cochran winced, picturing the headlines in the paper. "Go on."

"Anyway, they stayed up late last night and woke up late this morning. One kid went to take a dump in the woods and found her body." Saunooke pointed to the tall pine tree where the crows were perching. "Under that tree there."

"And nobody saw or heard a thing," Cochran finished Saunooke's account for him. He'd learned, over the past seven years, that whatever crime had transpired, never did anybody at the scene ever hear, see, or notice anything out of the ordinary.

"Right. Well, they thought they might have seen someone last night, but they'd all been drinking."

Cochran again regarded the five who now huddled like refugees in front of the battered old cabin. "Did they sleep inside or outside?"

"Inside. Lisa Wilson doubled up in her sleeping bag with one of the guys."

"Were they having sex or just sleeping?" asked Cochran.

"Just sleeping, according to the boy," said Saunooke. "He's upset, but not girlfriend-upset, if you know what I mean."

Ginger Malloy's strawberry-blonde hair flashed through Cochran's mind. He knew well what girlfriend-upset meant. "Which one of them found her?"

Saunooke glanced over his shoulder. "The dark-haired boy in the Duke sweatshirt."

"Is he the one she slept with?"

"No, she slept with the blonde kid who looks like a wrestler."

"Okay." Cochran looked at both boys, wondering if some love triangle had ended badly. "What else?"

"I was trying to sort things out when you arrived," said Saunooke "They're all scared, talking at once. They think a bear got her."

Cochran turned away from the interns, eyed the pine tree, hoping this might turn out to be just some errant sow protecting her cubs. "And did a bear get her?"

Saunooke shook his head. "No bear that I ever saw."

"What do you mean?" asked Cochran. Saunooke had come up through the ranks of the highway patrol—he'd seen plenty of death and dismemberment on the highways.

"You'll have to go see for yourself, sir."

"Okay," Cochran said "You confiscate all cell phones, cameras, anything these jokers have that might contain evidence or corroborate alibis. Then call Boots and get another squad car and the State Bureau of Investigation team from Asheville. I'll go check out the girl."

"Have you had breakfast?" asked Saunooke.

"Just coffee," replied Cochran.

"Good," said Saunooke, turning back to his little group of suspects. "You'll probably be able to keep that down."

Cochran kept the shotgun and headed toward the pine tree, steeling himself to see God only knew what. If a former highway patrol officer was blanching, then it must be bad.

The ancient pine trees stood like massive sentinels, their thick branches turning warm air cool, daylight into perpetual dusk. Little underbrush grew around them, and cast-off needles from countless autumns past had turned the ground into a spongy orange carpet. The cloying, metallic odor of blood engulfed him as he pushed his way through some feathery branches, then suddenly, he saw her.

"Sweet Jesus," he whispered. He stopped, realizing why Saunooke had been so undone, why Boots Gahagan's initial report was that some *thing* had torn a girl up. She lay naked in a small clearing, her arms stretched out as if she'd been crucified. Ligature marks scarred her throat, bulging her once pretty eyes, protruding a darkened tongue. Gnats and flies were hovering in a cloud above her face; already a crow had pecked at one of her eyes. But the scavengers did not make Cochran gasp. What brought his coffee roiling back up his throat was the bloody mess some *thing* had made of Lisa Wilson's body. Not only had the girl been stripped and strangled, but someone had turned her corpse into a scroll, carving hieroglyphic-like figures from her wrists all the way down to her pink-painted toes.

For a moment he truly thought he might vomit. He turned his eyes away, looking into the trees, swallowing the saliva that flooded his mouth. When he looked back, he tried to focus on just one, single part of her. Piecemeal, he could pretend it was just a puzzle on puckered skin. If he looked at her whole body, he didn't know if he could stand it.

Brushing away the gnats and flies, he concentrated on the reddish brown characters carved into the flesh of her right shoulder. The first figure resembled a Greek delta, the second one, closer to her clavicle, looked like something from the Cherokee syllabary. Slowly, he read his way across her torso, trying to find some figure he recognized. When he dropped down to her breasts, he realized sickly that the lower figures were just as dark as the ones across her shoulders. The bleeding had continued for all the wounds. Which meant someone had sliced Lisa Wilson up while she was still alive.

He backed away and began taking in deep breaths of the cool, pine-laced air. He'd seen a dozen homicides, a couple of real bear attacks. None of those came close to this. This was sick. This was territory he had no map for.

Suddenly, he heard footsteps behind him. Tightening his grip on the shotgun, he turned. To his astonishment, Buck Whaley came wheezing up through the trees, a toothpick lodged in the corner of his mouth, gold detective badge glinting from his belt. Quickly, Cochran cleared his throat. He didn't want Whaley to catch him on the verge of puking.

"Hidy, sheriff," Whaley greeted amiably, sweat glinting through his brush-cut gray hair. "I hear we've got some trouble."

"I thought you were on vacation," said Cochran.

"Got back last night. Heard Boots on the scanner and thought I'd come help out. What's up?"

"Take a look." Cochran stepped aside, revealing Lisa Wilson's body.

Whaley peered at the dead girl. "Holy fuck," he whispered, his little pig eyes widening. "What the hell got hold of her?"

"A bear, according to her friends," said Cochran.

"Yeah, and my granny's a Green Bay Packer." Whaley studied her face for a long moment. "She anybody we know?"

"You might have heard of her father," Cochran replied. "Jackson Carlisle Wilson."

Whaley removed the toothpick that dangled from his lip. "Are you serious?"

Cochran nodded.

"How'd that old fart get a daughter this young and pretty?"

"I guess he had sex with her mother," Cochran glanced at her driver's license. "Twenty-one years ago."

"What the hell was she doing up here?"

"She worked at that raptor center. She and her pals hiked over here on a ghost hunt. One of them found her this morning."

Whaley laughed. "Any of 'em see any ghosts?"

"Nobody saw anything."

"What a pile of shit." Moving closer, Whaley stood with arms akimbo, making a long, lingering appraisal of the girl's body. "Man, she's a peach."

Again Cochran thought of Ginger. A sudden protective rush surged through him, and he had to struggle not to push Whaley away from Lisa Carlisle Wilson's nakedness. "I hadn't noticed," he lied. "I was looking at everything carved on her body."

"Yeah, right." Whaley gave him a knowing wink. *You looked*, it said. *I know you looked. We all look, every time. We can't not look.*

"You want me to take over?" Whaley glanced at his watch. "You leave now, you can get back to town in time to schmooze with the honorable Governor Chandler."

"No," said Cochran. "I'm taking this case."

Whaley's brows lifted in surprise. "You?"

Cochran nodded. "Me and Saunooke and you and Clark, if he can walk. We'll work as a team. We've already got five suspects. You and Saunooke divide them up and take them downtown. You question the boys, let Saunooke take the girls. If Clark hobbles down there, he can help Saunooke out."

"What are you going to do?" demanded Whaley.

"I'm going to wait here for the SBI. I'll meet you downtown later."

Whaley opened his mouth to protest further, then, abruptly, changed his mind. "Okay," he said still sounding vaguely miffed. With a final glance at Lisa Carlisle Wilson, he started to waddle off toward the cabin. Cochran called him back with a warning.

"Don't go ape, Whaley," he said. "You work for me now, not Stump Logan. I don't want any black eyes or forced confessions."

Whaley gave a deep chuckle. "You just be careful yourself, sheriff. I hear there's ghosts up here."

23

Cochran remained under the tree, watching as Whaley conferred with Saunooke, then the two began to herd the suspects down the path to their cars. All of them, Cochran noted, walked with their heads down, their eyes averted from their fallen companion. When they disappeared from sight, he turned back to Lisa. Soon the SBI team would arrive with all their equipment. They would turn her into a number, a case, ultimately, a statistic. Right now, she still had a name, a face, was still a girl who people had loved. He would stay with her until that changed. It was the least he could do.

Stooping down, he looked closer. Her nails were unbroken, though a circle of paler skin around her left ring finger looked as if someone might have removed a ring. Her nipples were intact and her pudenda looked unswollen by sexual assault. The pine needles on which she lay were scattered and blood-stained, ranging from deep brownish to a vibrant red-orange.

"They killed you right here, didn't they?" he whispered, speaking to her as if she might sit up and answer back. "But who? And why?" He wondered if it was some kind of version of the choking game gone wrong, but carving someone up like that indicated a monstrous anger toward the victim. That led him again to suspect a romantic breakup. Had one of those boys choked her and mutilated her body while she was still alive?

"And then went back to sleep in the haunted house without waking a single soul?" he asked aloud.

No, came the answer. *It was either all of them, or none of them.*

Taking a different tack, he disregarded the five kids en route to questioning, and began to consider other possibilities. The Appalachians had their share of psychopaths—backwoodsmen who slithered through the trees, stalking their prey along trails instead of truck stops, campgrounds instead of bars. Had one of them come across these kids at the cabin and decided to have a little fun? Possibly, he decided. But why kill one and leave five sleeping like babies? And why carve her up like a Dead Sea scroll?

He stood up and gazed down at the cabin. It cowered beneath the trees like some beaten dog, in the middle of three hundred acres of thick forest, miles away from anything remotely resembling civilization. Even after all these years—even with a Winchester pump at his side—the place still gave him the willies. He felt like somewhere, in the midst of those three hundred acres, a man was looking at him with pale, wide eyes, and laughing.

"Fiddlesticks killed her with his razor; slit her throat and then forgave her," he repeated his mother's rhyme in a whisper, thinking that if some places were truly cursed, then this was one of them.

THREE

MARY CROW LOOKED UP as the huge eagle made a slow, sweeping circle of the amphitheater. Wings stretched wide, the bird glided over the large crowd of citizens who'd gathered for the grand opening of the new sports park. By Pisgah County standards, the festivities had been vast. Lige McCauley and his string band had fiddled, the Cherokee Drum circle had drummed, and the Hartsville High marching band had presented a mini-concert, complete with fire batons. Now upturned gazes followed Sequoia as he winged through the air. Of equal interest to Mary was the raptor's trainer, a man named Nick Stratton, whom she knew through three pre-festival phone conversations. From his crisp accent and straight-forward manner of speaking, she'd pictured him as a serious, bespectacled academic. That he was, in person, a rangy man who'd given her a funny little smile when he came out on the field, surprised her. Lately she was unaccustomed to any attractive man giving her any kind of smile, funny or otherwise.

She turned her attention back to the eagle, which made two complete circles of the amphitheater, then made a sharp turn and headed straight for the stage. Mary fought an urge to duck as the bird bore down toward her with talons extended, but at the last second Nick Stratton stepped forward and slapped his gloved arm twice. Sequoia instantly feathered his approach and landed gracefully on the man's arm.

"Our national bird in flight, ladies and gentlemen!" cried Mayor Tom Burkhart, the master of ceremonies. "Let's give Sequoia a hand!"

Everyone cheered. Stratton tossed Sequoia what looked like a bloody chunk of raw liver before the pair stepped forward and took their bows. As Stratton turned to acknowledge the dignitaries on stage, Mary was able to get a closer look at the man. Light brown hair streaked with blonde, deep set eyes, handsome except for a deeply scarred upper lip, Mary decided that either Nick Stratton had a deformity that had been surgically corrected, or Sequoia had, at some point, mistaken his mouth for another chunk of liver.

———

The dedication continued, with the Reverend Rosemary Brown of the First Methodist Church giving the invocation. As she asked the Lord's blessing on the park, Mary offered her own prayer of thanks, remembering what an uphill battle the Pisgah-Cherokee Sports Park had been. She'd spearheaded the project mostly to take herself out of a deadly dull stream of bankruptcies and estate planning, only to find that negotiating the project required the mediation skills of a diplomat. She'd had to wheedle and cajole tobacco farmers, land developers, swimming pool companies, and at one point, the governing body of the US Little League.

After the Reverend Brown ended her prayer, the mayor rose. He welcomed everybody in English, then Chief John Oocuma hopped up and said basically the same thing in Cherokee. Mary sneaked a quick glance at the crowd, looking for Jonathan and Lily. They promised they'd sit in the first row, but she couldn't find them anywhere. Suddenly, she turned, realizing that John Oocuma had switched from Cherokee to English.

"Now, I'd like to introduce someone whose hard work made all this possible—a true friend to both tribe and county, Mary Crow."

She blushed as the crowd began to applaud. Usually she spoke only to juries in courtrooms. Never had she addressed a crowd of thousands, as a "friend to tribe and county." Taking a deep breath, she clutched the notes she'd scribbled last night and walked to the podium.

"A year ago, our children had to pursue their sports dreams elsewhere. They had to go to Sylva to swim, to Swain County to play baseball, to Waynesville for their soccer and tennis matches," Mary said. "Today, all that is history. Today, we of Pisgah County can swim and compete on our home turf."

The crowd cheered. Someone blew a vuvuzela horn. Mary went on.

"Though I appreciate the credit Chief Oocuma gave me, this park would not have happened without the hard work of the citizens of Pisgah County, and the Eastern Band of the Cherokee Indians. But even beyond all our good efforts, this time we had an angel in Raleigh who loosened the state's purse strings and cut through several miles of red tape. We're lucky to have her with us today, to open the Pisgah-Cherokee Sports Park." As the crowd began to clap again, Mary turned to the dignitaries seated behind her. "Ladies and gentlemen, it's my privilege to introduce the honorable Ann Chandler, governor of North Carolina."

The cheering grew to a thunderous crescendo. The last governor to set foot in Pisgah County was Jackson Carlisle Wilson, back when Gerald Ford sat in the White House. That the current chief executive would take the time to come and open their sports park had the county bursting its collective buttons. Mary stepped back from the podium as a diminutive blonde in a white linen pantsuit rose from her chair. Chandler waved to the crowd as she came to the microphone. Mary was about to re-take her seat, when the governor pulled her close.

"Remind me again how to say 'play ball' in Cherokee."

"*Doyust uhlskult dah dahnay zohn.*" Mary whispered, hoping she could hear her above all the cheering.

"Got it." The governor winked at her and smiled. "Thanks."

Grateful to have finished her part of the program, Mary sat down. As the chief executive began her remarks, she again searched the crowd for Jonathan and Lily; again she could not find them. She guessed this was yet another example of Jonathan's recent strangeness. He'd spent the past month in Oklahoma with Lily, on a court-ordered visitation with his late wife's parents. She'd missed them terribly, and when they finally rolled back down the driveway, she assumed that their lives would go on as before. That had not happened. Lily had returned moody and petulant, and Mary had felt a coldness in Jonathan's kiss, as if something had disconnected his lips from his heart. As the weeks passed, she knew she should just ask him if he'd found someone younger or prettier in Oklahoma, but when an appropriate moment came, she always lost her nerve. She was thinking that today might be the day to ask that question when suddenly she heard the governor again call her name.

"Mary?" Ann Chandler smiled at her. "You're going to have to help me with this Cherokee again."

Mary hurried to the podium, ready to whisper the words in the governor's ear, but Ann Chandler put an arm around her waist. "Let's just say it together."

The two women leaned toward the microphone. *"Doyust uhl-skult dah dahnay zohn,"* Mary said assuredly while the governor stumbled along.

"Play ball, Pisgah County," the governor added, grabbing the last word for her English-speaking constituents. "Have fun!"

The biggest cheer yet went up from the crowd. The Hartsville High band struck up a spirited arrangement of "We Are the Champions." Representatives from Harrah's Casino released a huge flock of green and white balloons. Children in various team uniforms scattered to the playing fields while their parents surged toward the platform, eager to shake the governor's hand. Mary returned to her chair, feeling hollow inside. Her family had apparently decided not to come.

She grabbed her purse, hoping she could get a ride back to town with Tom Burkhart when she heard her name. There, beside one of the loud speakers, stood Jonathan and Lily—Lily in her red soccer uniform, Jonathan carrying the picnic basket she'd packed that morning.

"Hey, you guys!" She smiled, surprised. "I was about to think you stood me up."

"We got stuck in traffic," Jonathan complained. "Everybody in Pisgah County decided to come to this thing." His hair had grown long as his waistline had shrunk in Oklahoma, giving him a lean, noble savage appearance. *He looks incredible*, Mary thought. *He probably has a dozen women eyeing him up in Oklahoma.*

"Did you hear my speech?" she asked.

He nodded. "Good job."

"You pronounced *uhlskult* wrong," Lily informed her. "It's *oolskult*."

"Sorry," Mary replied. "Next time I'll let you do the translating." She looked over at the crowd around Ann Chandler. "Would you like to meet the governor?"

"I'd rather go see the eagle." Lily crossed her arms, pouty in the way of nine-year-olds.

"Well, let's go meet the governor first," Mary said. "And don't correct her Cherokee, Lily."

After waiting until the swarm of people surrounding the governor subsided, Mary stepped forward. "Governor Chandler, may I introduce my family? Jonathan and Lily Walkingstick."

"Hi, Jonathan." Ann Chandler gave Jonathan's hand a practiced pump, then reached down to greet Lily. "How proud you must be of your mother, young lady."

"She's not my mother," Lily snapped defiantly, pushing her glasses back on her nose.

"*Ooyohee!*" Jonathan shushed her in Cherokee. Mary was stunned by the child's rudeness, but Ann Chandler didn't miss a beat.

"Well, I know you must be proud of her, anyway. If it wasn't for Mary, you wouldn't have that nice new soccer field."

"If it wasn't for Mary, I'd ... "

"Lily!" Jonathan barked, his warning to the child clear. Lily stepped back, obviously re-thinking the comment she'd almost made.

"Mary?" called another voice. Mary turned to see Ginger Malloy bustling on to the stage, her red hair glowing like a lit match in the bright sunlight. An older man followed her, an impressive camera around his neck.

"Here comes our local press," Mary laughingly warned the governor, grateful that Ginger had broken the awkward moment Lily had caused in their conversation.

"Hey, partner." Ginger gave her a hug. "Great speech, great job on the park! I can't wait to hit the tennis courts with you."

"Thanks," Mary said. Though Mary gave most reporters a wide berth, Ginger had become a friend. They played tennis regularly, belonged to the same book club, had even hiked a couple of short sections of the Appalachian Trail. Still, she knew Ginger's present ebullience had less to do with the new tennis courts than getting an interview with Ann Chandler. "Something tells me this is not a strictly congratulatory embrace."

Ginger turned to the governor. "I was wondering if we could get a shot of you for the paper?"

"I'd be delighted," said Ann Chandler. She turned toward the photographer as Mary and Jonathan stepped back. "No, no," she said, putting an arm around both Lily and Mary. "Everybody get in the picture. We're having a party today."

They arranged themselves like stair steps—Jonathan, Mary, Ann Chandler, and Lily. Ginger stepped behind the man with the camera.

"On three," called the photographer.

Mary smiled. He took three quick shots, then nodded at Ginger.

"Thank you so much," Ginger said to the governor. "I'll send your press officer a copy."

"My pleasure," replied Ann Chandler. Her official duties finally finished, she shook hands again with Jonathan and Lily. "Nice meeting both of you. I know you'll enjoy this park for years to come."

"Thanks," said Jonathan.

Smiling, the governor turned back to Mary. "Could I possibly kidnap you for a few minutes?"

Mary looked at the governor, puzzled.

"My supporters are having a little reception for me. I'd love it if you could come. There's something I'd like to ask you about."

Mary didn't know what to say. As badly as she wanted to put on her bathing suit and relax for the rest of the day, turning down the governor seemed not the thing to do. "Certainly," she said. "I'd be happy to."

"Then come with me." The governor took Mary's arm and again smiled at Jonathan. "Don't worry. I'll have her back in time for the soccer game!"

Mary shot Jonathan a helpless look as the governor steered her toward a waiting bus. "See you in a few minutes," she called. "Don't forget our picnic with Jerry and Ginger."

She smiled, trying to convince herself that everything was all right between them. But she could tell by the expression on his face that it was a lie. Nothing was right between them at all. Lily's outburst had proved that something was dreadfully wrong with their little family. She started to thank the governor and tell her she would have to take a rain check on the party, but just then Tom Burkhart and John Oocuma came up to express their own congratulations. By the time she got a clear view of the podium again, Jonathan and Lily were gone.

FOUR

By mid-afternoon, the crows had given up any hope of scavenging Lisa Wilson's eyes. The SBI team from Asheville had scared them away by crawling over a hundred-foot radius of the pine tree. After they'd gleaned what evidence they could from inside the cabin and around the tree, two junior agents zipped her remains in a black body bag.

"I need a priority on this," Cochran told Agent Fred Brewer as two young men hauled Lisa Wilson down the hill. "This girl's got connections."

"Oh, yeah?" Twenty years and forty pounds ago Brewer had been a Marine. He still wore his gray hair side-walled, still barked commands at his evidence-gathering troops as if they were establishing a beachhead on some hostile coastline. Cochran guessed that, in a way, they were.

Brewer's gray eyes sparked with sudden interest. "What kind of connections?"

"Political."

"Who?"

Cochran knew this could go two ways. If the SBI needed some good press in Raleigh, Brewer would muscle in on the case. If the connection was too hot, Brewer would lead his troops to higher ground. "Carlisle Wilson," he finally replied.

Brewer frowned. "Governor Carlisle Wilson?"

"His daughter, by all reports."

"Aw, man," said Brewer, suddenly sympathetic. "This could get bad. That old bastard's got enemies in every county in the state."

"Enemies who'd go after his daughter?" asked Cochran.

"I don't know." Brewer shrugged. "Maybe."

Too much heat for Brewer, Cochran thought as the agents lifted Lisa Wilson into the back of an unmarked van. *This puppy's going to be all mine.*

"You know we'll help in any way we can," Brewer said tepidly, beginning to distance himself.

"Then when you get her to the lab, make sure John Merkel does the post-mortem," said Cochran.

Brewer snorted. "That fruit cake usually doesn't come into the lab until midnight."

"I'll get in touch with him," said Cochran. "He'll be waiting when you get there."

Brewer gazed at the now vacant spot under the pine tree. "Have you told Carlisle Wilson about this yet?"

Cochran shook his head. "I want to talk to the guy she was working for first."

Brewer gave him a sympathetic slap on the back. "I don't blame you, buddy. That's one next-of-kin call I'd put off as long as I could, too."

———

Brewer helped him cordon off as much of the area as possible—then he left to go to Winston-Salem, promising to return first thing in the morning. As Cochran headed back to his cruiser, he paused at the cabin, remembering his adolescent terror. Back then the place had seemed huge—dark and foreboding as a castle. Today, it was just a mean little shack, furred with moss, slowly being cannibalized by wild grapevine and trumpet flowers. Still—something about the place made him edgy.

"Your ghost was probably just some old brain-fried dude with a still," he told himself as he walked up on the porch and gazed in the open front door. "Probably laughed his ass off at the two little punks who didn't have the balls to steal a condom."

"Say what?" A voice ripped through the air behind him.

Cochran jumped, turning in mid-air. He was ready to rack a shell when he saw Saunooke standing at the bottom of the steps.

"What the hell are you doing here?" asked Cochran angrily.

"Detective Clark took over the interviews." The young Cherokee shrugged. "So I came back here. Sorry if I scared you."

"No problem." Cochran lowered the gun, his heart beating fast. "Though you might want to announce yourself next time you come up behind somebody holding a Winchester."

Saunooke walked up to stand next to Cochran. He peered into the graffiti-rich rooms, now speckled with white fingerprint powder. "Creepy as hell, isn't it?"

"Kids come up here to get scared for a reason," said Cochran.

"*Deegahdoli*," said Saunooke.

"What's that?"

Saunooke laughed. "That's what the Cherokees call this place."

"*Deegahdoli* means Fiddlesticks?"

"No. There's supposedly a ghost up here—*deegahdoli* means eyes."

"Come on," said Cochran, heading back down the steps. "Let's get over to the bird center. I want to positively ID this girl before I rattle Carlisle Wilson's cage."

———

Half an hour later Cochran and Saunooke pulled up in front of the staring faces of a totem pole that stood above a sign that read "Pisgah Raptor Rescue Center." Cochran got out of his car slowly, examining the totem pole for any of the same odd squiggles carved on Lisa Wilson's body. He didn't see any, but he still found it odd to come face to face with a Northwest Indian artifact here in Cherokee country. He turned to Saunooke.

"You guys don't put up totem poles now, do you?"

Saunooke laughed. "Only for the tourists."

"That's what I thought." Cochran frowned at the stylized faces of an eagle and an owl. "Let's go see what else is up there."

"Don't we need a warrant?"

"No. We're just informing of a death today," Cochran explained. "We're friendly and respectful, but we keep our eyes and ears open, just the same."

They turned left and walked along a gravel path that led uphill. Though the woods were just as thick as at Fiddlestick's cabin, Cochran sensed no silent, underlying malevolence here. Birds chirped, bees buzzed. An innate busy-ness hummed about this forest that made the silence at Fiddlesticks's place even stranger. They hadn't gone more than fifty feet when they met a wiry old man limping toward them, a huge bald eagle perched on his gloved right arm. When he caught sight of Cochran and Saunooke, he stopped immediately, the bird rousting its feathers at the abrupt surcease of motion.

"Howdy." The man respectfully touched the bill of an ancient Braves baseball cap with fingers that were sheered off at the second knuckle. "Something wrong?"

"Are you Nick Stratton?" asked Cochran.

He squinted up at him as if even this soft, leaf-filtered light was too bright. "No, sir. I'm Artie Slade. Nick's up yonder at the cabin."

"Can you take us to him?"

"Something wrong?" Slade asked again as the bird opened its beak and let out a shrill, whistling shriek.

"We'd prefer to talk with Mr. Stratton," said Cochran.

"Then come ahead on." The old man tightened his grip on a long leather strap that secured the eagle and turned around, heading back in the direction he'd come. Cochran and Saunooke followed, finally stopping at a cabin nestled between two tall sycamore trees. Recently built of new lumber, a wide porch surrounded it on three sides. On that porch two men stood talking. One slouched against the porch railing, smoking a cigarette while the other stood tall, with surfer-blonde hair.

"Yo, Nick!" called Artie Slade. "Law's here!"

The two looked up, startled. For an instant both gazed at Cochran with hard eyes, then the tall surfer came down the steps.

"Nick Stratton?" asked Cochran.

The lanky man nodded. "I'm Nick Stratton."

"Do you have an intern named Lisa Carlisle Wilson?" Cochran noticed a deep scar that bisected the man's upper lip.

Stratton frowned. "I do. Is she in some kind of trouble?"

"Mr. Stratton, at approximately nine a.m. this morning, we got a call from the east side of Burr Mountain. A twenty-one-year-old white female named Lisa Carlisle Wilson was found dead—the apparent victim of a homicide."

"A homicide?" Stratton looked at Cochran incredulous, as if he were someone dressed as a cop, playing a joke. "Are you serious?"

"Yes, sir."

"You mean Lisa's dead?"

Cochran nodded, knowing that it took awhile for people to wrap their heads around such grim news.

Stratton asked, "What about the other kids?"

"They're fine. Downtown now, giving statements."

"Holy shit!" The second man shook his head as he stubbed out his cigarette on the porch floor. "Here we were figuring they were just laid out drunk somewhere."

"I warned them that cabin was bad luck," said the man who held the eagle.

Stratton just stood there, looking like a man suddenly short of air.

"I understand that this Lisa is the daughter of former governor Jackson Carlisle Wilson," said Cochran.

Stratton nodded.

"Do you have any contact information for her?"

"Yeah," he said, his voice a croak. "Come inside and I'll get it."

While Stratton headed back to his cabin, Cochran turned to the other men who were standing there watching the proceedings. "Did you two men know Lisa Wilson?"

"We both worked with her." The smoker gave a leering giggle. "We didn't *know her* know her."

"You'll both still need to give Officer Saunooke a statement."

The eagle wrangler piped up. "Can I re-cage this bird first?"

Cochran nodded, then turned to Saunooke. "Interview this guy first, then get the other one after he ditches the bird."

Leaving Saunooke to the interviews, Cochran went inside the cabin. The place smelled of cedar and had Western décor, with the flag of Washington State draped over the fireplace, a hockey stick gracing the mantel. On one wall hung half a dozen musical instruments—fiddles and mandolins, a banjo and a guitar.

"You play all these instruments?" he asked Stratton, who was rummaging through a small file cabinet in the kitchen.

"Fiddle and mandolin. The kids play everything else."

Cochran wandered toward the kitchen, taking in the details of Stratton's home. He peered at the refrigerator, searching the array of calendars and notes for any of those strange, runic letters that decorated Lisa Wilson's body. He found nothing more exotic than a postcard from Costa Rica, written in Spanish.

"I can't believe this," said Stratton, finally extricating an envelope from the file. "Here's her information. What the hell happened to her up there?"

"We're not sure," Cochran said.

"But how can you not be sure, if she's dead?" Stratton's tone grew angry.

"The state medical examiner determines that, sir." Cochran always played his cards close to his vest. Maybe this bird guy would hang himself, if he was the killer.

Stratton ran a hand through his long locks. "To think we were getting pissed because they were late coming back to work."

"Who was getting pissed?" asked Cochran.

"Artie and Jenkins." Stratton nodded toward the porch, where Saunooke was still talking to the smoker. "They had to cover for the kids this morning while I went to the sports park opening."

Cochran thought of Ginger, the picnic they'd planned to have, the ring he'd hoped to put on her finger later that night. "What did you do at the sports park opening?"

"I took a couple of our ambassador owls and flew our eagle, Sequoia." Stratton returned to the file and pulled out a business card that had a cartoon depicting him with an eagle on one shoulder. "I do an avian educational show for kids. *Dr. Lovebird and Friends*."

"And your interns help you with that?"

He nodded. "They were supposed to. But yesterday they got a wild hair about going up to that old cabin. I figured they'd earned some time off, so I said okay."

"What exactly do they do here?" asked Cochran.

"They spend the summer rehabbing raptors. Learn avian anatomy, banding, helping fledge out young eagles on the hacking stand."

"Hacking stand?"

"A platform with open-faced cages, about thirty feet high. The eaglets learn to fly without human intervention."

"You a vet?"

"I've got my DVM, also a PhD. I run this rehabilitation center, plus teach adjunct at Duke and Appalachian."

Cochran nodded. This Stratton might look like a beach bum, but he spoke like a man accustomed to mortarboards and diplomas. He looked back at the wall of instruments. "Anything I should know about Lisa?"

"She was a nice girl. Good with birds, worked hard. Got along with everybody."

That strangled, mutilated body flashed across Cochran's mind. "Are you sure about that? She didn't get along so well with the person who killed her."

"I think a couple of the kids might have resented her," admitted Stratton. "But they certainly wouldn't have killed her."

"Why did they resent her?"

"Kind of a teacher's pet thing. She made sure I had a fresh pot of coffee every morning, that my porch was swept off." Stratton gave an apologetic smile. "Ultimately, it got embarrassing. I had to ask her to stop."

Cochran nodded, casually looking for scratch marks on Stratton's hands and arms. He wore a long-sleeved shirt buttoned to the wrists, but there were several cuts on the knuckles of his right hand. "Did Lisa have any problems with anybody else? Her family? Any old boyfriends come calling?"

"Seems like she said she'd broken up with some guy."

"Mention any names?"

"Honestly, I don't remember."

"You don't seem to know much about this girl, Mr. Stratton."

"It's not my job to know much about her." He frowned, defensive. "It's my job to teach her about raptors."

"And hopefully get her home in one piece."

Again, Stratton ran his hands through his hair. "I don't know what to tell you—she did her work, rehabbed a kestrel, tried to learn the guitar." He shrugged at Cochran. "I can take you to her room, if that would help."

Cochran gave a tight smile. "That might help considerably."

The two men went back outside. The late afternoon sun had heated the air, making the smell of pine so thick Cochran could feel it on his tongue. Saunooke had dismissed the smoker and was starting to interview the bird-wrangler. Stratton led him back toward the totem pole but then made a sharp left turn down another prong of the path. They finally came to two large cabins joined by a walkway. Laundry flapped in the breeze from both porches—jeans and tee shirts on one, bras and bikini pants on the other.

"The girls always claim that east cabin," Stratton explained. "It's got one more toilet and an extra sink."

Stratton walked to the cabin and opened the door. Inside, the room was divided into four cubicles, each appointed with bed and bureau, desk and bulletin board. They were what Cochran would expect from college girls. Pictures of friends decorated the walls, iPods rested next to laptop computers. Two of the girls had fiddles with beginning fiddle books. Another had a half-finished bracelet stretched across a beading loom and a deck of tarot cards.

"Which cubicle is Lisa's?" asked Cochran.

"Beats me," Stratton replied. "I never come down here."

Cochran walked around the room. Suddenly he stopped at the cubicle nearest the bathroom. "You think it might be this one?"

Stratton came over to stand beside him. Both men looked at a well-appointed cubicle that had every available inch of the wall above the bed covered in pictures of Nick Stratton. Stratton working with birds, playing the fiddle, coming out of a creek bare-chested and dripping wet. Cochran turned and looked at the tall man who was gaping at the display. "Are you sure you never came down here?"

"No." Stratton gulped, embarrassed. "I had no idea she'd taken all these."

Cochran gazed at the photos with interest. "Too bad," he said, pulling down a picture of Lisa beaming up at a shirtless Stratton, her missing ring clearly visible on her right hand. "Looks like your coming down here would have made Lisa's dreams come true."

FIVE

As it turned out, Mary missed every bit of the soccer game. Also the picnic as well as Jonathan's game-winning goal in the over-35 Cherokee men's stickball game. Between the governor—who wanted to appoint her special prosecutor for crimes against women—and Jake McKenna, chief arm-twister for the governor, she didn't get back to the sports park until well after dark. Now she sat, guilty and remorseful, as Jonathan sped them home, swerving up the tight mountain curves as overhanging limbs slapped against the roof of their car.

"I'm so sorry I missed everything," Mary apologized for the third time, breaking their sullen silence. "Did you guys have fun at the park?"

"It was great," said Jonathan. "Lily played an awesome game. After that we went swimming and had our picnic."

"Did you eat with Ginger and Jerry?"

"They never showed up," said Jonathan. "So we ate fast and went to the stickball game."

"Daddy scored a goal," Lily added. "Everybody cheered."

"I'm so sorry I wasn't there," Mary made apology number four. "It's just hard to turn down a direct invitation from the governor."

"What did she want?" asked Jonathan, a slight edge in his voice.

"Just to thank me for all my work on the sports park," Mary replied, deciding now was probably not the best time to bring up Ann Chandler's job offer.

"Wow," said Jonathan. "Get chummy with the governor, who knows what might happen?"

She started to tell him nothing was going to happen when suddenly Lily screamed.

"Daddy! Look out!"

Mary turned just in time to see a shadow swoop across Jonathan's side of the car. He braked hard, pitching them forward. Mary winced as her seatbelt dug into her shoulder.

The car fishtailed wildly, finally skidding to a stop diagonally across the narrow mountain road.

"Everybody okay?" With a brief glance at Mary, Jonathan turned his attention to his child.

Unharmed, Lily sat up between the front seats. "What happened?"

"Something flew in front of us," said Jonathan, backing the car into the proper side of the road.

"What was it?" Lily cried.

"Probably a bat," Jonathan replied.

"Wait! I want to get out and make sure it's okay."

"You don't need to mess around with bats, Lily."

"But it might be hurt!" Quickly, the child opened the door and scampered out of the backseat.

"Lily! Get back here!" cried Jonathan.

She paid no attention. Irritated, Jonathan thumped the steering wheel with the palm of his hand. "Damn it," he said, disgusted. "I've got to get some sleep tonight—I'm taking a fishing party up to Big Witch Creek at dawn."

Mary couldn't help but wonder why he'd played stickball if he'd had such a tough day coming tomorrow, but she made no comment. "Take it easy," she said, unbuckling her seatbelt. "I'll go get her."

She got out of the car. In the dim light, the backs of Lily's sneakers were two small bobbing orbs. Mary followed them, listening for Jonathan's door to open, his own footsteps to start following hers. Instead, all she heard was an abrupt silence as he turned off the engine. *Odd behavior*, she thought, *for a man who'd once spent half a day tracking a bobcat winged by an errant arrow.*

"I found it!" Lily shouted, from the far side of the road.

Mary jogged forward, wanting to stop the child if Jonathan had indeed hit a bat. "Don't touch it, Lily," she called. "Bats can be dangerous."

"It's not a bat!" Lily pointed to a quivering lump by the side of the road.

Mary hurried closer. As her eyes grew accustomed to the darkness, she began to make out not leathery wings, but white feathers, a yellowish beak. "Go get a flashlight, Lily. And tell your father it's not a bat."

Lily ran back to the car. A few moments later she returned with the flashlight, Jonathan behind her.

"Shine the light down here," Mary whispered. Lily pointed the flashlight at the creature on the ground. The lump became an owl. It had brown wing feathers, a cream-colored chest speckled with brown dots. The face was white but ringed in a delicate line of tan feathers that made the shape of a heart. With round black eyes, there was a kind of innocent sweetness about the bird's face. It looked terrified.

"Is it *Ugugu*?" Jonathan asked, using the Cherokee name for a Great Horned Owl, an animal that traditionally presaged death.

"No," said Mary. "Cut the flashlight, Lily. It's really scared."

As Lily doused the light, Mary turned to Jonathan. "It's some other kind of owl. It's hurt."

He made a soft grunt of regret. "I'll go take it up in the woods."

"What for?" asked Lily.

"To put it down, Lily. It can't fly."

"We can take it home and nurse it—"

"Lily, I hit it with the car. It will die soon. Better to let me kill it quickly, in the woods, than to let it flop here by this road."

"No!" cried Lily. "You can't kill him!"

"Lily, it's cruel to—"

"He's beautiful! His face is like a heart!"

"But Lily—"

The little girl started to cry. "He's alive. He wants to live!"

Jonathan knelt down in front of her. "Honey, you've seen wounded animals before. I've told you about the cycle of life."

"I don't care about the cycle of life. I don't want him to die!"

Mary bit her tongue and kept silent. This was a Walkingstick affair; she knew better than to intrude, uninvited, between father and daughter.

"I know somebody who'll help him!" Lily's tone rose in desperation. "Dr. Lovebird!"

Jonathan frowned. "Dr. who?"

"Dr. Lovebird. The man who flew the eagle today. I went over and talked to him. He heals birds when they get hurt."

Mary smiled, remembering Nick Stratton's stage name.

Jonathan took Lily's hand. "Honey, this owl probably has a broken wing—he'll never fly again. Even if Dr. Lovebird could save him, he'd have to stay in a cage the rest of his life. He could never do what he loved."

"But that's better than dying!"

Jonathan looked at her, his gaze serious. "You really think so?"

"Yes." Lily began to wail again. "He wasn't doing anything wrong. You're the one who hit him!"

"Accidents happen, Lily," he told her. "Sometimes bad things happen that are nobody's fault." He reached to pull her close, but she twisted away from him, her face streaked with tears.

"Dr. Lovebird can save him, Daddy. You hit him—you could at least take him there!"

"I'm not taking that owl anywhere, Lily. Dr. Lovebird flies eagles; he probably doesn't know a hoot owl from a hummingbird." Jonathan stood up and took a step toward the bird. Lily scurried to stand in front of him.

"No!" Her voice shook with rage as she tried to shove her father away. "You can't kill him! I won't let you!"

Stymied, Jonathan turned toward Mary. She could tell that he now wanted her input. Lily had inherited her father's stubbornness, and Mary had helped the two negotiate body-piercings (one hole per ear lobe only), tattoos (absolutely none), and late-night reading (until nine p.m., but only if all homework was completed). Tonight, she was going to have to find them common ground over this bird.

Mary looked at the owl, quivering by the side of the road, then she turned to Jonathan. "Let's take him home. Maybe he's just stunned. If he's okay in the morning, we can let him go."

"That's a good idea!" Lily said eagerly.

"But …" Jonathan began, then stopped as Mary lifted a silencing hand and turned to Lily.

"Lily, if he's not okay in the morning, then we'll have to release his spirit. It's cruel to let a wounded thing suffer."

Father and daughter glared at each other, neither willing to give ground.

"Is that agreeable?" asked Mary, thinking how much Lily's expression mirrored Jonathan's.

"Yes," said Lily.

Jonathan rolled his eyes. "Okay."

"Good," said Mary. "That's the deal. Lily, you stay here with the owl. Your father and I will go to the car and get something to put him in."

They left Lily with the flashlight and walked back to the car. "Don't you know that bird won't last the night?" whispered Jonathan.

"I do."

"Then why get her hopes up that he'll live?"

"Because she's almost hysterical, Jonathan. Wringing the bird's neck is not the answer." She turned to him, sudden tears stinging her own eyes. "Don't you think some things might be worth trying to save?"

He made a noise—a snorting kind of Cherokee phrase that had no real definition, but always meant disapproval. Still, he opened the trunk of the car and retrieved an old quilt they'd used for picnics. "Just remember that I'm leaving way before dawn. If that bird is still alive in the morning, you're the one who's going to have to kill it."

SIX

WHILE MARY CROW GRAPPLED with the injured owl, Jerry Cochran sat at his desk, steeling himself for his two most hated duties. The news conference he'd scheduled for ten p.m. was bad enough; far worse than that was his next-of-kin call to Carlisle Wilson. He'd been trying to reach the governor ever since he left Stratton's bird center. But the old man, according to some mush-mouthed aide, was "out fishing." Cochran finally decided if he hadn't reached the man before the press conference he would break the news without releasing the name of the victim. It would not make him look abundantly professional, but he couldn't sit on a homicide story for twenty-four hours. As Ginger often reminded him, the public has a right to know.

Impatient, he stared at the phone, willing the old man to call him back. As the thing sat mute and uncooperative, he started re-reading the statement he was going to give the press, striking through Lisa Wilson's name with a red pen. That presented a new set of problems. Giving the bare bones essentials—just saying that they'd found a twenty-one-year-old female dead on Burr Mountain would only make the reporters—Ginger especially—start digging for more. He could just picture their reaction if he told them the unvarnished truth—that Governor Carlisle Wilson's only daughter had been strangled and mutilated at a remote cabin reputedly haunted by ghosts.

Suddenly, the phone rang. Jumping, he grabbed the receiver, hoping Geneva had the real governor on the line and not just the aide she'd managed to come up with so far. "Hello?"

"This is Carlisle Wilson." The old man's voice sounded gravelly, as if he'd been asleep. "Who's this?"

"Sir, I'm Sheriff Gerald Cochran, Pisgah County, North Carolina." Jerry tightened his grip on the phone, retreating into cop speak. "I'm afraid I have some very bad news. This morning a twenty-one-year-old white female was found dead on the east face of Burr Mountain. Our investigation determined that she was Lisa Carlisle Wilson of 41 Princeton Mews, Raleigh. I'm afraid she was the victim of a homicide."

"But that's my daughter."

"Yes, sir."

"She's a victim? I—I don't understand."

"Sir, Lisa had gone on a campout with some fellow interns from the raptor center. One of those interns found her this morning. We've been trying to reach you for quite some time."

"You say she died on a campout? Did she fall off a cliff?"

"No sir." Cochran took a deep breath and started back at square one. "As I said earlier, your daughter was the victim of a homicide."

There was a long moment of silence. Finally, the old man spoke again. "You mean someone killed her?"

"Yes, sir. I am so sorry."

"But who would kill my Lisa? She's just a girl…"

"We're working very hard to determine that, sir. The SBI has joined our investigation, and her autopsy was given top priority at the state lab in Winston-Salem."

Carlisle Wilson began making a strange noise, somewhere between a cry and a choke. Cochran held the phone away from his ear. *No stranger*, he thought, *should be privy to this kind of grief.* At length Wilson's sobs abated and he spoke again, this time with the snap of a drill sergeant. "What did you say your name was?"

"Cochran. Sheriff Gerald Cochran."

"Well, Sheriff Gerald Cochran, I'm leaving right now. I'll be in your office first thing tomorrow morning."

"But sir, your daughter's remains are at the state lab. It might be better to—"

"Son, you just told me my Lisa was killed in your county," the old man growled, sounding every bit like the governor who once held all of North Carolina by the scruff of the neck. "You can bet your sorry ass I'm coming there. And I'm staying there. I'm going to roast your balls over a slow fire until you find out what the hell happened to my little girl."

Wilson slammed down the phone, leaving Cochran listening to the dial tone. He hung up the receiver slowly, thinking he'd probably just made the worst notification call in the history of law enforcement. He'd meant to express his sympathy, assure the governor he would find the girl's killer. Instead, he felt like he'd just thrown a rock at a hornet's nest.

He was wondering how Carlisle Wilson might roast his balls when someone knocked on his door. "Yeah?" he called, half expecting to see the old man already there, his eyes on fire.

Geneva peeked in, her gray hair newly permed into puffy curls. "I'm sorry, Jerry, but it's past ten. The reporters are … "

"Aw, nuts!" Cochran bolted up from his chair. Carlisle Wilson had pushed the press conference totally out of his mind. "I'm on it." He grabbed his coat. "You go on home, Geneva. You've gone above and beyond today, and I appreciate it."

"Thanks, Sheriff." She smiled a sweet, grandmotherly smile. "You get some rest, too."

He hurried down to the small room they used for official announcements. As he opened the door he found five reporters waiting—Tronda O'Brien from the Greenville paper, Shirley Heifner from Asheville, a couple of stringers he didn't know, and of course Ginger, who sat front and center, still dressed in the shorts she'd worn for the sports park ceremonies. She would, he knew, ask the toughest questions. He'd learned that the fact that they slept together did not make her go easy on him—if anything she doubled-down on the questions that made him squirm.

"Just doing my job," she would tell him later in bed, those green eyes coy behind dark lashes. As much as he loved her, he knew getting a story would always come first for her. And he respected her for that.

Clearing his throat, he stepped to the little podium Geneva had set up. "Sorry to have kept you waiting," he began, nodding at the five expectant faces looking up at him. By tomorrow, he knew they would be not five alone, but five in a sea of reporters clamoring for this story. He took a deep breath and began to read his statement.

"This morning at 8:57 a.m., we received a call that a body had been found on the east face of Burr Mountain. Officer Rob Saunooke was dispatched to the scene; I arrived approximately an hour later. We discovered that a twenty-one-year-old white female had been the victim of a homicide. She was one of six student interns from the Pisgah Raptor Rescue Center."

Shirley Heifner looked up from her laptop. "What was the cause of death?"

"The victim's at the state lab now," Cochran said. "I'll release that information when I have it." He thought of those cuts, all over her body. Never would he release that, not to anybody.

"Where are the other interns?"

Cochran said, "They are currently being interviewed."

"Are they college or high school students?"

"College. Two are from Duke, two from Carolina, one from NC State. The victim was enrolled at Carolina."

Ginger, who'd been taking notes but also watching him closely, raised her hand.

"Were they anywhere near the old Fiddlesticks cabin?"

He looked at her with a tight smile. His precious love had seen through his tap-dancing and asked the question he'd been dreading. "As a matter of fact, that was the location of their campsite."

She pressed on. "Can you identify the victim?"

He knew he couldn't evade her question. She would find out tomorrow anyway. "The victim was Lisa Carlisle Wilson, of Raleigh. Daughter of former governor Jackson Carlisle Wilson."

A moment of stunned silence enveloped the room, then the questions swarmed like gnats. *What was the governor's reaction? Has he released a statement? Have you brought in the SBI? Do you have any suspects or persons of interest?*

This was the part he hated. Reporters asked questions that, this early, he never had the answers to. Sometimes he wished he could reveal a murder investigation after the fact, when they'd caught the killer and tied up all the loose ends. Ongoing investigations always made cops sound so stupid.

After he'd said "We don't know" and "I can't say at this point," he stopped the grilling. "I really can't comment any more tonight. I'll schedule future press conferences as new information becomes available."

More questions erupted, but he left the podium and walked out of the room. He closed the door then paused to look back through the glass window. The reporters sat bent over their tablets, sending the story to their respective copy desks. Though it was late-breaking news, Lisa Wilson's murder would probably be on the front page of every paper in the region. He watched Ginger, pecking on her laptop and thought suddenly of the diamond ring in his dresser drawer. If the day had gone as he'd planned, that ring would be glittering on her finger now. She would not be typing, filing a story. He would not be trying to figure out what in the hell happened to the governor's daughter, and Lisa would not be on a slab in Winston-Salem with God knows what carved all over her body.

SEVEN

Mary Crow lay in a dream-tossed sleep, one minute trying to teach Ann Chandler Cherokee, the next trying to find a seat on the governor's bus. In the current one she and Jonathan were fighting over a dead hawk. They were pushing each other away from the bird when suddenly it came back to life and began to peck Mary's shoulder, hard and insistent. At that point, she awoke with a start, sitting up in bed to find Lily standing there in her pajamas, tapping her shoulder.

"Wake up, Meyli," she whispered urgently, using the Cherokee version of Mary's name. "I think the owl's dying."

"The what?" Mary asked, thinking she must still be dreaming.

"The owl. The one Daddy hit last night."

Mary blinked, trying to sort her dreams from reality. A hawk had not been pecking her shoulder—Lily had been trying to awaken her. She looked over at Jonathan sleeping beside her. As usual, he'd turned his back to her. The unwrinkled white sheets stretching like a snowfield between them.

"Get up, Meyli." Lily tugged at her arm. "Hurry!"

58

Mary slipped out of bed and hurried to Lily's bedroom. They'd put the injured bird in a cardboard box with some shredded newspaper. Jonathan had wanted to leave it on the back porch, but Lily had insisted on bringing it up to her room. Now it was struggling to fly—panting, reeling, vainly batting its wings against the sides of the box. In one corner of the box Mary saw a thick clump of dark red matter that could have been blood or vomit or both.

"Pleeeease can we call Dr. Lovebird?" Lily held up a business card that pictured a cartoon of Nick Stratton playing a fiddle with all sorts of birds perched on him. Beneath the picture was the line *Invite Dr. Lovebird and Friends to your next school event.*

"It's three in the morning, Lily. We can't call him now."

"But he said to call him if we ever found an injured raptor."

"He didn't mean in the middle of the night," Mary croaked, her throat like sandpaper.

"He said anytime!" Lily cried. As the bird squawked again new tears began rolling down her cheeks. "Please call him, Meyli. We can't let the owl die!"

Mary looked at the child. At that moment, pre-Oklahoma Lily was back. She stood there a sweet, loving little girl, weeping over an injured bird. Mary wondered—would calling Nick Stratton bring that little girl back to stay? And if Lily came back, might Jonathan return as well? She had no idea, but she figured it was worth a try. "Okay," she said. "I'll go call him."

She tiptoed downstairs to the kitchen, thinking that Nick Stratton had probably never dreamed some kid would take him at his word. Nonetheless, she punched in the number, for Lily as much as the bird. The phone rang once, twice, then a surprisingly alert male voice said, "Yes?"

Mary cleared her throat. "Uh, Nick?"

"This is Nick Stratton."

"Nick, this is Mary Crow. From the sports park opening?"

An awkward pause, then Stratton spoke. "Mary, right. What can I do for you?"

"I'm so sorry to bother you, but we've got an injured owl. My daughter got your Dr. Lovebird card today and insisted that I call."

"An owl?" Stratton sounded relieved, as if he'd expected much direr news.

"We accidentally hit it while driving home," said Mary. "We put him in a box. Now he's panting and batting his wings. I think he might be bleeding, too."

"Bleeding from where?"

"I'm not sure … there's a clump of dried blood in the box."

"That's probably a pellet," said Stratton. "Owls vomit undigested parts of their last mouse."

"Oh," said Mary, unaware that owls had that ability. "He still seems like a pretty sick bird."

There was another long pause, then Stratton spoke. "Okay," he said. "Bring it on over. God knows everybody else has tromped through here today."

"Where should I come?"

"At the end of Cashiers Branch Road, on Burr Mountain," said Stratton. "Keep the bird in that box and leave it alone. Don't shine lights on it or play the radio while you're driving up here. When you get to the totem pole, make a sharp left and follow the tire tracks."

"Thank you," Mary said, watching the hope flickering on Lily's face as she lingered in the doorway, listening to their conversation. "We'll be there as soon as we can."

She dressed in the dark, and she didn't bother to wake Jonathan; she knew he was already awake. He was a woodsman—he always slept lightly, attuned to any odd noise. He'd probably been awake since Lily first came into the room, and had just lain there, feigning sleep. She thought about telling him where they were going, but she decided not to bother. He would think them mad to drive a maimed owl halfway across the county in the middle of the night.

Mary followed Stratton's instructions, keeping the bird as quiet as she could. Lily followed her downstairs, insisting on going along.

"I can help," she told Mary. "I can hold him while you drive."

Mary's first reaction was to tell her to go back to bed. But her old, sweet Lily was still there, her eyes huge with concern over the owl.

"Okay," said Mary. "But we have to do exactly what Dr. Lovebird said. No talking, no lights, no radio."

They got in the car. For forty-five minutes they drove through the night, Lily making an occasional comment in a whisper. Mary shook her head at the incongruity of it all—a lone car speeding along mountain roads in the dead of night, its occupants as silent as if they sat in church.

Finally, they climbed up a gravel road that ended at a totem pole of leering faces. She turned left as Stratton had directed, churning up a rutted road that ended near a small cabin. A dim light burned on the porch, faintly illuminating a tall figure who paced from one end of the porch to the other. They got out of the car, Mary carrying the owl, Lily following. "Nick?" she called as they drew closer to the cabin. "Is that you?"

He stopped his circuit of the porch. "Is that friend to tribe and county Mary Crow?"

She laughed, flattered that he'd remembered John Oocuma's words. "It's me."

"Good," he said, his tone odd. "I was beginning to think I'd just dreamed you, along with everything else."

"I'm so sorry to get you up in the middle of the night," said Mary. "But this owl's in bad shape."

"No problem—I was awake." Stratton came down the porch steps and lifted the box from Mary's arms. "Let's go see what you've got."

He led them into the cabin. It was neat and cheery, built of new pine logs orange with varnish. A green flag hung over the fireplace while an array of stringed instruments hung on the wall beside the hearth. *Musician*, thought Mary, wondering what else Nick Stratton's talents included.

"Come on in the kitchen," he said.

He carried the owl into a small kitchen stuffed with everything from bread bowls to birdcages. For the first time, Mary got a look at Stratton, up close. He was even taller than she'd thought, with sun-streaked hair that grew into brown sideburns and dark stubble on his cheeks and chin. His eyes were greenish-blue and bloodshot; the scar that bisected his upper lip was tightly drawn as the ends of his mouth curved down in either irritation or disapproval. Despite his polite welcome, there was an edginess about Stratton that made her wonder if they'd interrupted something far more pleasurable than just a night's sleep. She decided that he must have a wife or a lover upstairs, now fuming because he'd left a warm bed to look after some bird.

"Where did you guys hit this owl?" he asked as he put the box on a long trestle table.

"Near our house," said Lily. "My daddy hit it. He wanted to kill it, but we wouldn't let him."

He frowned, disapproving. "Your daddy drive a pickup with a gun rack in the back?"

"Her father's Cherokee," Mary explained, not wanting Stratton to think she lived with some rifle-toting redneck. "They regard dispatching an injured animal as releasing its spirit."

"*Adonuhdo*." He used the Cherokee term.

"*Adonuhdo*." Mary nodded, surprised at Stratton's knowledge of Tsalagi.

He raised one eyebrow. "You disagree with the concept of *adonuhdo*?"

"I think certain things are worth fighting for," said Mary.

"But your husband didn't … "

"Lily's father didn't," she explained.

"Ah." Stratton's puzzled gaze lingered on her a moment, then he turned his attention to the box. "Well, then. Let's take a look at your bird."

He buttoned his shirtsleeves and looked at Mary. "Are you squeamish? Faint at the sight of blood?"

"Not especially," she replied.

"Then you can give me a hand with this. My regular staff is currently unavailable." His tone was bitter, as if his staff had quit and walked out in a huff, en masse.

"What do I do?" asked Mary.

"First, put those gloves on." He nodded to a long pair of leather gloves, hanging by the sink. "Injured birds still have eight sharp talons. I learned that years ago, when a big Golden Eagle decided to filet my upper lip."

So that's where the scar came from, Mary thought as she walked over and pulled on the gloves. Thick deerskin, they came up to her elbows and had the well-worn feel of silk.

"Can I do something?" asked Lily.

"Stand over by the light switch," said Stratton. "When I tell you, dim the lights."

Mary frowned. "We're going to do this in the dark?"

"It's only dark to us. To the owl, it's daylight." Stratton spread an old quilt on the table and spoke in a whisper. "I need you to hold the bird while I examine it. We need to move very slowly, very calmly, and whisper when we speak."

Mary crossed the kitchen to stand beside him. Lily stood at her post, one hand on the light switch as Stratton began.

"I'll get the bird out, and put it on its back. You just cradle it between your hands. Allow it to move, but not thrash." He looked at Mary. "We'll have to stand a lot closer together."

"That's okay," she said. God knows nobody else wanted to stand close to her.

He turned to Lily. "Okay, kiddo, dim the lights."

Lily darkened the room. Stratton opened the box and lifted the injured bird out. Its white feathers looked luminescent, a quivering froth in the darkness.

"Tyto alba," he whispered. "Barn owl."

He laid the bird down on its back. It flapped broad wings, made a couple of swipes at Stratton with his beak, then Stratton began to hum—a weird, mesmerizing kind of tune. Amazingly, the owl relaxed into the procedure.

"Just hold the bird gently and try to keep it still," he told Mary. "I'll do the rest."

Mary did as he asked. When she corralled the bird, Stratton stepped close and put his bare fingers between her gloved hands. He smelled of leather and oranges, and something else she could not name. She watched as he palpated the owl's neck; felt the line of feathers down the animal's chest. Using his fingers like calipers, he measured the width of the bird's breast. She noticed that his hands were strong and his long fingers went through their practiced motions precisely, as if he were playing one of those violins.

"I'm not feeling any internal deal-breakers," he whispered. "Let's check the wings."

He shifted slightly toward her and spread the owl's left wing. The bird struggled, the feathers under its beak quivering.

"Is he getting too hot?" whispered Mary.

"Just scared. She's stressed."

"He's a she?" Mary wondered how Stratton had determined the gender of the owl—to her it seemed all feathers and huge eyes.

"Probably. They're larger than the males. She likely has fledglings that just left the nest." He looked at Mary. "You live on a farm?"

She nodded.

"Then she's probably one of your tenants. Pays her rent by killing your mice."

Stratton continued examining the owl. Mary watched, fascinated as he felt the tiny bones and ligaments that made up the structure of flight.

"This bird flew in front of your car from the passenger's side, didn't she?"

Mary nodded, remembering how Jonathan had veered to the right.

"Well, you missed most of her. I only feel a slackness in the ligament that attaches the right wing to the shoulder."

"Can you fix it?" Mary asked.

"Unfortunately, not. Broken bones we can fix; ligaments we have to leave to Mother Nature." Stratton lifted the bird from Mary's grasp and put her in a tall cage that stood next to his refrigerator. Immediately, she climbed on a perch and rousted her feathers.

Stratton turned to Lily. "Lights, please."

Lily turned the light switch, craning her neck to see the owl. "Is she going to be okay?"

"I don't know, honey."

"But you won't kill her, will you?" Lily asked, her voice quivering.

"No," said Stratton. "*Adonuhdo* I leave to you Cherokees."

They stood there for a moment, watching the owl. She returned their stare with dark, glassy eyes, then she turned her back to them and faced the wall, as if offended by all the attention.

"What do we do now?" asked Mary.

"I'll keep her here, feed her mice, let her mend. If she starts flying again, we'll release her. If she can't fly anymore, we'll make her an ambassador bird, either here or somewhere else."

"So that's it?"

Stratton nodded. "That's it. We'll just have to wait and see."

"Well." Mary peeled off the long buckskin gloves. "I can't tell you how much we appreciate this. How much do I owe you?"

"Nothing. As a federally licensed rehabilitator, I don't charge for this."

"Can I at least make a donation?" Mary took her purse from Lily. "I know we got you up in the middle of the night, after a very long day."

"If you'd like to help out the Pisgah Raptor Rescue Center, that would be great. But it's really not necessary."

"No, I want to." Mary wrote a check for a hundred dollars and handed it to Stratton. "With many, many thanks."

"Thank you."

"Will you call us about the owl?" asked Lily.

"Sure," said Stratton. "What's your number?"

"Here." Mary dug a business card out of her purse. "You can reach me at my office."

Stratton's expression brightened as he took her card. "Are you kidding me? You're an attorney? I thought you worked for the mayor."

"No," said Mary. "I'm a lawyer. You need a will or a deed filed, give me a call. I'll give you the barn owl discount."

Abruptly, Stratton started laugh. "This is too good. A lawyer shows up with a barn owl. Don't tell me you defend people on murder raps?"

"I've defended capital charges before," Mary replied, wondering why Stratton found this so amusing.

"Then I'll put your card on my refrigerator," he said, still laughing at some private joke as he put her card on the door of the freezer. "You just never know when you might need a good lawyer."

EIGHT

THREE HUNDRED MILES TO the east, former governor Jackson Carlisle Wilson stood staring out at a hard rain that pelted the windows of the state police airplane hangar. The water dripped in rivulets down the glass, smearing the runway lights into streaks of electric blue.

"Are you okay, Governor?" asked a perky young blonde in a North Carolina Highway Patrol uniform.

He turned toward the girl. She looked a lot like Lisa—blue eyes, freckled face, a wide smile. Sweet Patootie, he and Marian had called their late-in-life daughter, singing her that old Fats Domino tune.

"Would you like to sit down?" The girl took his elbow. "Can I bring you some coffee, or a Coke?"

"I'd rather stay on my feet." That much he knew; that much he remembered from his high school football days. If you keep moving, you've got a chance, Coach Peebles had told them. Once you're down, it's all over.

"Well, if you need anything, just let me know." Squeezing his arm, she whispered, "We're all so sorry about your daughter, sir. If there's anything we can do to help … "

He nodded his thanks. Her words rang strange in a terminology new to him. He'd had people express sorrow over a bill that foundered in the legislature, or that his first wife had died much too early from cancer. But sorry about his daughter? His Tootie? The thought of it made him sick to his stomach. He turned away from the woman and strode over to a huge map of North Carolina that covered one wall. *Keep moving,* he reminded himself. *Keep moving and you've got a chance.*

He was staring at the map, thinking how the blue highway lines resembled the veins on the back of his hands when his wife emerged from the bathroom.

"Carlisle?"

He turned, looked at her. For a horrible moment, he couldn't think of her name. Was it Tootie? Marian? No, those were the women he loved. This woman was something else. She began walking toward him, preceded by the scent of coconut suntan lotion. He struggled hard, desperate for her name, then finally, blessedly, it came to him. Pauline.

She came over and put her arm around his waist. "Honey, are you all okay? You look awfully pale."

"I'm okay." Christ, how did she think you were supposed to look when some hayseed sheriff called to tell you that your daughter was the victim of a homicide?

She looked up at him, her nose slightly sunburned, a tiny dot of red lipstick on her front tooth. "Do you want anything to eat?"

"No."

"How about a drink? They can get you something from the airport bar."

"No."

"Then why don't you take one of my pills." She started digging in her purse. "It'll help you relax … "

"Because I don't want to relax!" He jerked away from her, hating her touch, hating her smell, hating her for everything she was not. Not his Marian. Not his Lisa. Not anybody, really, except a marginally acceptable fuck. "I want to find out what the hell is going on!"

"I understand, sweetheart," she said, talking to him as if he were a two-year-old. "I'll be right over here if you need me." Smiling at the young blonde officer behind the flight desk, she retreated to the other side of the waiting room, her sandals hitting the floor in a strident tattoo.

He turned back to the map, staring at the county lines, the cities, the little airplane symbols that indicated where a state chopper could land. Thirty years ago, this state had been his—a fiefdom that stretched from the Atlantic Ocean to the Appalachian Trail, with loyal lieutenants from Manteo to Murphy. He'd been the first governor since Zeb Vance to do anything more than wave at the western counties on his way to Raleigh.

"You're wasting precious time, going over there," his old mentor, Judd Thompson warned. "Everybody knows the state ends at Charlotte."

But he knew if he carried the western mountains along with his native eastern shore, then the fancy fat middle—the Charlotte bankers and the Raleigh pricks—could go fuck themselves.

So he'd gone and stumped at their Baptist churches, feasted on their fried chicken, winced as he sipped their moonshine. And on election day, the folks of Watauga and Buncombe and Pisgah counties pulled him through.

"Little Pisgah," he whispered, tracing the outline of the county with a liver-spotted finger. Of all of them, he'd liked Pisgah best. Half of the residents were fair-skinned Scots, the other half dark-eyed Cherokees. Most were poor, only a few well educated, but they weren't stupid. When they promised him their vote, they delivered it. In 1972, Pisgah County put him in Raleigh.

For that, he'd rewarded them nicely. Built them a new high school, three access roads to I-40, got the Cherokees a casino. Pisgah County was working now, staying in school. Hell, even the sheriff who called about Lisa sounded like he'd graduated from Harvard.

"And this is how you pay me back?" He whispered, his vision growing blurry again. "This is what you do to my little girl?"

He stood there with his hand on the map, swaying like an old tree in a windstorm. As awful as he'd felt when Marian had died, this was worse. With Tootie gone, he would now die alone, without any of the people who loved him. Softly, he began to cry.

"Sir?"

He heard a voice behind him. Wiping his eyes, he turned. Three young patrolmen stood at attention, uniforms spotless, brass buttons shining. They saluted him at once, snappy as a color guard.

"Sir, we've just received clearance from the tower. We can leave anytime you're ready."

He looked at the three young men, soldiers here to do his bidding. Suddenly he realized: he was not some washed-up old geezer. He was Jackson Carlisle Wilson, twice governor of North Carolina. He'd put books in the schools, money back in the taxpayer's pockets. He'd dragged Pisgah County off its mules and into the twentieth century. How dare they hurt his little girl?

"Okay, boys," he said, straightening his shoulders, feeling the old starch returning to his spine. "Let's go find out what the hell happened in Pisgah County."

———

As Carlisle Wilson boarded a plane, Jerry Cochran sat at his desk, studying the interns' interviews. While the two girls had been weepy and scared, they'd told basically the same story—that the group had changed their usual Asheville club plans to spend the night at the haunted cabin. They'd hiked up there, explored the place, listened to Chris Givens's account of the Fiddlesticks legend. After dark they built a campfire and passed around a bottle of tequila. Tony Blackman claimed to have seen somebody in the woods, but when the boys gave chase, they'd found only an old tree that gave the impression of a person when viewed from the right angle and aided, they admitted, with a fair amount of liquor. When it started to rain, they'd retreated to sleep inside the cabin.

"Lisa hated every minute of it," said Rachel Sykes, tears rimming her dark eyes. "The woods, the cabin, everything. She was just counting the minutes until she could get back to the dorm. And Nick."

"Did she and Nick have a special relationship?" asked Saunooke.

"Her old boyfriend had dumped her right before finals. So she glommed onto Nick as soon as she got here. She was really into him."

The less pretty Abby Turner corroborated the story. "The Fiddlesticks story really spooked Lisa. Then when Tony claimed he saw somebody up there, I thought she was going to run back down the mountain right then."

Two thoughts occurred to Cochran as he listened to the girls' interviews. The first was that Stratton wasn't admitting the full extent of his relationship with Lisa. The second was, in a way, more troubling: What if the Blackman kid had seen somebody up there? Somebody with hideously wide eyes and a rictus of a smile?

"Oh, come on," Cochran said to himself as he ejected the girls' disk and reached for the one with the boys.

The first track was Ryan Quarles, a muscular blonde who fought to keep his chin from quivering. He told the same story as the girls, adding that he and Lisa had slept in the same sleeping bag. "But we weren't into each other," he explained quickly. "It was just really cold, and we were both a little freaked out."

Next came Tony Blackman, a handsome boy who had the stunned look of someone who'd walked away from a train wreck. His narrative was disjointed, always returning to Lisa Wilson's corpse. "I've never seen anything like that ... she didn't look human ... flies were crawling inside her mouth."

"When did you see her?" asked Whaley.

"I found her first—I walked up there to go to the bathroom. She had things carved all over her body."

"And didn't you claim to see someone up there the night before?"

"I saw someone hiding behind the trees, I really did. It looked like a man, watching us. We chased him, but nobody was there." Roughly, he wiped his mouth with the back of his hand. "I think some bird had pecked at her eyes."

"They do that," Whaley said matter-of-factly. "Crows usually get the juicy pieces first."

Blackman completed the rest of the interview in tears. When it was over, Cochran stood up and paused the machine. "That one's going to need a little therapy," he whispered as he headed to the break room.

He poured a cup of coffee and grabbed a slice of the pound cake Geneva had brought in. When he came back and inserted the last disk, Chris Givens's face appeared on the screen. The boy sat slouched in his chair, lank brown hair combed back, his gaze insolent and sly.

"I'm Christopher Andrew Givens," he replied churlishly to Whaley's first question. "And I want a lawyer. I've been here since noon, with nothing to eat."

"Well, sure," Whaley replied agreeably. "It'll probably take us a few hours to get one off the golf course." He looked at his watch. "But we should be finished by midnight."

"Midnight?" Givens cried. "What the fuck kind of police department is this?"

"The kind that has your little hiney in jail," Whaley replied. "This ain't *Law & Order,* son. You're on our clock now."

"Where are my friends?" the boy asked.

"I think they're eating pizza. They just gave their statements, no big deal." Whaley shrugged. "They didn't have anything to hide."

"I don't have anything to hide, either." Givens snapped the bait like a bass hitting a grasshopper.

Whaley smiled. "Then I don't see that we have a problem. All I'm asking for is your version of what happened last night. No lawyer tricks here."

Givens squirmed in his chair for a moment, then he caved in. "Okay. Let's go ahead and get it over with."

Whaley turned to a fresh page on his legal pad. "Let her rip, buddy."

Cochran watched as Givens recounted his version of the story. They usually went up to Asheville for the weekend, but it was going to be a full moon and he wanted to film this haunted house.

"Why did you want to do that?" asked Whaley.

74

"There's this ghost show on TV. You can make a lot of money if you send them some good film."

"So you'd given this little expedition some thought," said Whaley.

Givens shrugged. "I've got a low-light video cam for shooting owls. The moon was going to be full that night, so I figured, what the hell."

"And you talked the others into it?"

"I didn't have to twist any arms."

"Not even Lisa Wilson's?"

"Actually, I was kind of surprised she came."

"How come?"

"She was into Nick. I figured with the rest of us gone, it would be fuck-a-rama time for them."

Cochran sat up straighter. This was the third person to mention Nick Stratton by name. He backed the scene up, played it again. Something in Givens's eyes made him think the kid looked jealous.

"That piss you off?" Whaley asked the boy, apparently sensing the same thing as Cochran.

Givens gave an oily smile. "Not enough to kill her, if that's where you're going."

Whaley backed off. "So tell me what happened next."

Givens told the same story as everybody else—he'd videoed them exploring the cabin, building a campfire, running after the figure Tony claimed to have seen lurking in the woods. "That really spooked the girls," he said.

"But not you?" asked Whaley.

"No, I figured Tony was just bullshitting. By the time everybody calmed down about that, it started to rain. So we went inside the house."

Whaley gave the boy a cold-cop stare that even chilled Cochran's blood. "Where you conveniently set up your camera."

"Yeah. Everybody spread out their sleeping bags. I put the camera up on the mantel, then I went to bed. The next thing I knew Tony was yelling that something terrible had happened to Lisa."

"That's pretty sound sleeping for people on a ghost hunt. Aren't you supposed to stay awake all night, listening for chains being rattled?"

Givens rubbed the stubble on his chin. "I tried to stay awake. But I guess I was too tired. We'd worked all day, and it took us four hours to hike up there. Plus we'd killed a bottle of Cuervo."

Whaley pressed on. "What did you do when you heard Tony yelling?"

"Honestly, I thought he was playing another joke. I tried to go back to sleep but everyone else was awake. The girls said Lisa had vanished, so I went outside to see what was going on. Tony was at the fire pit, pointing to a big tree, screaming his head off. I ran up there to see."

"And what did you find?"

"Lisa. She was dead."

Cochran watched the boy's image on the screen. Recalling Lisa's maimed body did not seem to cause him any particular distress. "Tony was really freaking, so I told him to go call 911. He had to run halfway down the mountain before he could get a signal."

"Why were you so sure she was dead?" asked Whaley.

"I've cut up mice and rabbits all summer," said Givens. "I know what dead looks like."

"What did you do after you decided she was dead?" asked Whaley.

The boy shrugged, suddenly uncomfortable. "I stayed up there a few minutes. Then I went down to the cabin. Tony came back and said the cops were on their way."

Whaley returned to the same statement that had caught Cochran's attention. "You say you stayed up there a few minutes. What did you do up there?"

The boy's eyes slid away, as if he were embarrassed. "I don't know. I guess I . . . I kind of looked at her."

"Ever see a naked girl before?"

"I've seen plenty of naked girls." Givens licked his lips, trying to maintain his fading bravado. "I've just never seen one cut up like that."

Cochran knew exactly what the boy was trying to say. Where Lisa's body had simply terrified Blackman and Quarles, Givens had dipped a toe into that monstrously seductive stream that flows between sex and death. Cops knew it but never spoke of it. Killers thrived on it, needed it no less than an addict needs a fix. Though Givens might forget the details of the morning he saw Lisa Wilson dead, the memory of her body would revisit him the rest of his life, whispering words he could not yet dream of.

NINE

"Something carved her up, but that didn't kill her, Jerry."

Cochran leaned back in his chair, putting his feet up on his desk. Though it was just past six a.m., he'd called the state forensic office, hoping to catch pathologist John Merkel before he left for the day. Merkel was a strange kid Cochran had known in pre-med, at Carolina. While Cochran had to drop out of the program when his father died, Merkel had gone on to become a forensic specialist. He'd become, however, no less strange. He gave his clients pet names, did autopsies at night with Puccini blaring through his iPod, claiming that the cool, slightly green light of the morgue allowed him to truly commune with his subjects. Despite his eccentricities, Merkel's professional reputation was impeccable, and Cochran always requested him whenever he sent a body to the state lab.

"Then what did kill her?" asked Cochran. "The girl's father is going to show up any minute. He's going to 'roast my balls over a slow fire' if I can't explain what happened to his daughter."

"Ugh." Merkel groaned. "I've seen roasted balls. They aren't pretty."

"So give a guy a break, okay? Give me something to tell him."

"Okay, okay."

Cochran heard shuffling on the line, then Merkel spoke again, his voice high-pitched and nasal.

"I don't have all the data in, but I'm fairly certain that Sweet Sue died from being sequentially strangled by a single piece of some non-abrasive material."

Cochran flinched at Merkel's nickname for the girl. "What do you mean, sequentially strangled?"

"Somebody strangled her to unconsciousness several times with something about an inch wide that lacked texture," explained Merkel. "They carved her up while she was out. When she started to wake up, they strangled her again."

"Wow," said Cochran. "That sounds a lot like torture."

"Sweet Sue would not have found it fun. The cuts would have been painful, but the killer was not going for exsanguination. I'm guessing they used her to send a message."

"What kind of message?" Cochran looked at the grisly close-up photos the SBI had dropped off.

"Beats me. The shapes make a repeating pattern, but they aren't recognizable letters in any known alphabet."

"It looks sort of cuneiform to me," Cochran replied. "I wonder if it's some kind of code."

"If it is, it's none my computer's familiar with."

Cochran swallowed hard, wondering how he could avoid telling the governor about this. "So after they finished writing this message, they killed her?"

"You got it, Sherlock."

"Had she been sexually assaulted?"

"Nope. Neither vaginally nor rectally."

"Was she pregnant?"

"Nope."

Cochran sighed—Merkel just trashed both his sex game and his pregnant girlfriend theories. "Any defensive wounds?"

"Fibers and dirt under two fingernails. Red clay soil with traces of mica, both indigenous to western North Carolina. And denim."

Cochran sat up a bit straighter. "Denim? As in blue jeans?"

"A thin weave of denim, made in China. Walmart sells them under the Levi's brand. Your perp was wearing cheap jeans when they killed Sweet Sue."

Again Cochran sighed. Most of Pisgah County wore cheap jeans, purchased at the new Super Walmart. "That's it?" he asked Merkel.

"That's all I've got so far." Merkel rattled some papers. "Look, I know you're probably going to go the FBI/VICAP route on these figures carved into her body, but I've got a pal over at Duke who might be able to help us out faster."

Cochran was skeptical. "He studies messages carved into corpses?"

"No, the guy's a cyber cryptologist. He has an IQ of about five thousand and is working on a new enigma machine. I think his Duke job's a cover for NSA."

"So why would he care about this?" asked Cochran.

"He wouldn't. He would just think it was fun."

"Thanks but no thanks, Merkel." Cochran knew if some spook leaked a photo of Lisa's body, he might as well take up residence at that cabin and pray that Fiddlesticks came for him. "Your buddy might find it fun, but my balls are the ones on the barbie."

"No, wait. He's a good guy who can keep a secret. How about I send him a picture of just the writing? No names or identifiable body parts."

Cochran still didn't like it. "I don't know."

"Jerry, it's your best shot at finding out what these figures mean. I don't have a clue. Usually the only messages I see on people's bodies are four-letter, one-syllable words. Your killer's written a novel."

Cochran considered Merkel's suggestion. Though having photos of the body sent to some geek at Duke felt a lot like losing control of his evidence, if the guy could identify those figures, it would be worth it. That much, he owed the poor girl. "Okay," he finally said. "But for God's sake, don't give him anything he can link back to the governor."

"Wilson's already called this office a dozen times," said Merkel. "I don't want him down on my ass any more than you do."

Cochran looked at his notes from their conversation. Though he had no real news to report, at least when Wilson showed up he could tell him that the best experts in the country were working on his daughter's case. "Okay, buddy," he said. "I appreciate your help. I'll buy you a beer next time I come over there."

"Could you bring me a couple of bottles of that kombucha they make in Asheville?"

Cochran remembered Merkel's drink of choice, a thick, soupy health drink that looked like swamp sludge. "You got it. Let me know ASAP what your pal at Duke says, okay?"

Cochran hung up the phone, disappointed. He'd hoped Merkel would have given him a fingerprint, or DNA from one of those kids at the haunted house. Cheap Walmart denim wasn't going to convict anybody of anything. Now the attack on the girl seemed even more bizarre. Repeated choking took strength, hard work. That kind of furious action connoted deep-seated rage. Yet the girl hadn't lifted a finger to defend herself.

He was considering that when his phone rang. He picked up the receiver to find an urgent male voice on the line.

"Sheriff? This is Scott at the front desk. I just wanted to give you a heads-up ... Carlisle Wilson is on his way to your office."

Cochran felt his stomach clench. The ball-roaster had arrived. "Thanks, Scott. Geneva will take care of him."

"I don't think she's come in yet," Scott replied. "The guy's got a trooper with him and they both look like they could spit nails. They're already halfway down the hall."

Cochran dropped the phone and scooped up the photos of Lisa Wilson's puckered, blood-spattered body. He stuffed them in a single manila envelope and shoved them in the bottom drawer of his desk just as his door burst open.

"You the sheriff?" A burly highway patrolman, looking official to the point of ridiculousness, strode into his office, side arm strapped around his waist, a Smoky-the-Bear hat pulled low on his forehead.

Cochran rose from his chair, irritated. "Yeah, I'm the sheriff. Who the hell are you?"

"He's my assistant." A tall man with a shock of white hair brushed past the trooper. Though he walked with a cane, his dark eyes were sharp, taking in Cochran and his office in a single glance. A much younger woman followed him, perky breasts bobbing, high heels clattering.

"I'm Jackson Carlisle Wilson," the old man growled, though there was no need of introduction—every North Carolinian over thirty knew the man's white hair and snapping eyes.

"Gerald Cochran." He extended his hand, but Wilson ignored it. Instead, he grabbed Cochran's chair with the hook end of his cane and pulled it in front of the desk.

"Tell me what the fuck happened to my little girl." Wilson sat down, his eyes boring into Cochran like hot coals.

Cochran glared at the highway patrolman, who stood by the door with his arms folded. He was willing to cut Carlisle Wilson some slack, but he did not intend to let some lumpy-assed traffic cop in on this. "I can only discuss this with the next of kin."

"Beat it, Fred," the governor ordered.

"Yes sir." With a sour look at Cochran, the assistant left the room immediately, closing the door behind him.

"Okay, Sheriff," the old man snarled. "Let's have it."

Cochran remained standing and reported the facts of the case, adding that he'd just talked to the chief pathologist in Winston-Salem, who'd determined that his daughter had died of strangulation. The woman gasped at the news; Carlisle Wilson pursed his lips in a tight line. Cochran hoped that would satisfy them. He didn't want to reveal any more details about how his daughter had died.

"Did Winston get any forensic evidence?" asked the governor, his voice firm and commanding.

"They found dirt under her nails and threads from a type of denim sold at Walmart."

"And that's all?" the old man thundered. "No fingerprints? No DNA? None of that shit they come up with on TV?"

Cochran shook his head. "No. But neither did your daughter have any defensive wounds, nor was there evidence of sexual assault." Maybe, he hoped, that would give the old man some comfort.

Wilson blinked, distinctly un-comforted. "So you're expecting me to believe that Lisa just lay down under a pine tree and let somebody choke her to death? What kind of moron are you?"

"Sir, this case is barely twenty-four hours old. I'm telling you exactly what we know at this point."

"Where are all those people she went camping with?"

"The interns are just now being released from jail. All freely gave detailed statements about this case. Unfortunately, none remember seeing or hearing anything out of the ordinary."

"And you believe them?" the former governor thundered.

"I neither believe nor disbelieve while I'm still gathering evidence," Cochran said, feeling like an idiot. He realized now how Wilson had gotten all his pet bills through the legislature—he'd simply browbeaten his opponents into submission. "Do you have any political enemies, sir?"

"Of course I do. You don't spend eight years in Raleigh throwing tea parties."

"Could you give me a list—of any who might bear this kind of animosity toward you?"

The old man stared at his cane, shook his head. "None of 'em would do this. None of 'em hate me this hard."

A silence fell in the room. Carlisle Wilson's wife attempted to rub his shoulders, but the old man brushed her away. "Sweet little Pisgah," he whispered, all the fury seeming to drain out of him. "I can't believe this happened here."

"It's a terrible tragedy, sir. I'm deeply, deeply sorry." Cochran was sorry. The governor had no idea how much he regretted this.

The old man sat there, resting his hands on his cane, a single tear rolling from his left eye down to the furrow that bracketed that side of his mouth. Its saltiness must have startled him, because suddenly he snapped out of whatever fugue had gripped him. He straightened his shoulders and looked up at Cochran. "I want to see the pictures."

"Excuse me?" Cochran's heart began to beat faster. *Please dear Christ*, he prayed. *Not the pictures.*

"You take pictures of bodies. I want to see Lisa's."

"Sir, it's not our policy to allow that. Those pictures are police property and—"

Wilson slammed his cane down on the floor. "I don't give a rat's ass about your policy! I want to see those pictures."

"Sir, it would be better if you didn't."

Suddenly the old man leapt to his feet, put both hands on the opposite corners of Cochran's desk. "Son, I was running this state when you were in diapers. Do not try to tell me what I should or should not see. Get me the pictures."

Cochran said, "Sir, wouldn't you rather remember her as she was rather tha—"

"Get me the goddamn pictures!" the governor screamed, spit flying into Cochran's face.

Cochran reached for his bottom drawer, suddenly fed up with the man's bullying. He wanted to see the pictures, fine. Cochran only hoped the sight of them wouldn't lay the old bastard out with a coronary in the middle of his office.

He pulled out the folder, but warned Carlisle Wilson once more. "Sir, these are truly nothing any parent—"

Wilson gave a snort of disgust as he ripped the pictures from Cochran's hand. He sat back down and opened the folder. The photo that Cochran had been studying while talking to Merkel was on the top of the pile. It was the worst of the lot—the one that showed in horrific detail what acts evil could visit upon flesh and bone.

For a moment, Carlisle Wilson just sat there staring at the photo, still as a statue. Then his old jaw dropped open and he made a sound unlike any Cochran had ever heard.

"Noooo!" he screamed, howling, it seemed, all the rage and grief and pain of every parent who'd ever lost a child. "Noooooo!"

Cochran lowered his eyes, not wanting to witness the old man's agony. He heard the woman clucking and shushing, but Carlisle Wilson suddenly grew deathly quiet. Cochran lifted his gaze to find the old man staring directly at him, snot running from his nose, tears from his eyes.

"Let me tell you something, you candy-ass college boy. I'm going to set up camp here in Hartsville and keep your feet to the fire until you find who did this to my little girl. I'll have this story on every front page in the state and believe me, everybody's going to be talking about Sheriff Gerald Cochran!"

"That's your prerogative, sir," said Cochran.

"Damn straight it is! Until you get Lisa's killer behind bars, you're going to have reporters crawling up your nose and out your ass." The old man struggled to his feet and wagged a gnarled finger at him. "I built this little pissant county up, son. And believe me, I can take it down just as fast. You want your tourists to keep coming, your rich Yankee retirees to keep planting their know-it-all asses up here, then you'd better find out what the fuck happened to my little girl!"

TEN

It was just past dawn when Mary Crow finally pulled back into her own driveway. Night had morphed into a colorless light that turned green trees gray, red roses black. She'd hoped to find Jonathan still drinking coffee before his trout fishing gig, but both he and his truck were gone.

"Where's Daddy?" asked Lily, who'd slept in the backseat all the way home.

"He's taking some clients fishing," said Mary.

Lily yawned. "Why do they always go so early?"

"Because that's when the fish bite." Mary opened the kitchen door. "Go on to bed. I'll take you to camp a little late today."

Mumbling something that sounded vaguely like "okay," Lily trudged up the stairs, leaving Mary alone in the kitchen. She looked around the room. Jonathan had, apparently, just left. The coffee pot was half-full, the iron skillet warm to her touch.

"We used to get up together," she said aloud, her voice ringing in the empty room. Unless she was knee-deep in some case, she would wake up with him, fix breakfast while he loaded his gear. They would eat, and then he would kiss her good-bye. She'd always loved those mornings—just the two of them sitting in a quiet house, drinking coffee at first light.

"See you later," he would say, his arms strong around her. "Save me a seat."

They'd used that old code phrase for the past twenty years—ever since they'd been sixteen, and in high school. He had not uttered it once since he'd returned from Oklahoma.

She poured herself a cup of coffee and sat down at the table, again wondering what had hijacked their lives into this alien terrain. A younger woman? A prettier woman? A woman who would totally devote herself to him and Lily? She didn't think so—he'd never been that self-centered a man. But something or someone had ridden back from Oklahoma with him, and they weren't letting him go.

"You can end this with six words," she reminded herself for the umpteenth time. *Jonathan, have you found someone new*? But those six words scared her—who knew what other words they might evoke? Sometimes she wanted to laugh at the irony of it. For years she'd questioned defendants mercilessly, dogged in pursuit of an answer. Now, every time she thought of uttering that simple six-word question, she felt sick to her stomach. The question itself wasn't so bad—it was the answer that terrified her.

"You need to end this," she told herself, her eyelids drooping despite the coffee. "Ask him tonight, after Lily goes to bed. Whatever he says will be better than not knowing." She put her head down on the table and closed her eyes, imagining all the ways the conversation might go. *I'm so sorry, but I've found someone new ... I'm so sorry, but I'm just not attracted to you anymore ... I'm so sorry, but I've decided to raise Lily by myself.* She was thinking of how she might respond to that when suddenly the telephone broke the silence of the kitchen.

"Hello?" She grabbed the receiver, hoping it was Jonathan.

"Ms. Crow?"

"Yes."

"This is Leonora Blackman, from Carmichael, California. I got your number from my cousin James Blackman, who lives in Sylva?"

Mary frowned. Why would a woman in California be calling her at six o'clock in the morning? "How can I help you?"

"I've never made a call like this, so I'm not really sure what to say, except that my son Tony just called me, and he's in jail! One of his friends was murdered last night and the sheriff thinks Tony did it. I'm just desperate to get some help for him, and James says you're the best lawyer in town. Won't you please take his case?" The woman's voice dissolved in tears.

Mary straightened in her chair and peered at the clock over the stove. 9:47. She blinked, unbelieving, wondering how she'd lost almost three hours of time. Then she saw the cup of cold coffee in front of her, her car keys tossed on the table. When she'd put her head down to think about Jonathan, she must have fallen asleep.

"Ma'am, where is your son in jail?" she asked the woman.

"Right there in Hartsville! They think he killed the governor's daughter, but he swears it was a ghost!"

Mary realized she was going to need a cup of hot coffee to deal with this. "I'm not in my office right now, Mrs. Blackman, but if you'll give me your name and number, I'll call you back as soon as I get downtown."

"You won't take any of the others, will you? Remember, I called first!"

Mary wrote down the woman's number, then reheated her coffee in the microwave. As she sat back down to make sense of everything, she turned the TV to the Asheville station. After five minutes of commercials, a mini-news break started. The lead story was that early yesterday morning, former governor Jackson Carlisle Wilson's daughter, Lisa, had been found strangled to death.

"We are questioning several persons of interest in this case," said Jerry Cochran, his bleary-eyed face suddenly filling the screen.

That's why he didn't show up at the dedication yesterday, thought Mary, remembering the lone empty chair on the stage. Her incredulity grew as the news continued.

"Lisa Wilson had been appointed to one of the coveted internships at the Pisgah Raptor Rescue Center," said a pretty blonde reporter. "She was specializing in raptor rehabilitation with Dr. Nicholas Stratton."

"Nick Stratton?" Mary almost choked on her coffee. "Dr. Lovebird?"

She watched, unbelieving, as a video of the sports park ceremony came on, showing Stratton flying Sequoia, the big bald eagle.

After that, the news skipped on to happier topics—new parking meters in downtown Asheville, Henderson County's burgeoning apple crop. Mary turned off the TV, stunned. Not six hours ago Stratton treated a wounded owl in a darkened kitchen. Now they were showing him on television, in connection with a murder.

"No wonder he acted odd last night," she said, remembering his strange laughter at her business card. At the time she'd chalked it up to fatigue, to his being awakened in the middle of the night with a bird emergency. But it wasn't that at all, she realized as she put a slice of bread in the toaster. One of his students had just been murdered. The guy was probably in shock.

"At least he appreciated the irony," she said. "The night after his intern gets bumped off, a lawyer shows up at his front door, hurt owl in hand."

———

She'd considered just taking the day off but then decided she'd better go into the office. Her partner, Sam Ravenel, was settling an estate in Charleston and she'd long ago learned that it was good for one of them to be on duty when something big broke in town. After dragging a cranky Lily to Camp Wadulisi, Mary arrived at her office. The Wilson murder story had grown like a crop of kudzu, and the town was now jammed with network TV vans uplinking to NBC, ABC, and a couple of BC's she didn't even recognize. Dodging three news crews clustered around the entrance of Sadie's coffee shop, she walked up the stairs to Ravenel & Crow. She headed immediately to her desk, where her answering machine blinked with fifty-six new messages.

"Wow," Mary whispered. Usually she got fifty-six messages a week rather than in a single morning. Sitting down at her desk, she punched the retrieve button and listened as voice after agitated voice filled the room. All were parents of the surviving interns, all were near panic, all were totally convinced of their child's innocence, and all wanted her to represent their offspring as soon as possible.

As Mary listened to their weepy desperation, she sat back in her chair and stared at the list of prospective clients. All of them sounded like intelligent, caring parents who never dreamed that the children they'd sent to learn about raptors would wind up as suspects in a murder investigation. She gave a wistful sigh. As much as she longed to call one of them and say she'd be happy to represent their child, she knew she could not do it. Long ago she'd promised Jonathan no murder cases. Right now they were travelling a bumpy enough road on their own. Defending a homicide charge might push them beyond the point of no return.

She'd just picked up the phone to call Mrs. Blackman in California, when suddenly she heard a loud speaker start blaring from the courthouse steps. Intrigued, she left her desk and went into the conference room, the one room that had a spectacular view of Main Street. The courthouse, the hotel, the chamber of commerce—the core of Hartsville spread out before the tall Palladian windows.

She walked over to a window and looked out. A tall man with a shock of white hair stood behind a makeshift podium, facing at least fifty reporters and three times as many citizens.

"I'll be damned!" she whispered aloud. "That's Carlisle Wilson."

Wilson thumped the end of the mike a couple of times, then started to speak. "I want to thank everyone for coming and being so supportive of an old guy like me." He began humbly, with an aw-shucks attitude.

"I don't know how many of you know this, but yesterday, my little girl Lisa was murdered. Right here in Pisgah County. I got the call last night in Wilmington."

His voice began to wobble. He stepped back from the microphone and wiped his eyes with a white handkerchief. A moment later, he spoke again.

"I guess I still can't believe something like this would happen in Pisgah County," he said, his tone choked. "I've always known it to be a county of good people, law-abiding citizens, the sons and daughters of pioneers who've led quiet, decent lives for generations. You've helped me out on election day many times in the past and I'm hoping that today, you'll find it in your hearts to help me out once more.

"Now you've got a good man as sheriff. Jerry Cochran's young and smart and his police department is working on this full-time. He's called in the SBI and the FBI and a bunch of folks in Washington. But you know, sometimes local folk do the best police work. Remember that Eric Rudolph? Them fancy federal guys spent years looking for him and came up empty every time. A mountain boy from Murphy found him, digging food out of a trash bin."

The crowd applauded, justifiably proud of one of their own. Mary smiled. The old politician really knew what buttons to push.

"Anyway—I'm convinced that somebody in this county knows something about what happened to my little girl. That's why I'm going to stay right here in Hartsville until I find out. And I'm putting my money where my mouth is—today I'm offering a reward to anyone who has information about Lisa's murder."

A low murmur went through the crowd. "No!" Mary whispered, fighting an urge to run down there and clamp a hand over the old man's mouth. She knew that a reward would muddle the case beyond all hope.

"How much of a reward?" someone called eagerly.

The governor's eyes blazed with a dark fire that promised to char anybody who dared stand in his way. "I'm offering one million dollars for any information that will bring my daughter's killer to justice."

A young man in jeans and a white tee shirt spoke up. "What if we bring him to justice ourselves?"

"Bring 'em in alive, the money's yours!"

The crowd gave a collective gasp.

ELEVEN

"Hey, Sheriff! How's it going?"

Cochran looked up from a photograph of Lisa Wilson's left clavicle to see Ginger Malloy peeking around his office door. A pleasurable jolt ran through him—though it had only been about twelve hours since he'd last seen her, it felt to him like several years had passed.

"May I come in?" she asked. "Geneva thought it might be okay."

Cochran turned the photograph over and grinned. "It is absolutely okay."

She slipped into his office, closing the door behind her. She wore a green dress that revealed long, well-shaped legs, and she carried a signature paper sack from Sadie's, Hartsville newest coffee shop.

"Brought your favorite—apple strudel," she said as she came over to the desk. Turning his chair toward her, she kissed him in a way that zinged electricity all the way down to his toes.

"Wow," he said, breaking the kiss only when he began to feel the insistent beginnings of an erection. "You take supporting your local sheriff to a whole new level."

"How's it going?" she asked, wiping a smudge of lipstick from the corner of his mouth.

"Not so hot," he replied.

"Have something to eat." She pulled the strudel from her paper sack, slyly casting a glance at the evidence files that lay on his desk. "I started over here with three of these, but Jessica Rusk stole one on the way over."

Cochran bit into the flaky, still-warm pastry. "Who's Jessica Rusk?"

"This utter bitch I used to work with at the *Richmond Times*. She's climbing her way to the top via the dead and dismembered."

Cochran thought of the sea of reporters who now clogged Main Street. "Why is the *Richmond Times* covering this?"

"They aren't. Rusk quit the *Times* to work for the Snatch."

Cochran blinked. "The Snatch?"

"The name real reporters have fondly given to *The Snitch*."

"That tabloid thing? What the hell are they doing here?"

"A politician's daughter getting murdered at a haunted cabin is huge. Add some famous pol like Wilson ponying up a million bucks and they get orgasmic. I'm surprised Jessica's eyes didn't roll back in her head when he announced it."

Cochran went cold inside. "What million dollars?"

"Didn't you know? Wilson just held a press conference in front of the courthouse. He offered a million-dollar reward for his daughter's killer and gave out your phone number."

"My phone number?" cried Cochran.

"The department's number." Ginger shook her head. "I figured a former chief executive would know that rewards only muddy the water of an investigation, but apparently not." Again she glanced at his evidence file, now under the sack from Sadie's. "Any new developments?"

Cochran didn't reply. Instead, he was thinking that he needed to call Tuffy Clark. Clark was already on the phone, interviewing Lisa Wilson's college pals, now he would have to field all the crackpot tips this million-dollar purse would generate.

"Wilson didn't elaborate on her actual murder, did he?" Cochran thought if that old fart had revealed that his daughter had been mutilated, he would go strangle him on the spot.

Ginger frowned. "What do you mean her actual murder?"

"I mean did he give details?"

"What details are you talking about?"

"None in particular," said Cochran. "I'm just asking my local reporter what he said."

"And your local reporter is asking you what details you're talking about. I have a job to do, too, Jerry. A story to cover."

He sighed. He didn't want to be accused of favoritism, just because he and Ginger were together. But he might need Ginger if Carlisle Wilson truly began his threatened ball-roast. He decided to give her the tiniest scoop. "I can't release any details about the murder, but I can tell you that all the interns are retaining counsel."

"So they've gone from persons of interest to suspects?"

"Not necessarily."

Ginger whipped out her notebook, ready to take notes. "Any one you like better than the others?"

"No. Anyway, we're looking at other people beyond these five students. They just happen to be the closest thing we've got to eyewitnesses."

"Do you think this murder might be politically motivated? Wilson made a lot of enemies while he was in office."

"He doesn't think so," said Cochran. "But I'm still looking into it."

She started to ask him something else when his cell phone beeped. He pulled it out. Whaley had texted him. FOUND SOMETHING INTERESTING IN THE GIVENS MOVIE. *Please God,* thought Cochran. *Anything interesting would be good, at this point.*

"Gotta go," he said, snapping his cell shut. "Duty calls."

"I know." Ginger put her notebook back in her purse. "I've got to get down to the paper." She leaned forward and kissed him again. "Will you call me later? If you find out anything?"

He laughed. Even while kissing she still thought of the story. "I'll try my best. Thanks for the strudel."

"Just be careful, okay?" she called over her shoulder as she walked toward the door. "And if a skinny blonde in a white Armani suit shows up, I strongly urge you to run the other way."

Cochran frowned. "Why?"

"Because it will be Jessica Rusk, the great succubus of trash journalism." In a chilling gesture, Ginger comically drew one finger across her neck. "Once she gets her hooks in you, it's all over."

"Thanks." He smiled. "I'll keep that in mind."

———

After Ginger left, his thoughts returned to Carlisle Wilson.

"Fucking asshole," he whispered. He couldn't believe the old bastard had been in town for less than three hours and had held a press conference and offered a million dollar reward. With the current economy, that could make for an awfully dicey situation. People already had far too many assault rifles in this county—add a rich reward and a killer running loose, and things could get tragic fast.

Disgusted, Cochran locked his office and walked up one flight of stairs to the "war room"—a large room they used for special investigations. He swiped his ID through the lock and the door opened, revealing Buck Whaley gazing at an oversized computer screen, a pile of empty Mountain Dew cans under his chair. He looked up when Cochran entered.

"What's the matter?" Whaley asked. "You look like you just ate a shit sandwich."

"Wilson held a news conference. Put out a million-dollar reward."

"Are you kidding me?" Whaley's mouth drew downward. "My dad hated that fucking old socialist. Said he wanted the government to run everything."

"Well, he apparently wants to run this investigation," said Cochran. "What did you find in that movie?"

"Sit down and I'll show you."

Cochran pulled a chair up next to Whaley.

"The first couple of hours are just kids farting around that cabin," the big man said. "I'll start where it gets interesting."

Cochran waited. In a moment, Chris Givens's ill-shaven face filled the screen.

"We're back inside the Fiddlesticks cabin." Givens spoke into the camera with a hushed voice, trying to sound serious over some ill-concealed giggling in the background. "We're going to bed now, but I'm keeping the camera rolling, in case Fiddlesticks comes in the night."

The picture fluctuated wildly, finally panning around the room to show the indistinct lumps of bodies on the floor. One of them lifted a hand, waved at the camera, calling "Hi, Mom!"

"Great picture," Cochran said, impressed by the sharp images in the dim light. "But I don't see anything other than kids in sleeping bags."

"Hang on," said Whaley.

Cochran watched as the campers settled down to sleep. Then the angle changed as Givens put the camera on the mantel. The sleepers were no longer visible, only a wide shot of a seemingly empty room, alternating between near dark and a hazy gray twilight.

"Why's the lighting so weird?" asked Cochran.

"High mountain clouds," Whaley replied. "I checked the weather. A front moved through, dumped a little rain up there."

Whaley fast-forwarded the video. "This is fifty-six minutes after they go to bed."

For a moment, Cochran still saw an empty room, then suddenly, someone's head appeared at the far right of the screen. Cochran recognized Lisa Wilson's curly blonde hair immediately. She tilted her head toward the window, a moment later lifted up on one elbow. Cochran leaned forward, holding his breath as he watched the murdered girl peer out into the darkness, then look around the room. A moment later she stood up, her boots in one hand, and started tiptoeing toward the door. She opened it slowly, looked around the room once more, and then stepped outside, closing the door behind her.

"That's it." Whaley stopped the film. "She never comes back. Until 5:32 a.m., all we see is an empty room."

"What happens at 5:32?"

"The batteries in the camera die."

"Play it again," Cochran ordered.

For the next two hours, they dissected Givens's movie, frame by frame, timing it, making notes. At 2:44 a.m., Lisa Wilson wakes up.

She looks out the window, around the room, out the window again. At 2:48 a.m., the girl who reputedly fears the forest at night gets up and tiptoes into the darkness, alone.

"What do you make of that?" asked Whaley.

Cochran tapped his pen on the yellow sheet of notes he'd taken. "I don't know. We can't tell what anybody else in that room is doing. Are they all there? Have they all gone out to play a trick on her? We only see Lisa."

"Pretty clever of Givens, to put the camera like that," said Whaley.

Cochran nodded. "Run it again."

Once more the two men bent close to the computer monitor. At 2:45, as Lisa turns from the window for the first time, Cochran stopped the film to study the girl's face. "You think she looks scared there?"

"Maybe." Whaley squinted at the screen. "But maybe excited, too."

"That's what I thought," said Cochran. "Bright-eyed, anyway."

Frame by frame they watched as Lisa Wilson looked around the interior of the cabin.

"She doesn't seem scared there," said Whaley.

"I know," Cochran agreed. "So her pals must be there. She would look scared if they'd left her alone."

"Unless she just thinks they're there." Whaley smirked at Cochran. "Didn't you ever pull sheets over your pillows so you could sneak out at night, when you were a kid?"

Cochran grunted, unwilling to admit that he'd never done such a thing. He'd spent most of his boyhood nights under the covers, reading by flashlight. "I don't think five kids could sneak out of that cabin without waking her up. They said she'd had the least to drink. She would have been the lightest sleeper."

Cochran re-started the film. He leaned close to watch Lisa Wilson gaze out the window, then he turned to Whaley and frowned. "Are you hearing a buzz on this machine? A high-pitched kind of whine?"

Whaley shook his head. "I can't hear shit anymore. Fired my pistol too many times."

"Never mind, then. Let's keep watching."

Once more, they studied the last moments of the girl's life.

"She doesn't call to the others," Cochran noted. "She doesn't want to wake them up."

"For a scaredy-cat like her, that's huge," Whaley said.

"Unless she's not scared at that point," replied Cochran. "Maybe she sees somebody she knows outside. Somebody she trusts."

"Like loverboy Nick Stratton?" asked Whaley.

"Possibly," Cochran agreed. With Lisa Wilson gone, they saw nothing but frame after frame of an empty room. Growing annoyed by the hiss of the machine, Cochran reached to turn the speakers off when abruptly, the extraneous noise stopped on its own. Cochran ran the video for another three minutes, but the noise never returned.

"Wait a minute." He turned to Whaley. "Back it up."

"Where to?" asked Whaley.

"To where she wakes up."

Whaley did as Cochran ordered The two men leaned forward as the movie started again, but this time Cochran turned the speakers up full blast. He put his ear to one as Lisa Carlisle Wilson woke up, looked around the room, and then tiptoed out the door to her death.

"Holy Fuck!" cried Cochran.

"What?" asked Whaley.

"Back it up five minutes!"

Whaley backed the video up even farther, to where there was nothing but an empty room on the screen. With one ear pressed to a speaker, Cochran nodded for him to start the video. He listened for a moment, then held up his hand.

"There!" he said, pointing at the clock/counter in the right corner of the screen. "It's starts at 2:39 a.m." He kept listening until Lisa Wilson left the cabin. "And it fades away at 2:54!"

"What starts?" cried Whaley, his face red with frustration. "What the fuck are you hearing?

"Exactly what you're supposed to hear up there." Cochran gave Whaley an odd look. "Fiddle music."

TWELVE

MARY WAS LATE PICKING Lily up at Camp Wadulisi. She'd handed all the desperate parents off to other defense attorneys and after that she'd had to thread her way out of a town newly congested with news vans and satellite uplinks. She caught a glimpse of DA George Turpin giving an interview on the courthouse steps, no doubt assuring the media that Pisgah County law enforcement was swift and would soon bring the killer to justice.

"A few years ago that was you," she said, a wave of nostalgia washing over her. Her boss, Jim Falkner, hated being on television, so he always made her comment on whatever case Atlantans found alarming. At first the bright lights and microphones intimidated her, but she soon learned the art of the sound bite, and ultimately started enjoying it. Criminal law, was, for her, like nothing else. She loved the excitement of starting a new case—piecing together the evidence, figuring out motive. Then going to trial and playing out the drama in front of a jury. Your heart raced a million miles an hour, your brain right along with it. It was almost better than sex, as best she could remember.

"Oh, stop it," she told herself as she turned on to the access road that led to Camp Wadulisi. "You don't do that anymore. Get over it."

She pulled into the pickup area to find Lily long-faced, the last Brownie still waiting for her ride. "I'm sorry I'm late," Mary apologized to the camp director as Lily climbed into the car. "My day got busier than I'd planned."

"Don't give it a thought." Mrs. Crawford smiled. "Lily was telling me all about the owl you rescued last night."

"Did you call about the owl?" Lily asked as they pulled away from camp.

"Not yet." Mary replied, wondering how Nick Stratton had spent his day, caught up in this intern mess. "But we can call after supper."

"She'll probably be dead by then," said Lily sourly, her face falling into the tight lines she'd acquired in Oklahoma.

Mary gripped the steering wheel tightly, wanting to remind the child that had it not been for her, the owl would most certainly be dead, but she kept her silence as they headed home. She'd learned that arguing with a nine-year-old was an exercise in futility.

———

Jonathan was in the kitchen when they got home, cleaning a string of rainbow trout. He looked up and frowned when she walked into the room.

"Hey," she said, walking over to hug him. "What's up?"

"Nothing. What's up with you?"

"Big news," said Mary. "Old Carlisle Wilson's daughter was murdered here the night before the sports park opened."

"Governor Carlisle Wilson? What was his daughter even doing up here?"

"Working at Nick Stratton's rescue center."

"The guy who flew the eagle yesterday?"

She nodded. "The guy Lily and I took the owl to last night."

Jonathan ignored her reference to the injured bird. "Cochran on the case?"

"I'm sure he is." She dropped her purse on a kitchen chair. "I think I'll go change my clothes."

"Dinner's in half an hour," he replied absently, returning to his fish.

———

They ate on the screened porch as thick, purplish clouds rolled in from Tennessee. The mood at the dinner table was as sullen as the sky. Lily had a long list of issues with Brownie camp, while Jonathan shared his own complaints about his fishing clients. Mary finally got up and started clearing the table, deciding that the clatter of washing dishes was more cheerful than their dismal carping. She was elbow-deep in soapsuds, when Lily came into the kitchen.

"Can we call Dr. Lovebird now?"

"Sure," said Mary. "Bring me his card—it's in my billfold."

Lily retrieved the card. Mary dried her hands, then punched in the number. Unsurprisingly, an answering machine advised that they'd reached Pisgah Raptor Rescue Center and to leave a message.

To Lily's disappointment, Mary left her name and number and asked Stratton to call them back.

"Sorry, Lily," she said as she hung up the phone. "He doesn't answer. I imagine he's pretty busy right now."

Her lower lip protruded. "I bet you could have talked to him if you'd called sooner. Now we'll have to wait for him to call us back. The owl's probably dead, anyway!" She started to stalk back out on the porch when Mary reached her limit.

"Lily!" she called, her voice courtroom stern.

The child turned. "What?"

"I did the best I could for that owl. Last night I had a full day of work behind me, and a full day of work waiting for me today. I think right now, you should say 'gee, Mary, thanks for all your help.'"

Lily lifted her chin, defiant. "I don't have to thank you for anything," she said. "You're not even my real mother. All you care about is yourself!"

Mary stood there slack-jawed as Lily thundered past her, down the hall, then upstairs to her bedroom, slamming her door so hard the kitchen windows rattled.

"What's going on?" Jonathan peered into the kitchen from the screened porch.

"You'll have to ask your daughter." Mary threw her damp dishtowel onto the counter. "Cause it sure beats the hell out of me."

She pushed past him, across the screened porch, and out into the field beyond. At that moment, she'd had it with the Walkingsticks. She needed to get away from their sour faces and hair-trigger tempers.

Off she ran along the path that the cows had made—a foot wide swath of trampled dirt that circled the perimeter of her pastures. Though the sky was the color of a plum and the air crackled with electricity, she ran toward the farthest edge of her property, enjoying the scent of pine mixed with ozone. What did she care if it stormed? She wished it would. The rumble of thunder would be a relief from the unvoiced discontent at home.

She ran past cows huddled under the trees, past the mended gap in the fence where a bear had broken through. When her breath came hot in her throat and her lungs felt close to bursting, she came to the weathered, silver-gray barn that Stratton said had been the owl's likely home. She ducked into the old structure. Once the home of mules and plow horses, now it housed only field mice and swallows. She peered up into the shadowy hayloft, looking for any more owls, but she saw nothing but old rafters that disappeared into the darkness.

When her breath came easier, she went back outside and picked up her run, her thoughts returning to Lily and Jonathan. This was her farm, left to her by her old mentor, Irene Hannah. Jonathan and Lily lived here at her invitation, yet ever since they'd come back from Oklahoma they'd treated her as if she were some kind of intruder in their private family circle.

But why? she wondered as the thunder boomed like distant cannons. *What have I done? Why on earth did Lily bring up the fact that I'm not her real mother?*

"A million reasons," she said to herself. "She's nearing puberty, she's been with a bunch of whippy kids all day, she's upset about the owl, she probably didn't get nearly enough sleep last night." That might explain Lily. But what about Jonathan? Why would he lie awake last night while they wrangled with the owl and not say a word? Why was he so distant, so uncaring?

She stopped on a little rise, at the very end of her property. In the distance, she could see the house—sitting easily between two great stands of trees. In the front yard was the creek, the swinging bridge, the tire swing. They had lived here happily for years. Then Jonathan and Lily made that trip to Oklahoma. Nothing had been the same since.

"It's time to ask the question," she told herself softly, knowing she could put it off no longer. "Whatever he says, it will be better than this."

She paused beneath an old oak tree to gather her courage, then she headed for home. Raindrops began to fall, fat as frogs, splatting on the leaves over her head. Keeping to the tree line, she ran to the house, pulling open the screened door as a fearsome clap of thunder broke overhead.

"Hey." Jonathan looked up from his new book on fly-tying. "I was beginning to worry about you."

"Oh, yeah?" She gasped, breathless and soaked as she brushed strands of wet hair from her forehead. She searched the porch and grabbed an old afghan they used on chilly nights. The only sign of Lily was her Kindle, lying next to Jonathan, its screen dark. "Where's Lily?"

"In her room, writing you a note of apology."

"At your suggestion?"

"At my insistence." He flipped the Kindle over. "She thinks we don't care about the owl."

"Oh, I care about the owl. You're the one who doesn't care about the owl." Mary remembered how angry he'd been, the night before.

"I care about the owl," he protested. "I just care more about other things."

She saw her opening; instinctively, she took it. "Do you care about me?"

He looked at her and frowned. For the first time in weeks, she felt as if she had his full attention. "What did you say?"

She swallowed hard, scared that this wasn't the right time, that she hadn't thought enough about what she wanted to say—but then she realized there would never be a time when she knew exactly what she wanted to say. She sat down beside him. "I asked if you cared about me. You have not been the same since you came back from Oklahoma. Neither has Lily."

His eyes were dark, unreadable. "How have we been different?"

"Lily's become a little brat. You treat me like I'm some tired old tire of a wife."

He shook his head. "That's not true."

"Jonathan, we've made love once since you've been back." She reached to touch his cheek. "If you've got somebody else in Oklahoma, then just tell me. I don't want to go on like this anymore."

For a long moment he said nothing. Her heart thumped in her chest, a counterpoint to the rain pinging down on the roof above them. When she thought she would burst from the waiting, he spoke. "There is something in Oklahoma, but it's not what you think."

Her mouth went dry. She seemed to float above her own body. *Remember this*, she told herself. *Remember that you were sitting on this back porch in the middle of a thunderstorm when everything changed.* "What is it, then?"

He leaned forward and rubbed his hands together, as if trying to choose the proper order of his words. Finally, he got up and went into the kitchen, pulling a thick, official-looking envelope from the highest shelf in the pantry. "This came a couple of weeks ago," he said, returning to the porch. "I don't know how to tell you, except to tell you. The Moons have filed another suit."

"The Moons?" She wanted to weep with relief. It was only Lily's grandparents! There was no other woman waiting; no other younger, more comely heart beating for him in Oklahoma. The Moons were nothing; she could conquer the Moons with her eyes closed.

"What do the Moons want?" she asked, almost giddy.

His voice was husky when he spoke. "Full custody of Lily."

THIRTEEN

COCHRAN SPENT THE REST of the day with Whaley in the war room. His dream of a rendezvous with Ginger vanished in an array of theories about the crime and its likely perpetrators, which Cochran diagrammed on a large whiteboard. Rob Saunooke and Tuffy Clark joined them around nine; Saunooke coming from working with the SBI, Clark hobbling in on one crutch, somehow managing to balance two pepperoni pizzas for supper.

"Looks like you guys have actually been doing some work." Clark glanced at the scribbled-on board and Whaley's growing pile of soft drink cans. "Sheriff's been dissecting the crime while Buck's gotten all ginned up on Mountain Dew."

"So what the fuck have you been doing?" snarled Whaley.

"Talking to Lisa Wilson's college buds and fielding reward tips," Clark replied.

"Get anything?" Cochran asked.

"According to her sorority sisters, Lisa was nursing a broken heart over a guy named Darren. Darren's currently banding birds in Costa Rica, so he's out of the picture. The tip line, though, was better than reality TV."

"Oh, yeah?" said Cochran.

"Yeah. One guy insisted Big Foot killed her. Said Big Foot liked to mate with fertile blonde females. He could smell them from miles away. 'You know they don't mate like we do'," Tuffy imitated a wheezy, slightly hysterical voice. "'They're wild! Rough! That's what killed her!'"

"I told that guy I'd turn in his tip," Tuffy continued, grinning. "If he'd introduce Big Foot to my ex-wife."

Everyone roared. "So I take it today was a wash?" asked Cochran when the laughter finally abated.

Clark put the pizzas in the middle of the long table. "I had a great time, but I think the governor's jackpot is safe."

Cochran turned to Saunooke. "What did you and the SBI come up with?"

"We staked a quarter-mile perimeter around that cabin and did a spiral search for evidence from daybreak to sundown. They brought dogs and a couple of guys on horseback."

"Find anything?" asked Whaley.

"A few broken twigs and tramped-down grass, but nothing a bear couldn't have made. Governor Wilson was mighty disappointed."

"He was up there?" Cochran was amazed at the old man's seemingly boundless energy. Wilson had reamed him out, held a press conference, issued a reward, and then joined up with the SBI, all in one day.

"He stood under that pine tree most of the afternoon," Saunooke replied. "Staring at where we found her."

The three older cops looked at each other, their light-heartedness gone. A girl had been killed on their watch. Regardless of who her father was, they wanted to catch who'd done it. After they'd finished their pizza, Cochran walked over to the oversized computer monitor. "You guys have a look at what Whaley and I came up with today."

He turned the screen in their direction and increased the volume on the new speakers he'd sent Whaley out to purchase. "This is Chris Givens's ghost movie. Welcome to the last night of Lisa Wilson's life."

Saunooke and Clark watched, for the first time, the movie that Cochran and Whaley had studied frame-by-frame. First came the shots of the six kids exploring the cabin, then Cochran cut to the scene where everyone was settling down to go to bed. After that, he skipped to when the faint strains of fiddle music started to come over the speakers.

"Are you kidding me?" Clark frowned, incredulous. "Am I actually hearing a fiddle?"

"Just watch," said Cochran.

They watched, no one making a sound. The strange, haunting melody continued when suddenly, Lisa Wilson sat up in her sleeping bag. She looked out the window, then looked around the room. A moment later she tiptoed out the door, shoes in hand. Three minutes later, there was only silence.

"We think she was killed shortly after that," said Cochran, stopping the playback. "There's nothing more on the video. The camera runs out of juice at 5:32 a.m."

"Whoa," said Tuffy. "Play it again."

Cochran played it through twice more. He'd watched it so many times he could anticipate the girl's every expression—fear turning to surprise, then turning to anticipation. He wondered if Clark and Saunooke were reading her the same way. "So what do you think?" he asked after the second run-through.

"She looks like she's trying to put something over on her friends," said Saunooke. "Sneaking out like that."

"Yeah," Tuffy agreed. "Like she was meeting someone." He launched into a high falsetto. "'Darling, I'll come out when I hear you fiddling in the moonlight.'"

Cochran walked over to the whiteboard, pleased that his staff was drawing conclusions similar to his own.

"Okay, then," he said, pointing to the first column on the board. "Have a look at this. We know from forensics that the killer wore jeans from Walmart, strangled Lisa with a smooth piece of leather-like material, and carved her up with a non-serrated curved blade less than three inches in length. She was not sexually assaulted, and the only item missing from her person was her mother's gold wedding ring, which, according to Rachel Sykes, she'd left in her dorm room."

He pointed to a second column. "From Chris Givens's movie, we've learned that fiddle music starts playing at 2:39 a.m., while all our suspects are supposedly asleep in that cabin. At 2:44, Lisa wakes up, looks outside. At 2:48, she tiptoes out the door, and at 2:54, the fiddle music becomes inaudible. The next thing we know of her is when Tony Blackman discovers her body, shortly before eight the next morning."

"Those are the facts." Cochran stepped over to a third column that listed the interns' names. "Whaley, tell us about our people of interest."

Whaley stood up like a kid in school and read from a sheaf of notes. "The interns don't have much in the adult database. The Sykes girl has a lead foot on the gas pedal; Chris Givens has a D&D charge in Chapel Hill. Three of them wore jeans that night, but none were from Walmart. All carried camp knives, but none had hooked blades. All the boys wore smooth leather belts. None of them had any musical instruments with them."

"But you could dump a knife and a fiddle pretty easily, up there." Clark frowned at the board. "Who put the star beside Givens's name?"

"I did," said Cochran. "Only because he dreamed up the whole trip, talked the others into it, and probably planned on pocketing whatever cash he might have gotten for the movie."

Clark shrugged. "His fingerprints are on a lot of it."

"But let's not ignore our other friends," said Cochran, moving over to the column that included the raptor center staff—Nick Stratton, Artie Slade, and Willy Jenkins. "Saunooke, tell us about these guys."

Saunooke pulled a pad from his back pocket. "Willy Jenkins is a fifty-six-year-old former security guard, fired from two different companies—one for insubordination, another for 'anger management issues.' He works at the bird center on an as-needed basis." Saunooke flipped to the next page. "Slade is seventy-two, works at the center full-time. He's got a gimpy leg, and he lost most of the fingers on his right hand in a metal press machine. "

"They got alibis?" asked Whaley.

"Stratton says he was at home alone all night. Jenkins claims he spent the night over in Tennessee, and he's on the surveillance camera at Weigel's gas station, near Knoxville shortly after midnight. Slade says he stayed at his brother's house, in Slade Holler. I talked to his brother, and he swears the two of them played cribbage until ten o'clock, then went to bed."

"Can you play cribbage with one hand?" asked Whaley.

"Sure," said Tuffy. "You can do a lot of fun things with one hand, Whaley."

"You ought to know," Whaley retorted.

Saunooke went on. "But get this—Slade insists that some crazy mountain man hangs out up there."

"What kind of mountain man?" asked Cochran.

"An old man dressed in shabby clothes. Slade says he's come for years, usually when the trees leaf out. Claims he stares at him from the edge of the woods and steals road kill from their freezer."

"Happens to me every time," said Tuffy. "Just put up a couple of squashed skunks and people beat a path to my door."

Though Cochran laughed, his memory flashed back to that wide-eyed face that scared him and Messer so long ago. "So that might corroborate the gray man the Blackman kid thought he saw up there that night."

"Except they decided it wasn't anything but tree limbs and shadows," said Whaley. "Plus they were half-drunk."

"Still," said Cochran. "Lots of people roam through the woods." He turned back to Saunooke. "So what do you think, Rob? Any of your guys warrant a second look?"

Saunooke studied his notes "Maybe Jenkins. He could have driven back from Knoxville in time."

Cochran remembered the way Jenkins's gaze had slid away from him, as if he were afraid to look him in the eye. "Anything else you like about him?"

"He wanted out of the bird business. According to Abby Turner, he kept pestering Lisa to get him a job with her father. Said Stratton didn't pay him shit."

"Anybody think somebody might have paid him to kill the girl?" asked Clark.

"Like who?" asked Cochran.

"Somebody who hated the governor. People take politics pretty seriously around here."

"I asked the governor that," said Cochran. "But he didn't think anybody hated him that bad." He walked over to the board and circled Jenkins's name. "I do happen to know this Jenkins character plays the fiddle."

"How do you know that?" asked Whaley.

"Stratton told me. Stratton plays, too. Has a whole wall of fiddles in his house."

"Whoa, Sheriff!" cried Tuffy. "You've been holding out on us!"

"It hasn't been my turn at bat," said Cochran.

"So tell us about Stratton."

"He's an academic from Seattle, adjunct faculty at Duke. He's run the raptor center for seven years. He has no record, not even a traffic ticket. He seemed shocked when I told him that Lisa had died. He freely invited me into his cabin, where I saw those fiddles. I asked him if he played, he said he and Jenkins played fiddle, while the rest of the group played other instruments.

"He said the other kids got along with Lisa but regarded her as an ass-kisser. Then he showed me her dorm room, where she had a hundred pictures of Stratton plastered above her bed."

Tuffy asked, "He didn't know about them?"

Cochran shook his head. "He claimed he'd never gone in there before. I'm inclined to believe him. He looked scared shitless when he saw them."

"Both girls and Chris Givens thought Lisa and Stratton had a thing going on," said Saunooke.

"Which Stratton denies," said Cochran.

"Wait a minute." Whaley's eyes grew bright. "Let's talk about Stratton. Maybe Lisa's stalking him—has him in a box he can't see a way out of. His kids go up to this haunted cabin and he sees his chance. He says he'll join her, play their special tune after everyone else is asleep. If the coast is clear, come out. He goes up there, plays; she sneaks out to meet him. He takes her up to that tree, then boom! Good-bye, Lisa. Shit, Stratton might have even been the ghost they claim to have seen."

"But why go to that much trouble?" asked Tuffy. "Why not just push her off a waterfall? Easiest mountain murder in the book."

"Or push her off that eagle hatching stand they've got up there," said Saunooke. "That thing must be thirty feet high."

"Right. If they're having a fling and she dies while they're on his eagle stand, then he's in a shit pot of suspicion," Whaley insisted.

"So how do you explain all that stuff carved on her body?" asked Cochran. "And why would Stratton kill her so close to the cabin? That would be risky, with all those hung-over college boys, peeing in the woods."

"I didn't say I had all the answers," Whaley sniffed, irritated. "So far, I just like Stratton better than an ex-security guard or some one-handed geezer who can't secure his road kill."

"Stratton's got the muscle to do it," said Cochran. "He was shirtless in most of Lisa's photos. The guy's pretty cut."

"It's still a lot to ask," said Clark. "Hike up there, kill the girl, hike home, destroy every shred of evidence, and then go fly your eagle at the sports park opening."

"Who said he hiked? He could have driven his car," replied Whaley. "Would have taken him an hour and half, round trip."

"Saunooke?" Cochran asked for their most junior member's opinion.

"I don't know," he replied, looking uncomfortable. "I still think they could have seen somebody up there that night. An *uluhnotski*." He struggled to translate his Cherokee. "A crazy person."

Cochran sighed, frustrated. Though they had an actual video of the last few minutes of Lisa Wilson's life, their evidence was still wispy, theoretical. Whaley liked Stratton, Tuffy didn't. Saunooke thought it was an *uluhnotski*; he was certain those figures meant more than just the random disfigurement of a body. They needed something more, in either motive or evidence. He studied the board another moment, then he spoke.

"Whaley, I want you to get a search warrant. List all structures at the Pisgah Raptor Rescue Center, including the personal quarters of Nick Stratton, Artie Slade, and Willy Jenkins. Plus all vehicles on site. Since we haven't found anything in the woods, let's see what we can turn up at the bird center. "

"When do you want it for?" asked Whaley.

"Tomorrow morning, six a.m."

"You don't want to go tonight?"

Cochran shook his head. "We all need some sleep, plus a few more warm bodies for the search. I'd rather go up there sharp tomorrow than half-assed tonight."

"You're the boss," said Whaley.

"That I am," said Cochran, capping the blue marker he'd used on the whiteboard. "Thanks, gentlemen, for your thoughts. I'll see you back here at five a.m."

Tuffy Clark leaned back in his chair. "You want me to go, or am I still on switchboard duty?"

"You stay on the board, Tuff. You're our official point man for Big Foot."

Laughing, Tuffy got up and hobbled out the door behind the others. Cochran listened as they made their way down the hall. *Good men, all of them*, he thought. *Sharp detectives*. He only wished one of them could figure out who the hell killed Lisa Wilson.

FOURTEEN

MARY CROW SAT ON her screened porch, not knowing whether to weep with relief or shriek with rage. No younger, prettier girl had stolen Jonathan's heart; Fred and Dulcy Moon simply wanted to take Lily away.

"Tell me why again," she asked, still not understanding why two people in their late sixties would suddenly want to raise a nine-year-old child. "Why now?"

"I heard they sold a piece of land and got some money," said Jonathan. "Enough to file this lawsuit."

"Wait a minute." She frowned. "Let me see that complaint."

He handed her the papers. She turned on the porch light, reading the thing line by line. Suddenly, she started to laugh. "Too bad they didn't get a smarter lawyer," she said. "This idiot's filed in Cherokee County, Oklahoma. You have to be a resident of a state before you can be sued there."

Jonathan's shoulders sank lower as a new wave of rain pounded the tin roof above them. "There's something else you don't know."

His words punctured her brief moment of joy. *Dear God*, she thought, *there's more.* "What?"

He gulped. "I am a resident of Oklahoma."

She cocked her head, thinking she must not have heard him correctly. "You what?"

"I bought a little duplex that was in foreclosure, the day I dropped Lily off at the Moons."

Once again, she felt too stunned to speak. For weeks he'd told her he'd rented a ground floor room at the Sooner Motel. For weeks, he'd lied.

He rubbed his forehead. "Mary, you just don't know what it was like. When Fred Moon took Lily's hand and pulled her inside his house he gave me this shit-eating grin. Then I saw a big-ass motor home parked behind his house. I knew that if they ever took off with Lily in that trailer, I'd never see her again."

"But you told me you stayed at the Sooner Motel." She couldn't get past his lie. It felt so much like a slap that her cheeks burned. "For a month!"

"I had to do something, Mary. The duplex was cheap, and it's so close to their house I could keep an eye on them. I've already got one side rented out, paying the note. I can use the other side myself if I ever take Lily out there again."

"And you just weren't ever going to tell me?" She stared at him. He'd changed, somehow, into someone she didn't know. Never had he been dishonest. Even when his words wounded, he'd always spoken the truth.

He lowered his eyes. "I didn't think you'd understand."

"Oh, I understand that you wanted to protect Lily," she said. "I just don't understand why you felt you had to lie to me about it."

She sat back in her chair, staring out into the rain. What a fool she'd been. She'd encouraged them to go together. She thought a father-daughter trip would be fun for them. She never dreamed their lives would be shattered when they returned.

In a few minutes he spoke again. "So I guess I have to respond to this?"

"Of course you have to respond, Jonathan. You can't just ignore a lawsuit. Buying that house gave them the toehold they needed. I can help you with it, though."

He walked to the edge of the porch, hands in his pockets, swaying slightly on his feet. She could tell he had more to say. Her stomach curdled as she waited. A moment later, he turned to her.

"I don't think you need to be involved in this, Mary."

"Not involved in this?" Again, she looked at him as if he'd turned into a stranger. "Jonathan, I've spent my entire career in the courtroom. Why would you not want me to respond to this lawsuit?"

"You're the reason the Moons are filing it," he said, his voice thick.

"What do you mean?"

He shook his head. "Just read the rest of those papers."

She began flipping through the pages. At first it was all the usual legalese, then she came to the bill of particulars. As she read the charges Fred and Dulcy Moon had levied, she went cold inside.

At no time has Mary Crow respected the bonds of matrimony that existed between our daughter Ruth and Jonathan Walkingstick.

Mary Crow has never acted in the best interest of Lily Bird Walkingstick, the natural daughter of Ruth and Jonathan Walkingstick, conspiring to keep her away from her biological relatives in Cherokee County, Oklahoma.

Mary Crow's jealousy of and hostility toward Ruth Moon Walkingstick culminated in a physical altercation that left our daughter dead, a crime for which Mary Crow has never been prosecuted.

We respectfully submit that Mary Crow, the woman responsible for our daughter's death, is neither loving nor trustworthy in her care of our granddaughter and maintains an emotionally toxic environment for our grandchild. As Lily Bird Walkingstick's biological grandparents, we, Fred Amos Moon and Dulcy Sims Moon, petition the court for full custody of said child.

"Oh my God." Mary looked up from the complaint, her hands shaking. "They're claiming I killed Ruth—that I got away with murder."

Jonathan walked over and grabbed the papers from her lap. "You know what I'm going to do? I'm going to treat this like the piece of shit it is." He ripped the first page in half.

"Don't do that, Jonathan!" She stood up and grabbed the papers back. "You've got a court date, in two weeks. If you don't show up, the Moons will get the judgment. Federal marshals will come here and take Lily away."

"The hell they will! I'll take her to Mexico. Or Canada."

"And live where? In the woods? Hiding from the Mounties?"

"If I have to." He turned to her, his eyes blazing. "Woods are woods. I could feed us."

"And what kind of life would that be for her?" Mary asked. "Or you? Or us?"

"I don't know," he replied. "All I know is I'm not letting the Moons have my child."

She walked back in the kitchen then. She couldn't talk to him anymore, he wasn't thinking rationally. She took the rest of the Moons' complaint and retreated into her study. Sitting down at her desk, she read the pages through twice more, each time her heart sinking further. This case was way out of her league—she was a former prosecutor, now a broker of ballparks. She knew nothing of Oklahoma law or child custody statutes. Still, she did know one person who might help. She grabbed the phone and punched one of the three phone numbers she knew by heart. Moments later, a sleepy male voice croaked something that sounded like "Yo?"

"Hello, Charlie? This is Mary Crow, calling from North Carolina."

"Hey, Mary." Charlie Carter's voice was rusty with sleep. "What's up?"

"Could I speak with your lovely wife?"

"Sure. Hang on."

She heard a rustling noise, then her oldest and dearest friend came on the line. "Mary?"

"Hey, Al," she said, tearing up at the sound of Alex Carter's soft Texas drawl.

"What's wrong, girlfriend?" Alex cut to the chase, apparently figuring that Mary wouldn't call at 2 a.m. to chat about old times.

Mary gulped, fought sudden tears. "Do you know anybody who can practice in Oklahoma?"

"I can. Why?"

"I need a lawyer."

"What on earth for?"

"The Moons are suing us for custody of Lily."

"Hang on a minute." The graininess had left Alex's voice. "Let me put on a robe and go down to the den."

By the time Alex picked up the phone again, Mary had dried her tears. Now was not the time to weep; now was the time to figure out what to do.

"Okay," said Alex. "Tell me what's up."

Mary told her how Jonathan had taken Lily to Oklahoma for a visitation with her grandparents. There, he'd become convinced that the Moons were going to kidnap her; how he'd foolishly bought a duplex to stop that from happening.

"He bought a house to live in for a month out of the year?" asked Alex. "Did you tell him that was a little over the top?"

"I didn't know he'd bought it until an hour ago." Mary felt her face grow hot; Alex must wonder what kind of relationship they had. Marriage-wise, she and Charlie always seemed to be exactly on the same page.

"Okaaaay," said Alex neutrally. "So Lily spent a month in Oklahoma with the Moons, being spied on by her father."

"Right." Mary pictured Jonathan in camouflage, belly down in a field, binoculars trained on Lily's every move.

"So what happened next?" asked Alex.

"A couple of weeks ago, Jonathan got a summons from Cherokee county civil court." Mary recapped the bill of particulars. "The Moons seek full custody, citing previous judgments of grandparental rights."

"Sounds like they're throwing shit against the wall to see if any will stick," said Alex.

"They've got a piece that might stick," said Mary.

"What?"

Mary took a deep breath, and slowly read the paragraphs that damned her. "'Mary Crow's jealousy of and hostility toward Ruth Moon Walkingstick culminated in a physical altercation that left our daughter dead, a crime for which Mary Crow has never been prosecuted'."

"Wow," said Alex, giving a low whistle. "They're actually arguing that you killed their daughter and the cops just let it slide."

"The cops did not let it slide," snapped Mary. "They ruled it self-defense. Ruth Moon was out of her frigging mind."

"I know, I know," Alex said soothingly. "I just wonder why the lawyer threw that in."

"They want to open the door to the night Ruth died," cried Mary. "They paint me evil enough and no judge will let me near Lily!" Again, her throat closed with tears.

"Okay, okay," said Alex. "We need to stay calm, Mary. And think."

"You're right." Mary took a gulp of air. "I'm sorry."

"What does Jonathan say about this?" asked Alex.

"He's threatening to take Lily out of the country. You know how he can get."

"Has he mentioned anything we can blow back on them? Any mistreatment or neglect of Lily?"

"Not unless we counter-sue for parking her in front of a television and letting her eat Cheetos all day."

Alex snorted. "That sounds vaguely like the Twinkie defense."

"I don't care," said Mary. "At this point, I'll take anything."

Alex gave a long sigh, as if reviewing the facts of the case. "Have you got a scanner there?"

"I do."

"Then scan the whole complaint into your computer and email it to me as soon as we get off the phone."

"Okay."

"Then tomorrow, you bundle up your boy and his little girl and send them back to Oklahoma."

"But the trial date's two weeks away."

"I'm going to try mediation first. If Jonathan shows up and makes nice with the Moons they may settle for something less than full custody."

"Jonathan will make nice with the Moons when pigs have wings, Alex."

"He may have to, or lose Lily until she turns eighteen."

Mary realized Alex was right. All of them needed to present their best selves to the judge in Oklahoma. "Okay," she said. "I don't have anything else on my plate. We'll hit the road first thing in the morning."

For a moment, Mary heard nothing, then her best friend spoke softly. "I'm afraid the invitation doesn't include you, Mary."

"Doesn't include me? Alex, I know the particulars of this case inside and out. I may not do child custody work, but I can read up on the statutes. I can—"

"Mary," Alex stopped her in mid-sentence. "You're an amazing attorney, a wonderful mother, and the best friend I'll ever have. But you cannot come to Oklahoma."

"Why not?"

"Because you and I both know where opposing council will go, Mary. The last thing we need is you on the witness stand, recounting the last night of Ruth Moon's life."

FIFTEEN

JERRY COCHRAN SAT IN the patrol car, watching wispy tendrils of fog caress the stylized faces of Nick Stratton's totem pole. Whaley had gotten Judge Barbee to sign off on all structures at Pisgah Raptor Rescue Center, but he'd also listed specifically all non-serrated knives, smooth leather straps, all denim jeans, and Lisa Wilson's gold ring. Now the two sat waiting for the sweep hand of Cochran's watch to pass 6:00 a.m. As he sat there Cochran thought of Ginger, home in bed, her hair a pile of fiery curls on her pillow. *How nice to be there with her*, he thought. Kissing her awake, lifting her on top of him, letting that long red hair cover him like silk.

"Ready to go?" Whaley interrupted his reverie, checking the time on his cell phone. "I've got 6:01."

"Okay," said Cochran, reluctantly leaving his dream of Ginger just as things were getting interesting.

He got out of the car and motioned to the phalanx of police cruisers that had accompanied them. Saunooke and three other officers emerged, ready to execute the search warrant for Stratton's domicile.

"Gentlemen, we need to go absolutely by the book," Cochran said. "All of you know what we're looking for. I want you to work carefully and in pairs. I don't want any evidence we may find thrown out because of a questionable search. Understand?"

They nodded.

"Okay. Whaley and Fields will take the intern dorms. Saunooke and Parker will do the bird barn, the staff cabins, and the hacking stand. Hastings and I will take Stratton's residence."

"Are the interns still here?" asked Fields.

"Nah, they all lawyered up and went home," said Whaley. "We can probably do the dorms pretty quick."

"Any more questions?" asked Cochran. When no one spoke, he gave a quick nod. "Okay, let's get going."

Silently, they hurried up the road to Stratton's cabin. With search warrants, Cochran always liked to maintain an element of surprise. A person's private face often differed vastly from the one they presented in public. Behind closed doors and under stress, Nick Stratton might be very different from his benevolent Dr. Lovebird persona.

They reached his cabin. Cochran walked up the steps and rapped on the door. "Nicholas Stratton?" he called. There was no answer. He knocked twice more, going from a knock to a near-pound. Just when he was about to have Whaley put his size thirteen shoes to the lock, the door swung open. Stratton stood there, wearing only a pair of canvas shorts.

"Nicholas Stratton?" Cochran read the warrant to him officially, feeling silly since he'd been up here just two days ago.

Stratton nodded.

"I've got a warrant duly issued by Judge James Barbee to search your domicile, your vehicles, and your livestock structures." He handed the warrant to Stratton, who looked at it as if it were written in Greek.

"Is this where you guys wreck the house?" he asked, frowning.

"My department doesn't," said Cochran.

"Do I get to call a lawyer?"

"You can call one," Cochran replied. "But it won't stop us."

"Well, okay." Stratton stepped away from the door. "Come on in."

Cochran remained on the porch, directing the other officers to their assigned locations.

"They won't unlock any of my bird cages will they?" Stratton asked, frowning at the two men headed to the bird barns.

Cochran shook his head. "Not unless they find evidence inside them."

As Whaley and Saunooke left with their partners, Pete Hastings moved in behind Cochran. Stratton stood there, blinking, his hair tousled from sleep.

"Mr. Stratton, we are looking for the items listed specifically on that warrant," Cochran explained. "If we find them, we will confiscate them as evidence against you. We cannot confiscate anything not listed on that writ. However, we can and may confiscate items belonging to the deceased Lisa Carlisle Wilson. We will not disturb your properties any more than necessary to execute a thorough search. Right now, you need to remain calm and allow us to do our work." Cochran looked at Al Sayles, a burly traffic cop he'd asked to come keep an eye on Stratton. "Officer?"

Sayles stepped forward, pistol snug in his holster. "Find a comfortable seat, sir," he told Stratton. "This may take awhile."

Stratton started to say something, then apparently changed his mind. With a shrug of his shoulders, he went over and sat down on the couch.

Cochran turned to Hastings. "Let's start in the kitchen."

———

They searched the kitchen carefully. Stratton had only four knives, all held by a magnetized strip over the sink. Though none had curved blades, Cochran put them in an evidence bag just the same. *You never knew*, he told himself. Again he glanced at the refrigerator, looking for anything written in the same shapes carved on Lisa Wilson's body. As before, he found none. But unlike before, he saw Mary Crow's business card, paper-clipped to a calendar.

Wonder when Stratton got that, he thought, taking note of the little gold-and-black card. It hadn't been there when they'd notified him of Lisa Wilson's death.

They found nothing else of interest in the kitchen, so they returned to the living room, ready to start on the rest of the house.

"Can I go in the kitchen now?" asked Stratton. "Make some coffee?"

"You may," said Cochran. Sayles followed Stratton into the kitchen while he and Hastings began to search the living room. It was, fortunately, minimally furnished. Stratton had a small couch, two filing cabinets that served as end tables, two chairs, and a reading lamp. What took up most of their time was a low bookcase, filled with books. Cochran and Hastings removed each volume and flipped through the pages, hoping something would fall out.

As they worked Cochran realized how much Stratton's library resembled his own—non-fiction titles about natural history, geology, tales of survival in extreme conditions. He pulled one small paperback off the shelf and smiled. A similarly battered copy of *The Boy Scout Handbook* rested on his own bookshelf.

Still, *The Boy Scout Handbook* yielded nothing, so he and Hasting moved upstairs, where a loft served as Stratton's office and bedroom. A huge topographic map hung above an unmade bed, flanked by expensively framed photographs of Stratton with a bald eagle, Stratton on skis, Stratton embracing a pretty, dark-haired woman dressed in buckskin and feathers.

They searched the bathroom, finding nothing more lethal than a large bottle of ibuprofen. The office consisted of a desk with a computer and printer, but contained none of the warranted items—not a penknife, not a leather strap, certainly not a ring.

They turned their attention to Stratton's bedroom. Cochran started with the closet, rifling through his clothes, hoping to find a pair of Walmart jeans. Again, he was disappointed. Not a single pair of jeans hung in Stratton's closet—all his pants were heavy twill trousers. Most of his shirts were pale blue and long-sleeved. He had a single black suit, a starched white dress shirt still in plastic from the dry cleaner, and a silk necktie that had some kind of hand-painted design on it. Cochran removed a black leather belt that hung from the hanger.

"Working man's wardrobe," he said, thinking how very much it looked like his own. One suit for special occasions, everything else no-nonsense, work-related, probably bought at the local Tractor Supply.

He closed the closet door and turned to Stratton's drawers, removing each one and dumping the contents on his bed. The first two held tee shirts, boxer shorts, a couple of wool sweaters. The bottom drawer was different—either swollen or out of alignment. Hastings had to tug hard on the thing to pull it open. Finally, though, he wrenched it free. It held nothing but long underwear and heavy wool socks. They were rifling through those when a dark, heavy thing rolled out from a sock and on to the floor.

"What's that?" asked Hastings. "Chewing tobacco?"

The thing bounced once, finally rolling lopsidedly underneath the bed. At first Cochran thought it was a can of shoe polish, then he realized it was an item beloved by northern boys.

"A hockey puck," he told Hastings. "Probably a memento. I'll get it." He knelt down on the floor just as he heard Whaley's voice booming up from the living room. Hoping that the overweight detective had better luck than he and Hastings, he lifted Stratton's rumpled bedspread and peered under the bed. It was empty, except for two pairs of boots and some dust bunnies. The puck had rolled near the head of the bed, where the frame met the wall. With Whaley thundering up the stairs, Cochran stretched out, reaching for the puck with one arm. As he pulled the thing from beneath the bed, something else caught his eye. A small, glittery thing. Tossing the puck to Hastings, he scooted forward to retrieve what he'd spotted.

"Where's Cochran?" he heard Whaley call.

He reached forward, the little item still just beyond his grasp.

"Under the bed," Hastings replied as Cochran stretched out farther.

"Look what I found in the dorm," said Whaley.

Cochran reached as far as he could, dust crawling up his nose, making him want to sneeze. Finally, his fingers curled around a small metal object.

"What?" asked Hastings.

"Lisa Wilson's iPhone and diary!" said Whaley. He moved closer, lifted the bedspread from the floor. "You hear what I said, Sheriff?"

"Yeah," said Cochran, scooting out from under the bed. He opened his hand. In it lay a gold filigreed ring, old-fashioned, but well-worn, the band noticeably thinner at the back. It was the same ring Lisa Wilson had worn in the picture where she'd smiled up at Nick Stratton, a look of utter devotion on her face.

SIXTEEN

MARY JERKED AWAKE, LIFTING her head from the desk, for an instant unable to remember why she'd fallen asleep there instead of in bed. She hazily recalled arguing with Jonathan, then talking with her old friend Alex. For a moment she wondered if it hadn't been some bizarre nightmare, then she saw the documents spread out before her. Her focus sharpened in an instant. The Moons were suing Jonathan for full custody of Lily.

"I've got to get them out there," she said, remembering Alex's last words. "To Oklahoma. As soon as possible." Willing herself awake, she hurried upstairs. Jonathan and Lily were still asleep, unaware of the journey ahead of them. Silently, she gathered Lily's dirty clothes, then tiptoed into the room she shared with Jonathan. He lay on his stomach with a pillow pulled over his head, as if trying to hide the woes that plagued him. For a moment she was tempted to snatch his covers off and again ask him to explain all his lies. An affair she could understand—pretty eyes and perky breasts could have sparked a reckless moment of passion. But to lie to her about a custody suit? And some stupid duplex? That required thought; they were acts of deception that required attention, like a garden of poisonous plants. And then to turn the whole thing back on her, saying she wouldn't understand...

"Sleep on, Walkingstick," she muttered, her anger again starting to simmer. "Enjoy your dreams."

She gathered up the rest of their clothes and went down to the utility room. She started a load of laundry, then headed back to the study to make hard copies of all the papers Alex needed in Oklahoma.

"I almost wish he'd had an affair," she whispered as she started the copier. "Then it would be just between him and me. Now it's between him and me and the Moons and some lawyer in Oklahoma."

By eight fifteen, she'd finished her copying and the laundry. Laden with fresh, still-warm clothes, she went back upstairs. Angrily, she stomped into their room and dropped the laundry basket on the bed. Jonathan sat up immediately.

"What's wrong?" he said, blinking in the morning light.

"Nothing." She started piling his clothes on the bed. "You need to pack. You're going to Oklahoma, so be sure and take your good suit."

"Huh?"

She separated his jeans from his underwear. "After I went through all those papers last night, I called Alex. She's meeting you at the Holiday Inn in Tulsa the day after tomorrow. She's graciously agreed to take your case."

He looked at her, uncomprehending. "Take my case?"

"The custody case the Moons brought against you?" A fresh wave of anger roiled inside her. "Alex wants you and Lily in Oklahoma, ASAP."

"Oklahoma?" He started to laugh. "You tell Alex I'll go to hell before I'll go to Oklahoma."

Mary looked at him, appalled. Never had it occurred to her that he might just refuse to go. "Are you out of your mind?"

"The Moons can shove that lawsuit up their ass. I'm not going back to Oklahoma."

"So you're just going to stay here and ignore their complaint?"

"I haven't committed any crime. They can't come and arrest me."

She folded her arms, furious. "Let me explain how this works, Jonathan," she spoke slowly, as if explaining some point of law to one of her backwoods clients. "If you don't answer this complaint, the court will render a judgment against you. The states honor each other's judgments. The Moons will present their Oklahoma order to Jerry Cochran, and he'll have to enforce it. There won't be a thing you can do."

"The fuck I can't!" he told her. "I'll take her into the woods, or Canada. I'll…"

"We explored Canada last night, Jonathan. Take her out of the country and you'll be a fugitive. Her photo will be on websites all over the Internet."

"I'm not going to give her to those goddamn Moons!" he cried. "She belongs with me."

"Then you need to go back to Oklahoma and work with Alex. Right now, it's your only shot."

He gave her an odd look. "You sound like you want us to go."

"I want you to obey the law," she replied.

"I'm sure you do. My obeying the law works pretty good for you."

"What do you mean?"

"It gets Lily out of your hair. She's a real pain in the butt. You said so not three days ago."

"Gosh, that must have been after I took her swimming. Or took that owl to the vet for her. Or picked her up at Brownie camp yesterday afternoon."

"See? You resent all those things. If we didn't have Lily, you'd be free to do what you want, take the clients you want and—"

"Work on murder trials?" she finished his sentence.

"Yeah. Work on murder trials. I know how you get off on them."

Her anger flared so quickly that she had to turn away to keep from slapping him. "You do what you want, Jonathan. Lily's your child. But I strongly advise you to pack your bags and get yourself and your daughter out to Oklahoma."

Furious, she stormed downstairs, back to the kitchen. Spooning coffee into the coffee pot, she told herself that Jonathan and Lily could do what they pleased; she was going to sit down and eat breakfast. She'd just retrieved eggs from the refrigerator when Lily came into the kitchen.

"Hi, Mary." The little girl yawned, still in her pajamas. Mary wondered if her angry words with Jonathan had awakened her, but she looked more sleepy than distressed.

"Morning, Lily." Mary tried to smile.

Lily rubbed her eyes. "Did Dr. Lovebird ever call back?"

"No," Mary replied, grateful that at least the child was concerned about the owl and not their argument. "You want some eggs?"

"I guess so."

Mary cracked two more eggs to the chipped blue bowl her mother had always used. Just as she reached to turn on the stove, she heard Jonathan coming downstairs. She was beating the eggs into a pale yellow froth when he sat down at the table, across from his child.

"Lily, there's something we need to talk about," he said, his voice raspy.

The little girl looked up, still sleepy. "What?"

"You and I are going to have to go back to Oklahoma."

"This summer?"

"No. Today."

"Today? But I have to finish my mask at camp. And tomorrow night is Debra Fisher's sleepover."

"I'm sorry, honey. We've got to go back today."

She looked as if she might cry. "But we just came back from there."

Mary handed Lily a glass of orange juice, waiting for Jonathan's response. "We have to go. Grandpa and Grandma Moon are suing me."

"What for?"

"They want a judge to say that you come and live with them."

"Live with them?" She put her juice down. "All the time?"

Jonathan nodded.

"But I don't want to," said Lily, her chin beginning to quiver for real. "All my friends are here."

"That's why we have to go to Oklahoma," said Jonathan. "To tell the judge that you like it here, and that you don't want to leave. Mary's friend Alex is going to help us."

Mary walked over to put an arm around Lily, but the child twisted out of her chair, pinioning her with a dark, hate-filled look. "This is all your fault."

"My fault?" Mary frowned. "Why is it my fault?"

"Because you killed my mother!"

"What?"

"You killed my mother! Grandpa Moon told me!"

Mary stood there stunned, unable to come up with a reply. Jonathan finally spoke.

"Nobody killed your mother, Lily. She was sick, then she died," he repeated the official explanation they'd used ever since Lily had been old enough to wonder about her biological mother.

"That's not what Grandpa Moon said," Lily cried, tears spilling down her cheeks. "He says Mary killed her! He says you two covered it up. That's why you've never told me what really happened!"

Jonathan's eyes flashed, angry. "Grandpa Moon doesn't know what he's talking about!"

"Yes, he does! He showed me the newspaper! Mary did kill my mother. Mary's a big liar, and I hate her!" Sobbing loudly, Lily ran back upstairs, again slamming her bedroom door so hard the windows shook.

A tomb-like quiet settled over the house. The skillet on the stove began to smoke; Mary turned off the burner. She'd lost her appetite.

Jonathan got up from the table and poured a cup of coffee. "If I could get my hands on that son of a bitch, I'd kill him."

Good idea, Mary thought. *Just like you buying the duplex and ignoring the custody suit.* But she said nothing. Reopening their argument would be like raking sharp fingernails over scalded flesh. She took the uncooked eggs and dumped them down the drain. "If you're going, you should get ready. Lily's clothes are washed—all you need to do is put them in her suitcase."

"You aren't going to help her pack?"

Mary thought of the dark fury in the little girl's eyes and shook her head. "I think I've done enough for Lily."

———

He left the kitchen in a huff. Mary slapped ham on rye bread as she listened to their footsteps overhead—Jonathan's heavy tread interspersed with Lily's lighter footsteps. She heard Lily crying, another door slam. Finally luggage began thunking down the stairs, hitting every riser with a loud thud. The front door opened and closed half a dozen times, then Jonathan stood in the doorway, his face as wooden as the tribal masks they sold in Cherokee.

"We're going," he announced.

She wiped her hands on a dish towel. "Then I'll come say goodbye."

She followed him to the truck, carrying a tote bag filled with sandwiches and a copy of the Moons' complaint. Lily sat buckled in the passenger seat, reading on her Kindle. Mary walked over and rapped briskly on the car door. "I want to talk to you, Lily."

Slowly, the child rolled down her window. "What?" she said, her eyes red and swollen.

"I want you to know this. Your mother was an extraordinary woman who loved you very much. Every day I see more of her face in yours, and you are both beautiful."

Lily gave her an odd look.

Mary continued. "Ruth Moon was a wonderful, talented woman who meant well. I'm sorry she got sick. I'm sorry you blame me for her death. But I'm very happy that so much of her lives on in you."

Lily frowned, not knowing how to respond. Mary took the opportunity to lean in the window. "My mother died when I was young, too, Lily. I know how badly that hurts." She kissed her on the cheek. "*Guh geh yu hee*, Lily-bird," she whispered. "Whatever happens, that's forever."

Mary stepped back from the truck. Lily rolled up the window, her head bowed, her face hidden by the dark curtain of her hair. Mary turned and walked over to Jonathan.

"I made you some sandwiches." She held out the tote bag. "Ham for you, turkey for Lily. And a hard copy of the complaint for Alex."

"Thanks," he said.

"Alex will be waiting for you. I wrote her cell phone number on the first page of the complaint. Try to keep in touch with her."

He put the tote bag in the backseat of the truck. Turning to her, he gave a sigh that seemed to come from deep inside him. "I don't know what to say."

She stood there. For a moment she wondered if he was going to kiss her, then it occurred to her that somewhere during the past night they'd gone beyond kissing—all the caresses in the world could not mend what had broken between them. "Don't do anything stupid, okay?"

"No." He gave a small, disgusted shake of his head and got in the truck. She backed away as he started the engine, then pulled down the driveway. He waved once, but Lily's gaze never left the Kindle on her lap. As they passed she etched them in her memory, two people in a red Chevy pickup, disappearing through tall green pines. *This is how it looked, this last day*, she thought. *From here on out, everything will be different.*

SEVENTEEN

"I TRIED TO STOP him!" Kristal Bridgewater fluttered her hands seemingly in an effort to cool off her ears. "But he came in here waving that cane like a crazy man. I put him in your office just to shut him up!"

"Who?" cried George Turpin. "What are you talking about?" Ten minutes ago he'd stepped out of a serene office to visit the sixth-floor men's room. Now he'd returned to find his secretary hysterical, looking as if she might jump out the window.

"Carlisle Wilson." Kristal sobbed. "And his wife."

Turpin's gut clenched. He knew that this day might come. He'd kept a close eye on Wilson from the cupola of the courthouse, hoping that Cochran might make a quick arrest and the old man would go bury his daughter somewhere at the other end of the state. But that had not happened. Cochran hadn't arrested anybody on as much as a jaywalking charge and the old man was now taking aim at the next person on the food chain: him.

"How long has he been in there?" Turpin whispered, eyeing his office door as if smoke and brimstone might come seeping out.

"Five minutes, maybe." Kristal shuddered. "I'm telling you, he's insane!"

Turpin considered his options. Having Kristal remain outside might be a good idea—she could call security if Wilson went totally off the rails. But by the same token, having Kristal within earshot might prove embarrassing, considering the potshots Wilson might fire at him. He didn't want to be the laughingstock of the ladies' room. "Why don't you go to lunch," Turpin finally suggested, the armpits of his shirt growing damp. "I'll take care of this."

Kristal's face brightened with relief. "Are you sure?" she asked, making a feeble show of loyalty. "I'll stay if you really want me to."

"It'll be fine." Turpin gave a high, girlish laugh. "You go eat lunch. No need to hurry back, either."

"Thanks." Kristal smiled. "And be careful!"

Turpin watched as she grabbed her purse and hurried to the door, her ample breasts bouncing in her blue knit dress. He waited until she was safely out of the office, then he straightened his tie, checked his zipper, mopped his forehead with a handkerchief. *Whatever happens*, he thought, *at least it won't go past this office.* He paused for a moment with his hand on the doorknob, then he took a final deep breath and opened the door. He found Carlisle Wilson pacing in front of his desk, one hand wielding his cane, the other clutching a newspaper. His wife sat in a chair, dabbing at her eyes with a tissue.

"Governor and Mrs. Wilson," said Turpin sonorously, walking over to shake hands with them. "I'm so sorry for your loss. Sybil and I both extend our deepest sympathies."

Wilson glowered at him with smoldering eyes. Mrs. Wilson mewed something he couldn't understand.

Turpin blathered on. "I can't express how upset everyone is about this. It's unthinkable that such a tragedy would happen in Pisgah County." Though Turpin had mastered the art of the sound bite, where he promised to prosecute criminals to the fullest extent of the law, he met with grieving relatives less comfortably. He found it hard to seem sincere when the greatest sorrow people would ever know was, to him, just another case on the docket. "What can I do for you today?"

"Do for me?" Wilson's face darkened as he held up a newspaper. "Have you seen this?"

"I-I'm not sure I have." Desperately, Turpin tried to remember what the *Hartsville Herald* had run this morning, but his brain seized up. All he could do was stare at the red filigree of blood vessels on the end of Wilson's nose.

Wilson slapped the paper down on his desk. To Turpin's surprise, it wasn't the *Herald* at all, but the latest issue of *The Snitch*. Turpin gaped at the cover photo of an NFL quarterback dressed in a bra, wondering what that had to do with anything when Wilson took his cane and flipped the rag to the centerfold. Turpin gasped. Under the headline MOUNTAIN MANIAC MUTILATES GOVERNOR'S DAUGHTER was a photo of Lisa Wilson nude, splayed out on the ground, her body covered in what looked like fuzzy, illegible tattoos.

"Jesus," whispered Turpin. He hadn't seen any of the crime scene photos—the picture of the girl's shredded body brought his lunchtime chicken salad roiling back up his throat.

"Do you have children, Mr. Turpin?" the old governor asked.

The room spun as his children's faces flashed before his eyes. "I do…a boy and a g-girl."

147

"Then can you imagine what it's like to lose your daughter, and then see her picture in trash like this?" Wilson's voice trembled with fury. "To know that strangers will gawk at her while they're waiting to buy frozen pizza?"

Turpin broke into such a clammy sweat that he wondered if he wasn't having a heart attack. "I'm s-so sorry," he sputtered again.

"What I want to ask you, Mr. DA, is what the hell kind of criminal justice operation are you running in this county?"

"What do you mean?"

"I mean why would that goddamned Cochran leak this?" thundered the old man.

"Are you sure he did?" asked Turpin. "Cochran usually plays his cards close to his vest."

"He told me he had the only photos of her. Said he was keeping them locked in his drawer. I believed, him, too. Until I saw this."

Turpin didn't know what to say. Though he and Cochran were not particular friends, the young sheriff had helped improve his own conviction rate in the past seven years. His evidence was always clean, scrupulously gathered. Compared to the corrupt Stump Logan, Cochran was a white hat, riding into Hartsville to clean up the town.

"I d-don't know, Governor," Turpin finally offered. Decorously, he closed the *Snitch*. "This doesn't sound like Cochran. But if he or his office leaked it, then I sincerely apologize on behalf of all Pisgah County."

"You're going to have to do better than that, boy."

Turpin reached for his handkerchief again. "I'll be happy to help in any way I can, sir, though I have no control over the sheriff's department. We—"

Suddenly, Wilson whipped his cane around, hooking the handle hard around Turpin's neck. "Then just what exactly do you have control over, sonny?"

"I have control over the prosecutor's office," said Turpin as Wilson twisted the cane so hard that his left arm went numb.

"Then stand still Mr. Prosecutor, and I'll tell you what you can do for me. First, get every copy of this garbage off the shelves. Seize it, buy it, steal it, I don't care. I don't want any more fucking Walmart shoppers ogling my little girl."

"Okay," gasped Turpin.

"Second, I want you to make sure that rag never prints another picture of my daughter."

"I'll f-file an injunction this afternoon. I'll claim they're polluting the jury pool, impeding an ongoing investigation." Turpin knew such an injunction would be laughed out of court, but he didn't care. He would do anything to remove this cane from his neck.

"Third, I want you to light a fire under Cochran's ass. I'm a mean old bastard, son. I want to see who did this to my little girl before I die."

"I'm sure Cochran's working as hard as he—"

Wilson wrenched the cane harder, pulling Turpin so close he could see the hairs sprouting from the old man's nostrils.

"You're not hearing me, son. I told you I'm a mean old bastard. You've got an election coming up in November. Right now you're running against Prentiss Herbert, a mealy-mouthed little ambulance chaser who couldn't get elected shit scooper."

Turpin nodded, the cane digging into his neck as Prentiss Herbert's thin, pale face appeared in his mind's eye.

With his free hand, Wilson withdrew a long white envelope from his coat pocket and tossed it on Turpin's desk. "In that envelope are some photos of you that will absolutely assure Herbert's election."

"Photos?" Turpin sputtered. "If you're talking about me and Kristal, it was just a one-time thing. A lapse. You know how women can get."

Wilson threw his head back and laughed. "I'm not talking about women, you moron. Women ain't shit anymore … women are notches on your gun these days." The old man gave an evil grin. "The pictures in there are of boys."

"Boys?" Turpin whispered, gaping into the old man's eyes—cold, dark voids that promised no mercy.

"You and boys." Wilson lowered his voice to a whisper. "You want to stay in this office with those nice big tits answering your telephone, you'll have Cochran find that killer. Otherwise, those photos are going to pop up in places you don't want 'em to."

"But it isn't true," Turpin whimpered. "I've never touched … "

Again, Wilson roared with laughter. "It doesn't have to be true, boy. All it has to be is out there!"

Turpin closed his eyes, sweat trickling down his cheeks.

Wilson twisted the cane again. "Now, do we understand each other?"

"Yes, sir."

"Good." Suddenly, Wilson unhooked the cane from Turpin's neck. "I knew you'd see it my way."

Turpin stepped back, rubbed his aching neck. He was shaking with equal parts of fear and rage. He wanted to kill Wilson, to stuff that fucking cane up his ass. But then he remembered the look in

Wilson's eyes, his sour old-man breath in his face, the smear campaign that he would spread like a plague. Instead of lifting his hand to him, Turpin stood there, red-faced as a schoolboy who'd just endured a paddling.

Like a storm that had spent its fury, Wilson turned and spoke softly to his wife. "Let's go, Pauline. I think we've taken up enough of Mr. Turpin's time."

She rose from her chair, keeping her eyes lowered, as if she didn't want to witness Turpin's humiliation. She took Wilson's arm and they started, blessedly, toward the door. Turpin thought their meeting was over, but the old man stopped and looked over his shoulder.

"I thank you and your wife for your condolences, Mr. Turpin," he murmured, now the soul of politeness. "I pray you and your family never have to go through anything like this."

They turned then and walked out, closing the door behind them. Turpin stood there weak-kneed, wondering if he was going to throw up. With trembling fingers, he opened the envelope Wilson had tossed on his desk. It contained three photos—all of him, with three boys he'd coached in Little League. He was hugging one, patting another's bottom, letting his arm rest across the shoulders of the third. Though each touch had been no more than a coach encouraging a player, he knew how the scenario would play out. First the whispered rumors, a snippet on YouTube. Then an unidentified victim would come forward, speak through an attorney and accuse him of the unthinkable. Though Sybil would stand beside him (he thought), the voters of Pisgah County would not. His career would be over, his life ruined.

"Maybe I'd better go have a little chat with Cochran," he wheezed to the empty space just vacated by Carlisle Wilson, which still seemed to glow darkly with his presence.

When his pulse calmed and his spaghetti legs stiffened, Turpin locked his office and walked all the way down Main Street, to the third floor of the jail, where he glared at a small red light that glowed above an interview room. Cochran was, according to his secretary, in that room, observing Buck Whaley interrogating a suspect in the Lisa Wilson case. *Thank God*, thought Turpin. *If they make an arrest, I'm going to shove those photos back up Wilson's ass.*

Brusquely, he knocked on the door and let himself into the room. Jerry Cochran looked up, surprised.

"Hey, George." Cochran nodded. "What brings you down here?"

Turpin rubbed the back of his neck. "I just got a visit from Carlisle Wilson."

"Quite a character, isn't he?"

Fuming with rage, Turpin tossed Cochran his copy of the *Snitch*. "You know anything about this?"

"No." Cochran shrugged. "I heard one of their reporters was in town."

"Check out the centerfold."

Cochran turned to the middle of the paper. As he looked at the picture of Lisa Wilson's body, his face grew pale. "What the fuck? Where did they get this?"

"That's what I was going to ask you. Governor Wilson brought it to my attention. He was outraged, to put it mildly."

"I keep those photos locked in a drawer, locked in my office." Cochran scanned the article quickly. "I bet that little NSA bastard at Duke leaked this."

"The who?"

"Nobody," Cochran said quickly. He closed the tabloid. "I'm going to find out who did this. If it was somebody on my staff, they're going to be looking at a lawsuit. Also a new job."

"We're both going to be looking for a new job if you don't arrest somebody for that girl's murder," said Turpin.

Cochran frowned. "Does being guilty of the crime matter? Or will just anybody do?"

"Of course he wants whoever's guilty of the crime." Turpin felt like a fool, lecturing Cochran like this. "I'm just telling you this guy's powerful and pissed, and he's not going away."

"Then I guess we'll just have to hunker down," said Cochran. "I'm not going to arrest somebody just because Carlisle Wilson's an asshole."

Turpin gulped back another wave of nausea as those Little League pictures flashed across his mind. He knew Cochran would react like this—any decent sheriff would. Yet he also knew what Carlisle Wilson would do with those photos. Panicky, he walked over to check out the two-way mirror that revealed the interview room. A tall man with longish blonde hair sat across the table from Buck Whaley. He wore a blue work shirt, buttoned at the wrists and a look of contempt on his face. "Who've you got in there now?"

"Nick Stratton."

"Who's he?"

"Head of the Pisgah Raptor Rescue Center. Lisa Wilson's boss."

Turpin's eyes brightened. "Got anything on him?"

Cochran shrugged. "We executed a search warrant early this morning and found some interesting items."

"What?"

"The girl's diary," replied Cochran. "Plus a lot of iPhone photos and a ring she took off for safekeeping."

"Oh, God," cried Turpin. "Please tell me you found it around his dick."

"No, under his bed."

"Hmm." Turpin turned back to the interrogation. This Stratton character would be handsome except for a scar on his upper lip. "What did the diary say?"

"I'm still going through it, but Lisa Wilson wrote some pretty hot pages about him."

Turpin frowned. Diaries were tough in court. Either side could paint them as accurate accounts of someone's life, or mere fantasies the diarist dreamed up. "Have you got anything else on this guy?"

"Some. But it's circumstantial. You'd have trouble with it in court."

"How do you know?" cried Turpin

"Because I know good evidence, George. And I know I don't have it yet."

"Why not?"

"That writing still bothers me."

"The writing in the diary?"

"No, George—all that stuff carved on the girl's body. It has to mean something."

Turpin grabbed the tabloid, gaped again at the centerfold. "You mean these are letters carved into her skin?"

"They're something. I've run them through every computer from Raleigh to Washington and come up with nothing."

"Then maybe they're nothing. A smokescreen." Turpin looked at Stratton through the mirror. "To make it look like some mountain psycho's loose."

They both stepped closer to the window. Cochran turned up the audio. Buck Whaley was oozing compassion, going on about how he could sure understand how a man might want out of an affair so badly that he'd kill for his freedom.

"Except we weren't *having* an affair," said Stratton. "I already had my freedom."

Whaley shrugged, as if he couldn't care less. "That's not what her diary says, buddy. Plus she had two hundred pictures of you on her iPhone."

Stratton shook his head. "I don't care if she had two thousand pictures. We weren't lovers."

Whaley needled him. "All your interns think you were."

Stratton laughed. "All my interns thought that cabin was full of ghosts."

"Then can you tell me why she wrote her father and told him she'd be staying with you after the semester ended?"

"I don't know."

"And why we found the ring she'd stored in her room underneath your bed?"

"I don't know."

Whaley leaned forward. "For a smart guy you don't know all that much, do you?"

For a long moment, Stratton just stared at him, then he withdrew something from his shirt pocket. "I know one thing," he said softly.

"What's that?" demanded Whaley.

"That I'm entitled to call a lawyer."

Whaley smiled. "Are you saying you need one?"

"I'm saying I'd like to call this one." Stratton held up the business card. "Mary Crow."

Behind the two-way mirror, Turpin's stomach curdled. He glared at Cochran. "The bastard's already got Mary Crow? That alone should tell you something, sheriff!"

"Getting good counsel doesn't make him guilty, George."

"Well, it makes him a hell of a suspect." Turpin turned away from the mirror, furious. "I want every piece of evidence you've got against this guy on my desk in an hour."

Cochran gave a bitter laugh. "Going to make the evidence fit the crime?"

"No. But I'm not going to let a bunch of carved-up squiggles scare me away from filing an indictment."

EIGHTEEN

MARY CROW HAD NOT lingered to watch Lily and Jonathan as they drove away; instead she'd stormed back inside the house and started to clean the kitchen.

"Why did you have to buy that damn duplex?" she asked the absent Jonathan, as she cleaned the grate in the woodstove they kept burning all winter. "Were you that scared of Fred Moon?"

She decided that yes, he was. When it came to Lily, Jonathan scared pretty easy. She scrubbed her way through the kitchen and hall, working her way upstairs, to their bedroom. In his packing, Jonathan had left the laundry basket overturned on the floor; all the dresser drawers empty and agape. The room reminded her of crime scenes she'd visited in Atlanta, where some family's day had started off like every other day until somebody went crazy and begun shooting up the people they loved.

"Just like Jonathan," she muttered as she slammed the dresser drawers shut. "Only he shoots lies instead of bullets."

She picked up his cast-off clothes from the floor and began to straighten the sheets he'd twisted into a knot. For an instant her anger abated, and she longed to curl up on his side of the bed, wrap herself in his smell. Then she remembered his coldness, Lily's ugly accusations about her killing Ruth Moon.

"Just get the sheets off the bed," she said. "Everything in this room needs a good washing."

She stripped the bed and went downstairs to run another load of laundry. As she walked through the dining room, she wondered if she ought to start the painting project she and Jonathan had discussed for months. One person could do it—they had a ladder long enough to reach the ceiling. But it would entail a trip to the hardware store, the purchase of brushes, the selection of paint. For some reason, the thought of that brought tears to her eyes. Looking at paint chips all by herself seemed like the loneliest task in the world.

"Eat some lunch first," she told herself. "You can decide about painting later."

She made a grilled cheese sandwich and took it into the study, eating at her desk. "My old refuge," she said, looking at a photo of her younger self, graduating from Emory Law. How proud she looked in her blue and gold gown! How ready to put every murderer on death row!

"And look at you now," she whispered. "Can't even pick out paint."

A wave of despair engulfed her. How could she and Jonathan have gotten to this place? She had done everything he'd ever asked. She'd brought them to her home, treated Lily as her own child, abandoned the one area of law she truly loved. And for what? A man who couldn't even tell her he was being sued and a whippy little brat who accused her of murder? Did Lily honestly believe that? And even if she didn't—even if she'd simply spoken in anger, how could they ever un-ring that awful bell? She sat there, growing sick to her stomach, when suddenly, her cell phone rang.

Jonathan! He was calling to apologize, to explain. She rummaged through the flotsam on top of her desk, finally finding her phone under the Moon's complaint. She grabbed it, cutting it off in mid-ring.

"Jonathan?"

"Mary?" A voice she did not recognize came sketchily through the mountain static.

"This is Mary Crow," she answered, her heart crumbling. Jonathan had not called to apologize. Jonathan had not called at all.

"This is Nick Stratton, from the Raptor Rescue Center?"

She closed her eyes. Nick Stratton, the man with Lily's owl; the man whose intern had been murdered. She didn't know whether to express her sympathy or just inquire about the bird. "Hi, Nick." She decided to go with a neutral response. "How's it going?"

"Well, your owl's doing better," he said awkwardly, as if trying to find the right words. "But the owl doctor's not so great."

"Oh?" Mary replied, puzzled.

"Uh, I'm here at the police station," Stratton's voice grew raspy. "They think I killed Lisa Wilson."

She wondered if they'd gotten a bad connection. "Excuse me?"

He cleared his throat. "The police think I killed Lisa Wilson."

Mary frowned. "But doesn't Cochran have your interns locked up?"

"He let them go," Stratton said disjointedly. "Then he came and got me."

Mary sat up straighter. "Have you been arrested, Nick?"

"I'm not sure. Mostly, they've just asked me a lot of questions."

She heard the edginess in his voice. Having cops fire questions at you scared most people—that's what it was meant to do. What most people didn't know was that it was largely smoke and mirrors. Still, without counsel, Stratton might incriminate himself badly. He went on.

"I think I need a lawyer, Mary. Could you help me out?"

His voice brought back a raft of old memories. Investigations, jury summations, the heady electricity when a jury foreman rose and gave you a conviction. If she took this case she'd be working the other side of the aisle, but at least she'd be practicing the kind of law she loved. *But what about your promise to Jonathan,* she wondered, gazing at the family photos lined across her desk. *Maybe the Moons happened to that promise*, she told herself. *The Moons and that duplex and the secret life he's been living in Oklahoma.*

"Mary? Did I lose you?"

"No, Nick." She took a deep breath. "Tell the police you've retained counsel. Don't answer another question until I get there."

"Thanks," he said. "I really appreciate it."

So do I, Mary thought as she hurried upstairs to change clothes. *A client in jail just beats the hell out of choosing new paint.*

———

An hour later she stood outside the interview room, briefcase in hand. Buck Whaley was sitting inside, sneering at Nick Stratton, who was sneering right back. Briskly, she opened the door. Whaley jumped, surprised.

"Detective Whaley," she greeted the beefy cop. "I'm representing Mr. Stratton." She dropped her briefcase on the table. "You want to tell me what this is about?"

Whaley gave a smug grin. "We're about to charge him with murder."

"Murder?" She gave Whaley a practiced look, implying he was crazy. "Who did he kill?"

"Lisa Wilson." Whaley folded his arms across his chest.

"I did not kill Lisa Wilson!" cried Stratton.

Mary put a hand on Stratton's arm. "I assume you have evidence, Detective?"

"We do."

"Well, then could you share it?" Mary feigned impatience, trying to take some of the wind out of Whaley's enormous sails. "I cancelled a tennis match to come down here."

"I can put Lisa Wilson's murder weapon in his bird barn, Lisa Wilson's ring under his bed, plus photos that indicate he had a pretty close relationship with Ms. Wilson." Whaley looked at Mary with a wide, triumphant grin. "What is it you tennis people say? Game, set, match?"

"We tennis people say you cannot be serious," Mary replied, though she realized that if Whaley was just blowing smoke, he seemed awfully cocky about it. "I think we're done with questions today."

"That's fine." Whaley gave an insouciant shrug. "We can talk again tomorrow."

Stratton leaned forward. "Look, I've got animals to take care of. Federally protected birds."

Whaley rose from his chair. "Guess you should have cleaned those cages before we got down here."

———

A few minutes later, Mary Crow sat across from Nick Stratton in a private meeting room. "I want to make this perfectly clear," he began. "I did not kill Lisa Wilson."

Mary smiled. She'd heard similar assurances from other clients. Marvin Sutton never drank when he drove, Tanya Foster had never taken matches and kerosene to her cheating boyfriend's apartment. Mary never paid much attention to her clients' protestations of innocence.

"That's great, but I don't care," she told him.

"But I didn't kill her," Stratton repeated, his eyes flashing with impatience.

"It's not necessary that I believe you, Nick," said Mary.

"It's necessary to me that you believe me," he replied.

"Alright." She held up her right hand. "I swear I believe you."

He sank back in his chair, as if extracting her vow of belief had used up all his energy. She took a legal pad from her briefcase. "Let's go over what they've asked you about."

For the next hour he told her about the blood-stained jesses—the leather bird leashes—they'd found in the barn, the fiddle music he loved to play, the ring that never left Lisa Wilson's finger. "I have no idea how it got under my bed. I was drinking coffee in the kitchen when Cochran came downstairs with it."

Mary started her third page of notes. "And that's why they think you and Lisa were lovers?"

"That, and the fact that she'd taken all these pictures of me. I didn't know anything about them until I took Cochran down to her room."

Mary frowned. "You took Cochran to her room?"

"Yeah. After he told me she'd been killed. We found all these pictures of me plastered all over her wall." He swallowed hard. "I guess that's why the others figured we were lovers, but we weren't."

"The other kids?" Mary shook her head. "Let's back up and begin at the beginning. Tell me when you first met Lisa."

He ran a hand through his hair. "She came a week late, after the other interns had gotten here. She was an eager, helpful girl, but there was something sad about her."

"Sad?" asked Mary.

"I think her home life was difficult. She once said her father was an alpha male who'd married a bleating sheep. I think Lisa was trying to find her place in the family zoo."

Mary caught her breath, wondering if some Oklahoma lawyer would soon describe her own family in similar terms.

Stratton went on. "For whatever reason, she latched on to me pretty quick. Followed me around like a puppy, always snapping pictures with her iPhone."

"And that's why everybody thought you were lovers?"

A twinge of discomfort flashed across his face. "I don't know how much the others knew, but one night Lisa came on to me."

"Oh?"

"I came home from playing a dance. I'd had a little too much to drink, so I went to bed. Woke up an hour later, to find her standing there, in the middle of my room. I asked her what was wrong, but all she did was pull off her T-shirt and step out of her shorts."

Mary wondered what it would be like to strip naked in front of a man like Nick Stratton. "And?" she finally asked, trying to keep her voice level.

"She climbed on top of me. We started kissing. I have to tell you, I was..."

Mary watched him, waiting to hear how he would finish his sentence.

"I was tempted," he finally admitted, squirming in his chair. "She was young, pretty. She wanted me."

"And you slapped her hands and sent her back to her room?"

"Yes," he told her, his blue-green gaze meeting hers directly. "That's exactly what happened. Sleeping with Lisa Wilson could have ruined everything I'd ever worked for."

Inwardly Mary groaned, wondering if she had run into another man like Jonathan, who turned hot, willing women out of their beds just because they were worried about something else. She tapped the table with her pen. "You do realize how ridiculous this is going to sound if the DA gets hold of it?"

"I can't help it," Stratton replied angrily. "It's what happened."

It sounded so incredible that Mary decided either he was telling the truth or he was the best liar on the planet. Regardless, she couldn't help but like Nick Stratton. He didn't have the nervous look of her other clients, as they weaved and dodged their way through a story. Dr. Lovebird just sat there and said what he had to say.

"Any more questions?" he asked.

"Oh, my, yes," she replied. "Thousands more. The police will probably question you again tomorrow, but I'll be with you."

"So you'll take my case?"

She put her legal pad back in her briefcase and snapped it shut. "For now," she said, smiling, finding something attractive in his scarred lip, something even more attractive in the prospect of returning to her office to think about something other than Jonathan and Lily. "For now, I'd be delighted."

NINETEEN

Seventy miles west of Nashville, Tennessee, Jonathan had already grown sick of the trip. All the way through the mountains he'd tried to come up with an answer for the accusation Lily had hurled at Mary, but he couldn't think of any good way to explain Ruth Moon's death. As they sped into a relentless Southern sun, he silently tried out several approaches. Finally, as they crossed the long span of the Tennessee River, he decided to just tell her, flat-out.

"There's something you need to know, Lily," he said, his voice sounding more severe than he'd intended.

"What?" She looked up from her Kindle, both sullen and defensive. She had not said more than ten words since they'd left Carolina.

"Mary did not kill your mother."

She returned her gaze to the e-reader. "That's not what Grandpa Moon says."

"Fred Moon is wrong," he said, refusing to give the bastard any familial title. "Fred Moon is a liar."

"But he showed me," Lily insisted. "In the newspaper."

He longed to pull off the road and talk to her face-to-face, but he was still on the bridge, trying to pass a semi that was doing at least eighty.

"What paper?" he asked. Ruth had died in Atlanta—of interest to no one locally. He couldn't imagine that the *Webbers Falls Gazette* had reporters across the country.

"I don't know," said Lily. "He keeps it in his wallet. It says Mary got mad at my mother, and shot her with a gun."

"That's not true," Jonathan said. "Mary wasn't mad at anybody. Your mother was sick, not in her right mind."

"That's what Grandpa said you'd say."

"But I'm telling the truth!" Jonathan gripped the steering wheel hard, wishing it were Fred Moon's throat. "Why would I lie about something like that?"

"Grandpa says because you always loved Mary best."

"That's not true, Lily." Actually, that was the one thing Fred Moon had gotten right. Never had Ruth taken Mary's place in his heart. He'd met Ruth after he and Mary had parted, each deciding that they were just too different to live together. He'd never intended to do more than shoot a game of pool with Ruth in Big Meat's bar. But she was sweet and had a nice smile. The next thing he knew she'd moved in with him; the next thing after that she was pregnant with his child. Though she assured him marriage was unnecessary, he drove her to the courthouse just the same. Mary was gone, both his parents dead. He wanted to pin his name on something before he died.

"What's not true?" Lily brought him back to the present moment.

"That I didn't love your mother. I loved her a lot. She'd been through a terrible time," he said. "She hadn't slept for days. She was scared you were dead." He searched for a way to explain insanity to a nine-year-old. *Crazy* didn't say anything, *schizophrenia* said far too

167

much. How about *confused*? Yes! *Confused* would work. "Sometimes when a lot of bad things happen, people get confused. Do weird things they wouldn't normally dream of doing."

"But why did she get confused?" She looked at him, her eyes huge. "Why would she try to shoot Mary?"

He sighed. How many times, over the years had he'd asked himself that question? He'd never come up with a satisfying answer. "I don't know why, Lily. Nobody knows why. All I can tell you is that she loved you. You were the most important thing in the world to her."

"Grandpa Moon says she wasn't confused at all. He says Mary was jealous and killed her. He said Mary might kill me someday, too."

Jonathan took a deep breath, willing himself to remain calm. "Lily, Mary didn't kill anybody. Mary isn't *going* to kill anybody. I wouldn't live with Mary if I thought she might harm you."

Lily sat back in her seat. Though she gazed out at the flat green acres of west Tennessee, he knew this discussion was not over. She was, in that respect, like him. She would think, then choose her words carefully, like the best-fletched arrow in a quiver. Twenty minutes later, she spoke again.

"Do you think I might get confused some day?"

Her voice was so thready that it scared him. For an instant, he wanted to weep. Lily now feared Mary far less than she feared her mother's madness.

"Absolutely not." He reached over and gently rubbed the back of her neck. "You will never get confused like that."

"How do you know?" Again, she turned huge eyes upon him.

"I just do. I promise that will never happen to you."

Though he knew that wasn't nearly enough, it seemed to satisfy her, seemed to quell, for now, whatever monsters Fred Moon had put inside the child's head. She gazed out the window for a few more miles, then she switched off her Kindle and went to sleep, looking so much like Ruth Moon that he suddenly felt as if he were driving three people to Oklahoma—Lily, himself, and the ghost of a woman he'd once loved.

Drained, he sped on toward Memphis. He couldn't have imagined a month with Fred Moon would damage Lily so. "I guess I've got some explaining to do, Lily," he whispered, looking over at her while she slept. Maybe they would stop for the night in Memphis. At a motel with a pool. They could swim, then talk, and he would tell her, for the first time, everything that had transpired that night. Though he did not have Mary's ease with words, he thought he could make Lily understand most of it. He was considering how to broach the subject when his cell phone rang. He dug down in the pocket of his jeans and flipped the thing open.

"Hello?" he answered as quietly as he could.

"Jonathan? This is Alex Carter." Unlike the sketchy reception in the mountains, Alex's voice came over so loud that he had to move the phone away from his ear.

"Hey, Alex."

"Where are you?" As always, Mary's best friend was direct.

"Just east of Memphis."

"Good. I wanted to let you know that I've scheduled a mediation with the Moons. Friday, in Tahlequah."

"Back alley or a courtroom?" Nothing would please him more than smashing Fred Moon's face into a brick wall.

"Actually, neither." She laughed. "Just a lawyer's office."

"Too bad," he replied. "I could have mediated like hell in a back alley."

"I know, but we'll have to do it this way. If we can come to terms in mediation, then we might not have to go to court at all."

"What do you mean, terms?" he asked, immediately suspicious. He wasn't going to give Fred Moon fucking ten minutes with his child.

"Some sort of visitation agreement. I've found some skeletons in their closet that I fully intend to rattle. They may not be so keen on going to court after that."

"So this might be over sooner?"

"Possibly," she told him. "If this is just a nuisance suit, they'll probably fold. If they're serious, they'll bring their big issues to trial."

He glanced over to make sure Lily was still asleep. "And their big issue would be Mary?"

"According to their complaint."

"That part doesn't look so good, does it?" There was no need to ask, he could hear it in her voice.

"Well, they're trying to load our girl up with some baggage."

"It's bullshit, Alex," he said, replaying the same argument he'd just made with Lily. "Mary didn't do anything that you or I wouldn't have done."

"I know. They're just putting the worst possible spin on it. But don't worry. We Texas gals can twirl a lasso pretty good, too."

He looked out the window, the sun searing his eyes. "You know, I'm thinking maybe I should just turn south and head to Mexico."

"No, Jonathan. Come to Oklahoma."

"But I can't let—"

She interrupted him. "You're starting to break up. I'll call you back in a few minutes."

He clicked off his phone angry all over again, hating Fred Moon and his wife, hating the day, hating himself for acting like such an asshole.

Suddenly, Lily sat up, blinking in the bright afternoon light. "Where are we?" she asked, her voice hoarse with sleep.

"Just past Jackson, Tennessee."

"I need to pee."

"I'll pull off at the next exit."

A few miles later they stopped at a rest area. Jonathan waited in the lobby while Lily went to use the bathroom. Though his first impulse was to call Mary, the idea made him uncomfortable. Lily had confided her deepest concerns about Mary—for him to call her now, behind Lily's back, felt like a betrayal. *Anyway,* he told himself, *what could I say? Trip's going fine, gas is a lot cheaper in Tennessee and, oh, by the way—Lily hates your guts?*

TWENTY

That night Cochran stormed out of the Justice Center by the back door. After ordering Tuffy Clark to find out who leaked the photos of Lisa Wilson, he then spent the rest of the evening going over evidence with Turpin. The two men had parted late and parted angry—Turpin insisting they had enough circumstantial evidence for an indictment, Cochran adamant that they hadn't yet looked under all the rocks. When Turpin finally retreated to the courthouse, Cochran headed out to the police parking lot where Angel, the department's unmarked Camaro, sat in one corner. They'd seized the sleek '98 black ragtop during a drug bust and turned her into their speed trap car. Though Cochran usually drove the standard Crown Vic, tonight he decided to indulge in one of the few perks of his job. He needed fresh air, speed, escape—everything that the Camaro both promised and delivered.

"Angel, I would have sold my soul for you when I was sixteen," Cochran told the car as he fired up the five hundred horses under her hood. "Everybody would have. Hell, everybody still would."

He lowered Angel's top, then headed up the hill, toward the courthouse. As he made a left on Keener Avenue, he noticed bright lights burning on the sixth floor. *Turpin's office*, he thought bitterly. *No doubt up there readying the charges against Stratton.* Usually, it went the opposite way, with him convincing the overly cautious Turpin that they had slam-dunk evidence against a suspect. Why Turpin's balls had turned brass now, he couldn't say, though he suspected Carlisle Wilson had something to do with it.

"Don't do it, George," he warned, punching Angel's accelerator. "Indict Stratton now and Mary Crow will eat you alive."

With a weary sigh, he put Turpin out of his mind and zoomed up to seventy. As Angel cruised effortlessly around the curves of Keener Avenue, a cool nighttime breeze caressed his face, carrying the croaking of tree frogs, the smell of fresh cut grass. Summer came back to him in a rush, and he thought of Ginger, and how they'd canoed down sleepy Walnut Creek, stopping for a picnic behind the fronds of a willow tree. That seemed a lifetime ago, yet it had been only last week. They'd talked little since then, and though he saw her at his daily news briefings, the ring he'd planned to put on her finger still lay in the top drawer of his dresser. As he skidded to a stop at the intersection of Keener and Golf Club Lane, he made a deal with himself. If he drove by and found Ginger's lights still on, he would stop. If they weren't, he would fly Angel down River Road and talk with her tomorrow. He turned down Golf Club Lane. Slowing to make the curve around the twelfth green, he peered into the darkness. Suddenly, he saw her cottage peeking from a rambling hedge of wild roses. To his great joy, lights glowed from her den window. Tires squealing, he pulled Angel in the driveway. As he got out of the car, he wished he'd brought that engagement ring; wished he had the nerve to ask her to marry him right now.

He walked to the back door and tapped softly. He heard footsteps, the click of a lock. The door opened and there she stood in her work-at-home outfit, one of his white oxford cloth shirts topping a pair of cut-off jeans, her flame-colored hair pinned up on her head.

She smiled. "Well, hey, sheriff."

"Hi," he said, his knees growing unreliable. The sight of her, the sound of her always sent a tremor through him.

Teasingly, she leaned against the doorjamb. "Is this a raid?"

"No. Just stopped by to say hello."

"Aw." She laughed. "I was hoping I might get frisked."

He took her in his arms. She smelled of apples and sunlight, linen sheets dried on a clothesline. He kissed her, reached to unclasp the barrette that held her hair. She wrapped long legs around his waist as he carried her inside. He kicked the door shut as she peeled off her shirt. He kissed her neck, her breasts. She wiggled free, unbuckled his belt, pulled his trousers down past his hips. He gasped as her fingers squeezed the tight muscles of his butt, then she began to unbutton his shirt. As his clothes fell away her lips made a warm, leisurely path down his chest. She pulled him to the floor, on top of a collection of newspapers. With their mouths and tongues seeking each other hungrily, they made love until both George Turpin and Carlisle Wilson faded away, ghosts consigned to another part of his life. Time stopped as they stayed on the floor, crumpling the newspapers beneath them, lying in sweet exhaustion until Ginger finally got up and padded into the kitchen.

"What's wrong?" she asked, returning to put an icy bottle of Yuengling on his bare belly.

"Yow!" He jumped from the sudden coldness. "What do you mean?"

"Earlier, when you first knocked on the door. You looked like you could chew nails. I'm not a reporter for nothing."

He scooted over to lean against her couch, wondering if the Fiddlesticks case had finally begun to ooze out his pores. "Just tired," he said. "I've spent the last eight hours arguing with Turpin about the Fiddlesticks case."

"Now there's a name I haven't heard lately," she said. "Where's our noble DA been these last few days?"

Cochran laughed. "Mostly hiding from Carlisle Wilson. Until today, anyway."

"What happened today?"

"Wilson paid him a visit at the courthouse. Turned Turpin into a true believer."

She looked at him, sensing a story. "Oh, yeah?"

"The DA's on the case now, big time."

"I'll ask for an interview tomorrow," she nestled against him. "See what I can find out."

He sat there on the floor, holding her. Crickets chirped, loud outside her window. In the distance he heard the quaver of a screech owl. He sipped his beer, loving the feel of her warmth. He was gazing at nothing—her darkened TV screen, the now cold fireplace—when he caught sight of her desk. The small green-shaded lamp illuminated several note pads, plus the centerfold of the *Snitch*, which dangled from the edge of the desk.

"What have you been working on?" he asked, his good mood turning sour.

"Oh, you know. My old crackpot theory that Lisa Wilson hasn't been the only girl killed up there."

He recalled her feature in last week's paper theorizing that other young women might have been killed after visiting the Fiddlesticks

175

cabin. Ginger had done her research, but the article only fanned the flames of controversy around that stupid cabin. "And did the *Snitch* photo prove your theory?"

"Jessica Rusk's piece?" She laughed. "Not hardly. I told you—Jessica's the queen of myth and misinformation. It did cause a pretty big stir at the grocery store, though."

He looked at her, all business. "Do you know where this Jessica got that photo?"

"No. I'm sure it's something she had Photoshopped. Everybody at the *Snitch* is bogus."

He frowned. "Ginger, that picture isn't a fake. That's real."

"What?" She sat up straight, her eyes wide. "Are you serious? What happened to that girl?"

"We don't know."

"Don't you dare leave me like that, Jerry. You must know something."

"Off the record?" Even with her, he was still cautious.

"Yes, Sheriff Cochran," she said, irked. "Off the damn record."

"Those marks are all cuts, made by a less than three-inch, non-serrated curved blade. Who did it and what those figures mean, we haven't a clue."

She reached over and grabbed the paper, squinting at the horrific image. "This is *writing* on this girl's body?"

"It's a repeating pattern of figures," said Cochran. "Though not one computer in all of law enforcement can read it."

"Wow." She sat back on her heels. "I thought Jessica had faked this. I wonder if those other girls were mutilated."

He recalled the old section-length feature on Fiddlesticks that was fast becoming her obsession. "They're probably just runaways, Ginger. Considering the number of kids who've gone up to that cabin over the years, three vanishing is not even a blip, statistically speaking."

"I'm sure their parents would love to hear you say that."

Cochran closed his eyes, his bones suddenly feeling heavy as lead. "Just let me clear this case first, then I'll get on those three cold ones. Wilson's already promised to roast my balls if I don't find out who killed his daughter."

"Are you kidding?"

"Not at all." He pulled her close. "We'd better make love quick, while I've still got the family jewels."

He took her in his arms, needing to feel her warmth. As they embraced, his gaze fell again on the *Snitch* centerfold. Though Lisa Wilson's face and breasts and crotch had been blurred out, the image was still horrific—a young girl who'd been carved up alive. He turned and kissed Ginger's neck, from her ear lobe down to the delicate knob of her collarbone. What if that had been her? What if someone had done that to this body, this flesh? In that instant, he forgave Carlisle Wilson everything—his cane, his bullying, his threats. You don't get over somebody doing that to someone you love. As he held her close, he grew even more convinced that Turpin was wrong. Carving that girl up hadn't been a smokescreen. Carving that girl up was the reason Lisa Wilson had been killed in the first place.

TWENTY-ONE

THE INSISTENT RING OF a telephone split the gauzy silence of the bedroom. Mary burrowed deeper under the covers, instinctively waiting for Jonathan to answer it—early callers were usually hunters or fishermen wanting to hire him as a day guide. But then she remembered that Jonathan was en route to Oklahoma; answering early calls was now her responsibility. Yawning, she sat up and stretched across the bed, reaching for the phone. A crisp British voice came over the line.

"Ms. Crow? Annette Henry here, from the criminal court clerk's office."

"Yes?" Mary croaked. Annette Henry usually called her at work, left messages on her answering machine. Mary felt like her accent always added a patina of respectability to her legal pleadings, as if Annette were summoning her to the Old Bailey instead of the Pisgah County Courthouse.

"Sorry to call so early, but I need to inform you that your client Nicholas Stratton is scheduled to be arraigned in Judge Barbee's court, at three this afternoon."

"Turpin's indicting?" Mary wondered if she was dreaming. "Are you sure? Yesterday the police were just holding him for questioning."

"I just received the papers." Annette rattled some pages. "Mr. Stratton is being charged with capital murder, in the death of Lisa Carlisle Wilson."

"When did you say? Whose court?" Mary fumbled for a pen on the bedside table. Annette's English precision always made her feel slightly disorganized.

"Judge Barbee's court, at three this afternoon."

"Okay." Mary scribbled the information on the back of one of Jonathan's crossword puzzle books. "Thanks, Annette."

She hung up the phone, blinking in disbelief. Though Pisgah County did not have the legal backlogs of larger jurisdictions, the wheels of justice rarely turned this swiftly. Had Cochran found some smoking gun of evidence? Had Stratton signed a confession? She doubted that—he was too smart and she'd warned him not to say or do anything without her. She stared at the phone a moment, then she realized—this was theatre. With Carlisle Wilson offering a million-dollar reward and that grotesque photo in the *Snitch* upping the ante, Turpin had to do something. Indicting Stratton would get the governor off his back plus it was good political strategy. And Turpin was up for re-election this November.

"He'll indict now, ask for remand, then go to trial after election day," she said aloud. "If he wins, great. If he loses, he'll blame it on sloppy police work. Either way he stays in office another four years." It was self-serving and unfair, but Turpin was a politician.

She'd disliked him since the day they met and nothing had warmed her feelings toward him since.

Still, even if the evidence was circumstantial, they must have found something. *Better hurry downtown*, Mary thought as she threw off her covers, *and find out what's going on.*

An hour later, she pulled up in the Justice Center parking lot. A deputy escorted her to the same interview room they'd used yesterday. She was opening her briefcase when they brought Stratton in. He looked tired and grizzly-cheeked, a surfer far from the sea.

"So what happened after I left yesterday?" Mary skipped the pleasantries of good morning and how are you feeling today.

"Nothing," said Stratton. "I walked five thousand laps around my cell. A lady named Charlotte brought me a hamburger for supper, and a drunk named Arliss sang Johnny Cash tunes all night."

"They didn't question you anymore?"

"No."

"You didn't sign anything, did you?"

"Of course not." He paced in front of the table, his steps quick, his shoulders hunched forward.

"Well, I hate to tell you, but the DA's going to arraign you this afternoon. They're charging you with Lisa Wilson's murder."

"What?" His eyes blazed with gray fire. "But that can't happen! I didn't kill that damn girl!"

"I know," said Mary. "But it looks like we may have to prove that in court. This is just the first step."

"To what?" Stratton looked wildly around the room. "A lethal injection?"

"No—this is just the first step in due process. We'll go over to the courthouse at three, the DA will charge you, and the judge will ask how you plead. I will say not guilty. Then the judge will set a date for a preliminary hearing. The DA will probably ask that you be remanded to custody."

"You mean stay in jail?"

She nodded. "But I'll argue for bail. I'll show what an upstanding citizen you are and how undeserving of incarceration." She uncapped a fountain pen. "But first, I need some more information— the court will want to know about your ties to the area."

He gave a great sigh—then started recounting his life. "I'm from Seattle. I've lived in North Carolina twenty years. Did my undergraduate work at Stanford, got my doctorate at Washington. I've run the raptor center since 1999. Never been arrested, never been in jail. Got a speeding ticket back in '97, in Idaho. My parents are dead. I have an ex-wife who lives in Portland, Oregon."

"Any children?" asked Mary, thinking of Jonathan and Lily.

"No."

"If there's anything I need to know, tell me now. Attorneys hate surprises."

"Anything like what?"

"Anything like charges that have been dismissed, drug busts you copped a plea to. Anything less than upstanding."

He thought a moment, then said, "I was stopped once for collecting road kill, in Tennessee."

Mary blinked. "Road kill?"

"For the birds," he explained. "Squirrels and opossums, mostly. Raptors love fresh meat."

"Okay," she said, making a note. "I don't think that will make you a flight risk. I'll be honest with you—yesterday a tabloid came out with a picture of Lisa Wilson's body. It's got everybody pretty riled up. I think that's why Turpin's moving so fast on this."

He frowned. "I'm not sure what you mean."

"It's an election year. George Turpin would much rather run as the man who put Lisa Wilson's killer behind bars than the man who let a homicidal maniac go free."

Stratton leaned forward. "Look," he said, his tone urgent. "I'm not a homicidal maniac. I can't stay in jail. I have work to do. Birds to take care of."

She'd heard this desperation before, in other clients. "I'll do the best I can for you. First, though, we need to get you cleaned up. Do you have a suit? A coat and tie?"

He nodded. "At home."

"Could somebody bring it down here?"

"One of my interns could."

She shook her head. "All your interns have gone home."

He flinched, as if someone had hit him. "Are Artie and Jenkins still there?"

"Who?"

"My two handymen. Call the Dr. Lovebird number. One of them should answer."

"And if they don't?"

He reached for Mary's pen and legal pad. "If they don't, forget about my suit and call this number."

"Who is that?" asked Mary, watching as Stratton scrawled an out-of-state area code.

"Doris Mager. The best raptor woman in the country. If you can't get me out of here, she'll have to come and get my birds."

———

Five hours later they pulled up in a police car at the back entrance of the courthouse. Much to Mary's relief, a funny little man named Artie Slade had answered the raptor center phone and agreed to bring Stratton his clothes. Now Stratton sat beside her freshly washed and shaven, looking elegant in a dark blue suit and gold tie. Mary smiled, knowing that Lady Justice was theoretically blind, but she still liked good-looking defendants.

"You want us to spread these photographers out a little, Ms. Crow?" asked Buddy Pease, an old cop for whom she'd just written a will.

"If you could, Buddy," she replied. She'd hoped to avoid the press, but reporters and photographers clustered thick around the door. Coupled with the throng of outraged citizens who stood in front of the building, the scene gave Mary an ominous feeling—all of Hartsville seemed bent on providing Carlisle Wilson with a suspect in his daughter's murder, purely as a matter of civic pride. "I'd like to get into the building with as little drama as possible."

"Why are all these people here?" Stratton peered out the window as cameras started flashing.

Mary said, "You're big news."

"I'm not walking in there hiding my face like some criminal," he warned.

"I don't want you to," said Mary. "You walk in there with shoulders square, head high. Remember, you're an innocent man."

Buddy Pease got out of the cruiser and starting pushing the press back, clearing a path for them. Mary got out next, then Stratton. As the photographers began jostling each other for the best shots, Stratton adjusted his tie and walked beside her, unflinching through all the commotion. They entered the building through the back door, then rode up to the sixth floor on a service elevator.

"Is it always like this?" Stratton asked.

"The process is always the same," said Mary. "There's seldom this much hoopla."

Finally, they reached the waiting room for Barbee's court. For a few moments they stood there, awkward, like two actors awaiting their cue. Then Virgil Starnes, the bailiff, cracked opened the court-room door.

"You're up, Ms. Crow."

"Thanks, Virgil." Smiling as the older man held the door, she whispered to Nick. "Okay—I know you're mad as hell, but you can't show it. Just stand up and answer whatever question the judge might ask. Say 'Yes Sir' and 'Your Honor.' Barbee's an ex-Marine who likes his law and his whiskey straight and without embellishments."

They entered the courtroom from a side door. Spectators filled the gallery, greeting them with a rumble of whispered comments as they entered. *Damn*, Mary thought, *everybody in the county must be here.* She strode over and took her place at the defense table, Stratton following. *Thank God he presents himself like an innocent man*, she thought as she laid her briefcase down on the table. She hated clients who skulked in like mangy dogs, guilt crawling over them like fleas.

She knew Judge Barbee appreciated crisp procedure, so she stepped up to the podium. Across the aisle, George Turpin gave her a brief nod as he took his corresponding place as prosecutor. She could tell he was enjoying this. Hell, it was a shitload of free publicity—what politician wouldn't love that?

Everyone rose as Barbee emerged from chambers, his trademark red tie bright against his black robe. "Well, Mr. Turpin?" he said as he sat down and looked at his docket. "It's your party. Let's get it rolling."

Turpin began to read a long indictment, charging Nicholas Macalester Stratton with the heinous murder of Lisa Carlisle Wilson.

Chapter and verse he elaborated, stating time of death, place of death, and claiming, with righteous indignation, that Nicholas Stratton had flouted the laws of all decency when he lured and most viciously strangled and mutilated this young girl to death. As the spectators gasped, he thundered like a preacher on fire with Sunday morning conviction; when he finished he looked at Mary with scorn, as if she were a worm for even thinking of defending such a piece of scum.

"Thank you, Mr. Turpin," Judge Barbee said calmly, unimpressed by the DA's hyperbolic oratory. He turned to the defense table, looked over his glasses at Stratton.

"Are you Nicholas Macalester Stratton?"

"Yes, sir."

"What say you to these charges?"

Mary took over. "Not guilty, Your Honor. Mr. Stratton completely and categorically denies all charges." She spoke strongly, telegraphing to Turpin that he was in for a fight.

Barbee marked something down on a piece of paper. "Alright, since the accused has counsel, I'll set the preliminary hearing for Monday, September seventeenth." He looked up. "Mr. Turpin, I'm assuming you want to remand?"

"I certainly do. The best way to keep the people of Pisgah County safe is to keep this man behind bars."

Mary started speaking almost before Turpin had finished. "We respectfully ask the court to review Mr. Stratton's past record, Your Honor. He is a doctor of avian biology, he's run the Pisgah County Raptor Rescue Center since 1999, his only prior offense was a traffic violation issued in 1997, by the state of Idaho."

Turpin pressed his case. "Your Honor, this crime is horrific. The daughter of a beloved governor has been, in our county, murdered without cause. May I also bring to the court's attention that Mr. Stratton is not a native Carolinian, with no long-term ties to the community."

"Your Honor, Mr. Stratton has lived in North Carolina for the past twenty years. He's an adjunct professor at Duke University, plus his commitment to the wildlife and ecology of these mountains is deep and long-standing."

"Okay, counselors, I get the picture." Judge Barbee shook his head. "Ms. Crow, your argument is persuasive, but I'm going to have to deny it. Your client's residence is too remote, and the mountains present a very easy escape route for someone so inclined. The accused is ordered remanded to custody."

Mary played her last card. "Without bail, Your Honor? My client has no criminal record, plus he has ongoing federal responsibilities to the endangered wildlife at his center."

"I'm sorry, Ms. Crow. This time the community trumps endangered wildlife."

Barbee tapped his gavel as a wave of noise enveloped the courtroom. Two officers appeared to take Stratton back to jail. Shrugging away from their grasp, he leaned toward Mary.

"Don't I get a shot at bail?" he asked, his voice hoarse.

Mary shook her head. "Not right now. But I'll start working on it immediately."

"Then call that number I gave you," he said as the two officers led him away. "Doris Mager. She'll need to come get my birds."

"I'll call her right away," said Mary. "Don't worry. We'll talk later this afternoon."

She watched as the officers hustled him out the door, then she felt someone tap her on the shoulder. She turned. George Turpin was standing there, case file in hand.

"Here's your homework, Ms. Crow," he said, his fat cheeks swelling as he smiled. "See you in nine weeks."

TWENTY-TWO

JONATHAN AND LILY PULLED into Tulsa just before suppertime. They'd gotten a late start out of Memphis, and most of the day had been an unremitting drive into a glaring summer sun. A headache had begun to flirt around Jonathan's temples between Little Rock and Fort Smith; by Tulsa it had grown into a full-blown hammer, pounding his forehead.

"Where are we?" Lily sat up and blinked, having slept through most of eastern Oklahoma.

"Tulsa. We're meeting Alex here."

"Why aren't we meeting her in Webbers Falls?"

"The hotel's nicer here," Jonathan replied. "They've got a big pool and in-room movies." Actually, Alex was hiding them, or at least Lily, from Fred Moon. She'd told him as much last night, when they'd talked on the phone.

Lily stuck her lower lip out. "I'd like it better in Webbers Falls, with Grandpa Moon."

He started to tell her that he'd like it better back home, or in Mexico or even on Mars, but he kept silent, ignoring her petulance. *She's only nine,* he told himself, *with a head full of Fred Moon's shit. She's doing the best she can.*

"Well, for now we're in Tulsa," he told her. "Let's go see if Alex is here."

"I don't even know Alex," said Lily, still full of complaint.

"She knows you."

"What does she look like?"

"Tall. Pretty." Jonathan remembered the first time he'd met the leggy blonde, when she'd strode into Little Jump Off. "She's smart and brave."

"As smart and brave as Mary?" Lily asked snidely.

"Yes," he said, thinking back to the long ago ordeal that had bonded Mary and Alex for life. "They're probably the two bravest people I know."

Lily had no response for that. They walked across the parking lot and into the lobby. A blast of cold air instantly chilled them. Jonathan looked around for Alex and found her, sitting on a leather sofa just outside the bar. She wore jeans and dusty cowboy boots, and had a briefcase open beside her.

"Alex?" he called.

"Jonathan!" She looked up and smiled, unfolding long legs as she got to her feet. "Lily! It's great to see you again!"

She hurried over and gave him a sisterly peck on the cheek. Though the Texas sun had freckled her nose and etched a few faint wrinkles around her deep blue eyes, her grin was still broad, and her voice still exuded a kind of no-shit confidence that made him feel like this might not be the end of the world.

"I'm so glad you're here," she whispered, then reached down and offered Lily her hand.

"I know how my two boys hate being kissed by strangers," she said. "So let's just shake hands."

Lily shook her hand but didn't say anything.

"It's been nearly five years since I've seen you," Alex continued. "You're growing up to be a very pretty girl."

"Thank you," Lily answered stiffly.

"So did you have a good trip?" Alex smiled at Jonathan.

"It was okay," he said, not bothering to hide the bitterness he felt.

"Well, I think you'll like it here." She pulled a key card from the pocket of her jeans. "Let's go see your room."

They rode an elevator up to the third floor. At the end of one hall, Alex unlocked a door that opened into a suite. Two large bedrooms were connected by a sitting area, which boasted a wet bar and large screen TV.

"Wow!" said Lily. "That's bigger than Grandpa Moon's!"

"Pretty cool, huh?" Alex walked over and lifted something that looked like a small ping-pong paddle. "Got a Wii, too." She walked over to the bedroom that opened to the right. "Hey, Cecilia. Come on out and meet Lily."

Jonathan watched as a small young woman dressed in jeans appeared. Her complexion was olive, her long dark hair clasped with a silver and turquoise barrette.

"Hi, Lily. Nice to meet you." Smiling, Cecilia offered her the same hand-pumping shake as Alex.

"Cecilia's my assistant," Alex explained to Jonathan. "Also the best Wii player in Fort Worth. I figured she could turn Lily into a Wii champ while you and I were busy."

"When do we go to court?" asked Lily flatly.

"Not for a while," replied Alex. "If we're lucky, maybe not at all."

———

An hour later Jonathan stood on the balcony of their suite, watching as Lily and Cecilia swam in the pool three stories below them. From a distance, they reminded him of two sleek brown otters, racing across a field of aquamarine. He was glad he'd taught Lily to swim early, cajoling her into the slow waters of the Little T when she was barely past walking. "Fim, Daddy!" she'd cry, as she dog-paddled to him, her expression wide-eyed and jubilant. "Fim!" *I would give almost anything*, he thought wistfully, *to go back to that time. I would do so many things differently*.

"You okay?" Alex came up to stand beside him, interrupting his melancholy reverie.

"Yeah. Just watching Lily."

"You don't have to worry," Alex said. "Cecilia will take care of her."

He looked at the other, slightly longer otter swimming beside Lily. "Oh, yeah?"

"She has a Masters in child psychology. Also a black belt in karate and a license to carry. I use her for all my custody cases. I can think of only one person Lily would be safer with."

"Who's that?" he asked.

"You."

He shook his head. "I don't know, Alex. I think I've fucked things up pretty bad."

She smiled. "Come inside and let's talk."

They went into the bedroom that Alex had set up as a quasi-office. As they sat down on the sofa, she told him to tell her the truth and tell her everything, that she would share it with no one.

"Not even Mary?" he asked.

She smiled. "That's precisely why I told Mary not to come. What you tell me is between you and me, alone. So tell me everything, but tell me the truth."

He squirmed on the sofa, feeling as if he were talking to some psychiatrist. He wasn't totally convinced that Alex would keep this confidential—he'd overheard her and Mary before, laughing over what some unnamed client had done. He supposed he had little choice in the matter, now, though.

"It started when I brought Lily out here for a month's visitation," he began. Alex took notes while he told her of Fred Moon, his Winnebago, his constant loading of the motor home with a sly grin on his face.

"Mary thinks I'm paranoid," he said. "But I knew Fred Moon was going to put Lily in that Winnebago and drive away. I would never have seen her again."

"Did he ever threaten to do that?" asked Alex.

"No," Jonathan replied. "But every day he'd be outside, getting that trailer ready to go somewhere."

"How did you know he was doing that?"

"I watched him from the lot across the street. With a pair of binoculars." He realized that he probably did sound like someone skirting the outer edges of paranoia, but he didn't care. Alex wanted the truth.

"Okay." Alex nodded. "Now tell me about Lily."

His rage grew hotter. Fred Moon was one thing—Fred Moon's damaging affect on Lily was what really let the monsters loose inside him. "Until Lily went to Oklahoma, her major concern was making a goal in soccer. Now she's worried that Mary might kill her."

"Kill her?" Alex looked up, stunned. "Why would she think that?"

"Moon showed her some kind of newspaper clipping he keeps in his wallet. Lily insists it says that Mary was jealous of Ruth and killed her to get rid of her. Moon told her we'd lied to her all these years because we'd gotten away with murder."

"So now Lily thinks Mary might kill her because she knows the truth."

"I guess." Jonathan hunched forward. "It's just crazy. Can you see why I don't want my child to go live with this bastard?"

Alex nodded. "That is a lot to lay on a nine-year-old."

"I told her that Fred Moon was lying, that Mary loved her. I pointed out all the things Mary did for her, every day. But she doesn't believe me." He got up and walked over to the balcony. Lily and Cecilia were now sunning on two bright green towels. Oddly he thought again of Alex and Mary, that long-ago day when they'd stopped by Little Jump Off before their hike into the woods. How incredible Mary had looked. Even the memory of it sent a ripple of desire through him. "But you know what the worst part of this is?"

"What?"

"Lily doesn't trust either one of us anymore."

"Because Fred Moon beat you to the punch about her mother?"

He nodded. "We were going to explain it, but she was so young. Telling a child her mother died struggling over a pistol is a lot tougher than revealing that Santa Claus is really your mom and dad."

"Refresh my memory," said Alex. "What happened that night?"

"We were in Atlanta, staying at Mary's grandmother's house. Lily was four months old. I think being on Mary's turf pushed Ruth over some kind of edge—she made an herbal tea that laid me out cold.

Then she came after Mary with a gun. They wrestled downstairs in the kitchen. One shot was fired. Mary was the one who got up, alive."

"Any witnesses?" asked Alex.

"No. Gabe Benge and the APD rolled up about five minutes later."

"Well," said Alex. "I can see why you wouldn't want to go into that with a nine-year-old." She flipped to a new page on her pad. "So what do you think Lily wants to do?"

Here comes the hard part, he thought. *Here comes the part she and Mary won't laugh about, on the phone at night.* He turned away from the window. "Lily doesn't want to live with Mary ever again."

Alex looked up from her notes, her blue eyes wide. "Does Mary know that?"

He shook his head. "I don't have the heart to tell her."

"I don't blame you," said Alex. "Mary adores Lily."

He gazed at the floor, thinking of Mary while Alex studied her notes. In a moment, she asked him a question that seemed to hang in the air between them. "What do you want, Jonathan?"

"For things to go back to the way they were before."

"Before what?" she pressed.

"Before Fred Moon."

"I think that horse has already left the barn, sugar," Alex said gently.

"I know." He turned back toward the balcony. He didn't want Alex to see how scared he was.

She was silent for a moment, then she walked over to stand beside him. "I've got to tell you, considering her history, the court may give some weight to Lily's wishes."

"You mean they'll put Lily on the stand? Make her repeat all that garbage about Mary?"

"I won't call her, but the judge might want to talk to her, in chambers."

Jonathan closed his eyes and pressed his forehead against the cool glass of the window. *This just gets worse and worse*, he thought. *I should have gotten some fake passports in Memphis and headed south to Mexico.*

Alex put her hand on his arm. "There's no need to panic, but I've got to know how you want me to proceed."

He frowned. "I'm not sure what you're asking."

"If you go for sole custody, they might ask Lily to testify. If we make a deal for joint custody, then I'll make sure she never gets called to the stand."

He looked down again, at the little girl swimming in the pool. He had no good options here. If he fought for Lily, she'd have to repeat every lie Fred Moon had ever told about Mary. If he made a deal with the Moons, he'd wage an unending war with Fred Moon for the heart and mind of his own child. Suddenly he remembered something his Aunt Little Tom had once told him: fight hard to fight only once.

"Shared custody with the Moons is not an option," he finally replied. "I will see Fred Moon dead before I see him with Lily Walkingstick."

TWENTY-THREE

MARY CROW SAT AT her desk, eating a sandwich from Sadie's coffee shop. She'd spent most of last night and much of the morning going over Turpin's evidence. She'd watched the ghost movie three times. It started off as a bunch of college kids explored an old cabin, then ended as strangely beautiful fiddle music lured Lisa Wilson out the door, to her death.

She knew it would be a fascinating case, and as much as she would love to take it, her old promise to Jonathan had begun to niggle at her. No murders, they'd agreed, as long as Lily lived with them. Reluctantly, she closed Turpin's evidence file and sent fellow attorney Dave Loveman an email, asking if he'd take the case. A couple of hours later he replied, saying he'd be happy to, if she could work on the preliminaries of a defense until he got back from vacation. *I'm in Israel with my family until August 15. Just piss on their evidence until then. Remember—all we need to create is a reasonable doubt.*

Okay, she wrote back, laughing. *I'll start pissing immediately.*

Happy to have something to take her mind off everything in Oklahoma, she started re-checking the notes she'd made. The most damning bit of physical evidence against Stratton was Lisa Wilson's ring beneath Stratton's bed. Beyond that, the cheap denim and mountain soil under Lisa's fingernails could have pointed to practically anyone in Pisgah County. The interns had opportunity, and motive if any were truly pissed about her brown-nosing. Same for Stratton's hired hands, particularly Jenkins, the one who'd asked for a job with her father. The fiddle music was a little more problematic, but not much. Who was to say it wasn't one of the interns who'd sneaked out underneath range of the camera? Who was to say one of them hadn't brought recorded fiddle music and played it to lure Lisa out of that cabin? Who was to say it wasn't some Appalachian loony tune who saw the kids and decided to have a little homicidal fun? Hell, plenty of drifters roamed these mountains—she'd run up against one of them once, though he'd communed with a pet snake instead of a musical instrument.

"Still," she admitted. "None of that explains the figures carved on the girl's body."

That was the most troubling aspect of this case. Strangling someone connoted deep-seated rage. Strangling someone and carving them up while they lay unconscious veered off into an evil Mary had no name for. When she first saw the crime scene photos she feared the killer was Cherokee and had carved characters from the syllabary into the girl. But closer examination revealed that the figures weren't Cherokee, or any other alphabet she knew. They were more like shapes than letters—rectangles, ovals, something that resembled a crescent moon, a trapezoid that looked like a lampshade. Had the figures all been geometric, she would have guessed it was some kind of mathematical language. But the crescent moon and the lampshade were whimsical—variables that didn't fit in with the geometry hypothesis. Yet the figures repeated, made a pattern. Somebody was trying to communicate something.

"Figure that out and you'll find the real killer," she whispered.

But finding the real killer was not her problem—like Dave said, all she had to do was come up with enough reasonable doubt to get Stratton off the hook. She put the evidence files aside, got out her Rolodex, and started flipping through her expert witnesses. Two hours later she had an Asheville psychiatrist lined up to interview Stratton, a retired ME who agreed to go over Lisa Wilson's autopsy results, and for the interns, Omer Peacock of China Grove, North Carolina, ex-SBI agent and her go-to private eye.

"You want the helicopter special?" Omer asked, sounding as if he were talking through a chaw of tobacco.

"What's that?" asked Mary, envisioning the little man rappelling down from the sky.

"It's for parents who want to know what their little college darlings are up to."

"Sounds perfect." Mary laughed. "Give me five helicopter specials to go."

"You got it, sweetheart. I'll be in touch."

She hung up the phone. Though she had set all the proper wheels in motion, she went through Cochran's evidence again and realized that it wouldn't be a bad idea to see inside the Fiddlesticks cabin. Her student-intern killer theories looked good enough on paper. Now she ought to find out if they worked in real life.

She stood up and stretched, surprised to find that it was nearing four o'clock. She checked her voicemail, on the outside chance that Jonathan might have called, but the only message was a call from Ginger Malloy. They'd spoken yesterday after the arraignment and had made tentative plans to play tennis, which she was now going to have to cancel. Quickly, she punched in Ginger's number.

"Ginger Malloy." Ginger always answered her phone breathlessly, as if the caller might be phoning in some hot news item.

"Hi Ginger, this is Mary. I—"

"Are we still on for this afternoon? Save me from working on this feature about mountain music?"

"I'm sorry, I can't. I've got to go out to the Fiddlesticks cabin."

"Don't waste your gas. Cochran's keeping a tape around it."

"I can go under the tape," Mary assured her.

"Oh, yeah? What makes you so special? I'm sleeping with Cochran and I can't even get under the tape."

"I'm counsel for Nick Stratton. Remember?"

"But I thought you were turning Stratton over to Dave Loveman."

"Loveman's on vacation." Mary replied. "I'm going to do Stratton's legwork until he gets back."

"Really?" Ginger sounded as if she sensed a story. "Gosh, Mary, Fiddlesticks is a lot more interesting than mountain music. Maybe I'll come with you."

"I'd love that, Ginger, but I don't think it would work. I'm a defense attorney, you're a reporter, plus you're sleeping with the sheriff. That's a conflict of interest on about ten different levels."

"But I'm also your tennis partner. And your friend. And I do fair and balanced reporting. Hell, I'll even drive. We can use the paper's SUV."

Mary considered that. Ginger had always been even-handed in her coverage, and given Hartsville's current vengefulness, Stratton might need a local reporter with a halfway open mind. "Can you leave right now? It gets dark fast back in those coves. I'd like to have the light for as long as we can."

"I'll honk for you in five minutes," she replied.

———

They drove high into the mountains, the *Herald*'s SUV chugging up twisting roads that had known more traffic in the past two weeks than they had in the past two decades. As they drove they drank Cokes and indulged in one of Ginger's guilty pleasures, a bag of barbecued potato chips.

"Did you ever come up here when you were a kid?" asked Ginger, downshifting into low gear.

"Once." Mary gazed into the summertime forest, thick with dog hobble and wild tangles of blackberry bushes. "In high school."

"Did you see any ghosts?"

Mary shook her head, remembering how she and Jonathan and three other couples had come up here full of anticipation over seeing a ghost. They left, however, after just a few minutes in the dank little house. Something about the place just hadn't felt right.

"Did you know that a number of girls have come up here and later vanished?" Ginger asked, a low hanging limb thwacking against the windshield.

Mary frowned. "I've never heard that."

"Didn't you read my feature? I wrote a whole flipping section on the Fiddlesticks cabin not a week ago!"

"Sorry," said Mary. "Lately I've been reading Oklahoma custody law. What did you write?'

"That every decade since 1986, at least one girl who's recently visited the Fiddlesticks cabin vanishes and is never heard from again."

"How old were these girls?" asked Mary.

"The three I wrote about were nineteen, sixteen, and almost twenty."

Mary shook her head. "That's ripe runaway-from-home age, Ginger. And three teenagers over three decades sounds more like coincidence than pattern."

"That's what Jerry said." Ginger licked orange barbecue salt from her fingers. "But I still think it's odd. And I haven't stopped investigating it."

———

A couple of bone-jarring miles later, the road narrowed to a mere footpath that led deep into towering pines. Ginger pulled over and parked in some weeds as a damp, November-like coldness raised goose bumps on their arms.

"*In the pines, in the pines, where the sun never shines,*" Ginger started singing, then stopped, embarrassed. "Sorry. I've been writing about mountain music all day."

"*And you shiver when the cold wind blows.*" Mary finished the old song with a shudder. "They probably composed those lyrics up here."

They got out of the car, Mary shouldering the backpack she'd brought from her office. As they walked toward the cabin, trumpet vines crowded the path, dangling lush red blossoms, lurid as tongues. They walked deeper into the woods, then suddenly, there it was: Fiddlesticks. Behind yellow crime scene tape crouched the most notorious cabin in Pisgah County. Mary stopped, studied it. It was smaller than she remembered. Meaner. A sour little runt of a house, so inconsequential it was hard to believe such evil had transpired here.

Ginger came up behind her. "Can you imagine spending the night there?" She shivered. "Even with all your friends?"

"No," said Mary, though when she'd come up here before she would have gladly spent the night, if Jonathan had asked. But the mood had not lent itself to romance—that part had come later. She put the memory away. "Come on. Let's go have a look."

Ducking under the tape, Ginger followed her up the rickety steps. "Just so I'm clear—what exactly are you looking for up here?"

"I want to take some measurements, see if any of my theories hold up."

"Theories of?" asked Ginger

"Alternate versions of Lisa Wilson's murder."

They crossed the sagging porch and entered the house. The front room was as Mary remembered—a low-ceilinged structure pungent with mold and mildew. Graffiti was splattered across the walls and the floor was covered with a fine, silt-like powder.

"Cochran's dusted for prints," said Mary.

"What are those red X's for?" Ginger pointed at six tape marks, spread around the room.

Mary pulled out her iPhone and began snapping pictures. "That's where the interns were sleeping." She pointed to another red X, on the mantel. "Givens set up his video cam there."

"At least the kid did his homework," said Ginger. "Most people think the ghost haunts the bedroom, but Fiddlesticks's wife, Bett, and Ray Hopson were killed in here."

"Oh, yeah?" said Mary.

"Performing an act of sexual perversion, as the DA so quaintly put it." Ginger shook her head. "You should read the transcript of that trial sometime. They said Hopson's male member was excised from his body with a single stroke of a knife."

"Jeez," said Mary. "What was he doing?"

"Getting a blow job from Fiddlesticks's wife. I guess in '58, they considered that perverted."

Mary walked over to the mantel and started shooting pictures of the room from the same angle as Givens's video cam. As she looked through her viewfinder, she pictured the scene the tape showed—Lisa Wilson and Ryan Quarles sleeping at the red X nearest the front window, while Tony Blackman and Rachel Sykes had slept on the other side of the front door. Abby Turner had bunked down with her head at the entrance to the kitchen. Those three X's were clearly visible in Mary's field of vision. Chris Givens, by his own admission, had slept opposite Abby, around the corner of the fireplace, conveniently out of camera range.

Ginger stood in the middle of the living room, watching as Mary took pictures. "Anything I can do to help?"

"Yeah," said Mary. "Go lie down under the front window. Put your head on that red X."

"I get to be the dead girl?"

"Just for a minute."

"Gee, thanks." Ginger walked over and stretched out beneath the window, while Mary went and lay down on the red X where Givens had slept.

"Can you see me?" she called to Ginger.

"I can see you from the waist down. The fireplace hides the rest of you."

"Thanks." Mary sat up and looked out the window nearest Givens's position. Though it was an easy jump to the ground outside, the panes had been shattered years ago, and long shards of glass extended like daggers toward the center. *Damn*, Mary thought, her theory imploding. It would take a skinny contortionist to get out of that jagged hole. Givens was at least six feet tall, already sporting a beer-and-cheeseburger waistline.

"Can't pin it on Givens, can you?" Ginger got up from the floor.

Mary frowned. "What makes you say that?"

"I've done my homework, too. I'm guessing you're trying to get Givens out of that window and into the woods, so he can kill the girl. You're pissed because you can't do it."

"How do you know that?"

"Because if you stare at those shards of glass any longer they'll melt."

Mary had to laugh. "That's why I needed to come out here. I can't let Dave go against Turpin half-assed."

"Don't feel bad. I think Jerry liked Givens, too, for a while."

Disappointed, Mary walked out on the porch. Fifty yards north of the cabin, Cochran had ringed an enormous pine tree with yellow crime scene tape. She recognized the spot immediately—Tony Blackman had found Lisa Wilson under that tree. She turned and called back inside to Ginger, who sat in the window sill, scribbling in a reporter's notebook. "I'm going up to that tree for a minute."

Ginger looked up. "You need me to be the dead girl again?"

"I'll holler if I do."

While Ginger returned to her writing, Mary started up the hill. Ten feet away from the house she felt it—a small frisson that traveled down her spine like an ice cube. She stopped, surprised, then she scolded herself. "Oh, come on," she whispered. "Big bad defense counsel, afraid of ghosts."

Shaking her head, she walked on toward the tree. The path was steep and slippery with pine straw and she looked as Jonathan had taught her to look—noticing which way the weeds were broken, if there were fresh paths trodden through the grass. The only thing unusual was the number of heavy lug footprints, left, no doubt, by Cochran and the SBI. She kept walking, pausing to let a long black snake slither across the ground in front of her. Finally, she reached the tree. A massive pine, its green needles seemed to sigh in the light breeze.

She checked for more snakes, then looked back at the cabin. "Ginger?" she called no more loudly than if they were standing at opposite ends of a tennis court. "Can you hear me?"

Ginger didn't move.

"Ginger?" Mary called again, louder. Ginger still remained engrossed in her writing.

Mary sighed. *Cochran's right again*, she thought. The wind would have to be blowing in exactly the right direction for anybody in that cabin to hear anything going on up at the tree. She was turning in a slow circle, surveying the thick forest around her, when once again, she felt something strange. Not a chill this time, but a noise. And not even a noise as much as an absence of noise, in the way that birds grow quiet when a predator nears. She glanced back at the cabin, thinking Ginger must be on her way up here, but the sun still caught the fiery highlights of her hair as she sat writing in the front window. Mary tensed. Something was strange here, something not quite right. She stood there listening when suddenly she heard a series of high-pitched sounds. Half a phrase, then it stopped, as quickly as it had begun. The hair lifted on the back of her neck. Someone was up here, playing a fiddle.

TWENTY-FOUR

MARY SWALLOWED HARD, FIGHTING a sick moment of panic. She and Ginger were a good half-mile away from their car. *Get a grip,* she told herself. *It's just your imagination.* But then, the noise came again. A bow, pulled across strings. She'd heard the sound all her life.

Quickly, she stashed her iPhone in her backpack. Zipping the thing shut made a loud rasp that set her teeth on edge. She looked around, as if that might flush out some fiddler full of teeth and claws and no remorse, but nothing—not a twig or a leaf or a bird—made a sound. Still, she knew somebody was watching her.

Grabbing her backpack, she headed toward the cabin. Though she longed to run, she forced herself to walk. Whatever animal you're up against, she remembered Jonathan once told her, don't show your fear.

She made her way down to the cabin on knees more jelly than bone. "Ginger," she called as she neared the porch. "Come on. Let's go."

Ginger looked up, surprised. "You're through?"

Mary nodded. "Let's go."

Ginger returned to her notebook. "Let me finish this paragraph."

"Ginger, we need to go." Mary risked a quick glance over her shoulder. "Now."

"What's the hurry? We just got here."

"We need to leave," Mary said slowly.

Ginger must have heard the urgency in Mary's voice. "Oh, shit," she whispered, her eyes wide. "Somebody's up here, aren't they?"

Mary gave the slightest of nods. "Let's just go," she said softly.

Closing her notebook, Ginger ducked through the open window. In three quick strides she was across the porch and standing beside Mary. "Who is it?" She craned her neck toward the tree. "Where are they?"

"Don't look up there!" Mary whispered. "I don't want them to know we're on to them. Let's just walk back to the car and get the hell out of here."

Ginger looked at her as if she were crazy. "Walk back to the car?"

Mary nodded, having long ago learned the value of a bluff. "Yep. Just pretend we're strolling out to the tennis court."

———

They started back down the twisting path. While Ginger was antsy, breathing hard, Mary kept listening to the woods behind her. Who would be up here in the middle of the afternoon—curious teenagers? That reporter from the *Snitch*? Some kind of sicko drawn to the Fiddlesticks cabin by all the notoriety? She didn't know; she didn't care. All she knew was that they needed to get away from whoever was playing that fiddle.

Suddenly, she could stand it no longer. She told Ginger to wait while she knelt on the ground, pretending to re-tie her shoe. As she tightened the laces, she risked a quick backward glance. A movement caught her eye—high up on the ridge to her right, forty yards behind them—a shadowy figure slipped behind a tree. With the lowering sun bright in her eyes, she couldn't tell if it was male or female, only that it was there and that it did not want to be discovered.

She tied her shoelace, trying to think of what to do. If only one person was up there, they weren't in bad shape. Already they were more than halfway to their car. But what if there were two? What if one person was near the tree and someone else was waiting for them at their car?

STOP, she told herself, willing her heart to slow down. *Next you'll be hearing the banjo music from* Deliverance. *Just deal with what is, not what might be. One person, following you along a ridgeline. They'll make noise coming down that ridge. Whatever they do, it won't surprise you.*

She stood up and smiled at Ginger, trying to hide her concern. "Okay, let's go."

"Can we run now?" asked Ginger.

"No," said Mary, sauntering along as if she enjoyed walking down pine-shrouded roads with her gut knotted in fear.

They went on, giving up on any chitchat. Though Mary longed to look back and see if the shadow was gaining on them, she forced herself to keep her gaze straight ahead. Every turn in the road presented a new tableau—bearberry bushes at one, another with a dead oak tree shrouded in grapevine. After the wide turn with the red trumpet flowers, suddenly the white SUV glimmered through the trees. Never had she been so happy to see an automobile. Still, she held her breath, knowing it wasn't over yet. If someone had disabled their car, they would be in deep trouble. She was almost afraid to look, but as they neared the car, she saw no slashed tires, no gaping hood with large chunks of the engine missing.

"Thank God," gasped Ginger, unlocking the doors.

"Now we can run," Mary said. "Fast."

They ran, jumping into the car, locking the doors behind them. Mary held her breath as Ginger shoved the key in the ignition. For an instant nothing happened, then the engine caught. Ginger whipped the vehicle around, making a tight turn on what felt like two wheels. Mary kept watch out the back window as they sped away, the SUV swerving around potholes, bouncing over tree roots and rocks. Neither woman spoke until they reached the paved road, then Ginger slowed down and turned to her.

"Did you really see somebody up there, or were you just playing make-the-reporter-shit-her-pants?"

"I really saw someone," said Mary, still peering into the woods behind them.

"Who?" Ginger demanded. "And if you say a ghost, I'm putting you out of this car."

Mary shook her head. "I didn't see a ghost."

"Who, then?"

She turned to Ginger and spoke quietly. "I may have seen whoever killed Lisa Wilson."

Ginger gasped, incredulous. "How do you know that?"

"Because someone was up there playing a fiddle."

———

An hour later they sat at John Bigmeat's Bar and Grill, a dark little joint that was an offshoot of John Bigmeat's Cherokee Trading

Post. They sat at a booth with Jerry Cochran, drinking cold beer, the eyes of a Cherokee bear mask glowering from the wall.

"Why the hell were you two up there anyway?" asked Cochran, keeping a protective arm around Ginger's shoulders. "It's still a roped-off crime scene."

"I can go up there," Mary reminded him. "I'm Stratton's counsel."

"I went as her assistant," Ginger added.

Cochran gave a disapproving frown but pulled out his notebook and pen."Then tell me again what happened up there—slowly."

Ginger recounted most of the tale, turning the narration over to Mary after she walked up to reconnoiter the tree.

"I was looking around, when everything got quiet," Mary said. "Like when a serious predator shows up."

"What do you mean a serious predator?" asked Ginger.

"A fox, a bear. Something that eats other, smaller things."

"Okay," said Cochran. "What happened next?"

Mary hesitated a moment, knowing this would sound crazy. "I had a gut feeling that someone was watching me, from not too far away. I shook it off. Then, I heard fiddle music. Twice. I started back to the cabin then. Later, when we were heading to the car, I saw some-one following us, along that upper ridge."

"You didn't tell me that!" cried Ginger.

Mary smiled, apologetic. "I didn't want to scare you."

"Wait a minute," Cochran said. "You say you heard fiddle music?"

"Two different times. Five or six notes, as if someone started to play, and then stopped."

Cochran gave her a hard look. "Are you sure it couldn't have been tree limbs, squeaking against each other?"

"I've grown up hearing fiddle music, Jerry. I know what it sounds like."

"So that's when you returned to the cabin?"

She nodded. "I told Ginger we needed to leave—"

"Can you believe she said we had to walk back to the car?" Ginger interrupted.

"If we'd run they would have known we were on to them," Mary explained. "That might have forced their hand."

Cochran asked, "What happened next?"

"Halfway to the car I pretended to tie my shoe. When I looked back over my shoulder, I saw a figure, moving from tree to tree along the ridgeline, about forty yards behind us. They were following us."

"Can you describe them?"

She tried to recall the shadowy figure. "It was an adult-sized individual with dark clothes."

"Man or a woman?"

"I couldn't tell."

"Only one person?" asked Cochran.

"I only saw one."

"Short? Fat? Thin? Any unusual type of walk?"

She sighed. "All I can tell you is that they were not fat and they knew the woods."

"Why do you say that?" asked Cochran.

"Because they followed us along the western side of the ridge, so the sun would always be in our eyes."

Ginger looked up from her notebook. "You sound like Jonathan."

Mary shrugged. "You live with a woodsman, you pick up a few things."

"What happened after you saw them?" asked Cochran.

"We went on to the car. I was afraid they might have disabled it, but it was okay. We got in and drove straight here."

"You didn't see them again?"

Mary shook her head. "Once we got to the car, we left pretty fast."

Cochran studied his notes for a few moments. "That's interesting, but not all that much to go on. Even if there was somebody up there, they made no threats against you."

"So you're not going to do anything?" cried Ginger.

"I'm sure going to log it in to my file, but since Turpin's already indicted a suspect, Lisa Wilson's case is off my desk. Carlisle Wilson came by and bid farewell to my troops this morning—Turpin and I are going to Wilmington tomorrow for the girl's funeral."

"But don't you think that fiddle music is strange?"

"I think it's creepy as hell," said Cochran. "But I also think it might also be just somebody up there, yanking your chain."

Ginger started to say something else when Bigmeat suddenly appeared with another round of drinks. Not beer this time, but single-malt scotch by the pale, honey-gold look of it.

"Whoa, John," said Cochran. "We didn't order these."

"Lady at the counter sent them over, with her compliments." Bigmeat pointed over his shoulder. A long-haired blonde in tight jeans and a black T-shirt waggled her fingers at them, then sauntered over to their booth.

"Hi, Ginger." She smiled, revealing long, slightly lupine teeth. "Sheriff Cochran, Ms. Crow."

"Hi, Jessica." Ginger scooted a millimeter closer to Cochran. "What brings you here to Bigmeat's?"

"Just getting my final bit of color on that poor girl's murder." Jessica tossed her blonde hair. "But I wanted to say that there's an extra seat on my flight to Wilmington tomorrow. If any of you are going to the Wilson funeral, you're welcome to ride with me, compliments of the *Snitch*."

Cochran's cheeks pinkened. "Thanks, but I'm going with the DA."

"And I'm going with him," Ginger added quickly.

"Well, if you change your mind, the plane leaves at eight thirty, county airport," said Jessica. She started to walk away, then turned back, this time aiming a smile at Mary.

"I also wanted to thank you, Ms. Crow, for keeping our circulation up one more week." She pulled a folded newspaper from her Gucci bag and dropped it in the middle of the table. "See you guys at the cemetery."

Jessica turned, then, and walked out the door, leaving the barest scent of citrus perfume. Ginger grabbed the paper she'd left on the table. "Let's see what Mary did for their circulation numbers."

As Ginger unfolded the tabloid, they all gasped. Mary was on the cover of the latest *Snitch*, leading Nick Stratton into the Pisgah County Courthouse. The caption beneath the photo read "Pocahontas now defending Fiddlesticks Killer."

TWENTY-FIVE

ALEX CARTER WOKE UP early the next morning. Though she'd had a sweet bedtime conversation with her husband and two little boys, she'd slept fitfully, worried about the mediation ahead. All day yesterday she'd tried to explain to Jonathan that it was supposed to be a compromise—that you gave up some smaller point in order to gain some larger one. But the man had seethed like a kettle on slow boil. "Look at the damage Moon did to Lily in a month," he insisted. "I'm never letting her go back there."

"But you've got to give me something to offer them," Alex had countered. "You're asking me to play poker with nothing in my hand."

"I don't care," he told her. "I'm not giving Lily up."

She'd considered, as she lay awake, calling the mediation off. *My client is intractable*, she would tell opposing counsel. *We'll just have to work this out in court*. But ultimately she decided to go ahead with it. Jonathan was already out here and she'd cleared her calendar just for this. If nothing else, she'd get a good look at the Moons and see if their attorney was anybody to worry about.

With a heavy sigh, she gave up on the last ten minutes of sleep and headed for the bathroom. She showered, brushed her teeth. As she wiped the condensation from the steamed-up mirror, she caught sight of the narrow white scar that stretched from her left collarbone midway down her chest. It was a lasting reminder of the camping trip from hell, where she'd been abducted by a lunatic trapper named Henry Brank. Had it not been for Mary Crow, she would not have survived it. She would not have lived to marry Charlie, or have two wonderful sons. She would have no law practice, no Little League games to cheer at, no sunsets that looked like all of west Texas had caught on fire. She sighed. All that she owed to Mary Crow.

"So don't fuck this up," she whispered to her reflection in the mirror. "If you don't win another judgment in your life, you've got to win this one."

She'd just started to put on her mascara when Cecilia knocked on the door.

"Alex? Sam Hodges is on the phone."

She pulled on her robe and opened the door. Cecilia stood there in a black yoga outfit, a cell phone in one hand, a cup of coffee in the other. "Which do you want first?" she asked.

"Both." Alex grabbed the coffee as she pressed the phone against her ear. Sam Hodges was a Tulsa attorney she'd worked with before, and a Cherokee graduate of Oklahoma law. She'd asked him to sit second chair on this, figuring it wouldn't hurt to have a male Cherokee presence on their side of the aisle. Even though today was just a mediation, she felt better with Sam there. "Hey, pardner. What's up?"

"Just wondered if your boy rode into town."

"Pissed off and ready to rumble." Alex remembered the flint in Jonathan's eyes, his angry, rigid posture.

"Then I'll put on my war bonnet and meet you in front of the Tahlequah courthouse. Eleven sharp."

"I appreciate it, Sam," she said. "We'll see you there."

She clicked off her phone. As she started to drink the rest of her coffee, she realized that she hadn't spoken with Jonathan this morning. For all she knew he could have gotten up last night and driven over to kill Fred Moon. She re-tied her robe and hurried to knock on his door. To her surprise, she found both Jonathan and Lily already in the sitting room, eating a copious room service breakfast.

"Good morning," she said, hoping both their moods had improved overnight.

"Morning." Jonathan wore jeans and a gray T-shirt. He sounded more sleepy than furious—a vast improvement over his storminess yesterday.

Alex grabbed a bagel as she turned to Lily. "How are you doing, sweetheart?"

"Fine," said Lily. "Daddy let me read my Kindle until eleven o'clock."

"I take it that's a rare treat?"

She nodded. "Most nights, I have to go to bed at nine."

"Well, I guess it's special, being in a motel and everything," said Alex.

"Yeah," Jonathan muttered. "Real special."

Alex sighed as she watched his mouth draw downward again. As far as lawsuits were concerned, this was only Jonathan's second rodeo. She needed to remind him of the ground rules. As she spread cream cheese on the bagel, she spoke to them seriously. "We need to leave pretty soon, so let's talk about what's going to happen."

They both looked up. She addressed Lily first. "Sweetheart, your father and I are going to what they call a mediation. All that means is that we're going to talk things over with your grandparents."

"And then do I go to Grandpa Moon's?"

"No. You're going to stay here and hang out with Cecilia."

Lily frowned, her expression mirroring her father's. At first Alex was afraid she might insist on going with them, but after a long moment, she asked, "Can we go swimming again?"

"You sure can. Cecilia also has a car and knows where there's a mall."

"Cool," said Lily, apparently satisfied with her options for the day.

Alex then turned to Jonathan. "We're scheduled to start at eleven, so we'll need to leave here in half an hour. We can go in my car."

"I'll be ready." He looked at her without blinking, his tone somewhere between a promise and a threat.

———

She returned to her room, went over her notes as she dressed, then it was time to go. She grabbed her briefcase and went into the sitting room. Jonathan stood alone, looking out the window. In a dark suit and silver-gray tie, he looked more New York than North Carolina. *Mary must have told him to dress up,* Alex thought. On his own, Jonathan would have probably shown up with a gun and a knife.

"Where's Lily?" she asked, hoping they weren't in for a tearful father-daughter farewell.

"Swimming with Cecilia," he said. "She gets a kick out of pools. We usually just swim in the creek."

"I'm glad she's having fun," Alex said. "You look terrific, by the way."

He grunted. "Wish I felt that way."

———

They got in Alex's Jetta and headed southeast on Highway 51. Jonathan sat in the passenger seat like a little boy forbidden to wrinkle his clothes before church. Again she urged him to offer something in the spirit of compromise—summers with the Moons, alternating Christmas vacations, but he refused to budge. All he could talk about was how Fred Moon had destroyed Lily's trust, Lily's relationship with Mary, Lily's once-steady emotional compass. By the time they pulled up at the courthouse, Alex was exhausted. *Thank God I married Charlie*, she thought as she reached for her briefcase. The only things he obsessed over were coffee in the morning and seven-year-old Bryan's potential as a pitcher for the Yankees.

As they headed toward the lawyer's building next to the courthouse, a short man wearing a black-and-white striped turban waved from across the street.

"Who's that?" asked Jonathan, chuckling at the man's outfit.

"Sam Hodges," Alex replied. "Our second chair."

"Does he always wear a turban?"

"When he goes to court," said Alex. "Hey, what's with you guys and turbans, anyway?"

"A bunch of Cherokee chiefs got them when they visited England, back in the 1700s. They liked them so much they came home wearing them."

Alex laughed. "And you've worn them ever since?"

"Some do," said Jonathan. "I don't."

———

They crossed the street. The two men shook hands, greeting each other in Tsalagi.

"There's one little wrinkle." Sam turned to Alex. "The second meeting room's not available, so we'll have to do this at one big table."

"Hmmm," Alex shot a look at Hodges. "That might present some problems."

"You want me to reschedule?"

"No, we're already here." She turned to Jonathan. "Look, we're going to have to do this in the same room with the Moons. That means you've got to remain calm. No histrionics, no threats. We'll hear them out, they'll hear us out. If we're lucky, we might find some common ground."

He looked at her with hard eyes. "I've told you, Alex. The only common ground between me and Fred Moon is Lily. And she's not up for negotiation."

Alex shot Sam a look, then they all went up to the second-floor office of one Laura S. Bagwell, a skinny, weak-chinned young woman who looked like a malevolent rabbit. Though she called Sam "Steve" and her "Mrs. Carver," Alex noted with amusement that Laura S. Bagwell was absolutely clear on Jonathan's name.

"We're so glad that you agreed to this meeting, Mr. Walking-stick," she said, smiling up at Lily's father. "We always prefer to avoid court when there's a child involved."

Jonathan shot her a look that could have turned her into roast rabbit.

"Are your clients ready to start?" asked Alex, noticing the sheen of sweat on Laura S. Bagwell's forehead.

"Absolutely." She led them into a conference room lined with law books. At one end of a long polished table sat the Moons. By Jonathan's account, Alex expected to see a man in a wife beater T-shirt, a woman in flip-flops and too-tight jeans. Instead, she found a chubby, dark-haired couple who sat like a solemn pair of salt-and-pepper shakers. Like Jonathan, they'd come in their Sunday best—a dandruff-speckled navy blazer for Fred while Dulcy wore a pale yellow pantsuit. Alex noted that the resemblance between Fred Moon and Lily was striking—both had broad Cherokee faces, with lively, wide-set eyes. The couple nodded politely as Laura S. Bagwell made the introductions.

"As I said, Mr. Walkingstick, we appreciate your coming." She took a seat between the two Moons. "We don't want to go to court any more than you do."

Alex smiled as she sat down next to Jonathan, knowing they would have a few more moments of genteel, kissy-face time before the gloves came off. "Since Mr. Walkingstick has traveled halfway across the country in an effort to get this settled, why don't you tell us exactly what the problem is. It seems to us that Mr. Walkingstick has complied fully with the family court decree in Pisgah County, North Carolina, dated 15 October of last year."

"He certainly has, Mrs. Carver," said Laura S. Bagwell. "But as our complaint states, we are gravely concerned over the propriety of having Ruth Moon's killer raising Ruth Moon's child."

"She didn't kill her and you know it," Jonathan glared at Fred Moon.

Gently, Alex shushed him. "I take it you're referring to Mary Crow?"

"Yes," Ms. Bagwell replied as both Moons nodded like bobblehead dolls. "We cited her in our complaint several times."

"Then let me remind you that Mary Crow was never charged in Ruth Moon's death. She was fully exonerated by the Deckard County police department, which determined it to be a case of self-defense."

Alex pulled the official police report from her briefcase and handed it to Laura S. Bagwell.

Bagwell took the papers with an indulgent smile. "Yes, but we also know that Mary Crow had been a long-time prosecutor in Deckard County. Their star prosecutor, according to the local newspaper. The police are known for protecting their own, Mrs. Carver. They would be unlikely to indict their prize attorney. "

"Especially if she wasn't guilty," said Jonathan. "They knew that and so do you."

"We don't know that." Fred Moon spoke for the first time. For a small man he had an amazingly deep voice. "Mary Crow had lots of friends in Atlanta. Ruth only had you."

Jonathan's voice grew louder. "Yeah. And after she poisoned me, she tried to kill Mary!"

"Let's not open old wounds!" Laura Bagwell cried, trying to drown out Jonathan's voice. "All my clients want is for their grandchild to be raised in a loving environment."

Jonathan leaned forward. "And what the hell makes you think she hasn't been?"

Alex squeezed Jonathan's arm harder. She knew if she didn't get a handle on him, this could go downhill fast. "Ms. Bagwell, Lily Bird Walkingstick lives in a lovely home, attends the Cherokee United Methodist Church, and maintains a straight A average at John Ross Elementary School." Alex gave Laura Bagwell a shrug. "I don't know how much family law you've practiced, but that does not connote a child being raised in a non-loving environment."

"If you love her so, then why is she scared?" Fred Moon lifted a crooked, tobacco-stained finger at Jonathan. "Why have you lied to her? Why do you keep living with the woman who killed her mother?"

221

Jonathan leapt from his chair before Alex could blink. In a heart-beat he was at the other end of the table, clutching Fred Moon by the lapels of his jacket. "Mary Crow did not kill your daughter!" He started to shake Fred Moon like a rag doll. Dulcy Moon bolted from her chair. "Lily was not afraid of anything until she spent a month with you."

Jonathan was lifting his fist to strike Fred Moon when Sam Hodges tackled him from behind, grabbing his arm at the very last moment.

"*Hahlee waysta!*" cried Hodges. "You can't do that in here!"

"I don't know why not." Jonathan shrugged Hodges off. "This bastard's filled my little girl's head with so much garbage she might never get over it."

"Gentlemen!" Laura Bagwell leapt to her feet. "This is a med-iation—"

"Oh, yeah?" Jonathan dropped Fred Moon and turned blazing eyes on Bagwell. "Then mediate this, sister. Before Lily came to Okla-homa, she was happy. She loved me, she loved her home, she espe-cially loved Mary." He turned and pointed a finger in Fred Moon's face. "Now all that's gone. You and your damn lies took all that away."

"Get out of my face!" Fred Moon brushed Jonathan's hand away. "At least you got a little girl left. I got nothing but a box of pictures!"

"Stop it!" Laura Bagwell banged her cell phone on the table. "This is a mediation. You're not supposed to do this!" Frightened, she turned to Alex. "Counselor, can you please control your client?"

Alex got up and walked over to the two men. "Come on, Jona-than," she said calmly, stepping between them. "Let's get out of here. I don't think we have anything more to say."

The unfocused rage in Jonathan's eyes vanished, replaced by a look of cold hatred. He gave a brief, dismissive glare at Dulcy Moon, who stood shivering in the corner, then he walked toward the door. As Sam held it open, he turned to aim one final salvo at Fred Moon.

"I don't know how you've got this rigged up, but the sun will not come up on the day Lily Walkingstick comes to live with you."

He stormed out the door, Sam following. The room was silent as Alex began putting her papers back in her briefcase.

"Gosh." Laura Bagwell gave a nervous laugh. "Mr. Walkingstick certainly has an interesting way of expressing himself."

"That he does," said Alex, continuing to pack her papers away.

"Are you leaving?" Laura Bagwell's rabbit nose twitched again.

"I don't think there's any real reason to continue."

"But we've got a lot on the table. Custody, visitation."

"I think my client summed up his position pretty clearly, Ms. Bagwell."

Laura Bagwell blinked. "You mean his refusal is final?"

"Yes." Alex picked up her briefcase. "From here on, I think we'd better work this out before a judge."

TWENTY-SIX

GHOSTS WERE NOT ON Mary Crow's mind as she grasped the telephone. She'd been pondering the Stratton case since noon, all the while waiting to hear about the mediation. Now, just as the sun was casting long shadows on her office wall, Alex finally called, spewing profanity that would do all Texans proud. Mary would have laughed at all the "bone-sucking shitheads" and the "four-eyed fucking assholes," had she not been so scared.

"Calm down, Al!" she cried, fearing that Jonathan had, as he'd threatened, knocked Fred Moon's ass into next Tuesday. "Quit swearing and tell me what happened."

"That little bitch is as smug as they come," Alex fumed. "Said she didn't want to re-open any old wounds, then proceeded to re-open every old wound she could think of."

Mary's heart sank. Some incredibly vicious litigator must be lurking in Tahlequah, Oklahoma.

"I go in there and think oh, boy, no sweat here. She's young, looks like a rabbit, almost swooned when Jonathan walked in. But no. Her shitty little rabbit nose started twitching and off she went."

"What did Jonathan do?"

"Oh, Jonathan perked things up quite a bit. Fred Moon made some stupid ass remark and before I know it, Jonathan's at the other end of the table shaking the guy like a rag doll."

"Oh, God." Mary closed her eyes, afraid something like this might happen. "Do I need to arrange bail?"

"No, Sam Hodges got him out of the room before he could throw any punches." Alex chuckled. "I think Moon's wife may have wet her pants, though. I gotta tell you Mary, your boy can be a pretty rank horse."

"Yes, he can." Mary rubbed the hard knot of tension that clamped down on the back of her neck. "I take it mediation is over for today?"

"Mediation is over forever. I don't think Dulcy Moon has that many pair of underpants. We're going to trial in ten days."

"So are Jonathan and Lily coming home?"

"No, I'm taking them to Texas with me. They can play cowboy with Charlie and the boys. I've got a therapist I'd like Lily to talk to."

"Good idea," said Mary. "Is Jonathan agreeable to that?"

"He balked at first, but he's come around. Lily's a mighty mixed-up little girl."

Mary's heart ached for the child. "Do you think I should come out? Make it a family thing?"

"No—I want to see what Dr. Pace says. She usually likes to talk to kids by themselves for a while. Anyway, if you came out here, you'd just drive everybody crazy."

"No, I wouldn't. I would—"

"Mary, we've gone over this before. The best place for you right now is in North Carolina, tending your own little legal practice."

"But I can help. I can—"

"Mary. I'll call you if I need you. Right now we're all fine."

"Are you sure?" Mary said, despising this feeling of utter helplessness.

"Positive. Now go sue somebody. It'll do you good."

"Okay, Alex." She sighed. "You win. I'll call you tomorrow.

She hung up the phone. A wave of sadness came over her—it seemed that everything was going wrong in Oklahoma and all she could do was wish them good luck.

———

For the next ten days, Mary worked hard on Stratton's defense. Every morning she visited him in jail, and though he tried to contain his frustration, she could tell that the Pisgah County Justice Center was wearing on him. He'd quit shaving and his complexion had gone from golden to sallow. He paced throughout their interviews like a scruffy animal trapped in a cage. All his interns had fled the raptor center after their release from jail. Doris Mager and a dozen other raptor rescuers had immediately volunteered to adopt Stratton's birds, but Artie Slade and Willy Jenkins agreed to stay and take care of the animals— Jenkins doing most of the bird cage cleaning, while Slade became the point man for the whole operation. Mary made a point to become friends with Artie, pumping him ever so slightly about the goings-on up there when Lisa Wilson had been alive.

"That gal was nice to me, but crazier than a bedbug when it came to Nick. Stuck to him like fly paper. 'Bout split her britches when he even talked to anybody else."

"How did Nick feel about her?"

Artie pulled his battered Braves cap lower on his head. "He told me once he'd be glad when she went back to school. I think she gave him the heebie-jeebies."

She made a note of that as she worked on the case. Evidence-wise, Omer Peacock had not exactly struck gold among the interns. His most damning find had been that Chris Givens had leaked Lisa Wilson's picture to the *Snitch*. "He's a slimy little bastard," Omer had told Mary. "It wouldn't surprise me if he'd carved the girl up just to sell the picture."

"But where did he get a picture of her?" asked Mary.

"Snapped it with his iPhone before the police got there. Somehow he got a signal out in the woods and sent it to his brother before deleting it so the police wouldn't know. The brother sat on it till Givens got out of jail then they sold it for twenty-five grand."

Though Omer confirmed Mary's low opinion of the boy, selling a picture of a dead body did not make someone a killer. Nothing Peacock dug up about the interns made her think they were anything other than self-indulgent college kids, so she decided to move on to Jenkins and Slade. She was sitting in her office, about to put Peacock on to them when someone rapped on her door.

"Come in," she said,

The door opened to reveal Buck Whaley standing there, a sly grin on his face, a small paper bag in his hand. Of all Cochran's detectives, Mary liked Whaley the least. He was an old-style holdover from Stump Logan's administration, full of swagger and stubbornness.

"What can I help you with, Detective?"

"The DA sent me over. I'm afraid we neglected to include some evidence in the Stratton case."

"Oh?"

"It's not much, but Mr. Turpin said you should have it." He stepped forward and handed her the paper bag, along with a folded copy of the *Snitch*. "Nice picture of you in the tabloids, by the way. Thought you might like an extra copy for your files."

"What's your evidence, Whaley?" she said, impatient with his snideness.

"Oh, just Lisa Wilson's diary. And a couple of hundred pictures off her cell phone."

She looked inside the bag and found a bound copy of the girl's diary in a manila envelope and half a dozen contact sheets of photographs. "You've held on to this for nearly two weeks?"

He gave a helpless shrug. "Sorry. Sometimes we get busy."

"You know I could go back to Judge Barbee and ask for a new trial date."

"Do what you gotta do, Ms. Crow," he said as he headed toward the door.

As his footsteps echoed down the stairwell, she considered filing a motion, but then decided to have a look at the stuff first. She pulled out the contact sheets and flipped through them quickly. Most were photos of Stratton, skimpily clad, either coming out of a swimming hole, or playing his fiddle.

"Taken by a girl in love" she whispered, tossing the photos on the desk and turning to the diary. "Let's see what Lisa wrote to Dear Diary."

She opened the envelope and pulled out certified Xeroxed copies of the pages of a small book. Neat blue writing spread across the pages, varying from print to script. The entries began May 24, the day Lisa arrived at the Raptor Center. *Met Nick Stratton today—he is so nice!* and went on to record Lisa's impressions of her fellow interns. Ryan Quarles she found sweet, Rachel Sykes nice. Abby Turner is a pain in the ass tattletale. Chris Givens she detested, calling him an arrogant dickhead. Laughing at some of Lisa's descriptions, Mary read on. The girl wrote about Jenkins pestering her about a job with her dad, how the mountains creeped her out at night, how Artie Slade had nailed up a shelf for her, even with most of his fingers missing. Then, on June 16, lightning struck both literally and figuratively. According to the diary, she and Nick were observing two young eagles on a hacking stand when a storm broke. *Lightning struck close by, just as Nick kissed me, she wrote. He really knows how to use his tongue!* After that, she barely mentions anything except intimate descriptions of liaisons behind waterfalls, quickies at the bird barn: *I never dreamed anyone could make me come so fast!* The last week of her life she recounts a breakup: *I can't believe he doesn't want me anymore.* And the day before she died she wrote, *I'll never leave Nick. I'm good for him, even if he doesn't know it yet!*

Mary put the diary down and took a deep breath, feeling as if she'd just read a volume of erotica. Though Lisa had included details only a lover would note (the scar on his thigh looks just like a crescent moon; his breath smells good, even when he drinks beer) Stratton had consistently denied any kind of sexual relationship with the girl. Mary shook her head. This was not good—before it was just Stratton's word that nothing had happened. Lisa had told quite a different tale to her diary. Turpin could do some major damage with this in court.

She put the pages in her briefcase and grabbed her purse. Stratton needed to come clean about his relationship with Lisa Wilson. It was strategic not to admit to murder. To lie to your attorney over an affair was just plain dumb.

———

Half an hour later she sat across from him in an interview room. He asked her the questions that had become a standing joke between them.

"Any chance of getting my fiddle?"

"No," she replied as usual. "Look Nick, we need to talk."

"About?"

She opened her briefcase and pulled out the pages from Lisa Wilson's diary. "This diary. Lisa writes that you two had quite an affair. There are passages in here that even made me blush…"

He started shaking his head. "She lied. I never laid a hand on her."

"Nick, it's okay if you did. She was over twenty-one. Having sex isn't illegal."

He slapped the diary pages down on the table. "But I didn't! At the very most, I put my arm around her shoulder."

"What about the night she came to your bed?"

"I told you! She kissed me, I responded. I'd been drinking earlier, or I wouldn't have even done that."

Suddenly, Mary saw a crack in the wall he'd put up. "So you two did have intercourse?"

"No."

"Nick, you can't expect a jury to believe that a pretty, young girl comes up to your room, takes off her clothes, kisses you, whereupon you tell her to get lost."

He closed his eyes, fighting some kind of battle within himself. "Okay. This is what happened. I was in bed—passed out. Lisa came in, woke me up, started taking off her clothes. She climbed on top of me and started kissing me. I got hard—I mean, sometimes your body just takes over. But I told her to get out before anything happened." He stopped and swallowed. "I was pretty drunk—I honestly don't remember much more after that."

"And that's the only time she came on to you?"

He looked at her, his gaze serious. "She kept flirting with me, but I avoided her. I don't get off on college girls."

"Are you gay?"

"No," he said sharply, giving her breasts an appreciative glance. "I just prefer women to girls."

She took back the diary pages and started thumbing through them. "Have you got a scar on your thigh?"

"Yeah."

"Let me see it."

He stood up and dropped his pants, revealing a crescent-shaped scar just above the hem of his boxer shorts. "A kid nailed me with his skate in a hockey game, back in junior high. Why?"

She ignored his question and asked another of her own. "Did Lisa Wilson get along with Rachel Sykes?"

He pulled up his trousers and sat back down. "Yeah, they were pals."

"How about Ryan Quarles?"

"I guess they were friends, I don't know."

"What did she think of Abby Turner?"

He laughed. "The same thing everybody thinks of Abby. That she's a bean-counting tattletale."

"Chris Givens?"

"Lisa hated Chris, and the feeling was mutual."

"Why?"

He shrugged. "Chris wanted to fly the eagles, but he didn't have the chops. Lisa did. He hated her for that. She hated him right back. Givens can be an asshole."

Mary looked up from Lisa's writing. "Do you realize that you've just corroborated everything Lisa wrote about your interns?"

He frowned, not understanding. "So?"

"Nick, you can't have it both ways. Why would Lisa write a totally accurate account of her fellow interns and then fabricate her relationship with you?"

He sat back, folding his arms across his chest. "The girl followed me around all summer—just because she wrote a lot of nonsense about me in her diary doesn't mean we were lovers."

"I guarantee you the DA will see this very differently."

"I can't help it," he replied. "I'm telling the truth."

With a deep sigh, she put the pages and the pictures back in her briefcase. This was a conundrum as old as humanity itself, she decided. He said, she said. The tragic thing about this was that the *she* was dead, and the *he* could well be hanged for her murder.

TWENTY-SEVEN

MARY RETURNED TO HER office, no less befuddled than when she'd left the jail. She climbed the stairs, dropped her briefcase on the floor, and flopped down on the sofa. Nothing about this Fiddlesticks case made sense. By Nick's own admission, all Lisa's descriptions were accurate, except the torrid pages about him. Those she had written with such detail that it raised Mary's pulse, yet Stratton insisted that beyond the one encounter, nothing had ever happened between them. She wondered if perhaps they'd had sex the night he was drunk and he just didn't remember it. If that was the case, then Lisa would have been a spurned lover the next day. Maybe that pissed her off. Maybe she threatened to tell her father, told Nick that the old man could ruin his career. Maybe Nick did kill her, in an effort to protect himself. Suddenly she was beginning to see Turpin's logic in indicting Stratton. He was close enough, strong enough, had the most to lose.

"Maybe he felt trapped," Mary said aloud. "Maybe it all boiled down to sex with the wrong person."

"What do you mean, sex with the wrong person?" asked a disembodied voice, just outside her door.

Mary sat up as Ginger peeked into her office, dressed in her work outfit of beige linen slacks and a blue blazer.

"Jeez!" Mary clutched her chest. "You almost gave me a heart attack!"

"Sorry." Ginger laughed. "Your door wasn't shut all the way. I was just about to knock when I heard you say something about having sex with the wrong person."

"I was just talking to myself," said Mary, irritated.

"About sex?" Ginger lifted an eyebrow at the quilt folded on one end of the sofa. "What all do you do up here?"

Mary ignored her glance at the quilt. "I work on Stratton's defense. Or I worry about Jonathan's defense. They're going to court tomorrow, you know."

"I've got to tell you, Mary, all that worrying doesn't sound like much of a life."

She shrugged, embarrassed to admit that except for the Jonathan part, she liked this life. She enjoyed being totally consumed by a murder case. She would move in up here if she could figure out some way to shower on a daily basis. *God help me,* she thought, *I must be a real sick ticket.*

"You need to get out more." Ginger grabbed her elbow. "Come with me."

"Where are you going?"

"To the Thursday night Sacred Harp singing at the Sugartree Baptist Church. It's the last installment of my mountain music feature."

Mary shook her head. "No, thanks. I need to stay here and work."

"Mary, lying up here talking to yourself about sex is not healthy. You need to get out, chat with non-incarcerated human beings."

"Take Cochran with you."

"Cochran's at Lisa Wilson's funeral, probably flirting with that horse-faced Jessica Rusk." She jingled her car keys. "Come on and go with me. This church is out in the boonies, and I'm still a little creeped out over that fiddler who followed us the other day."

Mary considered her options. Though she should keep working, it might do her good to breathe fresh, non-office air for a little while. "Okay," she finally agreed. "But we can't stay late. I've got a lot to do."

———

For an hour they drove through a soft, late-summer evening dotted with fireflies, loud with the rasp of katydids, finally pulling into the parking lot of a small white clapboard church called the Sugartree Baptist Assembly. They entered a large, brightly lit hall attached to the sanctuary, where about thirty people had gathered, ranging from early twenties to well past social security age. The men bustled around arranging chairs in the middle of the room, while the women arranged punch and cookies on a long table covered with a red-checked cloth.

"Ms. Malloy?" A chubby little man with thick glasses came forward, offering his hand to Ginger. He wore a plaid sport shirt buttoned to the neck and jeans pulled just shy of his armpits. "I'm Dermot Munro."

Ginger smiled. "So nice to finally meet you, Dr. Munro. This is my friend, Mary Crow. She's my assistant tonight."

"We're so thrilled that you've come." Munro included Mary in his broad smile. "People sing Sacred Harp all over the country, but we don't get much press."

"That's why we're here." Ginger got out her reporter's notepad. "So tell me about it."

"Well, it began in the 1800s, in the rural south. People didn't have printed music back then, so traveling music teachers had to invent different ways of teaching singing."

"Interesting." Ginger scribbled away.

"Our hymns are written in Walker's notation system, which dates from 1866. The term 'Sacred Harp' means the human voice."

Mary zoned out as Dr. Munro rambled on about shape note singing and how there were small but fervent shape-note societies in practically every state. Though her father had reputedly been able to sing like Elvis Presley, she had not inherited any of his musical DNA. She wandered over to the table, where a chubby, pink-cheeked woman in a long gingham skirt was stirring a pitcher of lemonade.

"Haven't seen you here before," she said sweetly. "This your first time singing?"

"I'm not really singing," explained Mary. "I just tagged along with my friend."

The woman poured Mary a glass of lemonade. As Ginger talked to Dr. Munro, more singers came up to welcome her. She met a woman who was doing her doctoral dissertation on Early American music, and an old tobacco farmer who wore coveralls over a starched white shirt. She'd just asked for a refill on her lemonade when Ginger came up.

"They're going to start in a few minutes," she said. "I'm going to look over my notes."

"I'll come with you," said Mary.

They walked to one end of the room and perched on the edge of a small stage. As Ginger reviewed what she'd written, Mary's thoughts drifted west, to Oklahoma. Tomorrow morning, Alex and Jonathan would go to court. Though Alex had sounded confident on the phone today and Jonathan reported that Lily was smiling more since her therapy, Mary still wondered how much damage the Moons had done to her family. If Jonathan did retain custody of Lily, what would they be like when they returned? Would Lily still smile in North Carolina? Would she and Jonathan ever crawl out from under the shadow the Moons had cast upon them?

She was sitting there, trying to foresee her own future when Dr. Munro walked over.

"Ladies, will you come join in the singing?"

"Thanks so much," Ginger demurred politely. "But we don't sing and anyway, I'm here to write a story."

"But you really need to experience this music," he cried, all enthusiasm. "At least come and sit in the cross. You'll be amazed!"

Mary shot Ginger a pleading look. She had Jonathan to worry about, reasonable doubts to come up with for Stratton. The last thing she needed to do was join in a hymn.

"Well, just for a little while," said Ginger. "We've both got deadlines to meet."

"Stay for three songs," chirped Dr. Munro. "And you'll be hooked for life!"

Reluctantly, they followed Dr. Munro to where the chairs had been arranged in a cross formation—four sections in a kind of north, south, east, west configuration, all facing inward, toward a podium in the middle. As Mary and Ginger took seats on the back row nearest the door, Dr. Munro walked to the center of the cross.

"Good evening!" he called. "It's good to see everyone again. Tonight, we have two special guests—Ginger Malloy and her friend Mary. Ginger's a reporter who's writing an article about us for the paper, so we need to be on our best behavior!"

Everyone laughed, turning to catch quick glances at the two of them. Mary suppressed a laugh of her own, wondering what connoted bad behavior for these people—an overdue library book? Twelve grocery items in the ten-item line? Dr. Munro went on.

"Okay, everybody. Let's start with page 197."

Pages rattled as Munro blew a single note on a pitch pipe. The singers hummed the proper pitch, then started singing a cappella—not words, but the do-re-mi scale. When they sang the song through once, Munro lifted his right arm and they began again, this time singing the lyrics.

As we travel through the desert, storms beset us by the way.
But beyond the river Jordan, lies a field of endless day.

Though the lyrics were standard Southern gospel, the sound was nothing like Mary had ever heard before. Beautiful and powerful, Dr. Munro's group sang in a raw, eerie harmony that lifted the hair on the back of her neck.

"*Farther on, still go farther, Count the milestones one by one,*" they sang, their song radiantly hopeful. "*Jesus will forsake you never, it is better farther on.*"

On they sang, the weird, compelling music filling the hall. Mary felt like God and Jesus might both, at any moment, descend from heaven and join in the chorus. When the song ended, she leaned over to Ginger. "Who are these people?"

Wide-eyed, Ginger shook her head. "I don't know. But I'm covered in goose flesh."

They'd barely recovered from the first tune when Dr. Munro called out another number. Again voices lifted in that strange harmony, this time singing a tune about friendship bands and parting hands.

It was an amazing, dazzling sound. Mary wanted to stay longer, but she had work to do, a final call to make to Jonathan before tomorrow morning. She was just about to whisper to Ginger that they needed to go when the woman in front of her turned around.

"Here," she said excitedly, thrusting hymnals at the two of them. "You girls sing the next one. We've got plenty of books to spare."

Mary started to explain that they had to leave, but the woman was too quick. She plopped the hymnals in their hands as Dr. Munro announced the next tune, on page 238.

"Come on," whispered Ginger, flipping to the correct page. "Let's not be rude. We'll sing one, then go."

Mary sighed as everyone did their do-re-mi run-through, then Dr. Munro lifted his arm and the singing began. She hummed along, only glancing at the lyrics. She hoped they might sing the song just once, but of course they launched into the second verse. Deciding that she may as well join in, she held the hymnal closer and began to pay attention to the words. As she began to sing, something about the musical notation caught her eye. Sacred Harp notes weren't the regular dark circles dotting the lines of a staff, but odd little squares and triangles. Suddenly, Mary caught her breath. The shapes that comprised Sacred Harp notation were the same figures someone had carved into Lisa Wilson's flesh!

Mary thought fast. The hymn was ending; Ginger promised they would leave. But she had to take a copy of this music with her, preferably without Ginger knowing. She sang until halfway through the last verse, then she faked a coughing fit. Ginger looked over, frowning with concern.

"I'm going to the bathroom," Mary rasped. "I'll be right back."

Scooping up her purse along with the songbook, she walked toward the back of the room. The same woman who'd given her lemonade pointed to a small door in one corner. Mary nodded her thanks and opened it to find an empty bathroom. Hurriedly, she locked the door behind her and ripped five pages from the center of the hymnal.

"That's ten different songs," she whispered. "Enough to figure out what's going on here."

She listened at the door until the singing stopped, then she made her move. Unlocking the bathroom, she headed straight for Ginger.

"Are you okay?" her friend asked.

"Just a frog in my throat," said Mary, trying to sound hoarse. "Are you ready to go?"

"Yeah," said Ginger. "Let me tell Dr. Munro good-bye."

"I'll go put these hymnals up." Mary put Ginger's hymnal on top and went over and gave both books to the lemonade lady. She felt guilty about defacing the church's property, but she would replace the hymnal later. If she could match these notes up with the shapes carved into Lisa Wilson, it would be a total game-changer for Nick Stratton.

Finally, Ginger made her farewells. "We're done," she said as they walked back out into the summer night. "It wasn't too horrible, was it?"

"It was great." Mary smiled. "I had so much fun, I got all choked up inside."

———

They drove back to Hartsville, Ginger going on about how weird but beautiful the music had been. She dropped Mary back at her office with another invitation to play tennis.

"Have you even bounced a ball on our new tennis courts yet?" Ginger asked.

"Not yet," Mary replied.

"Then let's play sometime this week."

"I'd love to," said Mary, anxious to get busy on her stolen pages. "Check your schedule and call me tomorrow."

She waited until Ginger drove away, then she hurried up to her office. She dug the pages from her purse, then rifled through the drawer that held the Wilson evidence files. Pulling out the photos, she spread them out in front of her fireplace. The police photographer who'd taken the close-ups of the body had numbered the shots sequentially, like a puzzle. In a few minutes an image of Lisa Wilson lay on Mary's floor, a grisly collage comprised of 8x10 glossy photos.

"Okay," Mary whispered. "Let's see what we've got here." She got out a magnifying glass, then compared the shape notes to the figures cut into Lisa Wilson's body. Discounting for blood smears and edema, the mutilations on the dead girl's skin and the musical shape notes were identical. The lampshade figure was do, the crescent moon re, the baseball diamond mi. Two triangles, an oval, and a rectangle made up so, fa, la, and ti. Eight repeating shapes for the eight notes of the scale.

"Holy shit!" she whispered. "Somebody carved shape-note music on this girl."

For a moment she just sat there, staring at the pictures, stunned by the enormity of what she'd discovered. There had been thirty people at that meeting tonight, and Dr. Monroe had gone on about how many shape-note societies there were. The suspect pool for Lisa Wilson's killer had just grown by hundreds, at the very least.

Still, she wasn't satisfied. Were the notes just willy-nilly, or did they compose a message, a tune? She grabbed a legal pad from her desk and made a grid on a sheet of paper. Then she began to copy the symbols down. Assuming the carver probably worked as most people read, she started at Lisa Wilson's wrist; an hour later she finished with a small, flag-shaped mark just above her left ankle. Somebody had cut sixty-four shape notes into this girl's skin.

"But why?" Mary said aloud. "What for? Was it a hymn? A warning of hell in the hereafter?"

She thumbed through the pages she'd stolen. Most of the tunes were simple—four lines of notes from start to finish. "Sixty-four cuts mean sixty-four notes. Sixteen notes to a line, four lines to a song."

Using a song called "Long Time Traveling" as a template, she drew five lines with four spaces between them. Laboriously, she copied down each shape note on its proper space on the staff. Do became C, re became D. Cursing the fact that she'd taken French in high school instead of music, she worked into the night—charting the notes going across the girl's body. Several times she tried to hum the tune, but she couldn't make it sound like anything. Finally, she put her pencil down as the courthouse clock struck two a.m.

"Okay," she said, flopping back on the sofa, her eyes burning with fatigue. "Right now, you've got the notes. Tomorrow you've got to find someone who can turn them into a tune."

TWENTY-EIGHT

THE NEXT MORNING, MORE contemporary notes poured from the iPod in Alex Carter's car. The songs comprised her special going-to-court playlist, ninety minutes of music that started with the Rolling Stones, traversed through Kate Bush and Duran Duran, and culminated with Bob Wills and his Texas Playboys.

As the music blared, Jonathan Walkingstick sat stiffly in the passenger seat, thinking how differently Mary prepared for court. With her, it was mostly silence—hours of pouring over case law or gazing at a computer screen. Her breaks consisted of either long, solitary walks in the woods, or fierce tennis matches with Ginger Malloy. If she ever listened to music, he'd never heard it.

"You okay?" asked Alex, turning down some song he remembered from high school.

"Yeah." *Okay covered it,* he thought. *Not great, but okay.*

"Did you get any sleep last night?"

"Enough," he said. Lily had slept well. He'd dozed in frustrating increments, waking up every fifteen minutes. At four a.m. he'd given up and gotten up, brewing a pot of in-room coffee while he watched the sun rise over the parking lot of the Holiday Inn.

"Lily's had a big time these last ten days," said Alex. "Riding Butterbean, playing with my boys."

Jonathan smiled. They'd both had fun at Alex's little forty-acre ranch, but Lily had truly blossomed. She'd learned how to ride a pony, played soccer with Alex's sons. Her laugh started coming easily again and the tightness around her mouth relaxed. Still, not once had he heard the child speak Mary's name.

"Has she said anything to you about Mary?" he asked, wondering if Lily might have shared her thoughts more easily with a woman.

"Not a word," said Alex. "How about you?"

He shook his head. "It's like she doesn't acknowledge Mary's existence anymore."

"Well, Ailene Pace said Lily still needed help. Probably you guys should get some counseling when you get back home."

He thought of home. It now seemed as distant as Shangri-La. "You don't think they'll make Lily testify, do you?"

"Probably not."

He sat back in the seat, his thoughts returning to Mary. He'd known, since he first signed the contract for that duplex, that he was going down the wrong path. But he'd seen the look in Fred Moon's eyes, the smirk on his face: you took my daughter, so now I'm going to take yours. Then, the lawsuit had come and he'd gone farther down that path, afraid to tell Mary what he'd done, afraid she would accuse him of deceit. Afraid, ultimately, of her looking at him without the love that he'd known since they were kids. He suddenly felt such a heaviness in his chest that he turned to Alex.

"So you think we'll do okay?"

"I feel better about this than I did ten days ago," she said, sipping her cup of Dunkin' Donuts coffee. "Aileen will testify that Lily is a healthy child whose current emotional difficulties were brought on by her recent stay with the Moons. Plus I've got a bunch of old DUI charges that don't exactly make Fred and Dulcy look like model grandparents."

"What about the Mary-Ruth thing?"

She shrugged. "They open the Mary door, I'll open the Ruth door. She comes across like a crazed poisoner."

Her words made him feel odd. Ruth had loved him, had worn his wedding ring. She'd wrapped her life around his like a little green vine. Now, Ruth was a ghost, haunting his nightmares, appearing in Lily's face when the light came at a certain angle.

"How do you feel about testifying?" asked Alex.

"I'm okay with it," he said, grateful to leave the subject of Ruth.

"Can you remember what we talked about? When you go on the stand?"

"Answer your questions in full. Answer Bagwell's questions briefly. Be polite, especially to the judge. Don't take any punches at Fred Moon."

"Even if they make you mad?" Alex said. "Even if they say awful things about you and Mary?"

He shook his head, feeling like a child promising never to call the playground bully a bad name. "Whatever anybody says, I stay polite."

"Then we're cool, buddy." Alex offered him a fist-bump. "I have every reason to believe that this will work out in your favor."

Please God, he thought, staring out at the flat farmland as Alex turned south on Highway 52. He had no idea what he would do if the judge gave Lily over to the Moons. Suddenly, his cell phone vibrated. He pulled it from the pocket of his jacket. It was a text message, from Mary.

Good luck today. Still saving you a seat in Carolina.

———

A thousand miles to the east, Mary put her cell phone on her table at Sadie's coffee shop, hoping that Jonathan would get her text message before he went into court. She'd gotten little sleep the night before, both excited over discovering the shape note figures and terrified about Jonathan's custody trial. About the trial she could nothing but offer her support; about the shape notes, she had quite a few more options. She'd done some Internet research last night and learned that Dr. Munro, the funny little man at the church, was one of the country's foremost authorities on Sacred Harp music. She'd decided, around five in the morning, to take her transcribed scribblings to him. Maybe he could figure out the tune carved into Lisa Wilson's body.

She waited through two more cups of coffee for Jonathan to text back, then she gave up and returned to her office. *He'll text when there's something to text about*, she told herself. *He's probably so nervous right now his fingers can't press the keys.*

She sat down at her desk and looked up the number for the Sugartree Baptist Assembly. A pleasant secretary answered her call, and happily gave her Dermot Munro's number. When he answered her call, she re-introduced herself and told him that she'd copied some old shape note music down and would he have a look at it?

"I'd be happy to." Munro sounded thrilled. "Just bring it to the next singing!"

"I may not be in town then," said Mary. "Could you possibly have a look this morning?"

Munro paused for an instant, then replied, chirpy as ever. "Of course. I live at 1414 Mulberry Street, in Sylva. I'll be here until three this afternoon."

"I'll be there in an hour."

She locked all of Lisa Wilson's photos in a drawer and headed down the stairs. Forty-five minutes later she stood ringing the door-bell of a modest brick home shaded by an old tree laden with ripening apples.

"My," Dermot Munro exclaimed as he opened his front door. "You are quick on the trigger."

"I apologize for coming so early," said Mary. "But this song has been driving me crazy."

"It's alright," said Munro. "My wife and I are retired teachers. We still get up early. Come on in."

Mary walked into the living room of a couple who'd obviously de-voted their lives to music. Small busts of Beethoven and Mozart stood on two end tables, while over-stuffed chintz chairs held stacks of sheet music. A grand piano commanded one corner of the room, a full-length mirror beside it.

"Hopefully, this won't take long," said Mary, pulling out the legal pad that held Lisa Wilson's notes. "I wondered if you recognized this tune."

Munro studied the scribbled music. "Does it have a title?"

"No." Mary thought of the old trunk in her office. "I just copied notes written inside an old trunk."

"Well, that's a new one on me," said Munro. "I've never heard of one written inside a trunk." Nonetheless, he sat down at the piano and began to play. The melody sounded odd and discordant, as if it were some composer's work-in-progress.

"Hmmm," said Dr. Munro. "Let's put this in minor key." He shifted his hands on the keyboard and played the song again. It sounded no better.

Frowning at the notes, he called to his wife. "Ima Lou, would you come in here and see if you recognize this?"

Mary turned as the lemonade lady from last night came bustling in "Well, hello!" she said, pumping Mary's hand. "How nice to see you again!"

"Nice to see you, too." Mary smiled. "I really enjoyed last night."

Dr. Munro looked up from the piano. "Sweetheart, see if you recognize this tune. This young lady found it written inside a trunk." He gave Mary a wink. "Ima Lou taught voice for thirty years. She has a sub-specialty in Southern Gospel traditions."

Ima Lou stood behind her husband, gazing at the music while Munro played the tune for a second time.

"Have you ever heard that before?" He looked up at her over his shoulder. "In the shape note literature?"

"Never." She shook her head. "It's so plaintive—it almost sounds like a string tune."

"You're right, Ima Lou!" cried Munro. "Violin, maybe. Or cello."

Mary gulped. Fiddle music at the cabin, fiddle notes carved on Lisa's body. Were two pieces of the puzzle fitting together?

"So you probably wouldn't find it in the shape note hymnal?" Mary wanted to be sure she understood this correctly.

"None that we know of." Munro nodded at a bookshelf stacked with books. "And we've got all the collections. If you found it in a trunk, it might just be a snippet of a tune somebody wrote down so they wouldn't forget it."

"Thank you so much." Mary smiled at the couple as she took back her scrawled musical transcription. "I can't tell you how much I appreciate this."

"Then give Ginger our best and come to the shape note singing again," Dr. Munro replied. "We meet the third Thursday of each month."

"I'll put it on my calendar," Mary said. "I feel like I've just scratched the surface of Sacred Harp singing."

———

She got back in her car. She checked her cell phone, but there was nothing from either Jonathan or Alex. *They're probably in court now*, she told herself, the pit of her stomach fluttery with nerves. *They'll call when they have something to call about.*

Keeping her phone plugged in to the dashboard, she turned her attention to the shape notes. Thanks to the Munros, she now had clues that weren't mere wisps of conjecture. The figures on Lisa Wilson's body comprised a tune, probably written for a stringed instrument.

"Which throws your canned-music theory in the toilet," she said aloud. "But doubles down on every fiddle player in the mountains, starting with Stratton."

But still, why cut this tune into someone's flesh? What did it mean? What she needed now was not a Sacred Harp expert, but someone who knew fiddle music.

"Lige McCauley," she said. She'd hired him and his string band to play the sports park ceremony. He was famous in the old-time music community, and was the current spiritual godfather of all mountain fiddlers. Now, all she had to do was find him. She remembered sending his check to an address sparse by current standards—simply Lige McCauley, Grapevine, Madison County, North Carolina.

"Okay, Lige. Here I come." She got back on the highway and headed north. Ninety minutes later she crossed into Madison County, a place of roaring creeks and woodsy hollers populated by mountain families who'd arrived in the mid 1700s and never left again. At a market she asked for directions to Grapevine and drove where she thought the clerk had told her, but she found no town, no church, not even a gas station. She was beginning to think that Grapevine might be one of those nebulous mountain communities that was more a state of mind than an actual place. If you lived there, you knew where it was. If you didn't, you could pass right through without ever knowing you'd visited.

After twisting along the Ivy River for a few miles, she came to a gap between two mountain ridges where the woods thinned out enough to allow a small, one-gas-pump country store and a row of industrial-sized garbage bins. Quickly, she turned into the parking lot. If this wasn't Grapevine, then maybe someone here could get her there. She parked her car and headed up the steps. Inside, the store was dimly lit and smelled of old wood fires. The narrow aisles were packed with everything from laundry detergent to lottery tickets. She walked to the counter, where a large woman with hair the color of soot sat behind an old brass cash register, frying apple tarts in an electric skillet.

"Help you?" the woman asked as she flipped one of the tarts over.

"I was wondering if you know where Grapevine is."

"This is Grapevine."

Mary smiled; she figured it might be someplace like this. "Then do you know where Lige McCauley lives?"

"Well, if you want to get to his house, you go a mile out the highway and take a left, then a right, then another left after you cross the bridge. If you want to get to Lige, just go over yonder." She pointed to the back of the store.

Mary returned her odd look. "He's here?" She figured finding McCauley would take the whole day and probably half the night.

The woman laughed. "He and Luke Lunsford have been here since breakfast. They play checkers all morning, music all afternoon."

"Thanks." Amazed at her good luck, Mary threaded her way to the back of the store. After passing two shelves of tattered paperbacks that made up the Grapevine Public Library, she found Lige McCauley folded into a rocking chair next to a cold Franklin stove, frowning as another old man jumped checkers across a board. She watched quietly as his opponent cleared all of Lige's men from the board, then she stepped forward.

"Lige?"

He looked up from under a brown felt fedora that had been stylish during World War II. "Why, hey there, girlie," he said, his blue eyes brightening with recognition. "How've you been?"

"Do you remember me?"

He nodded. "I surely do. You paid me and my boys in advance for that last gig. Fellers like us remember that."

Lige's opponent rose from his seat, politely offering her his chair. "Lige, I think I'll go get us some of Earlene's pies while they're hot."

Lige nodded. As his friend hobbled toward the front of the store, Mary took the chair he'd offered. "I need a favor, Lige."

"You got another park to open?"

"Not right now. I need to know if you can read music."

"I can," he said. "My mama taught me ... she played the organ at the Presbyterian Church."

Mary pulled out her scribbled notes. "Then I need to know if you've ever heard this tune before."

Lige studied the music for a long moment. With an odd look at Mary, he took his fiddle from its case, put the music on the checkerboard and started to play. While Dermot Munro had turned Mary's crude array of shapes into a real tune, Lige McCauley brought that tune to life. He coaxed and tickled the notes, bending them with time and tempo. The music that came from his fiddle was like nothing Mary had ever heard before—so sad and sweet that it made her ache for Jonathan and Lily and a thousand other things she could not put a name to. She got out the digital recorder she used in court and turned it on as Lige began to sing.

In my cabin in the woods, my dear sweet love lies bleeding.
In my cabin in the woods, my bloody knife lies reeking.
Though the one I love is gone today, her memory never leaves me.
Her cold gray lips and sightless eyes will forever grieve me.

McCauley sang the song twice, then put his fiddle down. "Where'd you get this?" he asked, his tone sharp.

"Why?" asked Mary. "Have you heard it before?"

He gave a somber nod. "That tune is cursed. Came straight out of Central Prison."

"Cursed?" Mary leaned forward, as if she hadn't heard him correctly. "What do you mean?"

"I spent some time there." He looked at her with unashamed eyes. "Before I met Jesus, I had some trouble with the law."

"When were you in prison?"

"April 12, 1970, to April 22, 1972." He rubbed his chin. "Two years that passed like two hundred."

"And you heard this tune while you were there?"

"Feller played it every night. It came from the building across from mine, where they kept the boys on death row. Every night the whole cellblock would go quiet, waiting for that tune to begin. It was pretty, but it tore your heart out. Little by little, we learned the words. Then everybody got to where they couldn't stand it ... the sadness just drove you crazy."

"Do you know who played it?" asked Mary.

McCauley shook his head. "I reckon just some poor bastard in prison."

"Were they still playing it when you were released?"

"Nope. We heard it for months, then one night we didn't hear it no more. Everybody got real antsy, waitin' for it to start again, but it never did. We figured they must have gassed the guy who played it, Lord bless his soul."

"Have you ever heard anybody else play it? Anybody around here?"

He shook his head. "Naw. The only people who'd know that tune would be dead by now. Or still locked up in prison."

"But it's so haunting, so beautiful," said Mary.

Lige McCauley's blue eyes flashed. "Maybe to you, girlie. To me it's somebody's soul, flying up out of that hell hole, trying to find a place to land."

TWENTY-NINE

HALFWAY HOME FROM GRAPEVINE, Mary's cell phone rang, a recorded voice announcing CALL FROM ALEX. Immediately she pulled off the road and put the thing to her ear.

"How did it go?" she asked, not bothering with hello.

"Okay," said her oldest friend.

Alex's flat tone chilled her. She took off her left earring and pressed the phone closer. "How did the judge rule?"

"She didn't. We're going back Monday."

"No!" cried Mary. "What happened?"

"Well, Jonathan did great, our Dr. Pace did great. Bagwell tried to argue the Ruth murder angle, but the judge wasn't buying. At three o'clock I thought we were done, but Bagwell said she still had a few more points to bring up. So back we go on Monday."

A thrum of unease passed through Mary. Bagwell had already proven herself sly. Now she had all weekend to come up with more mischief. "What more points could she have?"

"I'm guessing she'll dig up her own expert witness to rebut Dr. Pace."

"You think she'll call Lily?"

"I don't know," said Alex. She paused for a moment, then spoke again. "Mary, there's something I need to say to you."

Mary felt sick inside. Now she really didn't like the tone in Alex's voice. "What?"

"I think you should come out here. And I think you should come prepared to testify."

"What?" Mary could hardly believe what she was hearing. They must be in deep shit for Alex to reverse herself like this. "What's going on, Alex? And tell me the truth. Did Jonathan take a swing at Fred Moon again?"

"No, nobody hit anybody," Alex replied. "But most of the testimony was about you. I began to feel like you were the elephant in the room. Everyone was testifying about Mary Crow, but where was Mary Crow?"

"Did the judge say anything?"

"No, but I could tell she was frustrated. I mean, essentially, you are the child's mother. You should have been in court."

"That's what I've been saying all along, Alex," Mary reminded her. "I've wanted to come since day one."

"Mea culpa," Alex replied. "I called it wrong. I guess that's why you graduated first in our class and I came in twelfth. But can you come out now? Testify Monday?'

"I'll get a flight tomorrow," said Mary.

"Great." Alex gave a sigh of relief. "I'll pick you up at the airport."

———

The Saturday flights out of Atlanta had such long layovers that Mary bought a ticket for an early nonstop on Sunday. Shortly after noon that day, she landed in Tulsa. She'd spent the whole flight nervous and edgy, and as she waited for her red suitcase to start spinning around the baggage carousel, she kept looking for Jonathan, hoping that he had come to pick her up. But she saw only strangers at the baggage claim—cowboys in Stetson hats, college kids in flip-flops. Disappointed, she finally just waited for her bag. *All this way*, she thought. *All these years, and he can't even come to meet me.*

Luggage churned along the conveyor belt, then her bag emerged. She was reaching to grab it when she heard a familiar voice.

"Mary!"

She turned. Alex stood there, tall and grinning, wearing khaki shorts and an oversized white blouse. She opened her arms and wrapped Mary in a warm embrace.

"I'm so glad you're here!" she cried, hugging her close.

She smelled of sun and a distinct aroma Mary knew only as Texas—wind and hay, peppermint gum and suntan lotion. Still, she'd forgotten how tall Alex was, how strong her arms. Her old friend held her heartily, without any fussy little pats on the back.

"It's so good to see you." Mary blinked back sudden tears.

"Jonathan's at the motel," Alex replied, answering her unasked question.

"Did you tell him I was coming?"

Alex nodded.

"What did he say?"

"He asked me not to tell Lily."

"Oh." Mary was disappointed. She'd hoped the child might have softened toward her. Apparently that had not happened.

"Don't worry about it," Alex said, taking her bag. "He's just got a bad case of the mid-trial willies."

Him and me both, thought Mary.

They walked out into a bright Oklahoma afternoon, to Alex's once white Jetta, now beige with dust. "Have you had lunch?" asked Alex as she put Mary's suitcase in the trunk.

"Nothing beyond coffee and a bagel in Atlanta."

"Then let's get something to eat."

They left the airport, driving along shimmering, ruler-straight highways. Alex sped along with her blonde hair stuffed beneath a baseball cap, finally stopping at Pepe's, a tiny restaurant that operated out of a Silver Stream trailer parked on the edge of a flat, green pasture where horses grazed in the distance.

"Best tamales in town," she told Mary as she got out of the car. "And I'm an expert on tamales."

"Then order us some." Mary dug a twenty-dollar bill out of her purse. "Lunch is on me."

"*Si, senorita.*"

Alex walked over to the window of the trailer, where she ordered their lunch in rapid Spanish. A few minutes later she came back to the car, two large iced teas in hand.

"Let's go sit down," said Alex. "They'll bring us our food."

They went to a small table shaded by a bright red umbrella. "So tell me about Friday," said Mary. "How did I get to be the elephant in the room?"

Alex took a deep breath. "Well, Dr. Pace said Lily had been raised by an incredibly caring maternal parent, Jonathan said though Lily didn't call you 'mom' she regarded you as her mother, and that you two shared child-rearing responsibilities equally. Bagwell then went off on a financial tangent. What did Jonathan pay for, what did you pay for, how did he make his money, how did you make yours."

She's trying to make him look lazy, thought Mary. "What did Jonathan say?"

"He said he was a hunting guide and you were an attorney. Bagwell asked what kind of attorney you were. Jonathan said you were in general practice. Bagwell said she understood you were a prosecutor. Jonathan explained that you had agreed to give up capital crimes as long as Lily was in the home." Alex took a sip of tea. "I thought that was such a good point that I came back to it, on redirect, to show how committed you were to Lily."

Mary's mouth went dry. "Are you serious?"

Excited, Alex nodded. "It was a freebie. If stupid Bagwell hadn't asked the question, I couldn't have scored with the answer."

Suddenly a great humming noise enveloped Mary's brain. In slow motion she watched a young girl come and put a basket of steaming tamales on their table. She wore a silver and turquoise bracelet on her left arm; a crucifix around her neck. Mary heard nothing but the humming and the echoes of what Alex had just told her. *Jonathan said you'd agreed to give up capital crimes. It was such a good point that I came back to it, on re-direct.*

"Mary?" Alex reached across the table. "Are you okay?"

For a moment all she could do was stare at her friend. Finally, she spoke in a whisper. "There's something you need to know."

"What?"

Mary pulled out the copy of the *Snitch* she'd stashed in the bottom of her purse. She'd brought the thing along as a joke, thinking Alex would get a laugh out of seeing her in a supermarket tabloid. "This."

Alex unfolded the paper. When she saw the cover, she gasped. "You're Pocahontas? You're defending this Fiddlesticks guy?"

"I didn't mean to do it … it just happened."

Alex's eyes blazed. "What do you mean it just happened? Getting drunk just happens. Getting laid might just happen. But signing on as defense counsel in a murder trial? That doesn't just happen, Mary!"

"I'm sorry. The accused is a good guy. He saved an owl Jonathan hit with the car. Anyway, I've got Dave Loveman lined up to take over as soon as he gets back from Israel."

Fierce blotches of red bloomed in Alex's cheeks. "I've talked with you nearly every day for two weeks—could you not have at least mentioned this? Like, 'oh, by the way, Al—a pal of mine just got charged with homicide, so I'm going to help him out.'"

"You told me to take a new case to get my mind off this one," cried Mary. "This just fell in my lap. All the other criminal guys in town were representing the other suspects in the case. I never dreamed you'd base your custody argument on a promise I made to Jonathan seven years ago."

"Jonathan was the one who brought it up," Alex snapped. "And he brought it up proudly, I might add."

They fell into an awkward silence. Alex gazed miserably at her plate of tamales, then finally pushed it away. "Do you realize where Bagwell could go with this?"

"Yeah. I do." Mary closed her eyes. She was beyond tears, beyond anything except feeling a great numbness inside. She'd broken her promise to Jonathan, been deceitful with Alex, now she'd just torpedoed their custody case.

"Look—maybe my testifying isn't such a good idea. Maybe I should just catch the next plane out of Tulsa and just go home."

"No," said Alex. "Then you'd look too busy to testify for custody of Lily."

"Somehow, that still sounds better than being Pocahontas in the *Snitch*," said Mary.

Alex shook her head. "Damn, Mary. Why a murder trial? Couldn't you have just written a few wills? Or entered a tennis tournament?"

Suddenly, Mary's temper flared. "Because it's what I do, what I am. A good man is being railroaded by our asshole DA. I couldn't just tell him I was sorry for his bad luck, but I promised my boyfriend that I wouldn't take any nasty cases."

"Jonathan's a little more than your boyfriend, Mary."

"I don't know what Jonathan is anymore. Whatever he is, he can get over my not doing criminal work. So can you and everybody else."

Alex sat there, mulling their options. "Can you prove this Loveman is going to take over?" she finally asked.

"I've got his emails," said Mary. "I guess you could depose him, from Israel."

"Okay," Alex replied. "This is what we'll do. If by some stretch Bagwell knows about this case, we say the accused is a friend, this is his first criminal charge, and you've already made arrangements to turn the case over to another lawyer."

"No," said Mary.

"What do you mean no? Have you've got a better idea?"

"Yeah, Alex, I do," said Mary. "The truth. Thousands of criminal attorneys raise happy, healthy children. Why can't I?"

"Good question," Alex agreed. "Maybe you should pose it to Jonathan."

"I intend to," said Mary. "And sooner than later."

THIRTY

THE SAME SUNDAY AFTERNOON found Jerry Cochran staring up at Ginger Malloy's bedroom ceiling. After a lingering brunch on the patio, they'd retired to her room where they'd made love in the sunlight, a rare treat for both of them. Now they lay drowsy, attending the chirps of young wrens and the more distant laughter of golfers as they navigated the seventh-hole rough that bordered Ginger's backyard. Though Cochran knew he should treasure the moment—the feel of her body against his, the rhythmic, slightly hypnotic sound of her breathing, his thoughts kept going back to Lisa Wilson's funeral. It had been a political extravaganza—dozens of solemn-faced governors and congressmen lining up to express their condolences to Carlisle Wilson. He hadn't known how the governor would react to him, but the old man surprised him again—offering him a leathery handshake, whispering, "You're a good man, Gerald Cochran. I always knew you'd find who did it." But all the fire had vanished from the old man's snapping black eyes, and it seemed as if the only thing holding him up was sheer resolve. Though Turpin had driven them back home delirious to be re-admitted into Wilson's good graces, the doubts that had niggled at Cochran from the first had only grown worse. Every day he grew more convinced that Lisa Wilson's real killer was running free.

Suddenly, Ginger moved. Purposefully, as if deciding that now was the time to take action, she lifted up on one elbow and pinned him with a fierce green gaze. "I need to ask you something."

"What?" he asked, surprised. He thought she'd drifted off to sleep.

She brushed back a wisp of red hair. "Are we okay?"

"What do you mean?"

"I mean, are you still into this relationship as much as you were?"

"Of course I am." He raised up and kissed her. "Why would you ask that?"

"Because I'm here snuggling against you, while you're frowning at the ceiling. Looking, I might add, as if you wanted to check your watch."

"I'm sorry," he said. "I was just thinking about Lisa Wilson's funeral."

"Oh, God. Don't tell me you're lying here dreaming of the succubus."

"The what?"

"The succubus. Jessica Rusk in her white Armani suit."

"There were three thousand people there, Ginger. I didn't notice anybody in a white suit." Cochran sighed, as if confessing something shameful. "No, I'm not happy with Stratton."

"You told Mary you were."

"I told Mary my part of the investigation was over, which officially, it is. I'm not supposed to keep working cases once Turpin's filed an indictment."

"Even when two rational, non-hysterical women hear fiddle music up at that old cabin?"

"I told you both—no threat was made against you. Hell, it was probably your dopey pal from the *Snitch*. You've got to admit, she showed up at Bigmeat's right after you two."

Ginger snorted. "Jessica's way too girly to tromp around those woods. But if you're not buying that the killer was up there, then tell me what makes you unhappy with Stratton."

He thought of that long ago, leering face in the window. The fact that even the Cherokees considered the place haunted by a ghost they called Eyes. Should he tell her that he sometimes wondered if the killer wasn't the same person who'd terrified him a quarter of a century ago? No, he decided. She would think he was insane.

"I don't know," he finally told her. "Stratton just doesn't add up."

"Well, honey, if you've got a hunch, go with it. That's what I do in the newsroom."

He traced the line of her jaw down her neck and to her shoulder. "I think will. It sounds crazy, but I feel like I owe it to Carlisle Wilson."

———

They made love once more, then he left. He drove back toward his office, thinking about the case. All the suspects they'd interviewed had alibis. None of the interns could have left the cabin by any way other than the front door. And Givens's movie had clearly shown that the only person who left by that door was Lisa Wilson.

"Which leaves Stratton," he told himself aloud. He was pondering that when he suddenly remembered Artie Slade's wacky story about Fiddlesticks still being alive and stealing road kill from their freezer.

"Could that be it?" he whispered. "Some lunatic who's been roaming around up here for years?"

Stranger things have happened, he decided. It wasn't beyond the realm of possibility. Quickly, he turned Angel around and headed west into the mountains, up to the raptor center. After parking in front of the incongruous totem pole, he walked toward Stratton's cabin. As he crested the final curve in the gravel drive, he saw Jenkins and Slade, sitting on Stratton's porch. Jenkins was plucking the strings of a fiddle while Slade sat wearing his nasty Braves cap, blowing smoke rings from a cigarette.

"Good afternoon, gentlemen," Cochran called.

They both shot up like school boys caught in mid-mischief. Slade crunched his cigarette out on the porch while Jenkins stood awkwardly, holding his fiddle in front of his crotch.

"Hidy, sheriff," said the more amiable Slade. "What brings you up here? Does Nick need something at the jail?"

"Not that I know of," said Cochran. "I wanted to talk to you."

"Me?" Slade pointed to himself with his mangled hand.

"Both of you." Cochran walked up the steps to the porch. Slade smiled, squinting beneath his cap; Jenkins looked as if Cochran were a rattlesnake about to strike. "I wanted to ask you two about the guy who steals road kill from your freezer."

Jenkins gave a derisive chuckle. "That's Artie's ghost. I ain't had no truck with him."

Cochran turned to the older man. "You want to tell me about this guy?"

"I can probably show you better'n tell you."

"Okay," said Cochran. "Show me."

"Come on, then." Artie hobbled down the porch steps and started limping toward the bird barn. Cochran fell into step beside him.

"Mostly, I see that feller in the summertime, at the edge of the woods, when the leaves are thick," Artie began. "I've never seen him in winter, nor in early spring. I used to think he lived back in some holler, but now I think maybe he goes back and forth from somewhere else. Like a bird, you know?"

Wonderful, thought Cochran, *a migratory maniac*. "What does he look like?"

"He's probably your height, but thinner. Everything about him looks gray—his clothes, his hair—he's got a scraggly old beard."

"Does he carry a weapon?"

"Not that I've seen."

"How old does he look?"

"He ain't no spring chicken," said Slade. "Fifty, at least."

"You drink a lot?" asked Cochran.

"Not a drop in five years," Artie replied proudly. "That drinkin' cost me a leg."

"How's that?"

"I tried to climb up Nick's hacking stand one night after I'd had too much. Halfway up the ladder I fell. Broke my heel in three places. Gimped along ever since."

"Aren't those things thirty feet high?" asked Cochran.

Artie nodded. "Every bit."

"Then I guess it's a good thing you didn't make it to the top," said Cochran. "Otherwise, you'd be dead."

As they neared the bird barn, Slade veered off to one side, heading to the back of the building. Sticktights and poison ivy grew waist-high, making passage difficult. Slade pushed his way along a narrow path, then pointed up into a small gap in the tree line, fifty yards away. "I always see him there, eyeing this barn."

"Have you seen him lately?"

"I saw him early summer. The opossums were out with their babies. A lot of them don't make it across the road, so our freezers were pretty full. I came down here to thaw out some mice and half the opossums were gone."

"And you think this guy stole them?"

"Well, I know the birds didn't eat 'em. And them interns would've fainted if you'd served them up an opossum."

So would I, thought Cochran. "Did you tell Stratton?"

Slade shook his head. "Everybody rides me enough about Fiddlesticks, as it is. You heard Jenkins a few minutes ago. 'That's Artie's ghost'," he mimicked in a quavery falsetto. "'I ain't had no truck with him!'"

Cochran frowned. "So nobody but you ever sees this guy?"

"I'm the only one who ever comes over here!" cried Artie. "Them kids are scared of snakes, scared of poison ivy. Jenkins was supposed to grub all this out, but ever since Nick's been gone, all he does is sit on his lazy ass and play that damn fiddle."

Inching past the treacherous green vines, Cochran made his way to where Slade claimed to have seen the road-kill thief. He saw some mashed pine needles that might indicate where someone had sat or stood for a while, but beyond that, he saw only the same thick forest that covered the mountains.

Cochran turned to Slade, who'd limped up there behind him. "So would you say this guy is a woodsman?"

"I reckon so. Not many folks can just ooze in and out of the shadows like that."

"But he's never said anything to you?"

"Not a word. He just stands and stares with those queer eyes."

Cochran's heart skipped a beat. "Queer eyes?"

Slade made two circles with his thumbs and index fingers. "They're big as saucers. Something ain't right about them."

For a long moment Cochran stood there. This was the third time eyes had come up. First the face in the window, then Saunooke's ghost, now this phantom that appeared every summer to steal road kill from Stratton's freezer. *Somebody's out there*, he told himself. *Somebody's been out there, maybe for years. And doing what? Killing girls and carving other messages into their skin? Doing other things we have no name for? God only knows*, he thought.

THIRTY-ONE

OKLAHOMA WAS FLATTER THAN Mary had ever imagined. Though she remembered the fourth grade, when Lena Owle returned from visiting her Western relatives and told everyone how you could see all the way to the Rocky Mountains, Mary hadn't appreciated the unremitting flatness of the land. As she and Alex drove along, she felt as if she were some tiny ant, uncovered and vulnerable, scrambling for the refuge of a tree or a rock or a fallen log. She was glad that her mother's ancestors had hidden in the mountains while the soldiers rousted the rest of the tribe to Oklahoma.

"When was the last time you talked to Jonathan?" asked Alex, her eyes hidden behind dark sunglasses.

"Yesterday. He said you made Fred Moon look like a fool."

She laughed. "I never thought Bagwell would let it pass, but I asked him if he could produce the newspaper article he'd shown Lily. I was just fishing, but he pulled the thing out of his wallet."

"What paper was it?" asked Mary, remembering that bit of nastiness.

Alex snorted. "An op-ed piece he wrote for his hometown news!"

They laughed, though it wasn't really funny. Young Lily had assumed Moon's biased opinion was a straight news story—proof in black and white that Mary had killed her mother.

Alex broke the little silence that had sprung between them. "Does Jonathan know about the *Snitch*?"

Mary shook her head. "I doubt that he knows what the *Snitch* even is."

"Are you going to tell him about it?"

"I guess I'll have to," she replied uncomfortably. She looked at her old friend. "I don't guess there's any chance you could get him to stay away from court tomorrow?"

Alex gave her a knowing smile. "So you won't have to tell him at all?"

"I'm going to tell him," insisted Mary. "I'd just like to get through my testimony first."

"Mary, the man hasn't missed a minute of this case. If I were you, I'd break the news to him before you go to court. I'm sure Laura Bagwell reads those scandal rags in the grocery line like everybody else."

———

An hour later, Mary checked into her room at the motel. She saw Jonathan immediately, from her window. He was swimming laps in the pool, his long body glistening in the sun. She smiled at his concession to a bright yellow bathing suit—back home he swam, during the day, in cut-off jeans. At night, after Lily was asleep, they used to swim naked. How good he'd felt then—his muscles hard, his touch

271

knowing, his laugh low and easy as they glided first through the water, then later into each other, the dark creek buoying them, holding them as if they were something rare and precious. They had been, too, she realized. What a shame they were no longer.

"He's a beautiful man," said Alex, coming up behind her. "And one of the best fathers I've ever seen."

"He loves his child above all else," Mary replied, turning her gaze to Lily, who sat at a table shaded by a white umbrella, playing cards with a young woman. "Who's Lily's friend?"

"Cecilia Guarano, the best custody-case kid-minder in all of Texas."

"Does Lily like her?" Mary wondered if Lily was capable of liking anybody these days.

"Lily adores her. Cecilia doesn't have a dog in this fight."

Mary nodded, understanding how Lily might feel like a plug of taffy at a taffy pull. "Looks like she's teaching her poker."

"Texas Hold 'em." Alex laughed. "Lily's getting pretty good, too. I think she cleaned Cecilia out Friday."

"You think they'll call Lily to the stand?"

"Bagwell might if she gets desperate."

"Wonder what she would say," said Mary, turning back to the window.

"Good question." Alex gave a caustic laugh. "Lily may look exactly like her mother, but you know who she reminds me of?"

"Who?"

"You."

"Me?" Mary looked at her, astonished.

"She's smart and sweet, but she never lets you know what's going on behind her eyes." Alex laughed again. "She could be a hell of a lawyer some day."

"Did you know she hates me?" asked Mary, watching as Lily played a final card from her hand and gathered all the poker chips to her side of the table.

"Yeah. I also know she's just a kid, and a very confused one, to boot."

"I know, I know." Closing her eyes against her tears, Mary turned back to Alex. "Look, you've got to do me one more favor. Could you take Lily out tonight? I need to talk to Jonathan, alone."

"The big Fiddlesticks talk?"

Mary nodded, though the thought of it made her go cold inside.

"Okay." Alex nodded approvingly. "How about I go tell Jonathan you're here, sotto voce. While I'm down there, I'll suggest pizza and a movie to Lily and Cecilia."

"Thanks." Smiling gratefully, Mary added one final request. "Don't let Lily know I'm here, okay?"

"I won't." Alex put an arm around Mary's shoulders. "Don't worry, girl. We'll get through this."

———

Mary stared out the window, watching as Alex made her way out to the pool. She had a quick word with Jonathan, who frowned at the motel, then she strode over and spoke to Cecilia and Lily. Lily jumped up from her poker game excited, skipping over to Jonathan. The two conferred for a minute, then they all headed inside the motel, leaving Jonathan lying beside the pool. Mary stood there until she heard footsteps down the hall, a soft thump on her door that she knew was Alex. She waited a while longer, then more footsteps passed by her door again, this time going in the opposite direction.

"Lily, did you tell your dad we'd be back late?" Alex asked in a loud voice as they passed by.

"I told him we were going to the movies," the little girl replied, her voice high and piping. "I told him I'd be with you."

Hearing Lily's voice caught Mary off guard. How many times had she heard similar words directed at her? *Mary, I'm going to soccer practice with Jennifer Holmes. I'll be back after supper. Mary, can I go to Debra's sleepover on Friday night?* It was hard to believe that the child now hated her, blamed her fully for her mother's death.

"How have we come to this, Lily?" she whispered, fighting an urge to rush out into the hall and grab the little girl up in her arms. Tell her that she loved her, that she would never do anything to hurt her.

But that would not be the thing to do. Certainly not now, maybe even never. Now she had to work things out with the father before she could come anywhere near the child.

She was standing there, wondering what she was going to say to Jonathan when she heard another, softer, knock on her door. She went over and peered through the peephole. He stood there, hair slicked back from swimming, dressed in jeans and a blue shirt. With her heart thudding, she opened the door. He looked even better than he had in the pool. The sun had further bronzed his skin, and the small pooch of a belly that had begun to bloom at home had vanished. He looked now as lean as he had in high school.

"Hey," she said, her voice sticky in her throat. "Long time, no see."

"Yeah," he replied. "How about that?"

He made no move to enter her room, so she stepped back and held the door open. "Want to come in?"

He stepped inside, awkward, then opened his arms, holding her as if she were made of glass.

"It's okay, Jonathan," she said, rubbing his back, trying to ease the tension in his body. "It's only me."

"No, it's not," he said, his voice muffled. "It's never only you."

She started to ask him what he meant, but suddenly, he kissed her. Just as he had before—before Fred Moon, before Ruth Moon, before any of it—back when the only moon they knew was the one that rose over Snowcrop Mountain, a huge yellow disk that seemed to smile down on their secrets. She kissed him back, hungry for the taste of him in her mouth, the feel of him in her arms. She lifted her hands to cradle the back of his head then felt his arms drop low; his hands inside the waist of her jeans, his fingers loosening the zipper. In one swift motion he peeled away her jeans and underpants; in another he lifted her sweater and unhooked her bra. For a moment she stood before him naked, naked as she had that first time in the woods, so long ago. Then he joined her, shucking his own clothes off into a pile on the floor. He took her in his arms, carried her to the bed. They stretched full-length across the mattress, his flesh warming hers, his hands caressing her breasts; his mouth on her nipples. Fingers, legs, arms intertwined as easily as always, then he was inside her, his motion familiar but also unaccustomed, as if sex were a sport she'd once loved but hadn't played in years.

They made love twice in bed, then moved to the shower. He lathered her with motel soap, his hands slick as the minnows that brushed lightly against them when they swam in the shallows of the river. *We need to talk*, she tried to remind herself as they stood front to back, his hands caressing her breasts. *I need to tell him about Fiddlesticks.*

But Fiddlesticks seemed far away; another woman's trouble, a lonely woman's life. *I'll tell him later*, she promised herself. *After we've finished.*

But they didn't finish for a long time. They dried off and moved back into the bedroom, wrapping up in each other's arms all over again. It was as if he wanted to make up for all those nights at home, when he would turn his back to her, while she lay awake haunted and wondering. His kisses did not stop until they heard the ding of the elevator, then Lily's voice in the hall. "Do you think Daddy's asleep?"

As Alex murmured something Mary could not understand, Jonathan rolled off the bed and reached for his clothes.

"Do you have to go?" she asked, her skin feeling electric.

"Yeah," he replied brusquely.

Mary rose up on one elbow. "Jonathan, Lily knows we do this."

"She doesn't know you're here."

"I don't understand—why would that matter?"

"It's hard to explain." Suddenly pale beneath his tan, he zipped his jeans, pulled on his shirt.

She sat up in bed, covering herself with the sheet. "Then let me take a guess. You're afraid that if Lily knows that life with you will include me, she'll want to live with the Moons."

He gave a bitter laugh. "You aren't Mary Crow for nothing, are you?"

"It doesn't take much to put that together."

He came over and sat on the edge of the bed, ran his hands through his hair. "I don't know what to say."

Suddenly, she loved him more than she ever had and then with equal suddenness, she realized how impossible everything had become. He loved his child without reservation. He loved her, too, but within certain parameters. "Maybe there's nothing to say," she whispered.

"*Koga*," he used the old Cherokee word for crow as he lifted sad eyes to meet hers. "I love—

"It's okay," she said, interrupting him, not wanting to hear about who he loved. She knew that, already. "Maybe it's better not to talk anymore tonight."

"Maybe not," he said, leaning over to kiss her again. "Anyway, I'll see you in court tomorrow."

"Why don't you take the day off?" she suggested quickly. "Take Lily fishing. You've heard everything I have to say, a hundred times over."

He shook his head, his expression growing hawkish. "I wouldn't miss you taking on Fred Moon for the world. I want to watch you put the lie to his shit, once and for all."

She started to tremble, knowing that she should tell him about Fiddlesticks, knowing that Alex wanted no surprises in court, but she couldn't do it. If she told him that now, all their lovemaking would become farce. "Okay, then," she finally said. "I guess I'll see you tomorrow."

He kissed her once more, then he let himself out the door. She listened as his footsteps padded down the hall, then she reached over and turned on the light. She sat up in bed and listened to the thudding of her own heart, every beat bringing her a little closer to tomorrow, when she would raise her hand and swear to tell the truth about all the things she'd lied about today.

THIRTY-TWO

SHE AWOKE WITH THE memory of his body—his fingers on her skin, his breath tickling her neck, his long warmth enveloping her. She reached across the bed for him from years of practice; finding it empty came again as a surprise. She opened her eyes, saw tousled sheets, an anonymous motel room. For an instant she felt adrift in strange surroundings—then it all came back. Jonathan. Lily. Oklahoma. *Court.*

"Dear God," she whispered, remembering the night before. She'd planned to tell him about the Fiddlesticks case, had started to half a dozen times, but each time he would make love to her again, and then he'd left to go to Lily. "I didn't tell him. He still doesn't know."

She closed her eyes, imagining a courtroom, a rabbit-faced attorney waving a copy of the *Snitch* with her picture in it. *Aren't you involved in this case, Ms. Crow? Aren't you defending a man accused of mutilating this girl? Doesn't that dump your oh-so-noble promise to Mr. Walkingstick in the garbage can?* The lawyer would wave the tabloid in front of the judge, snidely paint her as a liar. She knew she would—it was exactly what she would do, were she representing the Moons.

She grabbed the phone, called Jonathan's room. *Maybe he can get away for five minutes,* she thought, *and leave Lily with the woman who's taking care of her.* The phone rang, but no one answered. She finally gave up and called Alex.

"Hey," she said when her old friend picked up the phone. "Do you know where Jonathan is?"

"He took Lily out for breakfast," she replied. "I think they wanted some father-daughter time, alone."

"Oh."

"Are you okay?"

"I'm fine," said Mary. There was no point in revealing any of this to Alex. She had enough on her plate already.

"Well, I'm taking Jonathan to court early. Sam Hodges will pick you up about quarter to nine. He wears one of those Cherokee turbans, so don't freak out."

"Okay—see you later." Mary hung up the phone, tempted to laugh. A man wearing a turban was the least of her worries.

She made a pot of coffee and took a quick shower. As she soaped her body, she again remembered the feel of Jonathan, next to her. "This will be okay," she tried to convince herself. "He'll see you were just doing your job."

Which was true, up to a point, she decided as she toweled off. And that point was Lily. If her involvement in the Fiddlesticks case hurt his chances of keeping Lily, then he would never forgive her.

"And what then?" she asked her reflection in the mirror. "Do I beg for mercy and go back to writing wills for the next ten years?"

The answer came swiftly, just as it had yesterday when she and Alex were having lunch. But now she had no time to deal with it. Instead she brushed her teeth and started dressing for court.

———

Twenty minutes later, someone knocked on her door. Hoping it might be Jonathan, she answered it quickly. A short, broad-faced man in a red and black turban stood in the hall, smiling.

"*Sheeoh*," he greeted her in Cherokee.

"Hi," she replied in English. She was sick of Cherokee, sick of the Moons, sick of this whole business. "You must be Sam."

He nodded. "*Ahyol diza*?"

"Fine, thanks. How are you?"

"I'm fine. Don't you speak Tsalagi?"

"Not before court," she snapped. "Catch me some other time, and I'll Tsalagi your ear off."

"Sorry." He shrugged. "Are you ready to go?"

"Just about." She walked over and grabbed her purse, checking herself in the mirror. Sapphire blue suit that brushed the tops of her knees, modest heels, and pearls. It was pretty in an afternoon tea sort of way, but so unlike her usual sexy court suits that she felt odd walking out the door in it. *Mary Crow as docile little help mate,* she thought, fighting back another laugh. If anybody in that courtroom bought that, she'd put on a turban and whistle Dixie.

They drove to Tahlequah, Sam filling her in on the trial.

"So how did Jonathan come across?" Mary asked him.

"Good, for the most part. Good provider, caring to the point of being a bit over-protective, but who's going to blame a father for that these days?"

"Nobody I know," said Mary.

"I actually thought the judge was going to rule Friday, for you guys. But Bagwell wanted to continue. Alex was already beginning to feel like you were the missing piece, so she jumped at the chance to get you out here." Sam looked at her. "Looks like it's all up to you, now."

———

They finally reached Tahlequah. Sam dropped her off in front of the courthouse and she rode the elevator up to the third floor, where Cherokee County family court was held, the Honorable Diane Haddad presiding.

She peeked in the door before she went inside. The Moons' half of the courtroom was filled with short, broad people wearing everything from suits to cowboy outfits. On the other side of the aisle, Jonathan and Alex sat alone. She opened the door. Though she'd planned to walk in a demure, wouldn't-hurt-a-fly gait, she changed her mind, walking in her regular, take-no-prisoners stride. She noticed heads turning as she passed, a low murmur going up from the Moons' side of the courtroom.

"I knew that was you." Alex stood up and hugged her when she reached their table. "Only Killer Crow would walk in here like that, spurs jingling."

"Old habits die hard." Mary hugged Alex, then turned to Jonathan. "How are you doing, Mr. Walkingstick?"

He wrapped her in a fierce embrace. "Ready to come back to you," he whispered.

"Me, too," she told him. She considered pulling him aside, telling him quickly about Fiddlesticks, but just as she started to take his arm, Judge Haddad swept into the room. The rest of the courtroom stood up as round two of Moon v. Walkingstick began.

———

Alex called her to the stand first, asked her the questions she wanted the judge to hear. Mary went on how much she loved Lily, how devoted she was to Jonathan and his child, how they had a good life in North Carolina. Then it was Laura Bagwell's turn. A skinny, beige woman with weak-looking eyes, she began her questioning from the plaintiff's table, as if she feared getting too close to Mary Crow.

"It's nice to see you, Ms. Crow. We're glad you finally decided to join us," she said, her sarcasm biting. "Just so I'm clear—how long have you and Mr. Walkingstick been married?"

"Mr. Walkingstick and I are not married. We've lived together for the past seven years."

"So doesn't that make you his common-law wife?" Laura Bagwell made it sound as if they lived in a dump and kept pit bulls chained up in their front yard.

"Actually not," said Mary. "North Carolina no longer recognizes common law marriage."

"So that would mean you're not married at all?"

"No, we are not."

Bagwell frowned. "Well, you just testified that you're quite devoted to Mr. Walkingstick and his daughter. Is there any reason that you two haven't married? Or you haven't petitioned to adopt Lily Walkingstick?"

"No," said Mary, unflustered. "It just never seemed necessary."

"Really?" Laura Bagwell made a note on a piece of paper. "So you think it's proper for a child to be raised by parents who feel that marriage and adoption are just silly formalities?"

"I believe there are more important factors in child-rearing than a marriage license," said Mary.

Laura Bagwell smiled. "And what would you consider those factors to be, Ms. Crow?"

"Love. Kindness. Meeting a child's needs."

"And you think you've helped Mr. Walkingstick meet Lily's needs?"

"Yes, I do. Until a few weeks ago, Lily was a happy child who was comfortable with her family and friends."

"And what do you think happened that made Lily change?"

Mary looked directly at the tubby little Cherokee couple seated next to Laura Bagwell. If she could get this next testimony out on the table, Alex might gain some ground with it on cross. "Lily spent the month of June with Fred and Dulcy Moon. She returned home convinced that nine years ago I killed her mother in a fit of jealousy, and that I have ever since hidden the true nature of my actions. Lily was, when she came back home, a changed and troubled child. "

Laura Bagwell fumbled with her papers, flustered. Mary gave Alex a quick smile, knowing she'd just taken Bagwell's lead away— now all she could do was follow where the witness led. *Sister, you have messed with the wrong Indian*, Mary thought gleefully.

"Uh, okay." Bagwell tried to recover. "Ms. Crow, do Mr. Walkingstick and his daughter live with you, in your house?"

"Yes."

"And you supply health insurance for them?"

"I do."

"And I assume you provide clothing for Lily, food for the family as well?"

"Partially. Mr. Walkingstick shares in those expenses."

"So Mr. Walkingstick does contribute something, to the family?" Bagwell's tone implied laziness on Jonathan's part, as if he slept till noon, then drank beer until suppertime.

"Mr. Walkingstick contributes quite a bit," said Mary. "He is Lily's primary caregiver."

"So in your family, the traditional roles are reversed—you go out and work, while Mr. Walkingstick tends the home front."

"Mr. Walkingstick's work is seasonal, so it's a successful arrangement for us."

"And you have a law firm?" asked Bagwell.

Here it comes. Mary's heart beat faster. "I'm in partnership with Sam Ravenel."

"And what sort of practice do you have?"

"A general practice."

"Wills, real estate closings, that sort of thing?"

"Yes."

"But no criminal work?"

"Rarely."

"Rarely?" Bagwell pretended to check her notes. "According to Mr. Walkingstick, you agreed not to do any criminal work as long as Lily lived with you."

"I did make that promise." Mary shifted uncomfortably in her chair. She knew where Bagwell was going.

"Do you recognize this, Ms. Crow?"

Mary's heart sank as Bagwell held up the issue of the *Snitch* that showed Mary and Nick Stratton fending off reporters. She showed the paper first to the judge, then to Jonathan and Alex. Alex's expression did not change, but Jonathan looked as if every drop of blood had evaporated from his body.

"Well, Ms. Crow? I ask again, do you recognize this?"

"Yes," Mary replied.

"Though this tabloid does, regrettably, refer to you as Pocahontas, is this not your picture?"

Mary swallowed hard. "It is."

Bagwell paused, holding the paper in front of Jonathan. "This is one of the most grisly murders I've ever read about, Ms. Crow. And they quote you on page 33, as saying, 'My client is innocent of all charges and looks forward to exonerating himself in court.'"

"I'm not quite as familiar as you are with the *Snitch*, but that sounds like something I probably said."

"That's a pretty strange quote for someone who claims to do only will and estate closings."

A smug, gotcha rumble went through the Moons' side of the courtroom. Mary sat still, tamping down the growing panic she felt inside.

"In fact, Ms. Crow, for someone who made a promise not to take criminal cases, I'd say you're either a sneak or a liar."

Alex leapt to her feet. "Your Honor, we don't need Ms. Bagwell to start name-calling."

The judge shot Bagwell a warning glance. "Be respectful, Ms. Bagwell."

Bagwell turned the *Snitch* to the page with Lisa Wilson's body and slowly walked it in front of the courtroom. "Just for the record, Ms. Crow. Are you or are you not representing the man who's been indicted for this murder?"

"Until the accused's chief counsel returns from Israel, yes," Mary said calmly. "I am."

Suddenly, Fred Moon stood up and pointed a finger at Mary. "All you are is death, Mary Crow. First to my Ruth, next to my Lily!"

The room erupted. Alex jumped up, objecting, then the court officer moved to restrain Fred Moon. Smiling at the ruckus she'd caused, Laura Bagwell dropped the *Snitch* on the table while the judge banged her gavel. Mary turned her gaze toward Jonathan, hoping to find some understanding in his eyes, but all she saw was his back as he walked down the center aisle of the courtroom, striding toward the door.

THIRTY-THREE

MARY WAS DESPERATE TO follow him and explain. *Nick Stratton is innocent, I couldn't turn him down. I'm turning the case over to Dave Loveman. I have emails to prove that.* But she couldn't leave. Court was still in session, and though Laura Bagwell was currently finished with her, she might be recalled to the stand. Reluctantly, she took Jonathan's seat at the defendant's table.

"Where did he go?" she leaned over and whispered to Alex.

"Out for air, probably. Don't worry—Sam will take care of him."

That calmed her a bit. Jonathan would need to walk off his anger, settle his nerves. Sam would bring him back when he calms down.

She returned her attention to court, where Bagwell was about to start her summation.

"Your Honor, I think we've painted an extremely clear picture of this case. On one hand, you have Fred and Dulcy Moon—two decent, hard-working, long-married people who want to raise their daughter's only child in a healthy environment of love and honesty." She walked over and pointed toward Mary. "On the other hand, you have Jonathan Walkingstick and Mary Crow—two people who have scoffed at marriage, scoffed at adoption, scoffed at being honest with Lily about her mother's tragic death. Even now they scoff—Ms. Crow by flaunting a broken promise in a national tabloid, Mr. Walkingstick by storming out of court when the most important decision of his life is about to be rendered."

Damn, Mary thought, *why did he have to leave?*

Bagwell walked slowly back to the plaintiff's table. "True, Fred and Dulcy have had their difficulties in the past. But they realized their mistakes and they've struggled hard to overcome them. For years they've been sober, upstanding members of their church, their tribe, and their community." Bagwell held out her hands, pleading. "It seems particularly unfair that these good, hard-working citizens must not only grieve for their daughter, but must also live, every day, with the knowledge that their daughter's killer is now raising their only grandchild."

"I didn't kill Ruth!" Mary whispered to Alex. "The woman had a gun pointed at my heart!"

"I know." Alex grabbed Mary's arm in a death grip. "Shut up!"

"All we are asking is that Fred and Dulcy Moon be allowed to bring up this beautiful little girl in a stable environment of love and respect, rather than the duplicitous, secret-ridden world of Jonathan Walkingstick and Mary Crow."

Bagwell went on for a few more beats, extolling the virtues of the Moons, the proximity of other close relatives, the sense of tribe Lily would enjoy in Oklahoma, then she sat down. Now, it was Alex's turn. Mary watched, nervous, as her leggy friend rose from her chair. She walked straight over to the Moons, and gave them a brilliant smile.

"Your Honor, I have absolutely no doubt that Fred and Dulcy Moon are people who have sought to better themselves. It takes an enormous amount of courage to dry out and remain sober, if you're an alcoholic. An equal amount of discipline to start resolving conflicts with your words rather than your fists. I can empathize with their grief at losing their daughter at such a young age; I can also understand their desire to raise their grandchild in what they consider a healthier atmosphere. What I don't believe the Moons have is the wisdom to discern what is best for this child."

Her heart thudding, Mary watched as Alex walked back to their side of the courtroom.

"American jurisprudence has always sought to keep biological families together. And what is best for this particular child is to remain with her biological father in North Carolina. Though the Walkingstick-Crow family may not be a traditional one, it is one of love and devotion to Lily Bird Walkingstick." Alex walked over and picked up a sheaf of papers. "Lily is a straight A student at John Ross Elementary school, she's the co-captain of her soccer team, and was the top seller of Girl Scout cookies for Brownie troop 112. Worthy achievements for a nine-year-old, would you not say?" Alex turned to look at the Moons. "Even her grandparents are smiling at that. Worthy achievements that indicate Lily is smart, Lily is well-liked by peers, that Lily is developing a strong sense of responsibility. This shows me that Lily is a happy child, a product of a happy home. Not a home built of lies. Not a home full of guilt or deception. Certainly not the home Ms. Bagwell portrayed."

Alex moved to block the sight of Jonathan's empty chair and pointed to Mary. "In this case, much has been made of Mary Crow's jealousy of Ruth Moon. I think not enough has been made of Ruth Moon's jealousy of Mary Crow, and her own actions that night.

Ruth Moon had already drugged Jonathan Walkingstick into a stupor and had attempted to drug Mary. Though she was mentally unbalanced at that tragic time, she clearly intended that Mary Crow die. She pointed a loaded pistol at Mary Crow's chest, at point-blank range. And as heartsick as the Moons are over their daughter's death, they need to remember that their Ruth was the perpetrator of this terrible act. Mary Crow was simply defending herself against a woman who had gone, sadly, insane."

Mary held her breath. Never had she heard Alex speak so eloquently.

"We maintain that both Jonathan Walkingstick and Mary Crow have provided a caring, nurturing environment that has given Lily strong roots. We respectfully ask the court to allow them to continue doing just that, so that Lily Bird Walkingstick can grow equally strong wings and soar into a happy, productive adulthood that both her parents and grandparents can be proud of."

Alex returned to her seat. Mary reached over and squeezed her arm. "Perfect," she whispered. "Absolutely perfect."

"Let's hope the court is so moved," Alex whispered back.

They turned their attention to the judge, who was pecking on her laptop. The moments stretched out, longer and longer; finally she looked up.

"This case is not an easy, clear decision. Both sides have strong arguments, and I feel like I've been asked to choose between reason and passion. Though this is not a tribal court, there are tribal precedents and traditions I'd like to take into consideration. That being said, let's reconvene at ten tomorrow morning."

After that, court adjourned. Everyone rose as Haddad left the bench and returned to her office. Mary stood there, frozen in place. Though she had risen for judicial egress probably a thousand times in her career, this time it felt different. This time she wasn't just a hired gun in the proceedings. This time, she had skin in the game. A lot of it. She turned to Alex.

"I don't know whether to laugh or cry."

Alex began gathering up her papers, a look of disgust on her face. "I was so hoping Haddad would call it today. Now it's one more night on pins and needles."

Mary looked around the courtroom. Jonathan was still not there. "I wonder where Jonathan went."

Alex turned to her, an odd look in her eyes. "You didn't tell him about Fiddlesticks, did you?"

Mary shook her head. "The right time never came along . . . "

"That's a shame," said Alex.

"Why? Did he say anything?"

"He didn't have to. I just watched his hands. His fists were clenched so hard his knuckles went white." Alex snapped her briefcase shut. "Come on, let's go."

Mary stared at the vacant bench, bracketed by Old Glory and the blue flag of Oklahoma. By this time tomorrow they would know. By this time tomorrow maybe he could start to forgive her.

She and Alex turned and headed for the door. Though most of the Moon entourage had filed out of the courtroom, Fred and Dulcy remained seated at the plaintiff's table, talking softly with Laura Bagwell. Mary considered going over there, telling them how sorry she was about Ruth's death, apologizing for whatever role they thought she'd played in it. She started toward them, then stopped. She was sick of apologizing. To the Moons, to Jonathan, to herself. She was a good attorney, a good person who'd nearly been killed by a crazy woman. Screw the Moons.

Alex nudged her. "You ready to go? Or do you want to gaze at Fred and Dulcy a few more minutes?"

"I'm way past ready," said Mary, turning her back on the couple. "Let's get out of here."

———

They left the courtroom together. Since they saw no one waiting for them, Alex guessed that Sam Hodges had taken Jonathan back to Tulsa. "I had Sam waiting just for this situation," she explained. "I figured I might need to keep Jonathan corralled."

"Good thinking," Mary agreed. She turned to her friend. "Listen, your summation was brilliant. Whatever else happens, I thank you for putting those words in the record."

Alex frowned. "If I'd been all that brilliant we'd have a judgment now."

Mary knew how she felt, from hundreds of her own summations. "You did a superb job, Al. Like I said, whatever happens, happens."

They sped back to the motel in a comfortable silence. They both knew from experience that there was no point in re-hashing the court proceedings. Bagwell had scored some blows; Alex had scored some counter-punches. Now it was all up to Judge Haddad.

"What do you want to do this afternoon?" asked Alex as she pulled into the motel parking lot.

"I guess I'd better have that talk with Jonathan," said Mary. "I'd also like to see Lily."

"They're probably at the swimming pool."

Mary followed Alex through the lobby, then out to the pool. Though the aqua water glistened in the sun, it was empty of swimmers, empty of people altogether, except for Lily's pal Cecilia, who lay on a chaise lounge, reading. She looked up when she saw Mary and Alex coming toward her.

"Hey," she said, smiling. "How did it go?"

"We won't know until tomorrow," said Alex. "Where are Jonathan and Lily?"

"Lily scraped her toe on the bottom of the pool. Jonathan took her up to their room to put some medicine on it."

Alex turned to Mary. "Maybe now would be a good time for you to go up there. Talk to them alone."

Mary nodded. "Good idea. I'll see you two in a little while."

Leaving Alex with Cecilia, Mary headed for the elevator. Jonathan, she knew, would be angry over her murder case. How Lily now felt about her she had no idea. Two months ago, she would have said the child loved her as her own mother. But that was two months ago—a lifetime for a nine-year-old. She pressed the elevator button, wondering what tack she should take. Apology? Appeasement?

"Just see how she feels, first," she said to herself. "Then you can start your fence-mending from there."

The elevator carried her up to the third floor. She walked down the thickly carpeted hall, past her room, finally coming to the suite that Jonathan and Lily shared with Alex. Taking a deep breath, she knocked on the door. The door swung open a bit, as if the latch hadn't caught. Opening it farther, she called to them.

"Jonathan? Lily? Are you okay?"

No one answered. *They must be in the bathroom*, she thought, opening the door a little wider.

"Jonathan?" she called again. "Are you guys okay?"

Again, she heard nothing. Holding on to the doorknob, she peeked inside the room. "Jonathan?"

The only thing she heard was a slight rattle as the air conditioning unit came on. She stepped into the room. Though the beds were made and damp towels hung over the shower curtain rod, the room was empty. No Jonathan. No Lily. No luggage, either. Nothing except a note underneath the telephone, scribbled in Jonathan's hand. She picked it up, trembling as she read his words.

I can't let the Moons have Lily. I hope you understand.
—Jonathan

THIRTY-FOUR

"I THINK YOU'RE BECOMING obsessed." Eleanor Cochran peered at her son as he sat glued to the computer screen.

"Really?" Jerry replied absently.

"Jerry, you're working on a closed case. Stratton's been indicted. He's awaiting trial. Yet when I went to bed at one thirty last night, you were still on that computer."

"Uh-huh."

"You and Ginger haven't had a fight have you?"

"No."

"Then why aren't you over at her house? You used to spend practically every night over there."

"We're both busy."

"Busy doing what?"

"She's writing about mountain music. I'm working on the Wilson case."

"Forgive my aged, chemo-addled brain, but as I said five seconds ago, hasn't Nick Stratton already been indicted for that girl's murder?"

Cochran took a deep breath and rolled his chair back from the desk, his eyes gritty with fatigue. He wondered how much he should share with his mother. With her new writing career, everything served as grist for her next plot. He wouldn't want to see this case thinly disguised in the paperback racks. On the other hand—his mother was a bright woman. Maybe running his theory by a mystery writer wasn't such a bad idea. "I'll tell you what I think, but you'll have to keep it confidential."

"Okay."

"I'm serious, Ma. No telling your agent or your writer cousin from Philly."

"I won't tell anybody, Jerry. I promise."

"It just seems improbable that a smart, successful, law-abiding guy would lure a girl into the woods, strangle her, carve indecipherable letters into her skin, then the next morning make an extremely public appearance at the sports park opening. I mean, why go to the trouble? Why not just push her off a waterfall at the end of the summer?"

"Because if he did that, you would immediately suspect foul play. You're always suspicious of waterfall deaths." Eleanor shook her head. "What he's set up now is perfect—he's miles away, the girl's killed at a haunted cabin, with strange figures cut into her body. Her pals don't find her until he's safely away, getting ready to fly his eagle. It's brilliant. He doesn't even need an alibi with a time frame like that."

Cochran frowned. "It's too dicey, Ma."

"So what's your theory?"

"I'm thinking there's some kind of connection to the Fiddlesticks cabin."

"Jerry, that was fifty years ago!" She gave him the same look of disgust she'd had when he was fifteen and wanted to join Streptococcus, Ricky Joyner's garage band.

"It's just a theory, Ma." Knowing how his mother loved charts, he took a piece of paper from the printer. "Let's say whoever killed Lisa Wilson was either connected to her or connected to that cabin." He drew a stick figure of a girl. "Everybody connected with her is accounted for—we've got a video that proves none of the interns left the cabin that night, Willy Jenkins was in Tennessee, and Artie Slade was playing pinochle with his brother. Even her ex-boyfriend was banding birds in Costa Rica."

"What about Stratton?" asked his mother.

"Stratton claims to have been at home alone, that entire night. But for argument's sake, let's say it's not Stratton." He drew a figure of a house. "Let's assume some mountain-man type killer has connected himself to that house. The interns thought they saw a gray man that night at the cabin. Artie Slade claims there's a gray man who stands at the edge of the forest and stares at him with abnormally wide eyes. Rob Saunooke told me that the Cherokees think a ghost named Eyes haunts that cabin. Even Butch Messer and I saw something weird up there, back in junior high school."

She frowned. "When did you and Butch Messer go to the Fiddlesticks cabin?"

He told her about Messer and Pearl Ann Reynolds and their ill-fated trip to steal condoms. She listened, fascinated.

"We were looking around the living room when suddenly, a face popped up in the window. A man, grinning. He had these wide, awful eyes."

"What did you do?"

"We jumped back on Butch's motor bike and rode like hell. I had nightmares for months."

"You never told me."

"I was thirteen, Ma. I wasn't going to tell my mother that I was afraid to go sleep at night."

She pursed her lips, skeptical. "Do you think Butch Messer really needed condoms at thirteen?"

"Probably not." Cochran chuckled. "But the trip made us both feel like read studs, until that guy popped up in the window."

She pulled a stool from the kitchen and sat down, intrigued. "How old did the man look?"

"Ancient, back then. Thinking about it now, he was probably in his forties."

Eleanor gazed at him, mental wheels turning. "Which would make him close to seventy now."

"Right." Cochran turned back to the computer. "Remember the girls Ginger wrote about in that Fiddlesticks piece? Officially, they're still missing persons. But shortly before they disappeared, every one was in or near the Fiddlesticks cabin."

"When did they vanish?" asked his mother.

Cochran clicked the mouse. A file popped on the screen, showing pictures of three young women. "Vicky Robbins disappeared in 2001, Carolyn James in 1992, Doris McFadden in 1986."

"One a decade," said Eleanor.

"Now Lisa Wilson," said Jerry.

"Good Lord," she whispered. "You might be on to something."

"I know. And I'm going to keep at it until I figure out what really happened up there."

Her mouth curled in a wistful smile. "You sound exactly like your father when you say that."

Cochran didn't know what to say. His father had been a teacher. A history professor who'd dropped dead when Jerry was a sophomore in college. He wondered, sometimes, if Lawrence Cochran would be pleased that his scrawny bookworm of a boy now wore a badge and locked people up on a regular basis.

"He would be so proud of you," said his mother, as if reading his mind.

He smiled, happy to think that his father would find him worthy. Then his gaze returned to the faces of those girls on the computer screen. "I'll be proud of me, too," he told his mother. "If I ever figure all this out."

THIRTY-FIVE

MARY LAY IN BED, trying to make sense of the day, re-reading Jonathan's note. Though the handwriting was his, the words typically terse and direct, she still couldn't believe he'd gone. Alex had immediately called Sam Hodges, then her husband Charlie in Texas. Hodges said Jonathan seemed fine when he dropped him off at the motel; Charlie had not heard a word. Since then she'd called him every fifteen minutes, explaining that court had gone well, that the judge would rule tomorrow, but Jonathan neither answered his phone nor returned any messages.

The endless afternoon had darkened into night. After a tasteless supper at the motel, she and Alex bid each other good night.

"Do you want me to call a detective?" asked Alex. "See if we can find him under the radar?"

Mary shook her head. "It would be a waste of time. If Jonathan doesn't want to be found, he won't be. I'm leaving him one more message, then it's up to him."

Alex looked at her, surprised. "Are you sure?"

"Yep."

"Okay, then. See you tomorrow. Call me if you need me."

That had been hours ago. Mary had left Jonathan a final message—apologizing for the surprise in court, telling him that the case still looked good and that she loved him. After that she'd simply lain in bed wondering where he was and if his two-sentence note would be the last she would ever hear of him.

For hours she twisted from one side of the bed to the other, the mattress too lumpy, the pillow too hot. Finally she sat up and turned on the light. The motel bar had long since closed, and she'd packed neither a novel nor any sleeping pills. She resigned herself to another long night of worry when her gaze fell on her laptop, sitting on the desk. That brought to mind Lige McCauley and the weird fiddle tune he'd learned in prison. Throwing off her clammy sheets, she walked over and unzipped her computer bag.

"I'll just play Nancy Drew," she whispered. "At least it'll give me something to do while I wait for Jonathan to call."

She booted up the machine, wondering where she should start her research—Central Prison? Fiddlesticks? Shape note music?

"Begin at the beginning," she whispered, quoting her favorite line from *Alice in Wonderland*. She Googled the *Hartsville Herald*, then did a document search for "Fiddlesticks." Ginger's special report filled the screen—columns of text, plus a picture of the original Fiddlesticks, Robert Thomas Smith, being escorted from the courthouse by two burly deputies. He was a slight man, with reddish hair and boyish features. He looked too insignificant to have killed much beyond a fly, but Mary had long ago learned that the most vicious killers could still look like choirboys.

She read Ginger's feature carefully—surprised at how close the ghost story mirrored the facts. On November 23, 1958, Robert Thomas Smith had come home unexpectedly and found his wife, Bett, having sex with a man named Ray Hopson. Smith flew into a rage and killed them both with a knife. Whether he'd stuck around fiddling while they died was up for grabs, but Smith disappeared. After a month-long manhunt, he was apprehended on Christmas Eve, coming out of the cemetery, having put two red roses on Bett's fresh grave.

"How romantic," Mary whispered. "A killer with a heart."

Ginger's article went on. Smith's trial began April 2, 1959, with spectators spilling out of the courtroom and into the halls. Testimony concluded after two days; the all-male jury deliberated only an hour. They found Smith guilty of two counts of capital murder. He was sentenced to death, due to the "particularly heinous nature of his crime." On May 8, 1971, Smith died in the gas chamber just after midnight at Central Prison in Raleigh. His unclaimed body was buried in the prison graveyard.

"Okay," Mary said. "Lige McCauley was in Central Prison the same time as Robert Thomas Smith. So maybe it was Smith McCauley heard fiddling from death row. But how does the same tune show up thirty years later, carved into Lisa Wilson's skin?"

She got up from the computer and heated some water in her in-room coffee pot. As she steeped some lemon-raspberry tea, she considered McCauley as a suspect. He'd been in prison the same time as Smith, had sung the tune carved on Lisa's body. But he was skinny as a pencil and had trouble getting out of a rocking chair. Plus, he lived nearly three hours away, in Grapevine. He probably wasn't the killer, but she still wondered if McCauley knew more about this than he was admitting.

"There's got to be a Central Prison connection here," she said. She returned to her computer, this time searching for "North Carolina prison records." A slick website came on the screen, but it was informational, for the families of inmates and victims. She needed the inside scoop, access to historical prison records.

Sipping her tea, she considered whom she might call. Jerry Cochran came to mind first, but she doubted he'd give her the tools to take the wheels off Turpin's case. She closed her eyes, trying to think, when suddenly it came to her. Her go-to PI, Omer Peacock, was retired SBI, retired detective of the High Point Police Department. He would help her out.

She grabbed her cell phone and punched in his number. The phone rang several times, then a recorded voice asked her to leave a message. She almost clicked off, thinking she would call him at a more decent hour, when Omer himself came on the line.

"Mary? That you?"

"All the way from Tulsa, Oklahoma."

"You in trouble?"

"No, I'm fine, but I need a favor."

"Shoot, girl, you scared me." He coughed, as if clearing phlegm from his throat. "What can I do for you?"

"Can you get into the North Carolina prison database?"

"Anybody can do that. You just Google—"

"No, I mean the restricted one. We had one in Georgia we called gofer—Georgia Official Felons Records. It was for police, DAs."

"I gotcha. You want NCLERC in Carolina."

"Can you get me in there?"

"You can use my password. It ain't exactly legal, but I won't tell if you won't."

"I won't."

"Then get a pencil and write this down."

She hurried to pull a pen from her computer case. A few minutes later, she had the website and Omer's password written on the palm of her hand. "Thanks, Omer," she said. "I'm sorry if I woke you up."

"Not a problem, sweetheart. I haven't had a late-night call from a pretty girl in a long time. I'll go back to sleep and dream of you."

Laughing, she clicked off the cell and returned to the computer, entering the web address Omer had given her. A screen appeared, giving dire warnings that this site was for law enforcement professionals only and all hackers would be summarily drawn and quartered. Ignoring that, she keyed in Omer's ID and password; a few seconds later she was in the system.

"Okay," she whispered. "First let's check out McCauley." She typed in his name. The computer whirred a moment, then a mug shot came on the screen. It showed a youthful version of the old man—his hair dark instead of white, jaw firm instead of flaccid. He'd served two years of a five-year stretch for bootlegging, released early on good behavior. The April dates matched exactly what he'd told her the other day.

"So far he's been straight," said Mary. "Let's try Robert Thomas Smith."

She typed in the name. The computer whirred for a moment, then produced a list of over five hundred variations of "Robert Thomas Smith," all having been in the North Carolina penal system at one time or another.

She narrowed the field, typing in Robert Thomas Smith, 1960. Still, over fifty names appeared. "Damn," she whispered. "This will take me forever." She thought for a moment, then remembered that Central Prison in Raleigh was the only place executions were carried out. She typed Smith's name and date in again, this time adding "Central Prison."

Once more, the computer whirred, this time coming up with only two names. Robert Thomas Smith from Pisgah County, and Robert Thomas Smith from Iredell County. "Bingo," she said. "There's our boy."

She clicked on the Robert Thomas Smith of Pisgah County. An enormous number of official records popped up—a warden's report, a witness report, the official order of rejection from the North Carolina court of appeals. She scrolled through them quickly, stopping at a death certificate, dated March 8, 1971. It stated that Robert Thomas Smith had died of asphyxiation by hydrogen cyanide, administered by Officer Harlan Howard and Officer Rufus Slocum, in accordance with said ruling of the North Carolina Appellate Court. Carlisle Wilson, governor, headed a long list of officials who signed the death certificate.

She scrolled down farther, going through an official inventory of Smith's possessions, then a notification of next-of-kin. Finally, she came to the end of the file—the coroner's report on Robert Thomas Smith. The date of death was May 8, 1971, time of death 12:16 a.m. deceased: Robert Thomas Smith, aged 27, residence Pisgah County. He had red hair, hazel eyes, stood 5'8" tall and weighed, at time of death, 147 pounds. Other identifying marks included a scar on his chin, a tattoo of a cross on his right forearm.

There were several more documents signed by witnesses, another form signed by a doctor, then, at the very end, was an autopsy photo. As that image came on the screen, she gasped. The autopsy photo showed a slack-jawed body lying on a table, covered from the waist down by a sheet. Though it was a white male, his features were thick and his hair dark. What made her gasp was not the dead man's appearance, but the fact that he looked absolutely nothing like the light-haired, boyish-looking man in Ginger's article.

THIRTY-SIX

"WHAT THE HELL?" CRIED Mary. She scrolled down, thinking there must be some kind of further addendum, but Pisgah County Smith's records ended there, his autopsy report showing the face of a totally different man.

She clicked back several screens, thinking she'd gotten the two Robert Thomas Smiths mixed up. Pulling up both sets of records, she compared them. The two men were similar in size—both 5'8", around 150 pounds, but where Pisgah County Smith was redheaded and young looking, Iredell County Smith had dark hair and coarser features. Iredell Smith's photo was the one attached to Pisgah Smith's autopsy report.

"Some clerk's messed this up," she muttered. She read on, amazed by the similarities between the two men. Both had been fingerprinted in August 1960, both had been sentenced to death for capital murder. But according to the Department of Corrections, Iredell County Smith's execution had been stayed twice on appeal by the ACLU, arguing grounds of mental competence. The last entry in his file was an appellate court case number, dated September 23, 1974. After that, nothing. She went back to Pisgah County Smith. According to the NCLERC records, he was executed on May 8, 1971. Iredell County Smith was still awaiting an appellate court ruling in September of 1974.

"So what happened?" Mary whispered, as she fished around the site. "Did they put the wrong picture with the wrong record?"

Exasperated, she left NCLERC and searched for North Carolina executions. She found that capital punishment had a varied history in the Tar Heel state, and in the early 1970s, North Carolina had squabbled with the Supreme Court over having a death penalty at all. In 1976, Washington slapped Raleigh's hand, overturning a long-standing mandatory execution statute.

"The Court vacated the sentences of over a hundred inmates awaiting execution," she read aloud. "Many received new trials, though most were re-sentenced to life in prison."

She tapped her pencil on the computer screen. "So they executed one Robert Thomas Smith in 1971. But what happened to the other one? And which is which?"

Her tea had grown cold, so she got up and fixed another cup. To her surprise, a pale, anemic dawn was beginning to lighten the room. She looked at her watch. It was 6:46. Abashed, as if she'd shirked some important duty, she hurried over to the window and looked for Jonathan's truck. She didn't see it—just a few cars in the parking lot and a white cat meandering toward the trash dumpster, its tail a curl in the air.

She checked her cell phone, but she'd gotten no messages, so she returned to the computer. "Let's see what Iredell County Smith was in for," she whispered.

She left Google, logged onto Lexis-Nexis, and typed in "Robert Smith, Iredell County, NC." The hourglass icon turned while the computer went through the files, then an index of records from the local paper appeared on the screen. The articles were ancient, dating from 1960, when Robby Smith of Troutman, North Carolina, was found guilty for the murder of Officer Frank Quinn of the Statesville police force. "Somebody put Robby up to this," his grandmother was quoted as saying, "I raised that child to be a good boy, but anybody could talk him into anything."

"Like change places with someone on death row?" asked Mary, scrolling through the articles. The paper reported that Smith was arrested, provided with a public defender, brought to trial in 1961, was found guilty, and received the death penalty.

At that point, the story died. She found only two more articles—one in 1962, describing how Smith spent his days open-mouthed and staring at the walls of an 8x8 cell. The last one appeared in 1974, stating that Smith remained on death row, awaiting a decision from the Court of Appeals.

"Which means he should be in the NCLERC database," Mary whispered. Logging out of Lexis-Nexis, she returned to the Department of Corrections website. As she waited for the home page to appear, she thought of Ginger. What a story this would make. At the very least it was grossly inept record keeping—at the worst, they may have executed the wrong man.

"Okay," she told herself. "Robert Thomas Smith, Iredell, gets you a guy still waiting on a court decision in 1974. Let's try Grandma's name for him—Robby Smith."

She keyed in "Robby Smith." The computer hummed, but no records appeared. She keyed in "Robby Thomas Smith," then "Robby Tommy Smith." Again, nothing.

"Well, nuts," she said. "The guy can't just evaporate." She thought a moment, then decided to widen the search. Still in the Central Prison database, she left the first name field blank and keyed in "Smith, Iredell, 1974." The computer churned for a second, then came up with four names. Audie Smith, Indigo Sayles Smith, Robert Thomas Smith, then Thomas Robert Smith.

"Did somebody reverse the names?" She clicked on the file. The information for Thomas Robert Smith was identical to the Robert Thomas Smith file, except it continued beyond 1974. Iredell County's Smith had lingered on death row from 1962 to 1977, then they transferred him to Naughton State Hospital.

"That's it!" she cried. Iredell Smith had been caught in the glitch when Raleigh and the Supreme Court were fighting it out over the death penalty. She scrolled down through a dozen more reports until finally, she came to the last record. She blinked, unbelieving. The last record was a mug shot—not of a coarse-featured, brown-haired man, but the same boyish-looking man pictured in Ginger's article. Though the red hair was graying and the face had grown pudgy, it was definitely the man who had walked down the courthouse steps in handcuffs.

"Fiddlesticks, alive and well."

THIRTY-SEVEN

BETT SCRATCHED AT HIS *window the night the moon was full. He thought she might—for days he'd felt a tingling in the pit of his stomach that wavered between terror and excitement. He'd gone to bed with a snootful of whiskey, hoping Dr. Jack Daniels might render him immune to her. But his eyes had flown open with her first rasp on the screen, as clear-headed as if he'd never touched a drop of liquor in his life. So much for Jack D. Even the mighty doctor is powerless against Bett Lovelace.*

She scratched again, cat's claws on slate. He sat up in bed and turned toward her. It always gave him goose flesh, the way she stood there, staring at him with those near-colorless eyes. Tonight her skin looked like untracked snow, her hair a mass of long, black curls. A scarlet cape draped across her shoulders. It matched the shade of her lips, exactly.

"Bobby?" Her voice sounded the same as always—low, but musical, as if he'd just done something she found amusing. "You awake?"

He nodded, knowing it was pointless to feign sleep. Bett never left until she got what she came for.

She smiled, coy and wheedling. "May I come in?"

Before he could answer she vanished from the window, a dark form swirling through the night. A moment later she stood at the foot of his bed, bringing the smell of lilacs and moldering earth.

"How have you been?"

He glanced wistfully at the half-empty bottle of whiskey. "I've been okay."

She sat down on the side of the bed. "Have you missed me?"

He looked down at her cape, a curl of crimson against his dirty sheets. That question was harder to answer. He loved her. He missed her. He'd been terrified of her since the day they met.

She reached forward, lifting his beard-stubbled chin. When his gaze met hers, she smiled. Those pale amber eyes flashed behind dark lashes, like distant lightning in mid-July. He caught his breath, once again wondering how anything this beautiful had ever been his.

"I think you've missed me, Bobby," she whispered.

She leaned forward and kissed him. Her lips were juicy as a plum, her tongue inebriating parts of him that not even Dr. Jack could touch.

"I think you've missed me quite a bit." Laughing, she pulled her lips from his and let her cape drop to the floor. She stood before him naked and luminous. She seemed composed of only three colors— white skin, black hair, and three touches of red—a succulent mouth and two rosy, erect nipples.

He felt himself grow hard as she pushed him down and climbed on top of him. With her breasts pendulous above him, she started kissing him, working her way by inches from his mouth to his throat, then down his chest. By the time she reached his waist, he was hard as a rock. Just as she began to move lower, she lifted her face to look up at him.

"They're talking about us again." Her voice was still low, but less musical now.

He couldn't speak; he felt as if he might explode.

"You know how that makes me feel."

He clung to the bedstead, as if some vortex might suck him up into space.

"They'll spread lies about us again. Call me a whore. And you a fool."

He tried to answer her, but he felt only her warmth on his hips, her breath on his skin, the agony of a release she would not allow.

"You need to stop that woman, Bobby." She licked him; a sweet, sick fire crackled through his whole body. "You need to make them leave us alone."

She might have spoken in English; she might haven spoken Chinese. He whimpered like a dog.

"Will you do it? Or should I get Ray?"

Ray Hopson: his oldest enemy. How like her to mention him now. He looked up at her and managed to shake his head.

She licked him again. "Do you mean no, you won't do it? Or no, don't get Ray?"

"Don't get Hopson," he croaked, a cold sweat soaking him. "I'll take care of it."

"Good. I thought I could persuade you."

She lowered her head—a sudden warmth enveloped him. All at once she granted him release—he exploded, every fiber in his body sending rage and shame and God knows what else out of him. As he screamed with the pure, hot pleasure of it, she lay back on the bed and laughed.

For a while he lay there helpless as a baby, his muscles drained, his body limp. When he could open his eyes, Bett again stood by the side of his bed, her red cape draped across her body.

"So you'll fix it, Bobby?" Her eyes glittered with the question.

"I'll fix it," he mumbled, his voice coming out dry as a corn husk.

"I knew you would." Smiling again, she knelt beside the bed. "You always were the best." She kissed him, all tongue and teeth and teasing, then as he felt himself grow hard again, she rose to leave.

"I've got to go now," she said. "But after you make things right, I'll come again." She laughed. "And so will you. Many times over."

He watched her leave, her cape swirling as she crossed his bedroom, then let herself out his front door. He heard soft footsteps on the gravel outside, then he heard nothing more but the hoot of an owl, far off in the night.

He closed his eyes, fighting tears. Always, he kept the small hope burning that she might be different, might be kind. But every time she flicked his hope out like a cheap match. Still, he knew he would do what she asked. He would do anything to see Bett Lovelace standing naked in front of him.

THIRTY-EIGHT

ABRUPTLY, SOMEONE KNOCKED ON her door. Mary jumped, startled. She'd been utterly enrapt in the unfolding drama in the databases on her screen. Hurriedly, she crossed the room and opened the door. Alex stood there in shorts and a T-shirt, bringing her a cup of coffee.

"Have you heard from Jonathan?" she asked.

"No," said Mary.

"Me neither."

"Damn," said Alex. "I was hoping he'd called you. Have you tried to call him?"

"Not since last night." Mary shrugged. "You can only leave so many desperate messages."

Alex peered over her shoulder, her gaze falling on the computer, the papers strewn out across the bed. "So what have you been doing?"

Mary felt sheepish, as if she'd been caught doing something wrong. "Working," she finally admitted.

Alex rolled her eyes. "On the Fiddlesticks case?"

"It seemed better than pacing around the room all night." Mary stepped back.

"Mary, you don't have to solve the case. If you're playing defense, all you have to do is cast reasonable doubt on the state's evidence."

"I know—but this is fascinating."

Sighing, Alex sat down on the bed while Mary gave her the short version of her night's research.

"My client Stratton is accused of a murder that occurred near a cabin where two other murders took place fifty years ago."

"Fiddlesticks," said Alex. "Killed his wife and her lover with a razor."

Mary frowned. "How do you know?"

"I read the *Snitch*, too, Pocahontas."

"Okay. Fiddlesticks, whose real name is Robert Thomas Smith, gets sent to death row in 1959. At the same time, another guy named Robert Thomas Smith is also sentenced to death row for killing a cop. Both are from North Carolina—one from Iredell County, the other from Pisgah."

"Okay." Alex took a sip of coffee.

"Somehow, Pisgah County Smith, aka Fiddlesticks, manages to switch places with the Iredell County Smith and was *not* executed as reported on May 8, 1971."

"How do you know?" asked Alex.

"The autopsy photo is totally different from the mug shot."

"It's a clerical error. Somebody must have gotten them confused when they digitized the records."

"I thought that, too," said Mary. "Only there's no autopsy report for Iredell County Smith."

Alex frowned. "Why not?"

"First, the ACLU kept appealing his conviction on grounds of mental incompetence. Then, North Carolina got in a huge flap with the feds over the legality of the death penalty. A lot of death row sentences got commuted to life."

"Then Iredell County Smith is still in prison."

"No. In April of 1977, Iredell County Smith was transferred from death row to Naughton Mental Hospital," said Mary. "As far as North Carolina is concerned, he's still there. No death records for this guy, no transfers back to prison or to any other hospital."

"No online obits? Nothing in the Social Security death index?"

Mary shook her head. "Nada."

"Well, shit, Mary." Alex sat up straight on the bed. "If your Fiddlesticks somehow switched identities with this Iredell guy, he could still be alive. There's your client's defense, right there."

Mary grinned. "Why do you think I stayed up all night?"

"Google the mental hospital," said Alex, moving closer to the computer. "See if they have any records."

Mary Googled the place that warehoused most of Western North Carolina's mentally ill felons. The computer hummed a moment, then a long list of hits came on the screen—one an official website that showed a pretty Victorian building in Morton, North Carolina, but gave little information about the place. Another whistle-blower website recounted a scandal where a caregiver had allegedly sat on a patient until he died from suffocation.

"Wow," said Alex, reading along with Mary. "This sounds like Texas. I thought North Carolina was more evolved."

"Not hardly," said Mary. "They just amended their constitution to deny marriage to same-sex couples."

They read on, through nearly a hundred posts about the place. Former patients accused the staff of being negligent and abusive;

former caregivers responded defensively, citing broken bones, missing teeth all due to unruly patients. Rape was an accusation levied at both sides; an undercurrent of rage and frustration seemed to flow darkly among all the posts.

"Look!" said Alex. "There's a woman from Texas, trying to find her brother."

"He was sent to Naughton in 1993," read Mary, picking up the story. "'We haven't heard from him since. That place is a hellhole. I'm sure they've killed him.'"

"Gosh," said Alex. "Can you imagine not hearing from somebody you love for eighteen years?"

"No," said Mary softly, Jonathan and Lily flashing across her mind. "I hope I won't have to find out."

Alex squeezed her shoulder. "You won't, honey. Jonathan loves you. That much I know for sure."

"I know he does," Mary said, staring at the bed they'd made love on just one night ago. "But children trump lovers, Al. And that's as it should be. I should have realized that from the get-go."

"But it may not be an either-or deal," cried Alex. "The judge hasn't ruled yet."

"The judge hasn't ruled, but I think Jonathan has." Mary turned back to the computer. "Anyway, let's look at this."

They returned to the Naughton Hospital website. Mary scrolled down, reading a few more distraught posts, then Alex said, "Naughton's pretty closed mouth about their patients."

"Yeah—if they won't tell that woman about her brother, they're sure as hell not going to tell me about Fiddlesticks," said Mary. "I'm nowhere near a relative."

"You could get a court order," said Alex.

"I don't necessarily want them to know I'm interested," Mary replied. "Once they see a court order, things get cleaned up, records disappear, patients become unavailable."

"You need someone to go undercover." Alex sprawled back on the bed and laughed. "Get your partner to go over there. Ravenel would fit right in a mental institution."

Mary laughed at the notion of Sam Ravenel among the inmates. "Ravenel can't do it—he's settling some historic estate in Charleston. But I do know somebody who might just love to go over there."

"Who?"

"Ginger Malloy. She's the reporter who wrote about Fiddlesticks in the first place."

"In the *Snitch*?" cried Alex.

"No, no," said Mary, reaching for her cell phone. "In our local paper. If she could tie an old ghost story to a botched execution and a killer in a mental institution, she'd probably win the Pulitzer Prize."

Alex glanced at her watch. "Mary, it's barely six a.m. in North Carolina."

"Trust me," Mary said as she punched in Ginger's number. "She won't mind waking up for this."

THIRTY-NINE

GINGER WAS SNUGGLING AGAINST Cochran when the phone jarred her awake. She grabbed it quickly, hoping to cut it off in mid-ring. She and Cochran had gone to sleep late and she didn't want him to wake up this early. Clutching the phone to her chest, she tiptoed into the bathroom and closed the door.

"Ginger Malloy," she answered in a whisper.

"Ginger?" Mary Crow's voice came over the line. "Are you okay?"

"Yeah," Ginger replied, surprised. "Jerry's asleep. I didn't want to wake him up."

"I'm sorry to call so early, but this is important."

Ginger sat down on the edge of the bathtub. "Don't tell me you've got bad news."

"No news at all—the judge hasn't ruled yet," said Mary. "Listen, last night I couldn't sleep, so I read your Fiddlesticks article, and you won't believe what I found out!"

"What?" Ginger was both surprised and flattered that Mary Crow had taken the time to read her piece with everything she had going on right now.

Mary then launched into a tale that sounded like a *Snitch* article—about how the original Fiddlesticks had changed identities with another inmate, escaped the gas chamber, and was transferred to a mental hospital.

"How did you find this out?" said Ginger, wondering if all this custody mess had pushed Mary over some kind of edge.

"I hacked into the penal system database."

Instantly, Ginger pictured the story in the paper. Front page, above the fold, her name in the by-line. "Well, it's a hell of a story."

"Why do you think I called you?" asked Mary. "I know just how you can get it, too."

Deciding that Mary was neither drunk nor hysterical, Ginger listened to her plan. She wanted her to go to Naughton Mental Hospital and look for a patient named Thomas Robert Smith from Iredell County. "But don't go as a reporter," said Mary. "They'll claim patient confidentiality and clam up."

"What should I go as?" asked Ginger.

"Say you're an attorney trying to settle an estate. Tell them Smith's been named in a will and has some money coming to him."

"Okay," Ginger whispered. "I can do that. But what do I do if I find him?"

"Just shoot the breeze with him. If he gets suspicious, then get out of there fast. Call me whatever happens."

"What if I don't find him?"

"Call me anyway. The story's still there—it just won't be quite as thrilling without Fiddlesticks."

"Can I have a look at your notes when you get home?" Ginger asked.

"Absolutely," Mary replied.

"Okay," she said hurriedly as she heard Cochran getting out of bed. "I gotta go ... I'll talk to you later."

She hung up the phone just as Cochran appeared at the bathroom door. "What's going on?" he asked, yawning.

"Mary called from Oklahoma."

"Did they get custody of Lily?" he asked, pulling her up from the edge of the bath tub.

"They don't know yet," she answered, as he carried her back to bed.

———

That had been three hours ago. Now Ginger was heading down the long driveway that led to Naughton Hospital. From the interstate, the place reminded her of one of those Victorian hotels in upstate New York. Red brick with sparkling white woodwork and tall turrets, the building commanded a long expanse of clipped lawn shaded by trees and dotted with flowerbeds. As she drove closer, she almost expected to see pale ladies in long white skirts, laughing as they played croquet. Only after she pulled into the parking lot did she realize that though the windows sparkled in the sun, a darkness hovered behind them, as if the building itself made a long practice of gazing inward, at its own shadowy corners.

She parked in a space marked for visitors. As a couple of vacant-looking men raked the lawn, she grabbed her briefcase and went over her cover story. She was Virginia Malloy, from Asheville. She had a deceased client who'd left one Thomas Robert Smith a rather large bequest in her will. She was trying to find Mr. Smith, whose last known address was here. The ruse was perfect, she decided. The news was non-threatening for everyone involved. Nobody was accusing Mr. Smith of being a psychotic felon; nobody was investigating Naughton Hospital for patient abuse. All she was trying to do was brighten the life of a patient with a nice fat check from his recently departed sister.

She got out of the car. A sudden breeze whispered through the leafy trees that surrounded the place. She glanced up at one of the turreted rooms above her head, feeling as if someone was watching her. Then she remembered where she was. *Somebody probably is watching you*, she told herself. *Any number of people could be peering out those dark windows.*

Squaring her shoulders, she took a deep breath and walked toward the front door. The brick steps had been swept of leaves; the wide veranda freshly painted a crisp gull gray. Whatever went on inside Naughton Hospital, outside it was painted and groomed to perfection.

She trotted up the steps and was about to enter the building when a face appeared in the windows next to the door. A young man with pale eyes sprayed cleaner on the glass. Their gazes met for a moment. Ginger smiled, but his expression did not change. He wiped the glass with a dull, robotic intensity, as if he did the chore a thousand times a day.

She opened the door. A cloying smell of geraniums mixed with antiseptic greeted her. She stepped into a smallish waiting room, with upholstered chairs and a coffee table that held a few tattered magazines about North Carolina. Opposite the front door was a windowed reception area, where a gray-haired woman sat at a computer. She looked up over silver reading glasses as Ginger entered.

"May I help you?" she asked, penciled-on eyebrows lifting.

"Gosh, I hope so," Ginger said, adopting the breezy charm that usually loosened even the most reluctant lips. She lugged the briefcase over to the desk as if it weighed a hundred pounds. "My name is Virginia Malloy," she said, pulling out the fake business card she'd printed up this morning. "From Asheville? I'm Mrs. Edith Ellington's attorney." She said Mrs. Edith Ellington as if anyone would surely snap to attention at the mention of the name.

"Yes?" The woman looked unimpressed with her or Edith Ellington.

"Mrs. Ellington passed away this April. I'm the executor of her estate. She left a rather sizable gift to someone who was once one of your patients."

The woman looked at her with cold eyes.

Ginger pulled out another fake form she'd downloaded off the Internet. "My research indicates that this gentleman has been here since 1977. Could you tell me if he's still a patient here?"

"I can't give out that information," the woman replied. "All patient records are private."

"I realize that," said Ginger. "But this man was not young, even in 1977. It's highly likely that he's deceased, too."

"And you can't determine that on your own?" the woman asked sharply.

"I haven't found him in the Social Security Death Index," Ginger said, bluffing her way through a source she often used at the paper.

Again, the woman shook her head. "I'm afraid I can't help you."

"I understand." Ginger smiled, playing her trump card. "I talked to Commissioner Hatch about this yesterday. Since this is a nonmedical inquiry on a patient who is likely deceased, he told me to try on-site first. He said if you all were sticklers, I'd have to come see him in Raleigh. So," she said, retrieving her business card. "I guess I'll go east and have a chat with Charlie Hatch. Thanks for your time."

Ginger grabbed her briefcase and headed for the door, letting Commissioner Hatch's name work inside the woman's head. She figured this would go one of two ways—either the woman would do nothing, happy to let her drive east to Raleigh or she might decide that Commissioner Hatch would not be pleased to have such unhelpful sticklers working the front desk at Naughton. Ginger was halfway to the door when she got her answer.

"Wait a minute," the woman called huffily. "I guess I could pull up a name for you."

Good girl, thought Ginger, *no point in wasting Charlie Hatch's time*. She turned back. "Thanks," she said, smiling. "It would save me a lot of time."

Lips pursed, the woman turned to her computer. "What's the name? Ellington?"

"Actually, it's Smith. Thomas Robert Smith of Iredell County. Mrs. Ellington's baby brother."

"Hang on." The woman pulled up a bright purple screen and typed in Smith's name. For a moment, nothing happened, then the screen changed to a softer blue.

"Smith, Thomas Robert, transferred from Central Prison in April of 1977?"

"That's him," said Ginger eagerly. "The black sheep of the family. Mrs. Ellington still loved him, though."

"Well, he's not here any longer," said the woman.

Ginger nodded, trying to hide her real disappointment. "I figured he might have passed away."

"I'm not saying he's dead." The receptionist scrolled down a long list of categories. "He was re-diagnosed and transferred to Pine

Valley Nursing home in Iredell County, in 1982. But he wasn't that old," she squinted at the computer screen. "Only forty-one."

"Which would make him around seventy today," Ginger whispered, amazed at the twists this man's life had taken.

"Well, if he's still alive, he should be at Pine Valley," the woman said, turning away from her computer. For the first time she gave Ginger a tight smile, undoubtedly pleased that the Thomas Robert Smith affair was off her desk.

"You don't happen to know where that is, do you?" asked Ginger.

She shrugged. "Somewhere in Iredell County. Once they leave here, they become their home county's problem."

"Thanks." Ginger smiled. "I'll be sure to let Commissioner Hatch know how helpful you were."

———

She hurried back to her car, passing the young man who was still cleaning the same pane of glass. Amazingly, Mary's fantastic theory seemed to be holding up—Thomas Robert Smith, who was really Robert Thomas Smith had, one way or another, traded places with a man on death row, gotten transferred out of prison to a mental facility, and then been released to a county nursing home. He was either the luckiest or the most devious man she'd ever heard of.

She got back in her car. *I should probably let Mary in on this,* she thought. *At least tell her what I've learned.* But the story was huge— if she found the real Fiddlesticks wheezing around in some nursing home, it would be the scoop of her life. She would leave Jessica Rusk laboring in the tabloids forever. Buckling her seatbelt, she keyed Pine Valley Nursing Home into her GPS.

An hour later, she pulled off I-40 and drove down a broad six-lane road flanked by fast food restaurants and strip malls. She passed a regional hospital, a Toyota dealership, and an amusement park called Carolina City. She'd just begun to think the smart-ass male voice on the GPS had totally screwed up when she saw a sign that read Pine Valley Heights Road.

She turned right. Within half a mile the commercial development gave way to houses set far back off the road. A mile past that, she was driving through undeveloped land. Just as she began to doubt the GPS again, she saw a battered sign that read PINE VALLEY HOME. She turned where it indicated and drove down a two-lane road that bordered acres of pasture land. Bright bluebirds perched on honeysuckled fencerows while cows chewed their cud beneath shady trees.

She drove along, finally coming to another sign that pointed to the right. She turned up a hill that overlooked the pastureland, wondering what she was going to say if Smith was indeed still alive. She'd felt safe asking for him at Naughton—mental hospitals had guards to deal with violent patients. Nursing homes were different. They rarely had more than a couple of beefy CNAs to turn the heavier patients.

"Oh, come on," she chided herself. "What's he going to do—run over you in his wheelchair?"

She went on. She passed one more sign advertising the home, then she drove under a cast-iron archway. She was just thinking what a good idea it was to have a nursing home out in the country when she crested a small hill. As she did so, she gasped. Though there was a driveway and a paved parking lot, all that remained of the Pine Valley Nursing Home was a burned-out shell.

"What the hell?" Stunned, she turned off her engine and got out of her car. Though the concrete walls of the structure still stood, there were great sagging holes in the roof. The windows had long been broken out and a family of wrens swooped in and out of what had once been the lobby. Dark smoke stains scorched the top level of the brick, just below the roof, as if something had caught on fire in the attic.

Instinctively, she reached for her iPad. She needed to know when this place burned down, what had happened to the patients inside. She tried to get online, but the signal was too weak. Figuring she'd have to drive to the nearest town, she started back down the road. She'd just reached the farm with the fencerow when she saw a man pitching bales of hay off a flatbed truck. She pulled over and got out of her car.

"Excuse me!" she called. "Sir?"

The man looked around, waved. He jumped off the truck and ambled over toward her. He wore a green John Deere cap and faded denim coveralls. "Help you?"

"I'm doing some family tree research—trying to find an old relative who used to live in that nursing home." She pointed up the hill. "When did it burn down?"

"Awww, probably thirty years ago." He squinted and looked up at the sky, as if he might find the answer written in the clouds. "Eighty-two or eighty-three, I reckon."

"What happened?"

"Fire marshal blamed it on the wiring. Ask me, I think some of them convicts burned it down."

Ginger played dumb. "Convicts?"

He nodded. "They used to keep a few who weren't dangerous up there. That didn't make 'em any less crazy, though."

"They kept crazy people up there?"

Again, he nodded. "One morning I found one of 'em in my hen house, squattin' down like he was gonna lay an egg. How he squeezed in there I'll never know, but it wasn't no egg that he left on that nest."

"Was anybody killed when the place burned down?" asked Ginger.

"Seems like a few of 'em might've died," he said. "I helped the firemen for a while, then I had to hose down m'barn. They were afraid a spark would set my hayloft on fire."

"That's terrible," said Ginger.

"It was a right bad night," the man agreed. "I'm sorry about your kinfolk, but that old nursin' home ain't no great loss. Not to me, anyway."

"Thanks for talking to me."

As the farmer headed back to his hay, Ginger hurried back to her car. She was going to call Mary Crow as soon as she got back to civilization. The saga of Fiddlesticks just kept getting stranger by the minute.

FORTY

AFTER MARY HUNG UP from calling Ginger in the early morning, she took a long, hot shower and readied herself for court. She put on the same blue suit, then she and Alex wandered over to the motel's breakfast buffet. Her earlier excitement over the Fiddlesticks case had ebbed into a worried anxiousness over Jonathan and Lily. She picked at her waffle, keeping an eye out for them, still hoping they might walk through the door. She and Alex lingered over coffee, talking about nothing, stalling as long as they dared. Finally, they could no longer put off leaving. Judge Diane Haddad would give her decision at eleven a.m.; they'd better be there to hear it. Alex sped them back to Tahlequah, parking next to the courthouse. As they crossed the street to enter the building, Mary put a hand on Alex's arm.

"Whatever happens, you've done a superb job. I can't thank you enough, Al."

"I owed you one, Ms. Crow." Though Alex smiled, her eyes were serious. "If it hadn't been for you, I would not be standing here, alive and breathing."

"Then I guess we're even," said Mary.

Arm in arm, in the way of old friends, they crossed the street and rode the elevator up to Haddad's courtroom. Apparently the Moons had told their cheering section to stay home, because only they and Laura Bagwell were sitting in the courtroom. Mary and Alex walked to the defendant's table, their footsteps echoing in the stillness. Bagwell nodded as they sat down, but the Moons maintained a stony-faced silence. The tension grew in the hushed room, then suddenly, everyone came in at once—the bailiff, the officer, the court reporter. Diane Haddad entered from the doorway behind the bench, an elegant lace collar topping her black judicial robe. Everyone rose as she took her seat.

"Glad to see everybody back," she said. "I know how hard it is to wait on a decision. Gloria, let the record show that this is day three of Moon v. Walkingstick," she told her court reporter, a chubby little woman whose fingers flew like sausages over her keyboard as Judge Haddad began.

"This has been an interesting case for a number of reasons and I wanted to consider all the aspects of it." She looked at Bagwell. "First off, let me say that I find the implication that criminal attorneys make less effective parents, specious. If anything, criminal attorneys make better parents, simply because they are more aware of how easily young people can take wrong turns in life that lead to pain and heartbreak. Never have I known a child of either prosecutor or defense counsel to be negatively affected by their parent's occupation."

"Damn!" whispered Alex. "If only Jonathan could hear that!"

The judge then turned to Alex and Mary. "Ms. Crow, you have been thrust into an unusual situation. Though it is beyond the jurisdiction of this court to determine your culpability in Mrs. Walkingstick's death, I am convinced that you have raised Lily Bird Walkingstick in a loving, responsible way. By all indications, she is a bright, happy child who is well-liked by her peers. Any step-parent would be envious of your success."

She turned back to the Moons. "However, Mr. and Mrs. Moon have an equally compelling argument. Through no fault of their own, they've tragically lost their only daughter in circumstances that are at best murky. This court can clearly see that having Ms. Crow raising their only grandchild would be akin to rubbing salt in an open wound."

Mary shot Alex a nervous glance, sensing this might not go the way they'd hoped.

"Seldom are custody cases easy—this one is particularly difficult. As commendable a job that Mr. Walkingstick and Ms. Crow have done, Mr. and Mrs. Moon have rights as well—not only do Oklahoma statutes address grandparental rights, but among the Cherokee people, orphaned children are traditionally raised by the mother's family. Though this is not tribal court, I would like to respect Cherokee precedent as much as I can.

"So, given that Mr. Walkingstick and Ms. Crow have made no effort to formalize their relationship by marriage, that Mr. Walkingstick already owns a home near the Moons' residence and has no regular, full-time employment that specifically requires his residence in North Carolina, I'm awarding custody of Lily Bird Walkingstick jointly to both her biological father, Jonathan Walkingstick and her maternal grandparents, Fred and Dulcy Moon. Commencing August first of this year, Lily Bird Walkingstick will spend weekdays with Mr. Walkingstick here in Oklahoma and weekends with

Mr. and Mrs. Moon." Haddad looked at Alex and Bagwell. "Counselors, I'm charging you two with working out an equitable arrangement regarding holidays, subject to this court approval."

Haddad gave Mary a sad smile. "I know this is not what you wanted, Ms. Crow, and probably far less than you deserve. But Oklahoma needs good criminal attorneys. Perhaps you will see your way clear to join us on this side of the Mississippi."

The judge tapped her gavel once, lightly, and rose from her chair. Mary stood, stunned, as the judge disappeared through the doorway behind the bench. Her practicing criminal law hadn't hurt them a bit—their case had been sunk by their lack of a marriage license and Jonathan's purchase of that duplex. For an instant she thought she might vomit. Jonathan and Lily would not be returning to North Carolina; she would be going home alone, a brand-new family of one.

"Mrs. Carter?" Laura Bagwell plunked her briefcase down on their table. "When shall we work this out? I imagine Mr. Walkingstick will need to be involved."

"Mr. Walkingstick will be involved," Alex assured her. "He's just out with his daughter today."

Bagwell's eyes narrowed with suspicion. "He does know that he'll be in contempt if he doesn't surrender the child on August first?"

"It won't be a problem," said Alex.

"Shall we begin this afternoon?" asked Bagwell. "My clients are anxious to get started."

"I need to get back to Texas, Ms. Bagwell. My associate, Sam Hodges, will take over from here." Alex pulled one of Sam's card from her briefcase. "I'll inform him about this as soon as I leave court. You two can set up a time to meet."

Bagwell took the card. "We'd like to get started on this ASAP."

"As does Mr. Walkingstick."

Mary could tell Bagwell wasn't particularly happy, but there was nothing she could do. She followed Alex out of the courtroom with just a single glance at Fred and Dulcy Moon, who held each other close, their faces wet with happy tears.

Foolishly, Mary looked again for Jonathan when they got outside, thinking maybe he'd taken all their phone calls to heart and had come back to hear the verdict. But no tall, dark-haired man with a child waited for them, nor did she see his truck parked anywhere nearby.

"Wow," said Alex, blinking in the bright sun. "What now?"

Mary shrugged. "You go back to Texas, I go back to North Carolina."

"What about Jonathan?"

"Let's both call and give him Haddad's decision, though I doubt he'll come back."

Alex shook her head. "He'll be in a shit load of trouble."

"I know. But he won't care. He will never let Fred Moon have Lily."

They walked back to Alex's car, each lost in their own thoughts. "You know what I hate about this the most?" Alex finally blurted as they crossed the street.

"What?"

"That Jonathan didn't hear what Haddad said about you. She totally vindicated you, Mary. You never needed to make that silly promise about criminal law."

"I did then." Mary looked at her old friend. "But I don't anymore."

They drove back to the motel. Mary got on her cell phone and amazingly, found a seat on an afternoon flight. She was changing from her blue suit to a comfortable pair of jeans, when she found the pillow she'd taken from Jonathan's bed. She picked it up, pressed it to her face. Already, his smell was fainter. Tomorrow it would be fainter still, the next day gone. She considered packing it in her suitcase, enclosing what remained of him, like a treasure in a box. But after a moment she let the pillow fall back on the bed. Jonathan was gone. Lily was gone. From here on, she would have to recall them in memory only. She had a plane to catch, a client to defend, a new life that needed her active participation.

FORTY-ONE

SHE'D JUST GOTTEN IN line to board the plane when her cell phone rang. She answered it immediately, hoping, for the thousandth time, that it was Jonathan. Her heart fell when a woman's voice came over the phone.

"Mary? This is Ginger."

"Hey." Mary felt odd, as if her friend were calling from another world, another life.

Ginger went on, breathless. "Are you sitting down?"

"No," said Mary. "I'm in line to board a plane."

"Well, listen carefully and I'll talk fast. I found Fiddlesticks!"

"You what?" Mary sounded so surprised that the man in front of her turned around to stare.

"I found Fiddlesticks! I had to do some tap dancing at Naughton, but I found out that Smith was there until 1977, when they released him as a low-risk lifer to a nursing home in Iredell County."

"Are you serious?" Mary held the phone close to her ear as a garbled airport voice paged a passenger.

"Yes! And it gets even crazier! I drove to the nursing home, and guess what—it's nothing but a shell! An old farmer said it burned down back in the early eighties."

"So what happened to the patients?" Mary retreated to the rear of the boarding line.

"That's what I'm working on now," Ginger replied. "But it's like grabbing at air. You figure out one question and find fifty more to answer."

"That's the most incredible story I've ever heard," said Mary.

"I know." Ginger cackled, full of glee. "And it's all mine! No Jessica Rusk on this one!"

Mary smiled. "You go, girl."

"Hey, what put you on to this?" Ginger asked. "How did you put Fiddlesticks in Naughton?"

"I'll tell you later," said Mary. "I've got to get on the plane. But our trip to the Sacred Harp singing had a lot to do with it."

"When will you be home?" asked Ginger.

"Early evening, if we land on time."

"Well, promise you'll call me, okay? Whatever time you get here. I've got lots more to tell you."

"Will do. Talk to you in a few hours."

———

Shaking her head at the craziness of the Fiddlesticks case, Mary was the last person to board the plane. A few minutes later, it lifted her into the sky. She gazed out the window as Tulsa spread out below her, oddly looking for Jonathan's red truck on the interstate below. Then the plane banked right, and all she saw was clouds and sky. *I still can't believe it*, she thought bitterly. *All those years, all that love, ending with two sentences on Holiday Inn stationery. Don't think about it*, she told herself, pulling the shade down over the window. *Think about what Ginger found out at Naughton. If only half of it's true, then you've just gotten Stratton off the hook for murder.*

———

Two hours later she landed in Atlanta. She bailed her car out of long-term parking and headed north, into the mountains. Though she knew she'd promised to call Ginger, she decided that a visit to Nick Stratton might be first in order. She hadn't seen her client in nearly a week and giving him some good news might cheer them both up.

She drove up Highway 441, cutting through the hills of north Georgia and then snaking into Carolina. The mountain breeze blew cool and damp, so different from the dry winds of Oklahoma. As the aromas of cedar and pine filled her car, a strange feeling overcame her—that Jonathan was not hiding, nor had he fled to Mexico. Jonathan was here. He'd come back to the place he knew best. He and Lily were waiting for her at home, right now. Her sense of him was so strong that she slowed down, started to turn left on Goose Pen Road. But then a more sober notion pulled her back, reminding her that she'd spent the last two days frantically trying to reach the man and receiving nothing in return.

"Just go on and see Stratton," she whispered, moving out of the turn lane. "If Jonathan's at home now, he'll still be there an hour from now."

———

A little while later, she again sat in interview room three. A female officer she did not know escorted Stratton into the room, closing the door behind him. He walked over to the table in strangely small steps, now more accustomed to the parameters of his cell. His clean-shaven, handsome courtroom appearance was gone—replaced by a scruffy dark beard and bloodshot eyes. "Hey," he said, sitting down across from her. "Long time, no see."

"I had to leave town unexpectedly," she explained.

"No problem." He gave a bitter laugh. "It's not like I'm going anywhere."

"Well, I think I've got some real good news."

"What?"

"I've just found lots of irregularities in the old Fiddlesticks case."

He frowned, apparently unable to connect the dots. "I'm sorry—what does the old Fiddlesticks case have to do with me?"

She told him, briefly, the whole saga of Robert Thomas Smith—the original Fiddlesticks who'd avoided the gas chamber, gotten re-assigned to a mental hospital, and then possibly walked away from a nursing home fire.

"Are you serious?" Stratton looked at her, incredulous.

"That's what the records indicate. I don't know how much of it's true, but it will certainly muddy the waters in your case."

He ran a hand through his hair. "I'm still not sure I understand."

"We don't have any proof that the original Fiddlesticks is dead. Remember how someone carved those strange figures into Lisa Wilson's body?"

He nodded.

"Those figures are musical shape notes, well known to people who do Sacred Harp singing."

"So a Sacred Harp singer killed Lisa?"

"Possibly. It widens the suspect pool enormously. But here's what's really interesting. Those notes on Lisa's body make up an arcane little tune that some fiddler played at Central Prison, the same time Smith was on death row. Whoever carved that tune was in prison the same time as Smith."

"So you're saying that Smith killed Lisa?"

"It's not impossible."

"But wouldn't he be too old?"

"He'd be in his seventies. Not prime of life, but if he kept himself fit, he could be our guy."

"Saved by a ghost," he whispered. He shook his head, then for the first time in weeks, his mouth curled in a smile. "Hey, I've got a bit of news for you, too."

"What?"

"Rachel Sykes and Tony Blackman drove over from Charlotte this afternoon. They'd been up to the center and said the barn owl you brought in was ready to be released."

Mary had forgotten about the little creature she and Lily had worked so hard to save—it seemed like a lifetime ago.

"They're going to help Artie release it tonight."

"Tonight? Where?"

"Up on a bald, on the back of our land. It's clear there; she can find a tree to roost in."

Mary remembered the strange sense she had of Jonathan and Lily being home, waiting for her. If they were there, bringing the owl back home might be a promise of mended fences, healing. "Do you think they might release it at my house?" she asked. "At my barn?"

"Sure," said Stratton. "But you need to get in touch with them fast. They'll start for that bald pretty soon."

She whipped out her cell phone and called Artie, but all she got was Dr. Lovebird's answering machine.

"They're probably at the bird barn," said Stratton.

Mary frowned. "Where's that?"

"Take the path to the right at the totem pole. If you drive like hell, you might get there in time," said Stratton.

"Thanks!" Mary leapt from her chair. "I'll see you tomorrow."

———

She hurried to her car, still trying to raise Artie on the phone. In the parking lot she saw Cochran, revving up the black Camaro he loved to drive.

"Hey," he called, lifting a hand in greeting. "When did you get back from Oklahoma?"

"Just now," she said, backing her car out of its space. "Gotta go out to the bird center. See you!"

She waved, squealing her tires as she sped out of the parking lot. For a moment she feared he might give her a ticket, but he turned right as she turned left, out of town and into the mountains.

She drove fast, her little Miata hugging the curves. Once again she came to the turnoff to her farm; once again she ignored it and drove deeper into the mountains. She turned on to the road that led to the raptor center, her car skidding on the gravel pavement. She smiled at the memory of the night she and Lily had driven up here holding the owl in a cardboard box. "Please let me get there in time," she whispered. "Maybe if we had something like this, we could all start out fresh."

She twisted up countless switchbacks, then finally, her headlights flashed across Nick's totem pole. Pulling to the side of the structure, she got out of her car and followed Nick's directions up the right prong of the path. The gravel was several inches thick and in her light sandals she felt as if she were trudging through damp sand. As she hurried up the steep hill a clammy sweat began to dampen the back of her neck. She was wishing she'd changed out of her jeans and into shorts, when she heard the screech of a bird just ahead. She started to run, thinking it must be the interns with the barn owl. As the gravel path curved into a clearing, she saw the high roof and narrow windows of the bird barn.

Quickly, she headed toward the open door. She'd just stepped on to the porch when suddenly, she heard the sound of a bow scraping across the strings of a fiddle. The noise took her by surprise; then she remembered that all Stratton's interns seemed to strum or pluck some kind of instrument.

She hurried to announce herself, to tell them that they needed to release the owl at her place. She was almost inside the door when the fiddle scraping became real notes, a real tune. Mary listened for a moment, then a gravelly voice began to sing.

In my cabin in the woods, my dear sweet love lies bleeding.
In my cabin in the woods, my bloody knife lies reeking.
Though the one I love is gone today, her memory never leaves me
Her cold lips and sightless eyes will forever grieve me.

She listened, horrified. Someone was singing the tune Lige Mc-Cauley had learned in Central Prison—the same tune carved on Lisa Wilson's body!

For an instant she stood there, unable to move, then some deeper instinct took over. She turned and started to run, except her right foot caught on one of the pillars that supported the porch. Down she went, her ankle twisting as her body thudded on the wide plank floor. She lay there for an instant, stunned, then she realized the music had stopped.

Oh, God, she thought. *They heard me.*

She rolled off the porch, trying to scramble to her feet. Her ankle wobbled more than supported her, making a funny crunch with each step. Still, she forced herself to go on, limping across the clearing, her footsteps scuttling through the gravel. She lumbered along as fast as she could, seeking the forgiving darkness of the trees. Down the mountain she went, racing toward her car. She listened, desperate for the sound of that fiddle to start again but all she could hear was the ragged sound of her own breath. Then, all at once she heard a new sound—not fiddle music, but footsteps running in the gravel behind her.

Ignoring the pain in her ankle, she willed her legs to pump faster, not daring to glance back. She considered veering off into the woods, but a twisted ankle would only slow her down more in the thick underbrush that grew along the path.

She ran, gulping deep breaths of air. Finally, blessedly, she saw the totem pole, her car just beyond that. *A hundred more feet,* she told herself, digging in her pocket for her key fob as the footsteps behind her grew louder. *A hundred more feet, then you're inside the car, locking the door, getting the hell off this mountain.* She raced on, growing aware of a ragged kind of grunting joining the footsteps behind her. She slipped once in the gravel but regained her footing. Now she was coming up to the totem pole—the raven, owl, and hawks all staring into the darkness with cold, raptor eyes. *You're almost there,* she told herself. *Just fifty more feet ....*

Suddenly, a massive weight struck her on her shoulders. Arms twisted around her torso, another pair of legs entwined around hers. Though she tried to keep running, she couldn't. Her car keys slipped from her fingers and she hit the ground hard, gravel digging into one side of her face. As hands grasped at her clothes, hot, sour breath enveloped her face. It was then she realized that Lige's tune was, indeed, cursed. It presaged death just as surely as a rope around your neck or a knifeblade to your heart.

FORTY-TWO

BEFORE SHE COULD DRAW a breath, he'd flipped her over, on her back. She looked up. Immediately, she recognized him. Though the red hair was now a fringe of snowy white and the boyish face now wrinkled, it was an older version of the picture in Ginger's article. The only thing different was the eyes—the ones she'd only known squinting beneath a baseball cap were now grotesquely wide.

"Artie?" she gasped, astonished.

He laughed, his eyes seeming to take up half his face. "Who'd you think it was? That pissant Jenkins?"

She grabbed a handful of gravel from the path, hurled it into his face, then rammed the heel of her right hand into his nose. He screamed as blood spurted on both of them. She felt his weight lift off her. She tried to squirm into the darkness of the trees, but he grabbed her arms, twisting a leather cord around her wrists as a cowboy might rope a calf. After he'd bound her hands numbingly tight, he pulled a razor from his pocket and held the blade so close against her throat that it quivered with her every heartbeat. *Fiddlesticks killed her with his razor. Slit her throat and then forgave her.* The old jump rope rhyme in Ginger's article echoed in her head.

"Now you just lie the hell still," Artie snarled, straddling her. He grabbed at his crotch. She panicked, anticipating rape, or his penis forced down her throat. *I can endure the one*, she thought, *but not the other.*

The notion of either made the bile bubble up her throat. She turned her head and vomited, bits of complimentary airline peanuts spilling all over her left shoulder and Artie's right knee.

"You little bitch!" he cried. Furious, he scrambled to his feet, kicking her in the head, the shoulder. New waves of pain crashed over her as her vision shimmered with white lights and shooting stars.

"Fucking cunt!" He wiped the vomit from his trousers. "You're all alike. Every damn one of you spewing something from one end or the other!"

She lay there, her pain a monster with a life of its own. As it reached to claim new territory along her neck and spine, she heard his footsteps on the gravel close to her head. *Keep him talking*, she told herself. *Keep him talking and maybe he won't kick you again.*

"Where's Rachel? And Jenkins?" she croaked. "Stratton said you were letting my owl loose."

"Jenkins has gone to his cockfights," Artie replied, wheezing for air. "Them interns didn't want to hang around after dark." He cackled. "They're afraid the murdering lunatic might get 'em!"

She tried to answer, but breathing seemed to require all her effort. She watched dimly as he grabbed her purse, pulled money from her wallet. He dug deeper, examining her cell phone and makeup bag. Finally he pulled out her little recorder. As he toyed with the buttons, Lige McCauley's fiddling began wafting into the air. Artie cocked his head, listened. "Where'd you get this? Who's singing my tune?"

"A guy who knew you back at Central."

Artie punched more of the buttons. When he managed to get the music turned off, he tossed the recorder and the rest of her purse to the ground. "You play that for anybody else?"

"Lots of people," she lied, each word sending a new jolt of agony through her neck and jaw. "I'm surprised Sheriff Cochran's not here already."

He frowned, as if trying to decide whether to believe her, then gave a snide little laugh. "If Cochran knows so fucking much, how come he's still got Stratton in jail?"

She had no answer for that. All she knew was that her only chance was to keep him talking. Maybe if she could get him to drop his guard, she could plaster his nose again and crawl off into the woods.

"Cochran knows you killed Lisa Wilson," she said. "He's just trying to figure out how you did it."

"Well, it wasn't too hard. I just played my tune and out she came. Any fool could have done it."

"How can you play the fiddle with only half your fingers?"

He held up a mangled hand. "I bow with this one. Play the notes with the other."

"But why kill Lisa Wilson? She liked you ... I read it in her diary."

Smith fingered his swollen nose. She must have done some damage when she'd hit him. "I didn't have nothing against her," he said, "She was just the easiest one to get ... I knew she'd slip out if she thought Nick was waiting."

Mary swallowed hard. Smith had held no grudge against the old governor; any of the interns would have sufficed. "But why kill any of them? They were just a bunch of dumb kids in an old rotten shack."

Those wide eyes sharpened. "Because that rotten shack was my home! They were mockin' it, mockin' my wife! Everyone that goes up there mocks my Bett!"

She'd punched his hot button. He started twirling the razor between his good fingers, his eyes on fire.

"You know how long people have been tromping through my house? Lookin' for Bett, telling terrible tales about me and her. And that little Givens prick was going to make a TV show out of us!" He shook his head. "Bett comes to see me when people start doin' that. She makes me take care of 'em. People should know better than to mess with holy places."

"Holy places?" As she looked up at him she saw how close the woods came to the graveled path. If she could scoot over just a little, she might be able to make a run for it. Woozy with pain, she sat up. "What makes that old shack so holy?"

"My wife died there. My best friend, too."

"Yeah," she said, inching toward the trees. "You killed them."

"I did not!" He kicked her hip so hard her body left the ground. "Ray, yes; I never laid a hand on Bett."

She fought a wave of nausea, wondering if he'd broken her leg. "That's not ... not what they said in court."

"You think I'm gonna tell the whole county my wife was suckin' off another man? No way. But she was. I came in the door and they were hard at it—her on her knees, right in front of the fireplace. You should have seen the look on Ray's face. 'Bobby!' he cries. 'You ain't supposed to be back yet!'"

"But you came back early," Mary said, holding her hip as she inched closer to the woods.

"Surprised 'em. Ray went white as a sheet. Bett turned, looked at me over her shoulder. Next thing I knew Ray grabbed her by the hair and dragged her up in front of him, a knife at her throat. She was naked. His britches were to his knees. 'Stay away from me, Bobby,' he said. 'If you don't, I'll kill her.'"

Smith gazed into the darkness, back into that long-ago night. "I couldn't stand the thought of him touching her. I lunged for him, thinking he'd just push Bett away. But he didn't. He took that knife and raked it hard across her throat." He shuddered as he spoke. "I never knew one little girl could have so much blood."

Mary remained silent, moving another half-inch.

"He made to get away, then. Tried to jump out the window, but he couldn't run because of his britches. I went after him like a crazy man. I got the knife away from him and he started to cry. 'Please, Bobby. I didn't mean anything. She wasn't nothing but a whore, anyway.'

"I grabbed him by his collar. I was short, but I'd long since made it my business to be mean. 'Your first mistake was pulling down your pants,' I told him, turning his own knife on him. 'And your last mistake was calling my wife a whore.' I cut his dick off, then. He grabbed the thing and ran around that cabin, howling like some animal, clawing to get out the door, but I blocked the way. Finally, I guess he just ran out of juice. He lay down on the hearth and died."

She watched as he stood there, reliving a murder fifty years past. His story was vastly different from the transcript of the trial. "So you only killed Ray Hopson?"

He nodded. "I took the blame for both of 'em. But I swore I'd never hang for it. And I didn't. At Central I buddied up with a simpleton and bribed a couple of guards with my grandmaw's money. That got me off death row. Then I laid low and acted addle-pated. They sent me first to the nut house, then to some old nursing home. That place was almost fun—cases of rubbing alcohol, all over the attic." He laughed. "It just took two matches to get those old folks up and running for their lives."

"All to come back here and kill young girls?"

He looked at her. "I got to do what Bett says—she doesn't like it when strangers go there."

"But isn't Bett dead?" Mary asked.

"Not to me, she ain't."

He stood there for a moment, then he took off his belt and looped it around her neck. Wrapping one end around his good hand, he jerked her to her feet. "Come on."

He'd just begun to push her toward the bird barn when she made her move. She shoved him, hard, catching him off balance. As he struggled to regain his footing she drew her bound hands back over her shoulder, as if clutching an imaginary baseball bat. She was just about to swing into his jaw with all her weight when he stepped to one side. He flicked her once with his razor. She heard a sound like ripping silk as blood began to gush from her shoulder to her elbow. For an instant she felt nothing, then a new, different pain began to zip up her arm.

"Don't fuck with me, Mary Crow," he warned, tightening the belt around her throat. "Or I'll write a new verse of my tune all over you."

FORTY-THREE

FOR THE LAST NINETY minutes, Ginger had squirmed through dinner at Tony's restaurant. Though they'd ordered their favorite meal—chicken calabrese and a bottle of ciro rosso, all she'd done was pick at her food and check her cell phone every five minutes. Cochran had brought the engagement ring; tonight was the night. After dinner he was going to ask her to be his wife.

"Are you okay?" he finally asked.

"Yeah." She gave him a distracted smile. "Why do you ask?"

"Because all you've done tonight is check your messages."

"Sorry—I'm expecting an important call."

Suddenly he grew irked—what could possibly be more important than dinner with the man who hoped to make her his fiancée? "About your mountain music feature?"

"No, something else," she said, checking her phone yet again

"Some other boyfriend promise to call you?"

"Mary Crow promised to call me the minute she got home," she replied, irritated. "I just wonder if her plane was delayed."

"No, she's here," said Cochran.

Ginger's green eyes flashed. "How do you know?"

"Because she almost broadsided me as I was leaving work."

Ginger frowned. "She was at the jail?"

"She was around six thirty."

"Then she must be home by now." Ginger whipped out her cell phone again. "I'm sorry, Jerry, but I really need to talk to her."

He sat back, exasperated, sipping his wine as Ginger called Mary's home, then Mary's office, then, finally, Mary's cell phone. No one answered at any number; each time Ginger left a growingly insistent call-me-immediately message. When she finally put the phone aside, he'd drained his glass.

"You know, I'm getting a bad feeling about this," she said, frowning. "Mary promised she would call me. Was Jonathan with her when you saw her?"

"No. Just Mary, driving like a bat out of hell."

"But it doesn't make any sense," said Ginger. "Why would she leave the jail like that? Why would she be at the jail in the first place?"

"She has a client there, Ginger. She's been out of town, she probably went to see him."

"Which way was she going when she left?"

"West," Cochran replied, growing impatient with the Mary Crow drama. "Probably home to turn off her phone and go to bed."

Ginger shook her head. "She wouldn't do that without calling me first."

She got back on her phone, again trying to reach Mary. Disgusted, Cochran pulled out his own cell phone. A few moments later he was talking to Simp Mathews, on the night desk.

"I need a favor, Simp," said Cochran. "Go back to the cells and ask that guy Stratton if he knows where Mary Crow is."

"Mary Crow the lawyer?" asked Simp.

"Yeah. She's Stratton's attorney. She was over there earlier."

"Think he'll tell me?" Simp asked dubiously.

"Probably," said Cochran. "He's still a rookie, jail-wise."

"Okay," he said. "Hang on." Cochran waited while Mathews put him on hold. *This night might still be salvageable,* he told himself, his right leg twitching with nerves, *if I can just find out where Mary Crow went.* He heard a scraping noise, then Simp came back on the line.

"Sheriff?"

"Yeah?"

"According to Stratton, she went up to his bird center to let some owl loose."

"Thanks, Simp," said Cochran. He clicked off his phone and smiled at Ginger. "I found out where Mary is."

"Where?"

"Stratton's place."

Ginger's eyes grew wide. "What's she doing up there?"

"Releasing an owl, according to Stratton."

"She must have found something else out," Ginger said softly. For a moment, she just stared at her glass of wine. Then she grabbed his wrist, pulled him to his feet. "Come on—we've got to get up there!"

"Why?" he cried. "Ginger, she went up there to let an owl loose."

"There are things you don't know, Jerry," she explained. "Things that we've only just found out."

FORTY-FOUR

For what seemed like hours, Artie Slade pushed Mary Crow along a hidden path that went from the bird barn deep into the woods. As she limped onward, thorns tore at her jeans as Artie's belt buckle dug into her throat. She kept searching for a way to escape, or even a dead limb to hit him with, but the trees were thick and dark, and if there were fallen branches, she did not see them. Finally, she retreated to her default plan—keep him talking until she could think of something else to do.

"I need to catch my breath," she gasped after they'd crested a steep rise.

He looked at her with disgust. "I thought you were supposed to be some big, bad Cherokee."

"Yeah, well I thought you died in the gas chamber."

He laughed. "I guess we're both full of surprises."

As he loosened the belt around her neck, she looked up and caught a glimpse of the moon, a hard white pearl peeking through the black lace of the trees. "Why did you frame Nick?"

"I learned at Central that somebody has to take the blame." He snorted through his swollen nose. "Lisa was a regular bitch in heat over Nick. I figured if I linked the two of them, nobody would take much of a look at an old, one-handed feller like me."

"So you put her ring in Nick's bedroom?"

He nodded. "While he was at that sports park thing. I figured she'd have no more need of it, and it might come in handy for me."

"But why carve a shape note tune all over her?"

"That was Bett's tune ... I wrote it for her in prison. Them shape notes are the only way I can write music."

"But how did you fake out Cochran? He's pretty smart."

"I got an old buddy who lives in Hell's Acre, at the end of Slade Holler. We got a deal worked out for alibis. Cochran's deputy was in and out of there in about five minutes. You don't live in Slade Holler, you ain't exactly made to feel welcome."

He looked up at the sky, noted the ascendant moon. "Come on. We've got to get going."

"Wait a minute," she said. "Just out of curiosity ... how many other people have you killed up here?"

He shrugged. "I don't know—I lose count. You'd have to go down in that old mica mine and do a skull count."

He pulled her to her feet, then shoved her farther along the trail. Up they climbed, through trees so thick they hid the moon. Rhododendron grew shoulder-high, while unseen animals rustled through the underbrush ahead of them. She figured he was going to take her to the mine he'd pushed his other victims down. As she walked she fought a rising panic—she didn't want to die in some dark hole where no one would ever find her.

"You know Stratton's expecting me back at the jail tomorrow," she told him, chatting him up again. "He knows I came up here. People are going to come looking for me pretty soon."

"So? I'm gonna call Cochran up here myself, once I finish with you."

"You're going to tell Cochran I fell down a mine?"

"Naw, honey. I got something different planned for you."

They climbed up several steep switchbacks, then, abruptly, he stopped.

"Come on," he said, turning right. "This way."

Pushing her through more trees, they finally stepped onto a grassy mountain bald. The little field glowed in the moonlight, and Mary saw that at one end, six tall and white poles stretched high into the air, supporting a platform at the top.

"That's a hack box," Artie answered her unvoiced question. "Where little eagles learn to fly." He grabbed her arm. "You're about to have a bad accident up there. You went to watch me set your owl free. Only you slipped and fell."

She faked a laugh. "You honestly think Cochran's going to buy that?"

"You won't be any more banged up than you are now. I'll tell him you snagged your arm on a nail, going over the edge. Cochran ain't that hard to fool."

"Oh?"

Again Artie cackled. "He came up here the other day, all official, looking for the ghost with the big eyes. I showed it to him, too. He just never realized the ghost was me."

She shook her head. "I don't get it, Artie. How can you trick all these people?"

He grinned. "You just figure out what they want and you give it to them."

She realized then that he probably could convince Cochran that she'd fallen—he had a slimy sixth sense that had gotten him out of jams far greater than pushing one woman off a hack box. She struggled to twist away from his grasp, but he held his end of the belt too firmly. With the buckle pushed painfully into her flesh, he shoved her across the bald, over to where a long ladder stretched up to back of the platform.

At the base, he cut the strap that bound her hands. "Start climbing," he said. "I'll be right behind you, at the end of this belt."

She eyed the ladder, desperate for a plan. If she could stay just a little bit ahead of him, she might be able to kick him off.

"And don't get any ideas." He twirled his razor, as if he'd read her mind. "With those little sandals you're wearing, I can lame you faster than I can cut hot butter."

She knew he was right. Two swipes of his razor and her Achilles tendons would be useless, leaving her feet flopping at the ends of her legs. Again, she was tempted to kick and scratch and fight it out here, but he held the belt too firmly around her neck. If he tightened it at all, she'd pass out, just like Lisa Wilson.

She grabbed the ladder. The thick rungs were rough and splintery. Desperate for a plan, she started to climb. As she made her way upward she realized she had one advantage over Artie. She could grasp the ladder with both hands and go faster. He had to hang on to the razor, the belt around her neck, and the ladder itself. If she could manage to jerk the belt out of his grip and scamper up to the platform first, she might have a chance.

FORTY-FIVE

GINGER'S STORY SOUNDED LIKE something his mother might dream up—Central Prison screwing up executions; death row inmates switching identities. But she remained adamant that her facts were correct. "Remember when I was in the bathroom this morning, talking to Mary?"

He nodded, disgusted at his own gullibility. He'd thought they were talking about Mary's custody suit.

"She'd spent the night researching all this. I spent today double-checking her theory, and it's true."

"That Smith was never executed?" he cried.

Ginger nodded. "He was transferred to a mental hospital, then an Iredell County nursing home that burned down a few years after he got there."

"And?"

"And nothing," she replied. "Not a single death record on any index in the country. Smith could be up in those woods, killing women as we speak."

"And now you think he's at Stratton's place?"

She shrugged. "I've just got a hunch, Jerry. I don't think Mary Crow would rush up there just to let an owl loose. She must have figured something out on her trip home."

He didn't know what to think. To go on a wild goose chase at his girlfriend's insistence made him feel like a fool. Yet on a deeper level, he had to admit that Ginger's hunch was resonating with something that felt a lot like an awful truth. "Okay," he said, unlocking Angel's doors. "Just to ease your mind, I'll drop you off at your car, then I'll go up to Stratton's."

"But can't I come with?"

"Absolutely not. You go straight home." He looked at her without smiling. "If you come up there, I'll have you arrested."

"Okay," she said, her voice strangely small. "Will you call me when you find out something?"

"I'll come by your house when I'm done."

———

He drove Ginger to her car, waiting until she pulled out of the police lot, then he raced out of town, driving the Angel like a black shadow through the night. Up the mountain they climbed, Ginger's words ringing in his head. *Robert Thomas Smith was never executed ... he could be killing women even as we speak.*

"It's not possible," he told himself. "The guy would be a fossil. He couldn't have survived forty years up here in these mountains."

But that odd feeling still remained. Artie Slade said an old man with wide eyes had stared at him from the trees. Thirty years ago someone with wide eyes had scared him and Messer shitless.

"It's not possible," he repeated. He made the turn to Stratton's place on two wheels, then punched Angel up a series of switchbacks, his headlights flickering through the thick woods. Finally, he reached Stratton's totem pole. His mouth went dry as he saw Mary Crow's black Miata, parked to the side of the thing.

He treated it like a regular traffic stop, leaving Angel running, his radio on, shining a bright flashlight inside the little convertible. He saw that a red suitcase took up most of the passenger seat; Mary's purse and keys were gone.

"Okay," he said. "She's up here releasing a bird. Where would that take place?"

He looked up the left prong of the gravel path that led to Stratton's cabin. "Probably not there," he said. "Try the bird barn."

He turned off Angel's engine and reached for his shotgun. Shouldering the weapon, he grabbed his flashlight and started walking up the path. He listened for any wisps of laughter or conversation, but all he could hear was the crunch of his own footsteps in the thick gravel.

Up he went, the shotgun tight against his back, his flashlight making a wide sweep of the path in front of him. Once he thought he heard a bird-like scream, but the sound died on the damp night air and did not come again. He wondered, as he trudged up the hill, what he was going to tell Mary when he found her. That Ginger had a hunch and made him come? That the twelve-year-old boy inside him was terrified that Fiddlesticks was still alive? *Just find her*, he told himself. *Make sure she's okay and you can have a laugh about this over a beer at Bigmeat's.*

He walked on, his breath coming harder. Up the trail, to his left, he could see lights twinkling through the trees. He quickened his pace, anxious to get all this behind him. Cresting the hill, he saw the bird barn. He'd almost reached the structure when the beam of his flashlight caught something shiny beside the gravel path. He hurried over to it—there, on the ground, lay the same kind of brass-buckled purse that Ginger carried, a digital recorder with the power still on. He picked up the purse and found a wallet inside—empty of cash, but full of identification. As he read the driver's license by the glare of his flashlight, his heart began to sink. The owner of the purse was a thirty-five-year-old black-haired, hazel-eyed female named Mary Crow.

FORTY-SIX

HALFWAY UP THE LADDER she thought of a plan. It seemed ridiculous, but at least it was something. She started to cough, and then began sucking great gulps of air. Below her, Artie jerked the belt tighter around her neck. "Go on, girl. Get up there."

She looked down at him, pretending to sway. "This is so high... I think I might throw up..."

"Don't you puke on me again!" he cried. He popped her lower back with one end of his belt as he shifted to one side of the ladder. That was exactly what she hoped he'd do. Just as he moved, she pulled hard on the belt loop around her neck. It slithered out of his hand, one end flicking him hard across the nose.

"You bitch!" he cried, tearing up from the sharp blow. As he clung to the ladder with one hand and wiped his eyes with the other, she made her move.

Up she climbed, reaching for the next rung. The leather sandals that had been such a breeze at airport security were useless on the steps—their soles were too slick to gain any traction. So she pulled with her arms and scrambled for purchase with her legs. Higher she climbed, driving a splinter deep into the palm of her hand. With her breath burning in her throat, she looked up. Only ten more feet to the platform. Already she could hear Artie scrambling up behind her.

Ignoring the throbbing in her hand, she struggled on. She had to get to the platform before he could cut her legs with that razor. She grasped the next rung. It was crusty with dried bird shit, but she grabbed it without hesitation, pulling herself upward. Risking a glance over her shoulder, she saw that Artie was now climbing with both hands, holding his razor pirate-like, between his teeth. His face was purple with rage, his eyes embers from hell.

"Come on," she told herself. "You're almost there."

She grasped the next rung and willed herself upward. As she did she suddenly felt something warm and slick on her right foot. She looked down. Artie had swiped her heel with his razor. He'd missed the tendon, but a hot pain was zinging up her leg as blood dripped down into Artie's face.

"You ain't get away!" he screamed. "Nobody gets away from me!"

She lifted her right foot and shook it, hoping more blood would drip on him. Her arms on fire, she gripped the last rung of the ladder hard and flung herself forward, skidding on the dew-slick surface of the platform.

She knew she had only seconds before Artie would be there. Crawling on her hands and knees, she raced for what looked like a tall cage and looked for something she could use as a weapon. She found nothing inside the nesting box except perches and a pile of twigs.

She looked toward the ladder. Already she could see the top of his baseball cap, lumbering up over the edge of the platform. She turned back to the cage, frantic, wondering if she could somehow confuse him with a shower of twigs and push him off the ladder. She was making a dash for the twigs when suddenly, she noticed that one of the perches was sagging away from the cage wall. It was a thick oak branch, drooping at an angle, as if the nails supporting it had worked loose. As Artie gave a mad cackle, she rushed forward and pulled on the thing with all her weight. Two of the three long nails popped out immediately; the third had been driven into a knot in the wood and wasn't giving way.

"Damn it!" she whispered, desperately trying to wrestle the thing away from the wall.

"Okay, girlie," called Smith, now halfway on the platform. "Time to find out how you crows fly."

Her mouth chalky with fear, she pulled the branch once, twice. The thing moved, but still did not pull free of the wall. As Smith clambered to his feet, she focused all the strength she had left and gave a mighty wrench. The heavy branch came loose all at once, twisting, practically throwing her out the cage door. She made a grab for the thing just as Smith was coming around the corner.

"What are you doing?"

She didn't bother to answer. She swung the board as hard as she could, catching him just below his ear. His knees buckled but he didn't go down. She hit him again, driving the end of the perch into his chest. He stumbled backward on the slick platform. She was about to hit him a third time when he stepped on one of the long nails she'd just dislodged. His right leg flew out from under him. Arms pinwheeling, he scrambled backward, trying to regain his balance. She watched in horror as his legs pumped frantically, then he fell backward into the darkness, a death angel falling, screaming like one of the raptors he'd once helped to fly.

EPILOGUE

Eight months later...

"Do I look okay?" Mary turned away from the mirror, her eyes bright.

"Yes," said Ginger. "You look beautiful. Do I look okay?"

"You look incredible." Mary tried to peer out of a slit in the tent. "What's going on out there?"

Ginger peeked out to gaze at the crowd sitting beneath another white tent erected in the middle of Mary's cow pasture. "I see Cochran and Tuffy Clark and Judge Barbee and about a hundred other people sitting down. I think everybody's waiting for us!"

"Then grab your flowers," said Mary. "It's show time!"

Ginger picked up a bouquet of blue forget-me-nots. "Are you nervous?" she asked.

"Kind of," said Mary. "But I just keep telling myself to do what we did in rehearsal last night, and it'll be over before we know it."

"Good idea," Ginger said, taking a deep breath as Mary gathered her own bouquet of blue hydrangeas. "Well, here we go. See you on the other side!"

Their bouquets in place, Mary and Ginger walked decorously over to the other tent. As Lige McCauley and three other ancient musicians struck up a string band version of the "Wedding March," Mary gave Ginger a wink, then started to make her way slowly down the aisle. As she walked she nodded to a few of the guests— Dave and Jackie Loveman back from Israel, Nick Stratton in the same suit he'd worn to court, and Sam Ravenel, recently returned from Charleston. Standing pale but proud, Jerry Cochran smiled at her from the little grapevine altar, backed up by his best man, Tuffy Clark. She walked to the spot marked for the maid of honor, then turned. As Lige and his band began playing with greater gusto, Ginger started coming down the aisle, wearing a short white frock that swirled like thick meringue. Mary smiled. Never had she seen her friend look so lovely. She walked to stand beside Cochran, then they all turned to Judge Wilson Barbee.

Five minutes later, it was over. Cochran said "I do" and "I will" with absolute conviction, his voice command-strong. Ginger responded more softly, but no less lovingly. After Barbee pronounced them husband and wife, they walked back down the aisle to an Irish jig and the happy applause of the guests. Mary took Tuffy Clark's arm as the best man escorted the maid of honor from the altar.

"That's a load off," whispered Tuffy, still walking with a slight hitch. "Now we can move on to important things. Are you playing tennis this summer?"

"Probably," Mary said, nodding at Rob Saunooke. "Why?"

"Just wondered if you'd like to partner up for mixed doubles. They've got some good tournaments coming up. Folding money for the winners."

"Give me a call," she replied. "If I'm in town, I'd love to play."

The party funneled out of the wedding tent into a much larger one that held chairs and tables, food, and a dance floor. Later everyone would feast on barbecue and form squares for a square dance. Now all gathered to watch Jerry and Ginger slice a flower-bedecked cake, then take the first turn on the dance floor, twirling to Lige's version of the "Waltz of the Wind."

"They make a lovely couple, don't they?"

Mary turned. Eleanor Cochran stood there, a white corsage pinned to her lavender suit.

"They certainly do," Mary agreed. "I had no idea Jerry could dance so well."

"He couldn't until about a month ago." Eleanor's eyes twinkled. "I took him down in the basement and gave him emergency waltz lessons."

"Well, you did a great job," said Mary. "He looks like he's been at it for years."

Eleanor laughed. "As long as he sticks with the waltz, he'll do alright." She put a hand on Mary's arm and leaned close. "You know, I used to think maybe you and Jerry would get married."

Mary smiled as Cochran waltzed by, gazing at Ginger. "I appreciate the compliment, but I think he's found the perfect girl for him."

Eleanor's impish look faded to one of concern. "Have you heard anything from Jonathan?"

Mary knew someone would ask that question today. For weeks she'd wondered how badly it would hurt to answer it. To her surprise, her words came out with unusual ease. "No. Not a word."

"I'm so sorry," Eleanor said. "I thought you two made such a handsome couple."

"We did, for a while," Mary said. "But I guess we both changed."

"Still," Eleanor squeezed her hand, sympathetic. "You'd be surprised how things can work out. Last year I was dying of cancer, today I'm going to dance at Jerry's wedding." She started to say something else when a tall, elegantly dressed couple approached.

"Eleanor?" the woman asked. "Is this the famous Mary Crow?"

"Why, yes it is!" Eleanor reached up to hug both the woman and her equally tall husband. "Let me introduce you. Mary, these are my cousins from Philadelphia, Rhonda and Larry Ross. Rhonda's a mystery writer, just like me."

"Hello," Mary smiled as she greeted the couple.

"It's a pleasure to meet you," said Rhonda. "Eleanor's told us so much about you."

"About me?"

Rhonda nodded. "About how you and Jerry and Ginger were on the same track with that Fiddlesticks case. Fascinating."

Mary shrugged, not wanting Fiddlesticks to darken the wedding festivities. "Actually, Ginger and Jerry did the heavy lifting. I just did what I could to keep from going off a hacking stand."

Rhonda's gaze sharpened. "What do you mean Jerry did the heavy lifting?"

"Jerry showed up about five minutes after Smith died," said Mary. "He found my recorder that accidentally recorded Smith's confession and then he figured out where the mica mine was."

"That's where he dumped those other poor girls," added Eleanor.

"What I don't understand is why nobody caught on to him sooner," said Larry.

"Smith had a real gift for the con," Mary replied. "He had a buddy in the toughest holler in the county giving him an alibi, which one of our rookie detectives bought. Until he tried to kill me, I thought he was just an eccentric old codger who worked for Nick Stratton."

Larry gave a sly grin. "So did you get the million-dollar reward?"

"No, the governor came back and endowed the Lisa Wilson scholarship in environmental studies at Western."

"Fiddlesticks never got over losing his wife," Eleanor chimed in. "It'll all be in my next book, which, by the way, my editor already adores!"

"How nice for you." Rhonda gave an envious smile.

"Well, I'll leave you two authors to chat," Mary said, extricating herself from the trio. "I need to make sure the party keeps rolling along."

She left as Eleanor went on, rhapsodic about her new book. Wondering how Jerry would find life with two writers in the family, Mary strolled over to the refreshment table, where a white-coated waiter served her a slice of wedding cake. She'd just taken her first bite when Nick Stratton walked up.

"Hey," he said, leaning over to kiss her cheek. "You look gorgeous."

"Thanks." Even though she knew all eyes were rightfully on Ginger, she was still pleased that someone had noticed the pale peach dress she'd driven all the way to Atlanta for.

"And you did a terrific job as maid of honor."

"It's not hard," she said. "Just walk down the aisle and try not to fall on your face."

"They look mighty happy, don't they?" Stratton gazed at the pair, who were now greeting people in a receiving line.

"They do." In a way, it surprised Mary that Jerry and Ginger had invited Stratton to their wedding, and that Stratton had decided to come. But the two men had gotten past whatever awkwardness existed between arrester and arrestee, mutually agreeing that Cochran had simply been doing his job. Mary noted that the real villain of the piece, George Turpin, had been omitted from the guest list.

"Want to dance?" Stratton asked as Lige and his band launched in to another waltz.

"If you don't mind your feet getting stepped on," said Mary. "Twinkletoes I'm not."

"Me, neither."

He took her hand. They started off around the edges of the floor, steering clear of the more adept couples swirling in the center. After two cumbersome, knee-bumping circuits, Tuffy Clark cut in. One waltz with Tuffy led to one with bumbling Ravenel, then someone across the room requested a square dance. Rob Saunooke grabbed her as the squares began to form. With Lige calling, they do-si-do'd and flutterwheeled away as the spring afternoon turned into a lingering dusk. She was just about to launch into the Farmer's Quadrille with Dave Loveman when Stratton again took her arm. "Can you leave for a few minutes?" he asked.

"I think I'd better." Mary fanned herself. "Before I do-si-do myself into a heart attack."

"Then come on," he grabbed her hand. "I want to show you something."

He led her out of the tent and through the field that comprised the rest of her front pasture. The sun was just beginning to set, casting her land in a pinkish twilight. Though the air still held a slight chill, it carried the damp, earthy scent of new growth. Birds she had not heard since last fall chirped along her fencerows and the world looked freshly painted in the tender pastels of spring.

"Where are we going?" Mary asked as they walked toward the back of her property.

"Take a guess."

"The barn? To see the shy Mrs. Owl?"

He nodded.

Mary smiled. "I heard her the other night when I was helping John Sanders move his cows out of the pasture for the wedding. She wailed like some kind of banshee."

Stratton laughed. "They don't call them ghost owls for nothing."

They walked through the meadow, into the cool, sweet-smelling dimness of the barn. Stratton started climbing up the ladder to the hayloft. Kicking off her pumps, Mary followed him. He helped her up through the last steps, then he headed over to the far corner of the barn. He knelt down on the floor, motioning to Mary. She walked over to stand beside him.

"Look at all these pellets she's regurgitated," he whispered, pointing at a dozen or so grayish looking balls. "That means she's hunting regularly."

"You think she has babies?" asked Mary.

"Probably." He peered up into the shadowy rafters. "I could climb up there and look."

"No. Let's leave her alone. It's enough that she's back home and thriving."

"Yeah." Stratton nodded. "You're right."

They walked back to gaze out the wide hayloft door. All of her farm lay spread out before her—the house, the woods that surrounded the fields, the just-lit Japanese lanterns that now bobbed like fireflies around the party tents.

"Having second thoughts about leaving?" asked Stratton.

Mary leaned against the rough wood of the barn. "No. It's just hard to say good-bye."

"You don't have to go. You've still got your practice here."

She looked over at her house. Though his words tempted her, in her heart she knew it was time for a change. The honorable Ann Chandler had offered her a job, was giving her a chance to do what she'd been meant to do since her first day in law school. On June 1 she would move to Asheville as the special prosecutor for all the counties of western North Carolina, serving at the pleasure of the governor.

"Ravenel can mind the practice," she said. "Sometimes you have to go away. Then you can come back new."

"I understand." He sat down on the hayloft floor, letting his long legs dangle out the window. "Sometimes I feel like last year was a long, bad dream I'm just now waking up from."

She gazed out at her farm, lost in thought. The past eight months had not been easy for her, either. She'd daily climbed up in this hayloft and watched for a red truck to come down the driveway; for a tall driver and small passenger to get out, cross the swinging bridge, and run into the house. But as the green summer turned into a golden fall, she began to realize that it wasn't going to happen. Though she held on to a slim hope throughout Thanksgiving, and Christmas, on New Year's Eve she gave up and turned her porch light off. She had not turned it on since.

She resolved to live the new year differently—brushing up on her French, painting her dining room a rich shade of gold. As she worked, she started re-joining the world—hosting a dinner party for the Legal Aid society, going to a movie with Stratton. It felt odd, as if she were learning the art of enjoyment all over again. Then, in late January, on the night of her birthday, something awakened her. She woke up and looked out her window. New snow covered the ground and the inky sky shimmered with stars. As she looked across her back field she noticed a line of footprints. They emerged from the woods behind her house, traveled in a single line to her backyard gate and then vanished. She could tell they were human, but what caught her attention was that they'd been made in the way of the ancient Cherokees—a single-track, heel-to-toe pattern that, in the old days, made it difficult to count the number of men in a war party. Jonathan Walkingstick was the only person she knew who walked like that.

Hurriedly, she put on boots, threw a parka over her pajamas, and went outside. As she hurried through the frozen snow, she looked for him—leaning against the fence, or hovering in the shadowy edge of the woods. She didn't see anybody, but when she reached the back gate she found a smooth stone studded with garnets carefully placed on the post. She grasped it, pressed it against her cheek. In that instant a curious sense of peace came over her. She knew he had come back; knew that someday, months or even years hence, they would meet again. "We are not finished yet, Walkingstick," she'd whispered, her words a frost in the air. "Not even close to being through."

"Mary?" Stratton's voice brought her back from that long-ago night. "Are you okay?"

"Yeah, I'm fine, in fact." She turned as the breeze carried the strains of a new square dance.

He stood up and grabbed her hand. "Then shall we rejoin the dance?"

"Absolutely," she replied, smiling as he pulled her toward the ladder and the life that awaited. "I think we both have a lot to celebrate."

ACKNOWLEDGMENTS

No book is written without the help of angels and ghosts. My ghosts know who they are; my angels are as follows:

Ann Lewis, friend, activist, partner in the delicious crime of novel research. I owe you much, MSP.

Doris Mager, founder of Save Our American Raptors, who taught me a lot about birds, but a lot more about living your passion.

Mary Beth Brynam and Susie Wright, co-founders of Asheville's Wild For Life, whose kindness and generosity extended to me, along with their furred and feathered friends.

Bob Lewis, good pal and good tennis player, without whom I would have been computer-less at a critical junction.

Clare Fisher, who helped me re-visit undergraduate life.

Cynthia Perkins, my go-to first reader whose enthusiasm has never faltered.

Robbie Anna Hare, agent extraordinaire.

Finally, to my friends and fans who waited so patiently for more Mary Crow—my thanks to you all.

ABOUT THE AUTHOR

Sallie Bissell is a native of Nashville, Tennessee, and a graduate of George Peabody College. She won first place in her second grade essay contest and has, in varying capacities, been writing ever since. A former ghost writer for Bonnie Bryant's Saddle Club series, Bissell introduced her character Mary Crow in her first adult novel, *In the Forest Of Harm*. *Music of Ghosts* is Bissell's fifth Mary Crow book, and she has a sixth one in progress. Bissell is a Shamus Award nominee and her work has been translated into six foreign languages. She currently divides her time between Nashville and Asheville, North Carolina, where she enjoys tennis and an occasional horseback ride.

www.MidnightInkBooks.com

From the gritty streets of New York City to sacred tombs in the Middle East, it's always midnight somewhere. Join us online at any hour for fresh new voices in mystery fiction.

At midnightinkbooks.com you'll also find our author blog, new and upcoming books, events, book club questions, excerpts, mystery resources, and more.

MIDNIGHT INK ORDERING INFORMATION

 ### Order Online:
- Visit our website www.midnightinkbooks.com, select your books, and order them on our secure server.

 ### Order by Phone:
- Call toll-free within the U.S. and Canada at 1-888-NITE-INK (1-888-648-3465)
- We accept VISA, MasterCard, and American Express

 ### Order by Mail:
Send the full price of your order (MN residents add 6.5% sales tax) in U.S. funds, plus postage & handling to:

> Midnight Ink
> 2143 Wooddale Drive
> Woodbury, MN 55125-2989

Postage & Handling:

Standard (U.S. & Canada). If your order is:
$24.99 and under, add $4.00
$25.00 and over, FREE STANDARD SHIPPING

AK, HI, PR: $16.00 for one book plus $2.00 for each additional book.

International Orders (airmail only):
$16.00 for one book plus $3.00 for each additional book

Orders are processed within 12 business days. Please allow for normal shipping time. Postage and handling rates subject to change.